Praise for the Farlander novels

'Something special . . . Buchanan writes vividly and well, and
the story grips from the astonishing opening sequence to
the unexpected conclusion'
The Times

'Two pages into *Farlander* I was hooked . . .
Nice one Mr Buchanan'
Neal Asher

'With steampunk, magical and historical influences, this is
one of the most refreshing new fantasies out there'
SFX

'If you're a fan of blood-drenched epic fantasy then this is
a series that you should keep an eye on'
Fantasy Book Review

'The battle scenes are intense and brilliantly written . . .
If you like your fantasy grand in scope but intimate in detail
and character-driven, then the series is perfect for you'
Civilian Reader

'I'm a sucker for political intrigue in my fantasy books, and *Stands a
Shadow* delivers this in bucketloads . . . A brilliant read'
Mithril Wisdom

'A searing new fantasy series that sets the blood pumping . . . this is
a series to be reckoned with. Everyone take note'
The Truth about Books

The Black Dream

Col Buchanan is an Irish writer who was born in Lisburn in 1973, and now lives on the west coast of Connemara. In recent years he has mostly settled down, and loves nothing more than late-night gatherings around a fire with good friends. *The Black Dream* is the third of the Farlander novels.

By Col Buchanan

The Farlander Novels

FARLANDER

STANDS A SHADOW

THE BLACK DREAM

COL BUCHANAN

The Black Dream

THE FARLANDER NOVELS
Book Three

TOR

First published 2015 by Tor
an imprint of Pan Macmillan, a division of Macmillan Publishers Limited
Pan Macmillan, 20 New Wharf Road, London N1 9RR
Basingstoke and Oxford
Associated companies throughout the world
www.panmacmillan.com

ISBN 978-1-4472-1118-1

1 3 5 7 9 8 6 4 2

A CIP catalogue record for this book is available from the British Library.

Typeset by Ellipsis Digital Limited, Glasgow
Printed and bound by CPI Group (UK) Ltd, Croydon, CR0 4YY

Visit **www.panmacmillan.com** to read more about all our books
and to buy them. You will also find features, author interviews and
news of any author events, and you can sign up for e-newsletters
so that you're always first to hear about our new releases.

For the wild

'If you chance upon your master
on the road - kill him.'

OLD SAYING OF THE TRAVELLING TUCHONI

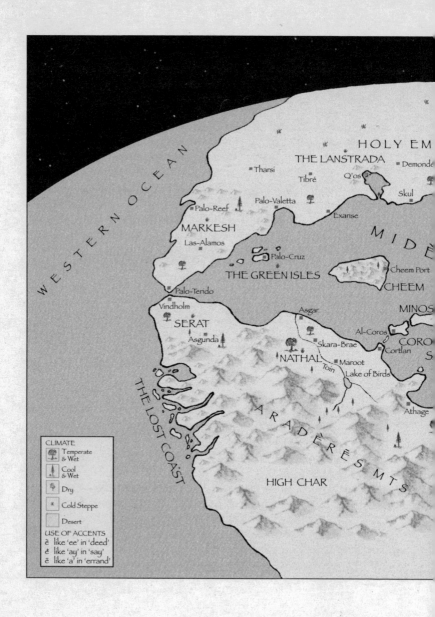

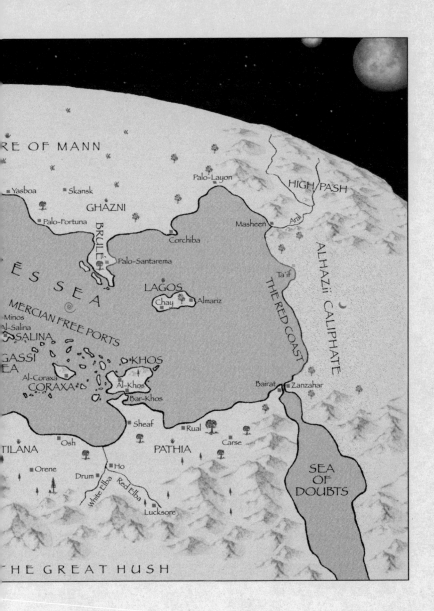

RE OF MANN

HIGH PASH

Yasboa   Skansk   Palo-Layon

GHAZNI   Corchiba   Masheen   Aral

Palo-Fortuna   BRULE   Ta'if

ALHAZii CALIPHATE

Palo-Santarema

ESSEA   LAGOS

Chay   Almariz

THE RED COAST

MERCIAN FREE PORTS

Minos

Al-Salina

SALINA

GASSI   KHOS

EA   Al-Coraxa   Al-Khos   Bairat   Zanzahar

CORAXA   Bar-Khos

Sheaf   Rual

TILANA   Osh   Carse

Orene   PATHIA   SEA OF DOUBTS

Drum   Ho

White Elba   Red Elba

Lucksore

THE GREAT HUSH

Fast Falling Rocks

Over the man's head a star was falling.

He looked up as it streaked across the night sky, blazing in a display of unlikely brilliance, and had time enough to track its course as it fell through the constellations to the west, fading even as his own fierce spirit continued to wane.

The old farlander blinked the sweat from his eyes, and forgot for a moment the ring of men that surrounded him in the fire-struck darkness, pressing closer even now; a thousand figures nervously eyeing his black skin and his curved sword, while beyond them thousands more surged towards the distant wall, roaring their fear and rage at its defenders.

Instead Ash's stare lingered on the stars of the night sky, his thin eyes narrowed further by the bright twin moons hanging there in a deeper blackness of their own making, the Sisters of Loss and Longing.

Right overhead – the band of stars that was the Great Wheel, glowing with faint smudges of colour. And there, low to the east – the red planet known as *Obos* by his people, its delicate string of moons stretching like a necklace from its body. Cold air swirled in his open mouth while the constellations shone with a hard intensity. Names of myth enshrined upon the cosmic sky: the supreme wilderness, he supposed, up there where anything could be possible; whilst here, down in the mud which clung so hungrily to his boots, there was only blood and carnage.

Around Ash the heat from the thousand men formed a cloud of mist in the wintry air through which their faces stared at him, flickering in the torchlight.

The enemy host bore features drawn from every corner of the

known world, and languages too. Over the din and clash of the greater battle they jabbered their excitement, coaxing each other closer towards the old Rōshun who stood with bloody sword over those he had already slain.

Not long now, Ash supposed, with a wipe of a hand across his mouth. He was losing blood fast from the bandaged wound in his side, and two arrows stuck out from his back like quills. Exhaustion hammered down on him in waves that he was growing too unsteady to resist.

His balance suddenly swinging on a pendulum, Ash sagged against the belly of his fallen zel to save what little strength was left to him, aware that it could be counted in heartbeats now. With a grimace he spat the bitter coppery taste from his mouth; glanced back over the black and white stripes of the zel to his fellow Rōshun, lying dead against the creature's saddle.

A cluster of arrows stood out from the Alhazii's barrel chest. Baracha stared with lifeless eyes that still caught the light of the moons, a fixed expression darkened with the tattooed words of his Prophet.

At least you saved your daughter, Baracha. You were right to stop her. She lives now because of you.

Past the heads of the enemy, explosions ripped through the air where the defenders' shells rained down amongst the attackers. Roars sounded from the throats of men cutting each other down.

Ash breathed deeply to quieten his racing heart, his many pains. He saw the naked steel in their hands and the ropes to bind him. He would die before he fell into their hands. He would rip open the wound in his side and bleed out right there in front of them all, before that happened.

How did it come to this? he asked himself now through the fog of his mind, and it seemed that the closing pressure of the enemy was precisely enough to focus his memory, for suddenly it came back to him.

Ash recalled the Great Hush and the hordes of kree deep in their warrens . . . His captivity in the Isles of Sky and his dead apprentice Nico . . . The tragic fate of the *Falcon* and her crew . . . All of it and further back, every step in his life leading him to the space and time he occupied now with his final breaths.

'Huh,' the old farlander grunted with a tilt of his head, seeing the full picture of it at last.

CHAPTER ONE

Captive States

In silence a young thunderhawk glided across the black surface of the canal, landing with a squeak from its pinned prey: a thick-bodied rat that had been squirming through the grasses by the water's edge. At once, another thunderhawk cried out from the opposite side of the water, a harrowing screech joined again by a third bird nearby, so that their triumph rang out across the moonstruck rooftops of the city, drowning out even the gunfire of the endless siege.

Ash lifted his chin to the sudden hoots and howls that answered from the other side of the high wall he was facing, the animals of the menagerie provoked from their slumber by the sudden cries of the birds. His lips curled as a roar from a desert lion stilled them all, restoring silence again to the night. Nothing stirred save for the thunderhawk lifting off with its prey, and the soft tread of the night-sentry's boots as he strolled along the gravel path following the canal.

Ash was well hidden here, deep within the shadows of a ruined and solitary archway by the edge of the water. He was sweating in this heat. It was like a Honshu high summer in the Sea of Wind and Grasses, those endless plains of his homeland where the tindergrass was so dry it exploded with each drop of sweat that touched it. At least the nights there had offered some relief, with the vast cloudless sky sucking the heat from the land. Here in Bar-Khos, the city's million stones seemed to release the heat of the summer sun all night long.

He would be glad to be gone from here once the repairs to the skyship were completed, returned to the cooler climes of mountainous Cheem and the Rōshun order. Glad to be home.

In the muggy darkness of the archway, his new apprentice

occupied himself by chewing the inside of his mouth, bored like most youths with the simple task of waiting. Ash could hear it, the soft rhythmic clacking of the boy's teeth, a sound not dissimilar to the canal water dripping occasionally from their sodden clothes onto the stone flagging.

Click, click, click.

Ash blinked rapidly, suddenly caught in this moment which he felt he had lived through before.

There was a name in the old country for this kind of experience, *way-wei*, a vivid sense of having already lived the same moment, prompting nostalgia before it was even gone. With such a mood upon him, the old farlander studied the curly-haired, half-starved young man called Nico Calvone, eighteen years of age and primed with all the life still owed him – and wondered if he hadn't made a mistake by taking him on as his first and only apprentice.

A few days ago, Ash had wakened alone in a Bar-Khos taverna from dreams of his past, of his life before the failed revolution. He had awoken to find himself not in his homeland after all but on the far side of the world, a dying exile blinded by tears and hearing movement next to his bed – this boy Nico stealing his purse – but thinking, for the briefest of moments, that it was his dead son instead.

His son Lin, who had fallen all those decades ago in battle right before Ash's eyes – for all that Ash had promised to protect him.

Amazing, the power of memories, to make him feel pain after all this time, like an accusing finger stabbing at his chest.

Such times as those he would never wish to live through again. Yet somehow he had just made a promise to a different mother, Reese Calvone; having sworn to keep her son safe from harm. Safe – in this line of work!

What if it all ended in tragedy once more?

Ash swayed in the shadows of the archway, feeling the sudden pain in his chest pulsing up into his skull, where the vice that had been there all day tightened a little further. In the moonlight his vision dimmed for a few trembling heartbeats. The old farlander winced, chewing faster on the bitter dulce leaves bundled in his mouth for relief.

His head pains had been worsening for months now. Soon he would be cast blind from them, unable to see at all, and then death would take him swiftly, as it had taken his father and grandfather before him, in the same way.

Not long now.

Nico's eyes were two lamps in the darkness. 'What?' the young man muttered through a yawn, and the luminescence of his stare caught Ash for a moment, startled him. He hadn't realized he had spoken aloud.

Instead of answering the boy Ash straightened, blew these ghosts of his away with a silent exhalation.

He rocked his boots against the stone of the ground, rooting himself to the world again, to the heart of the moment and what needed to be done.

'Come,' he said. 'Let us try this.'

*

Quickly, Ash stepped onto the gravel path and crossed to the shadows of the wall, where he pressed his back against the stone and looked back to see Nico standing out in plain sight, bent over something as he tried to scoop it up with awkward sleepiness. It was the heavy wool blanket he had been carrying.

'Boy!' Ash hissed at him sharply, chancing a glance along the path. The sentry was lost in the gloom.

Against his back, the wall was ten feet high and topped with broken shards of coloured glass that glinted from lights on the other side.

'I still can't see why you had to wake me in the middle of the night for all this,' grumbled the boy, throwing the blanket over the top of it.

'I told you. If you are to be Rōshun, and that remains to be seen, you must learn to perform your work when tired, exhausted even. Besides, we would not make it far with this in broad daylight. Now, give me your foot,' he snapped, and cupped his hands into a stirrup. 'You go first.'

Nico studied him with narrowed-eyed suspicion. On the other side of the wall the desert lion roared again into the darkness. Ash imagined he could see the process of the boy's thoughts: the memory of the recent gaol he had been imprisoned in for his theft of Ash's purse; the need to make a good impression here, on this man who had saved him from punishment in exchange for becoming his apprentice.

'Consider it part of the lesson,' Ash prompted.

'A lesson in what, I'm starting to wonder?'

'Consider it courage.'

A roll of the eyes, and then the boy placed one of his new boots into Ash's hands, and in an instant had scrambled up over the wall. A fine climber, Ash noted.

Just as quickly he followed after him, ignoring his protesting joints and the hammering weight of his head. Ash saw colours dance when he landed on the other side. He gritted his teeth and crouched down next to Nico, where the blades of long grasses hid them from sight.

In the distance, he could hear the music of plucked strings and a woman or young boy singing. Ash parted the grasses to peer at the mansion up on the hill. The house was brilliantly lit up there, bordered by lawns struck by the light flooding from its interior. The odd scrap of laughter could be heard amongst the notes of music spilling from its open windows: people socializing on a patio, their shapes black against the open doorways. It was as though the siege of the city and the imperial army massed against them were only a distant dream.

'Your father,' enquired Ash of his apprentice, while he scanned for nearby guards. 'You said he fought beneath the walls. What became of him?'

'Dead, most likely.'

'He went missing in battle?'

'No,' replied the boy's quiet voice. 'He ran off on us. Deserted everything.'

Ash thought of the visitors' vault in the gaol again where he had met with the boy's mother, Reese Calvone. The way she had dismissed her younger lover from the room. The emotional armour she had worn about herself.

'Your mother. She still loves him.'

'And hates him. Is this part of the lesson too?'

Anger in the boy's voice. Clearly he was sensitive to questions about his family. It only made Ash want to enquire more, but instead he chewed the bitter dulce leaves for relief and stared out across the grounds beyond, staying his tongue.

Below the mansion and its lawns, a large expanse of hedges ran out towards the perimeter wall where they hid. Gravel pathways threaded between them, past cages covered by sheets of canvas from which the odd noise of a captive animal arose into the night; the grand menagerie of the Santobar family, one of the wealthiest Michinè bloodlines on the island of Khos.

'Come,' he said, and they rose to amble onto a path that led into the menagerie, their boots scrunching lightly on the gravel.

'Loose coral,' he noted aloud for Nico to see, 'difficult to run in,' but the boy was peering around him nervously instead, as though an ambush or trap awaited them.

'I'd feel better if you'd brought that sword with you.'

'I told you, we must not harm anyone tonight. If it comes to it, we will flee.'

'At least with a sword you could wave it around a little, scare them with it.'

Ash had paused in front of a long cage not much higher than himself, fashioned by thin bars of tiq. Shapes could be seen moving inside the cage. Claws clacked on the floor. They crowded towards him, making soft snapping sounds with their beaks. Ash had never seen such animals before. Their bulbous heads swayed on impossibly long necks; their feathered bodies rested on bony stilts.

'You watch too many Tales of the Fish in the street,' he told his nervous apprentice. 'A naked blade has a hunger for blood. It will seek it out or draw the blood to it. Either way,' he stepped closer to the cage, reached out a hand as though to stroke one of the animals through the bars, 'it is rarely only a threat.'

The nearest creature poked its head out through the bars, stretched its long neck in an attempt to reach his outstretched fingers. 'Birds, would you believe. Here, try touching one. They are tame.'

Again that boyish suspicion. Still, Nico was game enough to reach out with a finger, and prod one of the feathered flank pressed against the bars.

In an instant a beak came flashing out at him, snapping loudly as he snatched back his hand.

'Hey!'

Ash chuckled softly. Moved on.

There were more cages, many more. Some were silent in their darkness, no sign of what might be contained within them. In others, the animals came to the bars in open curiosity. Monkeys hooted and grinned with their lips peeled back from their gums. A beaked kerido hung from the bars of one cage, its eyes round and forlorn. Stinkrats scurried through the sawdust of another. The last cage at which he lingered held a black panther, prowling back and forth as though demented by its confines.

Frowning, Ash headed inwards. In the distance a lone guard patrolled the lawns around the mansion, but he spotted no one closer. Abruptly he stopped, raised a hand to stroke his stubby wedge of beard.

Somehow, he'd expected more of a challenge.

The old farlander cast his gaze around until it settled on a hut of small cages, where small colourful birds sat on perches within. They chirped and fluffed up their feathers at his approach.

'*What are you doing?*' Nico demanded as Ash opened up the cages one by one, the birds chirping wildly now. The boy hissed and crouched down on the path as animal sounds erupted all about them, making a drama of their presence there. Ash was too absorbed in the birds hopping from the open cages to answer him. Some tried their wings first while others launched themselves straight into the air.

A few lingered within the cages, chirping quietly, refusing to leave their captivity. It provoked Ash, those remaining birds fearful of their freedom. It spurred him further, so that he began to jog around the area, opening larger cages, even releasing the prowling panther so that it set off into the darkness with a growl.

'Are you mad?' Nico whispered, then jerked around as a wolf pattered past him, though the animal only gave him a cursory, canine glance, seemed to be smiling with its toothy open mouth. 'They'll know we're here now!'

The young man's breathing needed working on; his sense of stillness.

'Calm yourself, boy. Focus on your breathing.'

Nico opened his mouth to protest but stopped, swung his head around in alarm.

Ash had already heard them though. Clawed feet racing along coral paths towards their location. Guard dogs perhaps, or worse.

'Get behind me,' he advised his stunned apprentice, and began the deep breathing exercise that would allow him to project his voice.

For a short time the sound of running feet disappeared – the animals loping over grass – then returned with a splash of gravel, nearer now, off to their left.

Ash swept around.

The first creature came into view with a speed and muscled grace that made his blood sing. A banthu – a larger, running cousin of the kerido, no doubt trained to strip the flesh from men. First one and then two, three, four of the animals sprinting towards them.

'I knew you should have brought your sword!'

With his body telling him to run, the old farlander stepped forwards to meet the creatures head-on, throwing all his power into his voice as he did so.

'*Ssqhuon!*' he exclaimed as he raised his arms high. '*Ssqhuon!*'

He had only ever tried the trick with dogs – yet the animals faltered in mid-step, kicking coral up around them, and then they were drawing up in sudden confusion. '*Ssqhuon!*' he tried once more, risking another step forwards with arms flung high, and they clacked their razor beaks and turned to flee, speeding back from where they had come.

'I don't believe it,' said Nico with a gasp.

Calls now from the great house. Voices raised in enquiry.

We must be quick!

Ash scattered a pair of spotted cats with his stride, following the distinctive scent of tallow flowers in the air until he came at last to a darker area of ponds and marshy ground to the west of the menagerie.

'Here. This must be it.'

Frogs croaked in the darkness as he stopped next to one of the pools covered by domes of wire mesh.

'I doubt we have long,' Nico said breathlessly, curious now.

'Then pay attention.'

Opening the lock took a matter of moments with his picks. Inside the wire dome, Ash hunkered down on his belly and looked out across the dark water, his exhalations sending tiny shivers across the surface. He saw a brilliant white tendril as thin as a hair rise and float amongst the surface tension before disappearing again.

'Fresh-water pelloma,' he explained to the boy. 'The estate sells their eggs to the local restaurants.'

'We came here for eggs?'

'Precious eggs, renowned for their benefits to health and spirit. They will make an excellent parting gift for your mother.'

Nico was down next to him, panting fast. 'How do we get them?'

'Put your hand in the water. You'll feel them.'

The boy gave a long, studied gaze at the black surface; saw another swirl of a tendril in the centre of the pool. 'Whatever that is, it looks dangerous.'

'I can think of worse stings, but not many.'

'Then *you* do it!'

'I will, after you. Don't worry. I know how to deal with it if you're stung.'

They could both hear guards in the distance. A panther roared and a rifle shot fired out in response. Women screamed from the house.

Nico was ready to bolt for it, he saw. No good for the boy's confidence if he did.

'Consider it another part of the lesson.'

'Of what, simple-mindedness?'

'Call it trust.'

'Admit it, you're making this up as you go along.'

Too early to admit to such a truth yet. Ash grunted and lifted his hand towards the water, prepared to do it himself, but the boy stopped him, slipped his own hand into the pool with a gasp.

'Feel around the edge until you come upon their bubble nest,' Ash advised the young man as he groped frantically around the pool. 'The eggs are the size of your fist.'

Ash followed the trembling of the water. If they were in luck then the pelloma in the pond would be in their usual sluggish night mode. If not though . . .

A ripple erupted in the centre of the pool. More tendrils broached the surface. Nico yanked his hand out with water and bubbles raining off it. He held aloft a small translucent egg in triumph.

'Here,' the boy exclaimed and tossed it into his hands. Ash gripped the slippery egg and returned the boy's gaze, which glanced towards the sounds of approaching guards and then back again, as though he no longer cared about their danger. His blood was stirred. The spirit of the challenge was upon him.

He has heart, Ash thought with a surprising spark of pride, and realized then what the test had been tonight, and that Nico had just passed it; for heart, most of all, was the one thing Ash could not teach him.

Thrashing in the water now. Ash was glad the boy's hand was out of it and that he'd been spared the pain and shock of a sting. Let him wait until later in his training for such lessons as those.

Nico's teeth shone white in the darkness.

'Your turn.'

CHAPTER TWO

The Great Hush

In the afternoon daylight a fierce odour drifted from the hole, a stench that caused the flying insects to swerve away from its vicinity, seemed even to have leached the colours from the nearest fronds of tropical grasses.

The hole was a vertical opening in the foot of a clay-brown cliff of earth, small compared to most of the other openings in the earth, the same size as the mouth of a wine barrel, though the daylight that entered a few feet inside it showed a tunnel widening downwards into blackness. The earth was hard and bare around it, covered with traces of a faint, milky membrane.

Beyond the hundreds of other openings that pocked the base of the cliff, the ground was a pan of beaten earth with islands of faded grasses. No animals were to be seen but the hundreds of six-legged kree scuttling back and forth in their work beneath the afternoon sun, an orange disc way up past the highest flanks of the rift valley, way up in a sky that was like a wide river of running blue.

From the tunnel a sudden sound emerged. The blackened tip of a velvety-blue limb protruded from the orifice to be followed by others; a young worker kree, squeezing its great size through the dimensions of the opening.

It was out and away as quickly as it had appeared. Behind it, a long time later, the same sound of movement returned. Another limb extended from the hole – though this one had fingers, a hand, a greasy arm.

With a gasp, a heavily scarred face pushed its way outwards; a slick and gleaming skull with a crop of dark hair; eyes that were slits squeezed tight against the daylight. Finally a pair of shoulders popped out, and then the rest of the body slithered free behind it, naked, coated in oily grime, reeking of kree.

With deep, sobbing breaths of air, the longhunter hauled out the net bag after him filled with clinking wooden jars.

Sweet Holy Mercy! thought the man with relief as he finally rolled away from the opening of the kree nest, and lay back against the slope of earth wiping his eyes clear of grime, the scars of his face rough against his shaking palm. The longhunter gulped down the fresh breeze and shook with the elation roaring through him.

He felt reborn, as he always felt reborn upon emerging into the light.

Cole breathed deep until his shaking subsided, though the elation remained as a surging flow of his blood. The jars were still intact. The Royal Milk gurgled heavily inside them when he gave the netting a jostle. He looked up and watched countless kree coming back and forth across the ground before him, blinking as though in surprise.

'This is the last time, you hear me?' Cole breathed to himself as he climbed shakily to his feet. 'The last time!'

*

On those nights, returning alone through the wilderness of the Great Hush, Cole would bed down in his sleeping furs fully aware that he might never waken from his slumbers again, or worse still, that he might awaken as prey in the midst of some gory feeding frenzy; a few awful moments of agony and terror, he always supposed, a few brief glimpses of their barbed lashes thrashing against his face and the dark sheen of their carapaces, before he was gone.

Cole felt this more strongly the longer he remained so close to the rift valley known as the Edge – an actual sensation like stones rolling around in his stomach and a light prickling of his scalp, knowing that he was prey in a predator's land.

It was the beginning of the cool season, the traditional time for expeditions into the Great Hush, this endless continent to the south of the Broken Spine of the World; for in the more tepid air the kree were slower and less likely to rush at you out of nowhere. It had taken him more than a month to make it from the Aradērēs mountains to the great rift valley of the kree, and a further week to prepare and then descend into the rift itself before returning with his haul of Royal Milk.

Now, ahead of Cole, over the thousand and more laqs of grass-lands he had ridden on his way here, a string of small supply caches stretched back all the way to the Broken Spine of the World, his only assured means of getting back to the known world without starving in the trying – for he would need the food stored in them, and the black powder to hunt for more. The line of caches was like a rope holding him over a void, and so he thought of them often, along with the haul of Milk he carried with him, and tried not to dwell on those things that could go wrong.

All about him, as he headed home across the badlands bordering the rift valley, he saw sign of the kree everywhere: stripped trees and the bones of killing grounds scattered across the grasslands, where the kree had ingested the liquefied innards of large animals, entire herds of them.

Diligently, each morning the lone man continued to smear him-self from head to toe with the kree blood he carried with him, and smeared his remaining zels and his hunting cat too until they all stank from it. The reeking grease made his clothes stick to his skin, but Cole tolerated the discomfort, knowing that it helped to mask their scents from the native kree.

It was his only protection in this barren land, that and making sure to keep his distance whenever he sighted the scuttling creatures through his eyeglass. During the nights he simply hoped that his camp would not be discovered by chance, and bedded down listening to the chirp of the small birds in their cage that would be his first and only warning of attack, brought all this way on the back of a zel.

This close to the Edge, nothing lived on the ground but the grasses and trees and the small animals that buried themselves deep in their warrens during the hours of daylight. In every direction, the horizon maintained the same unremarkable flatness, save for the occasional grassy hummock standing there like an island, topped by stands of the strange boli trees. While riding, Cole would never tire of watching the trees at this time of the year, their crowns of resinous leaves ablaze with flames, trailing smoke into the sky that carried their sweet scents and seeds. Or at night, burning like stands of torches against the stars.

The longhunter saw no birds in the sky, none at all. It was believed the birds were afflicted by the air here, afflicted in the same way that humans were whenever they stayed too long in the Hush, rendered infertile, melancholic, even mad.

Indeed, his own moods only worsened, just as they had done during his previous solo expeditions. Cole snapped at the big cat that accompanied him whenever she got in the way; a lean domesticated prairie lynx with reddish fur and a manner more doglike than feline. Always she growled back at him just as moodily. The zels snickered and nipped at each other's necks, and the birds in the small cage grew silent. He started talking to himself and the animals more often. It became hard to focus on simple tasks, and Cole's heavily scarred face set itself into a permanent scowl of concentration beneath the brim of his hat.

At night, the dreams oozed into his head whispering of dark and lonely things. Cole would waken with his hands trembling and his mind filled with isolation, wondering for the hundredth time why he was here in this forsaken place, why he insisted on putting himself through this misery year after year so far from home and family.

But then he knew the answer, even if he did not wish to face it.

Deep down, he knew that he was a coward.

*

It was the first wind of the night and it came without prelude, a sudden tussle of air that made the badlands all around him sough in their empty vastness. Its breath rattled the bare limbs of the tree beneath which Cole lay deep in troubled sleep, though the long-hunter did not stir.

Above him in the tree, a solitary seedwing swung from a bare and twisting branch, the last of this year's crop tugging as though for its release. Somewhere out in the corrugated badlands, a mott called out beneath a sky made bright by the low hanging moons.

From his dreams the longhunter cried out and then fell silent. The cat too, curled and sleeping against him, whimpered in distress. Moonlight from the Sisters shone on Cole's white, clammy face, painted shadows in the folds of canvas wrapped around the longrifle propped against the trunk, before they faded behind drifting clouds. The breeze across the Hush faded to a trickle.

In the sudden darkness of his night camp, in the small wicker cage he had brought all this way, the pair of chirl birds suddenly ceased in their chirping.

Nearby, where his three zels stood out as slashes of chalky white in the blackness, heads went up as the birds fell dead to the floor of their cage and a little bell tinkled into the night. Nostrils flaring, ears twitching, the zels scented the air and listened to the nearing murmurs in the ground.

Still Cole did not awaken.

From the east the pack of kree scuttled towards the sleeping man's position, the breeze carrying their hunting spores before them. In silence the predators split up to surround the camp from every direction, scrabbling on their six legs across the scrubby ground with tiny puffs of dust.

The zels tensed for flight, but the hunting scents of the kree seized them and froze their bodies to the spot, their muscles locked and trembling. They could make no sounds from their throats. Eyes rolled animal-wild in their heads. Cole too sniffed the air and croaked in sudden despair. Next to him the cat pricked up her ears, opened her eyes into slits. She tried to stagger to her feet, fell over onto her side. With a surge she tried again and forced herself up, where she stood rooted to the spot unable to growl, her glassy eyes staring out at the darkness, fixed on the motions of an approaching kree.

Again the wind came, stronger this time. It was enough to tug the solitary seedwing in the tree above the man. Once, twice, three times it tugged before the seedwing detached itself with an inaudible snap and fell spinning towards the ground, where it settled on the man's right cheek.

His face flinched.

In an instant, Cole was struggling up from his sleeping furs with bile and the reek of kree burning his throat, knowing that he was in danger, and that his worst fears were about to come true. Instinctively, he swung for the longrifle and grabbed it up, then swung back again to appraise his chances, seeing the shivering rumps of his zels and the dark form of the cat rooted there on the spot. The hairs on her back were standing up on end.

A zel cried out, and then something hidden by the darkness dragged it to the ground.

No time for his pack or saddle. No time for anything but to run.

Sweet Erēs, the Milk! he thought, seeing the bundle of jars sitting next to the bird cage, everything he had worked so hard to gain. But then he spotted the oily dark sheens of kree carapaces coming right at him, and he thought no more of anything but escape.

'*Cat!*' the longhunter shouted as he ran for the nearest zel.

At the sound of her name the cat snapped from her spell and launched herself snarling into the darkness ahead. Cole grabbed a fistful of the zel's mane and leapt onto its back. The animal came to life beneath his weight, and he spun it around in a kicking panic, searching for a way out. Movement all around them now. He spotted the cat loping past, choosing a direction of escape.

'Yah!' Cole yelled, kicking the zel to follow after her, and his young mount sprang forwards. Cole rocked into its lengthening stride and with his teeth tried to pull the canvas wrapping free from his rifle, jouncing wildly without a saddle and stirrups.

He chanced a glance over his shoulder. The second zel was following behind them with white foam frothing from its mouth. Shapes were closing fast on its tail.

Cole brought the wrapped longrifle down behind him and aimed it at the creature – his fingers seeking out the trigger through the canvas – and on the next upstride he fired, the end of the wrapping bursting into flames.

In the momentary flash of light Cole glimpsed the zel falling, and instantly set upon by dark carapaces.

The Milk! his rattled mind cried again, knowing it was lost to him now, a fortune in Milk; that they would sniff it out and bring it back with them to their warrens.

Cursing bitterly, the longhunter leaned forward with the rifle held out to one side for balance, his muscles sinking deeper into the rhythms of his mount while he kicked it for all it was worth, keenly aware that other kree might still be in pursuit of them.

They followed hard after the cat like refugees cast from a dream, man and zel bearing the last guttering light through the emptiness of the Great Hush, for the end of his canvas-wrapped rifle was still burning, trailing a thread of sparks and smoke through the long night.

CHAPTER THREE

Cheōs

Halfway up the mountain path the Dreamer staggered and dropped to one knee, slapping a palm against the rocky track whilst the gusts roared and shoved at her back like bullying giants. Cursing, she raised the borrowed shield above her head again for protection against the falling hail, and looked out at the black storm clouds rushing in over the Painted Mountain, hardly believing what she saw.

The hailstones were growing larger now, chunks of white ice dropping from the broiling sky the size of fists, hammering against the wooden shield in her grasp and bursting noisily all around her on the boulders and scree of the slope. In panic, a family of mountain goats brayed and scampered downwards in leaping kicks. The Dreamer gritted her teeth, pieces of ice almost knocking the target shield from her grasp. With keenly narrowed eyes she scanned for cover, and when she spotted a nearby outcrop and set off for it through the barrage, Shard was thinking fiercely: *this is no ordinary storm.*

Beneath the overhang of rock, she bent her long body under its shelter and watched the deluge of ice turning the mountain slope white with frozen debris. Shivering, she pulled the fur collar of her longcoat about her neck against the blasts of frigid wind, and tossed the chipped and splintered shield to the ground.

Shard gasped aloud, running a hand over her dark, slicked hair while she felt the mirrored half-mask growing chill against her face. It was the first real storm of winter here in the Free Ports, by far the worst she had ever seen on the island of Salina, and she was starting to realize how crazy she was to be out in it.

Thank Erēs the hail was lessening, vanishing with a last few clattering strikes on the slope, though in its absence the blasts of wind grew fierce enough to pin her to the rock, flattening her dark hair and the black and white feathers sprouting from her collar.

Should I risk it? she considered in all seriousness, but then a tree limb went whipping past in a gust and the air whistled in warning, and Shard leaned back to reconsider her options.

Some help would be needed if she hoped to make it any further. Her numb hand plucked a vial from one of the many leather pockets on her belt, and she twisted it open, took a good long sniff from the powdery contents within it, bitter and numbing at the back of her throat. The Dreamer gasped from the dazzling effects of the narcotic now surging through her blood. Her eyes dilated, senses sharpening towards a point where time was slowing down. Details leapt out at her.

A linen shirt flew through the air, flapping its arms as though trying to return to the washing line it had just been swept from. Not far from the lines of washing below, some of the garrisoned troops were trying to stop the zels in the corral from breaking out in their collective fright. Behind the struggling figures rose the white build-ings and domes of Cheōs, her beloved Academy of Salina, nestled in descending terraces on a broad shoulder of the Painted Mountain, which itself rose as bare rock from the tree line below, ringed by bands of colour, stripes of ochre and honey.

From the many chimneys, grey smoke blew to nothing in the blasts of wind. Sparks flew from the wires of the Sky Batteries hang-ing between the domes. Even as Shard watched it, a turning water-wheel on the side of the foundry seemed to slow in its motion. A few students hurried from the library across the open spaces, their feet kicking aside bits of ice, heading for the exotic gardens where broken glass gaped from the glasshouse roofs – worried, no doubt, over their personal crops of hazii weed and stimulants. Mandalay would be in a fine lather over the damage to her glasshouses, where the Observer grew all manner of experimental plants for their medicinal properties.

Over the gleaming dome of the sky observatory, used on cloudless nights to study the cosmos though closed now and shedding ice in the gale, she could see down the mountain slope to the coastal low-lands of the island and the blue sparkle of the Midèrēs beyond, where a fleet of League warships patrolled for Mannian incursions.

The sun was still shining down there. Apparently the storm was a localized phenomenon, streaming in from the west in a narrow band of dark clouds. More evidence that this was anything but natural. Shard wondered what they were making of it in the shack of exotics at the very top of the mountain, where wizened old Observers pursued their obsession of understanding and predicting the weather.

Shard, are you there?

The voice in her head came through the farcry she wore like a belt beneath her clothing, a warm and fleshy object pressed against her skin. For a moment she thought it was Remedy again, one of her rooks in her private eyrie further up the slope, contacting her to ask what was taking so long. But when the voice spoke again in her head she realized instead that it was Coya Zeziké, her contact within the Few. Shard frowned with impatience.

What is it Coya? This isn't the best time for chat.

Trouble?

A storm just hit the island. And one of my rooks is in trouble. Where are you anyway?

Are we secure? Can we talk?

Of course.

I'm on Breaker's Island, a few hundred laqs south-east of you. I'm using the farcry on my skyboat. Listen, Shard, I'm with the Rōshun. I finally recruited their aid!

The Rōshun? You found them? As usual, Coya's news was of the most surprising kind. *Where were they hiding all this time?*

In Cheem, just like I said! The Empire has destroyed their monastery there. Now they're keen to join us and take them on.

The war, Shard realized with growing unease; he was contacting her because of the war.

For ten years now the people of the Free Ports had lived under siege and blockade by the Empire of Mann. It was an ongoing struggle for their existence, in which the most crucial front lay in the easternmost island of Khos, where the famed city of Bar-Khos stood right on the throat of the Lansway – that bridge of land connecting the island with the occupied continent to the south – blocking the Empire's endless assaults with the colossal walls of the Shield.

Shard had arrived in the midst of it a year into the siege, as a young girl and refugee from the southern continent. An awful and harrowing business, and she had been glad to be gone from it when her family had moved elsewhere in the Free Ports. But now the Empire was attacking again with all its might, stirring up the coals of the war once more. Already they had landed a force in Khos by sea, an Expeditionary Force that had threatened to storm Bar-Khos from behind – before General Creed, Lord Protector of the island, had stalled them by launching a surprise night attack with a much smaller army, in the process felling their leader in battle, the Holy Matriarch of Mann herself.

Shard, I'm going to Bar-Khos after I finish this business with the Rōshun. The city is in trouble. The Empire closes in on them again.

A frown formed on her fine Contrarè features.

But I thought there was a lull in the fighting, now that the Holy Matriarch is dead? You said last week the Expeditionary Force were stalled in the middle of Khos, fighting amongst themselves?

They still are. But now trouble comes from the south, in Pathia, against the Shield. An old villain returns to the scene of his crime. General Mokabi, previous Archgeneral of the Empire. The man who launched the first assaults against the Shield of Bar-Khos, and was retired when he failed to take the walls. He's leaving Sheaf now with a quarter of a million mercenaries, intent on finishing what he started.

You're joking. How many?

Enough, Shard, he's bringing enough to storm the walls of the Shield no matter how many reinforcements the League sends to the city. Bar-Khos can't hope to hold on without intervention.

No doubt he was making it sound worse than it really was. Which was his usual tactic whenever he was about to ask her a favour, something else on top of all those things she was already undertaking for the Few – this secret network that she had somehow been made a part of, by Coya, yet about which she still knew very little, save that they were a scattering of individuals throughout the Free Ports, working behind the scenes to maintain the spirit of the democras – *people without rulers.*

Well she wouldn't have it, not this time, not with everything they were already doing in aid of the war. For all that Shard knew, one of her rooks was up there even now in her eyrie losing her mind for the cause. They could give no more.

Shard?

You've always said the Lord Protector knows what he's doing. I doubt he will make it easy for them.

Creed? He's still recovering from his heart attack. From what I hear he's hardly his old self.

You haven't spoken with him?

He ignores my missives. But his people say he's in a bad way. I'll be travelling there myself soon to see what aid I can lend them. Many of us are heading to Bar-Khos right now. It's where we need to be.

The lump in her throat grew sharper. She knew now what he was going to ask her, and Shard no longer felt the cold against her skin, no longer felt the wind at all.

Shard, I need you to come with me to Bar-Khos.

Now you really are joking. Have you any idea how much I have on my plate right now?

Bah. So you always say whenever I ask you to leave the Academy. You're the only Dreamer we have, Shard. Not to mention the best rook in the Free Ports. This time I really need you. The democras needs you.

I'm not your pet Dreamer, Coya. I'm not here to be dragged in front of an army every time you need to scare them witless with some fancy light and dazzle show.

That isn't – strictly – the only reason why I need you there.

Then why?

Because . . . you're Contrarè.

The woman straightened at that, banging her head against the overhang of rock. It was the last thing she had expected him to say.

In blood only, she hotly replied. *I was raised in a town, Coya. I went to school. I'm no more Contrarè than those fake totems your bodyguard keeps sending me for his own ridiculous reasons.*

He wants you, that's why he keeps sending you those baubles, Shard.

I know what he wants – you're avoiding my point!

You're still Contrarè, Shard, no matter how much you try to hide the fact. We need you. Marlo suggested the plan and he's right. If we are to save Khos, we must make another effort at gaining the aid of the Contrarè in the Windrush forest, bring them into the war on our side. They can help tie up the Expeditionary Force indefinitely in the north, while the Khosians focus on dealing with Mokabi's threat to the south. Which means I need to go there personally and speak with the Contrarè. Which means I need our resident

Contrarè Dreamer along to show them whose side I'm on. Which would be you, Walks With Herself, unless you know of another.

Shard was twenty-three years of age, but she felt altogether older than her years as she crouched beneath the rock, blasted by the storm, feeling herself pulled this way and that by the demands of her abilities.

Barkbeaters was the derogatory name for her people, the indigenous Contrarè of the region. In the city of Sheaf where she had grown up, the local Pathians had treated her kind like dogs – those Contrarè living there after their tribes had been pacified, driven from the diminishing forests of northern Pathia to work whatever sweat jobs they could find in the cities. Shard barely knew what it was to be Contrarè, save for old myths told by her parents and how to sing songs during dances and, much later, how to pretend she hadn't noticed the fascination of eyes upon her features and the grasping of preconceptions.

I can't, she told Coya firmly. *I have too much going on here to just drop it all and leave.*

Shard!

Contact me later. This isn't a good time right now.

With a command of will she broke the connection between their two farcrys, then offered a shake of her head and a few worthy Contrarè curses to the gale; another legacy of her parents.

Coya's words echoed in her mind like ghostly accusations.

How she loathed this war with the Empire, resenting the time it robbed from her studies of the raw bindee, her attempts at exploring these abilities she still barely understood as a fledgling Dreamer.

Thank kush her parents had gotten her out in time, not long after Pathia had fallen to Mann. And thank kush she had gone on to find her place in this world, right here on the slopes of the Painted Mountain, in this academy which welcomed anyone of ability regardless of their fortunes or their blood or their gender, and which supported itself and its students largely through donations and outreach colleges in the towns and city, where its name of Cheōs, reflecting the spirit of open-minded learning, had become synonymous with wisdom itself.

After so many years spent studying here, Shard held a deep love for this place where she now lived as a rare prize to the Academy, a

Dreamer in residency – indeed the only Dreamer in the Free Ports. Certainly, she had no wish to leave again any time soon.

Absently, Shard's gaze was drawn to the open palm of her hand, where the rainbow colours of her glimmersuit swirled like oil on water, a transparent second skin that lived upon the entirety of her own.

Before the storm had hit, she'd been down in the culture-tanks checking on the latest experiment for the glimmersuits – trying to create a method that would reproduce them from samples taken from her own. But the results remained unsatisfactory, the secrets of the second skin still largely a mystery; something else the Few would no doubt be pestering her about soon, even as Coya tried to persuade her to drop everything and come with him into the maws of the war.

Shard, please respond.

Coya, I'm serious, this isn't—

It's Remedy, cut in the voice of one of her rooks.

What is it?

Just suggesting you hurry if you can. Moon's worse than we thought.

Is she conscious?

Her eyes are open. But I don't think anyone's home.

Thunder cracked the sky open, shook the mountain and the air and the juices in the pit of her belly. All day Shard had carried a feeling of sick anticipation in her stomach without knowing that it was for this moment now. Moon had been her finest, her brightest. Now the girl was likely gone.

Stay clear of the Black until I get there. I'm doing my best.

Understood.

Lightning flashed and struck the iron conductor of one of the domes, for an instant coursing along the dangling lines of the Sky Batteries.

The Dreamer could do little about the lightning just now, but at least she could do something about the wind. When the height of her narcotic rush began to subside at last, Shard knew she was deep enough to work a glyph, and pictured one in her mind, a golden shining thing she had crafted from the bindee with such occasions in mind.

Her glimmersuit began to warm against her skin, colours swirling faster across the backs of her hands; a conduit of her will, rousing itself to the raw bindee around her. For three years now she had worn this second skin upon her own, ever since stepping from a hidden pool in the Alhazii desert; the shell of living liquid reaching into every orifice of her body, never to dry. Yet still she could feel the touch of things. Still she perspired.

When Shard willed the mental glyph to life the wind around her fluttered and began to lessen. She stepped out from cover, the worst of the gusts deflected around her by the subtle manipulations of chance some distance upwind.

Normally it took little effort to maintain this kind of glyph, for it was always easier to manipulate non-living things such as the movements of the air. But she was still drained from last night's work, and her mind was buffeted by the elements. She needed to be quick.

Shard ducked out from the rocks and hurried upwards along the track, propelled by the steady eagerness of the wind. At least it was no longer trying to barge her flat to the ground.

She was panting by the time she reached the steps leading to her eyrie, though she maintained her pace as she stamped up to the log house above, perched on an outcrop of rock amongst a lone stand of shaking dwarf pine.

Reaching the front door, Shard dropped the glyph in her mind and stepped inside, her longcoat suddenly billowing with air.

CHAPTER FOUR

Terravana

In the frigid darkness of a cave the farlander Ash stood alone, smiling to himself in reverie.

Through his mind and heart ran a memory of his lost apprentice Nico; the night in Bar-Khos when they had stolen into the menagerie, creatures calling out into the darkness all around them. The boy's sly humour as he turned from the pond with the dripping egg in his hand, thrilled at his own bravery.

Your turn!

A smile tugged at the corners of the old Rōshun's mouth. Eyes opening to slits, Ash gazed into a small alcove carved into the wall of the cave, where a candle flickered warmly, blackening the rock above it with smoke.

The small alcove had been empty when they had first arrived here a day earlier by skyship, at this ancient island Hermitage in the sea. Now it was swept clean and occupied by the candle, along with two stout urns of clay.

In the larger urn were the bones and ashes of Oshō, leader of the Rōshun order, his friend and mentor fallen in the defence of their monastery in Cheem. Next to it, the smaller vessel held the remains of his young apprentice Nico, months passed now since the boy's death in the far imperial capital of Q'os.

Swaying in something of a trance, the farlander was filled only with the lingering impressions of the boy who still haunted him, still lived on in his mind where his son and his wife also lived on, all three in some way entwined. At his back, the never-ending growl of the Terravana lulled Ash into a peaceful stillness, sent a vibration through his bones that soothed the pain in his lower spine. He

26

basked in the strange sounds, carried along by their rhythms and the flow of emotions washing through him.

A place of memories, this cave in the side of the sea cliff. So Meer the fake hedgemonk had told him. Its curious flute of singing stone was said to stir the past into life again.

In the cool air of the cave, the column of white rock behind him rose from the flattened floor into the jagged roof overhead, glittering with the same mineral deposits that sparkled across the walls. There were small holes along the height of the Terravana, like nostrils on the undersides and uppersides of carved knobs of rock. The deep growling sound was coming from these openings; a panting, wavering, never-ending force of air gusting up and down within the hollow column itself, a growl accompanied by the distant booms of crashing waves far below.

The first holy men of the Hermitage had carved and refined what they'd found in this cave until they had achieved what they believed were perfect notes of harmony. For fourteen hundred years the same sonorous tones had been echoing in this space without interruption, longer than the Oreos of Lagos had been standing, older even than the city states of Markesh; and now they rode through Ash too, physically vibrating the fibres of his being.

The hermit shamans were gone now, their community of Istafari having faded into obscurity. Now all that remained was the ancient sea-cliff Hermitage itself and its empty spaces running through the solid rock, echoing with old ghosts.

Ash blinked, staring at the candle flame as it flickered in a sudden draught. He glimpsed a bonfire on the sandy floor of an arena, Nico's face smothered by the rising flames before a crossbow bolt shot into the boy's forehead, one that Ash had shot himself from the heights of the Shay-Madi, hoping to end his misery.

I had to do it, he told the trace of the boy that still lingered on. *There was no other way, or I would have taken it.*

Silence, save for the wavering tones of the Terravana.

Perhaps the sudden pain in his head was an answer. Ash winced and chewed on the bundle of leaves in his mouth all the harder. How long was left to him now, he wondered . . . A few months perhaps. A few weeks even.

There was a time when such reflections would have spurred him to seize the moment for all that it was worth, to make the most of his time while he still could. But now the knowledge of his nearing demise seemed only to lessen the long weariness of his soul. In a way Ash would be glad to lay down the struggle, glad to rest his bones in peace.

Only one last thing left to do, if he still had the time.

Ash stared at the urn of Nico's ashes and wondered once more if it was possible, this desperate plan of his.

Chasing miracles, my boy. What more can I do than that?

*

'Ash, my man. I've been looking for you all over.'

Ash turned his head to see a crooked figure standing in the tunnel that led out to the steps carved on the side of the sea cliff, blocking what little daylight made it this far. It was Coya, leaning on his walking cane as he stepped closer into the dim glow of the candle.

'And now you have found me.'

'Thanks to Meer. He suggested you might be hiding down here.'

The old farlander exhaled softly and regarded Coya with his hooded gaze, this man who had flown the Rōshun from their destroyed monastery in Cheem to here, the deserted island Hermitage that was their new sanctuary in the Free Ports. Coya stood hunched over his cane by the burdens of his contorted body, though his young face looked serene within its frame of lustrous blond hair.

High on the hazii weed again, as so many of these people in the Free Ports seemed to be, where the growing of the weed approached a form of artful worship, and where the herb itself was used for all kinds of ailments of both body and mind, including the aching joints of Coya.

'How goes the unpacking?'

'Noise and dust everywhere. Though your people seem in good spirits. I think they're satisfied with their new home.'

He referred to the surviving Rōshun, many of them apprentices, up above in the empty chambers and passages of the Hermitage carved by its community of shamans now long gone.

'Aye, you did well to bring us here,' Ash consented.

Coya Zeziké, Delegate for the League of Free Ports and member of that secret network known as the Few, lowered his head by way of acknowledgement. 'You seemed lost in thought when I entered,' he remarked. 'Thinking of the past, by any chance?'

'A little. Meer warned me this place can bring memories to life. Something about the sound that it makes.'

He said nothing more, for he had come here to be alone and the desire still persisted. Coya cleared his throat, perhaps sensing as much. Still, he did not leave, instead favouring Ash with his striking gaze, this fellow in his mid-twenties whose stoop and walking cane gave him the appearance of a withered old man.

Here was a person who made the most of his appearance as best he could, as witnessed by his oiled blond curls and his manicured nails and his elaborate, splendid robe of cream silk; a vanity that seemed incongruous to the rest of his modest ways, though not, Ash supposed, for the direct descendant of the spiritual rebel Zeziké, philosopher of the democras.

'Thirty years in exile living as Rōshun,' Coya murmured. 'You farlanders have come a long way since your cause was broken all that time ago.'

He spoke of the old country, Honshu, and the failed people's revolution there, and of the three old farlanders still alive within the order.

'Our cause was never broken,' grumbled Ash. 'Only betrayed.'

Coya eyed him standing there with his sword leaning against the wall within easy reach. 'I'm told you're still something of a revolutionary, in your own way. You like to take on tyrants when you can.'

'I hear glamour in your voice, Coya. Careful you do not make a romance of things from afar.'

'Afar,' Coya chuckled dryly. 'Revolution is my business, Ash, or hadn't you gathered that yet? I've been studying our uprising here in the Free Ports ever since I was a youth, the good and the bad of it. Even now, more than a century later, that same revolution carries on thanks to people like myself, people who help this experiment of the democras to survive.'

He was speaking of *the Few*, Ash knew. That invisible web of individuals scattered throughout the Free Ports and perhaps further, chosen how or why he didn't know, but working for the benefit of the democras, otherwise known as the Mercian Free Ports.

The network was still mostly a mystery to Ash save for what little Coya and Meer had so far offered him, just enough to know that they could be trusted, perhaps, and that the equally secretive Rōshun could work with them, for they shared a common enemy after all, and they were both followers of the Way with its emphasis on *Balance In All Things*. How long the Few had been around and how powerful they really were seemed a matter best left unspoken. He suspected they had been here since the very beginning, working through shadow-play and cunning as they did even now.

'You were lucky here in the Free Ports,' said Ash at last. 'Your revolution turned out well for you and is yet to be subverted. You have nurtured a respect for the land and the spirit here. The people have a voice that is heard, a say in their daily lives free of masters.

'In Honshu though, even before we were betrayed, we did not know if we were fighting for a different set of rulers to replace the old. And in imperial Q'os, their own revolution spawned the Empire of Mann, and their sham representation of those they govern. A revolution that is also ongoing even now.'

'Bah,' said Coya with a scowl. 'Theirs was a coup without the support of the people. Besides, madness always lay at the heart of the Mannian cult. What can you expect from a people who worship their own selves and believe that everything is to be exploited? No wonder they spawned an empire of oppression. No wonder they hate the Free Ports so explicitly, and try in the blackest of ways to undermine us, and conquer us.'

Coya lightly rapped the tip of his cane. 'But regardless, it's good that you are here, taking a side at last.'

Yes, here they were, the remnants of the Rōshun order, preparing to take the war to the Empire despite their beliefs in neutrality; bent on revenge, on seeking justice for all those who had been lost back in Cheem at the hands of the Empire.

'The Rōshun. You will resume your vendetta trade from here, do you think?'

Ash ignored the subtle inflection of judgement in the man's voice, directed at the Rōshun trade of violent retribution. Instead he looked off to one side, where the boxes of seals had been stored under canvas for the time being in the driest part of the cave; all of them rescued from the Watching House beneath the monastery ruins in Cheem.

A faint rustling could be heard from the boxes of Rōshun seals. The hundreds of living leathery things inhaling and exhaling in their straw padding.

Another memory flashed through his mind with the startling whiteness of snow. His very first solo vendetta as Rōshun. Following the footprints of pilgrims for a hundred laqs through the passes of the High Pash, leading him to a windy shrine to a god with no name, where he had found the man he had tracked all that way to kill.

Yet his target had seemed to have only redemption in mind, not escape. The fellow had swayed on the lip of a rocky precipice not far from the shrine, readying himself to jump; a murderer unable to live with the shame of having slain his older lover. Ash had sensed her just then, the slain woman, for he wore a seal on a thong about his neck which was the twin of the seal she had worn herself for protection, and even though it was dead now, like its twin, it still contained a trace of her.

Wait – she forgives you! Ash had called out to the man through the buffets of wind, but he was too late, for even as he spoke the fellow stepped forward off the rocks, and disappeared over the edge.

Ash had shaken his head in wonder. His first lone vendetta, completed without drawing blood.

'We still hold protection contracts with many people,' he informed Coya now in the cave of the Terravana. 'And the gold they paid us for that protection. Yes, we Rōshun will restore our numbers, and we will resume our work once we are done with this war against the Empire.'

'Assuming it's over soon.'

'Yes. And that the Free Ports win. It would be a shame to have to move again if they do not.'

'Oh, it would be shame in many ways. The difficulties of the Rōshun order is certainly amongst them.'

Ash frowned at his own insensitivity. He knew well enough what the people of the Free Ports were facing, surrounded by the Empire's blockade. Most of all the besieged people of Bar-Khos, clinging by their fingertips on the brink.

'Forgive my levity. A habit of mine when dealing with the horrors of this world.'

In response, Coya's smile was replaced by a sudden seriousness; as though his relaxed spirit rode above a deep well of anger. Something from his youth no doubt, a crippled boy who always had to prove himself, a boy in constant pain.

'If you knew the imperial forces now approaching the Shield, you would be truly horrified. A host of mercenaries from all over the world led by the previous Archgeneral, Mokabi. I head to Bar-Khos when I'm done here to see for myself. Which reminds me, I have some good news for you. A skyship is on its way to pick you up.'

'At last.'

'Hush now, you've only been waiting a day. You might be pleased to know the *Falcon* was available as requested. A good choice, I'm told. The fastest flyer in all the Free Ports.'

It was good news indeed.

'The *Falcon* and her crew once carried me to the southern ice and back. I would like that kind of expertise again.'

'Well you shall have it, though the captain needed some persuasion. He tells me the crew are ragged from lack of shore leave. You will need to go easy on them, Ash.'

'Easy? We fly over the Broken Spine of the World during winter and from there into the Great Hush. Then we must search out the Isles of Sky. There is nothing easy about this venture. You are certain they volunteered for this?'

'They know the risks, Ash. And yes, they volunteered . . . after I explained the importance of this voyage you wish to undertake.'

'Important to me. Hardly to these men.'

'Important because we live up to our promises. You helped to bring the Rōshun order to the Free Ports. They will be a great boon to our struggle against the Empire right now.'

Ash clenched his fists by his side, feeling the momentum of his actions accelerating now even as his heart beat faster. Once more, he wondered if he was justified in seeing this through to the end, in risking the lives of an entire crew for the sake of a single boy, for the crazy notion that somehow – in the legendary Isles of Sky where the people were said to live forever – he might bring his apprentice back to life.

He didn't even know if the feat was possible, for all that Meer the hedgemonk assured him so. Yet it had been the price of his bargain with the Few, his price for agreeing to bring the Rōshun here.

'If we make it back, the crew must be rewarded well. Their families too, if they do not survive. I consider this part of our bargain.'

'Of course. I'll see to it personally. And in return, you must remember your promise to me.'

'Which one?'

'Ash, please.'

'You mean, *do not get caught*.'

'Do not get caught by the *Alhazii*. We rely upon the Caliphate for all our vital trade. Most of all for black powder. If you are unfortunate enough to be caught by them anywhere near the Isles of Sky, they must know that this is to be a private venture by the Rōshun and nothing more. Hence why your contract with the captain will be in writing. And why the *Falcon* has been registered falsely with a bondsman in Cheem using a forged port pass. The Free Ports cannot be implicated in any way with this endeavour of yours.'

'Relax. I have no intention of starting a dispute with the only trading partners you have left.'

'We are agreed then,' said Coya Zeziké, nodding in satisfaction.

Ash inclined his head to one side and studied the man closely. He knew that Coya was holding something back here, and had suspected as much from the very beginning of their arrangement.

The young fellow had every right to be concerned though. They spoke of the most dangerous secret in the known world here, the location of the Isles of Sky. For centuries, the Alhazii Caliphate's monopoly on exotics – those materials obtained from the mysterious Isles of Sky and nowhere else, most of all black powder – had been based solely on the jealously guarded knowledge of how to find those secret islands. Their monopoly had allowed them to garner riches in long-lasting peace while kingdoms rose and fell around them, using embargoes to cripple those nations who dared seek the location of the Isles for themselves.

Only with the promised guidance of the fake hedgemonk, Meer, did Ash hope to find the Isles too. Meer, another member of the Few, claimed to have once visited the Isles as a hidden stowaway on an Alhazii trading ship, seeing just enough to discern their general location – somewhere along the eastern coast of the Great Hush.

In a flash it came to Ash, his suspicions fully formed.

'You want the location of the Isles for yourselves. That is why you have loaned me this skyship for my own task.'

Coya glanced back at the entrance to the tunnel. 'Be careful what you speak aloud, Ash,' he said in a hoarse whisper. 'Even here.'

'You do not deny it.'

Coya frowned and gripped the head of his cane tightly.

'Come,' he said. 'Follow me.' And Coya picked up the candle from the alcove and led the way across the uneven floor of the cave towards a low far wall.

There was another tunnel back there leading downwards, dark as pitch. Coya's head barely cleared it as he ventured inside, the small flickering candle flame lighting his way.

'Come,' he said again, drawing Ash after him.

*

They stood in a cave larger than the one above containing the Terravana, and silent as a grave.

Slowly Coya searched the walls with the guttering flame until he came to a stop, holding up the candle to a flat expanse of rock.

'Ah yes,' he said breathlessly. 'Just where I remember them to be.'

Ash followed his gaze. On the wall were a series of faded paintings, ancient designs much older than the Hermitage itself, pictures of zels and bison on the run, men with spears loping after them. A time before the rise of civilizations.

In the first painting, green pine trees rose above a herd of strangely shaped, four-legged creatures peacefully grazing. In the second painting the scene was the same, save for a striking object descending from a sky filled with starry crosses, its descent marked by symbols like arrowheads or the tracks of a bird. A third image portrayed the vessel settled on the ground, with the shapes of tears falling from its body and scattering around it, where new plants were sprouting upwards. The last showed the squat object buried in a hill, and around it the original herd replaced by creatures familiar to the eye, most of all naked humans, women and men and babes.

They were depictions of the creation myth of the Sky Tribes. Ash had seen similar pictures in the desert of western Honshu, painted on the sides of an outcropping where the shadows would have made it comfortable to sketch. They were said to be found throughout the world.

Once again he wondered if the myths of the Sky Tribes were true, these seed ships landing from the stars.

Why not? They had to come from somewhere?

Now that they were further from daylight and deeper in the darkness, Coya set the candle on the floor and turned to face Ash squarely.

'The skyship is yours because of our deal, Ash. You may have use of the *Falcon* for as long as it takes. But yes, of course, there are more hopes pinned on this voyage than your own. Some people believe that with our backs to the wall it is time to take this chance at last. With Meer's guidance you may well find the Isles of Sky for yourselves. If you do, he will return to us detailed charts of how to get there and back.'

Ah, it was starting to make sense.

In the ongoing war between the Empire and the Free Ports, it was common knowledge that the neutral Alhazii Caliphate wished to preserve the present balance of power, for their profits in black powder remained sky high so long as they supplied both sides in the conflict. Which was why they maintained trade with the embattled islands of the democras, helping them to survive against the Empire's ever tightening grip; maintaining the status quo without becoming embroiled in the war themselves.

But Coya was hoping to change that stance, using the leverage of the Isles of Sky and the knowledge of their location.

No wonder the man was so fearful of the *Falcon* falling into Alhazii hands and the Free Ports being implicated. An embargo of black powder could ensue, and that would mean the rapid end of the democras.

'I hope the risk is worth it,' Ash rumbled.

'Great rewards must demand great risks. With detailed charts to the Isles we can negotiate with the Caliphate for more aid against the Empire. If they threaten embargo we can threaten to sell the location to the highest bidder. We can tip the Alhazii into taking more of a side in this war, more of a risk. At the very least, it's a chance for us.'

'Yes. I can see that.'

'You are fine with this then?'

'If it helps the people of the Free Ports, I am all for it.'

Coya's breathing was loud over the silence that befell them. He was staring at the wall paintings again, fascinated by what he saw.

'There is more riding on this than the fate of the Free Ports,' he said.

'How so?'

'The Empire of Mann threatens our entire world, Ash. Their greed is a void like no other. More than death it is anti-life. Unless we stop them here, the Mannian creed of the divine self will turn all cultures into their own through conquest and the promise of plenty, and their greed will go on to strip the entire planet.

'I have seen it in my nightmares, Ash. Great pulsing hive cities covering the globe and sucking the life from it, and all the civilized peoples believing themselves to be separate from the world and each other, so they are as malleable as cattle in their master's hands. If the Mannians win here they will carry on victorious until they have ravaged Erēs to the bone, and then the entire world will burn.'

With a sniff, Ash swayed back from the wall. He had noticed before how Coya tended to speak with a subtle inflection of fear whenever he mentioned the Empire. No wonder, when he understood their nature so precisely.

To travel the Empire extensively, as Ash had done, was to see such things in a state of acceleration. Fences and stone walls cutting through previously open ranges. Hills of sterile white bones where once there had been herds of plenty. Waterways discoloured with poison for the sake of quick harvests of fish. Endless laqs of singular, pest-prone crops where the soil grew salty through over-irrigation, or was swept away as dust for lack of tree roots, never to be restored. Mountains with their flanks blown off for coal or precious metals. Much of the great forests of the heartlands felled to stumps and memories. Species after species going extinct as their habitats were destroyed.

People grew affluent from the race to fully exploit the land, some much more than others and many not at all, and all the while the world about their lives grew ever more poor and enclosed.

It was enough to cast the mind far ahead as Coya seemed to have done, and imagine where all of it was heading.

Maybe they really had come from the stars, he reflected now, staring at the image of a vessel descending from the sky. Maybe they had even devoured their old world and this was their final act of desperation, sending out ships to seed another.

'Make it fast, Ash. We need those charts to the Isles. If we are to save it all we must stop the Empire here in its tracks!'

CHAPTER FIVE

The Black Stuff

The Dreamer Shard was dreading what was coming next, but she pressed on regardless, barging into the house with the storm winds chasing her inside.

From their oval worktable her two frightened rooks turned to blink their surprise, then blinked again when she banged the door shut behind her.

The wind was howling down the chimneys of her eyrie, rattling the panes of watery glass in the window frames and a few tiles that had been loosened on the high roof arching overhead. In the criss-crossing draughts an Alhazii desert-canvas swayed on a wall next to some Contrarè vine writing, while the pages of open notebooks ruffled on tables filled with the miscellanea of Shard's work: exotics from the Isles of Sky and vials of stimulants, relaxants, entrancers. Her ears still ringing from the fading crashes of thunder, Shard could barely hear what the younger men were saying to her, babbling in their eager fright.

Ignoring them both, the Dreamer approached Sholene on the opposite side of the worktable, where the young woman still sat connected to her farcry. The object squatted before her on the table, breathing lightly; a living egg-shaped mass of flesh and veins and nerve tissue the size of a wooden pail, still glistening wet from a recent dousing in the feeding tank. One of its fleshy connection cables was held in her grasp as though she was in silent communication with someone on a distant farcry, or simply *rooking* them – eavesdropping on a conversation, stealing into their memories, playing them in some other way.

But no, the girl's eyes were partly open. Sholene gazed as though oblivious to the outer world.

Shard checked that she was still breathing, and carefully took her pulse.

'What was she working on?' she asked of her two surviving rooks now watching over her shoulder.

'Rooking a Mannian farcry in Sheaf,' Remedy said, talking over the howls of the wind.

'Claimed she was listening in on General Mokabi,' Blame added with a shrug. 'We thought she was joking.'

Shard grunted. She snapped her fingers before the girl's face, but there was nothing there.

'Get juiced up, the both of you. We're going in.'

*

They were up for it, even Blame – a young man who had only joined her team in the previous week, chosen from the many student rooks of the Academy because most of all he was good at what he did, but also because he was startlingly attractive.

Both were eager young rooks obsessed with the artificial reality that was the Black Dream – just as Shard had once been – even as they remained keenly aware of the dangers of their craft. How could they not, when one of their own sat there with her mind blown away? It was the storm outside that had really spooked them, Shard realized now as she watched them eagerly clutch the fleshy connections in their grips, take dabs of rush oil to quicken their minds, before closing their eyes to settle into the Black.

Shard had no need for the farcrys that sat before them on the table. Beneath her embroidered vest, pressed against the second skin of the glimmersuit, hung a living belt she had purchased from a Zanzahar exotics smuggler for the price of a Dreamer's miracle in return. It had been smuggled from the Isles of Sky themselves where their foreign sale was prohibited, or so the blackmarketeer had claimed: a portable farcry that could be worn and used anywhere at any time.

Without fuss she took to a seat and closed her eyes, and after a few moments felt her mind sinking downwards, and then she was in.

*

Seat of Wisdom, meant the name Cheōs. The renowned Academy of Salina was perched high on the slopes of the Painted Mountain, where it had been founded centuries ago as a place of intellectual training for the young sons of the Michinè, those families of aristocracy who had once ruled across the islands. In Cheōs, these young men had been taught the importance of competition, titles and costumed pageantry, and most of all how to lead rather than follow.

Within its walls, Ateziké himself, famed philosopher and spiritual father to the democras, had once taught his persuasive style of rhetoric to the fresh-faced young nobles in attendance, hoping to breathe some air into the status quo of the islands' many royal and merchant families from within. But eventually Zeziké had been cast out for his ever more obvious polemic. Even his name had been banned within its walls.

Now, ironically, a statue of the man stood before the front entrance of Cheōs, for in the following centuries his imagined democras had indeed flourished into life, thanks to the revolution, and a different spirit had filled the halls of the Academy, one of open learning for all.

Ever since then, other Academies had been blooming into existence across the Free Ports, closely following the lead set by the newly dynamic Cheōs, including its shift into the field of exotics, those living materials bought from the fabled Isles of Sky through the monopoly of the Zanzahar Guildsmen. As a rising movement, one which created all manner of unexpected boons for the Free Ports, the most surprising developments of all had come only recently, and from the students themselves.

With the decade-long war against the Empire setting a keener edge to all their lives, the students had turned their time and initiative towards finding new and unexpected ways of using those exotic materials they were daily instructed in. Most crucially of all, they had begun to spend more time playing with the communications device known as a farcry, which offered access to other farcrys through a medium that had long remained a mystery, the Black Dream.

*

Stars shone in a field as black as the night sky, though instead of suns they were distant farcrys, entire constellations of them set against a firmament smeared with the faintest of colours. Even now Shards's pulse quickened at the sight of it. Next to her roared the white glows of the rooks' three farcrys, their surfaces alive like colourless suns in miniature. Movement caught her eye: two orbs emerging from them to join her disembodied form, beating slowly like hearts.

Weightlessness. An experience Shard could never take for granted. Dolphins must feel this way. Soaring birds. People falling far to their deaths.

Slowly, Shard spun in place, taking in the far Horizon, a band of pale and tangled lines like bird scratchings across a slate, belting the entirety of obsidian space. Her mind was crystal, and she saw everything in the sharpest of detail as clear as an eagle's gaze.

Somewhere back in that other dream of the waking world, the Dreamer's features relaxed as though she was home.

Sholene, she willed in her mind. *Moon!*

Faraway, a star pulsed brightly.

You see it?

Yes, came the responses of her two rooks.

We jumping in? asked the younger rook Blame.

Not a chance. We'll fly there and approach from a distance. Enable your cloaking suites and follow my lead.

Even now it still thrilled to venture out across this open vastness. Outwards the trio sped, streaking across the Black leaving trails of light in their wakes, accelerating ever faster until the nearest stars began to shift and take on colours, while behind, they left a tiny constellation of suns that were at first their own farcrys, then all of those of the Academy, then all the farcrys in the Free Ports; an archipelago of stars hanging there in the Black.

What are we thinking here, a Mirror? came Remedy's voice, as cool as he always was when nearing a threat.

Unless someone has thought of a new way to scramble a person's mind.

I hope it's something new, said Blame eagerly, tactlessly.

Across empty space they flew with the stars drifting by on every side. Far to the left passed the constellation of the Alhazii Caliphate, arrayed around a tight cluster that was their capital city of Zanzahar. Directly ahead, growing larger now, spanned a reef of stars that was the southern continent under Mannian occupation, the odd light streaking between one pin-point to another.

Other movements flickered out there in the Black, the ghost-light of old trails still slowly fading; a matter of days sometimes to fully fade away, weeks even. Shard called up her suite of defensive glyphs and willed all but two of them into life. Her cloak was the last thing she activated, and she watched as Remedy and Blame did likewise, their light dimming to almost full translucence.

Together they fell towards the reef of stars and the pulsing Mannian farcry where Sholene was located; the port city of Sheaf in northern Pathia. The city closest to the besieged Shield of Bar-Khos.

As they decelerated, Shard activated a sniffer and sent the faint ball of light ahead of them to take a look. It found nothing but the nearing farcry itself and the hovering presence of Sholene. The girl's orb was beating as delicately as her pulse.

They stopped and scanned the area, close enough to see Sholene hanging like a moon around the Mannian farcry, still seeing nothing out of place.

Hang back, Shard told her two rooks as she dived down to Sholene.

*

Seven years ago, Shard had come to the Academy of Salina to find herself in the midst of a quickening revolution. In those early days of rooking, the Academy's only ageing farcry had been used for practice sessions or for conferences between the Observers of different Academies; a bulbous living thing squatting under a dusty cloth upon a table, breathing lightly. In secret, through trial and error, the students had learned how to take covert cuttings from the priceless device, and from those cuttings how to germinate their very own rudimentary farcrys.

Back then the results from the cuttings, grown without notice alongside sanctioned experiments in the tanks, were small and delicate things which barely breathed, though they had been alive – just enough – to project the students into the dimensions of the Black Dream.

The visual definition had been dreadful. So low it was like flying through a fog. But the replicas allowed them to play in the Black Dream with limitless freedom, and most of all that was the key to their ensuing success.

From the students' official lessons of the farcry, they had known how there were established methods of manipulation within the

Black Dream, traditional ways to operate and find your way around. It was a mutual communications device after all. But with practice, they discovered there were fewer limitations to these methods than they had been taught, that there were ways to nudge and influence what you could do by using creative visualizations of the mind and efforts of will, much as Shard was later able to manipulate reality as a Dreamer, though in the Great Dream – the waking world itself.

Within the Black Dream of the farcrys, the students had been doing things that no one had ever heard of or even considered before, overcoming the limitations of their sickly replicas with endless patience, youthful cunning, and strong doses of stimulants to quicken their minds.

The simple trick of secretly listening in on another farcry was passed on in the back circles of their daily lectures and consciousness lessons. Soon the first River had been discovered in the Black. Ghosts were seen in the hinterlands of its dark expanse. A student from the Academy of Coraxa claimed to have discovered a series of farcrys so far away they couldn't possibly be of this world, and then others reported seeing them too, hysterically, before the devices suddenly vanished without a trace. Myths grew and mysteries deepened.

To the exclusion of all others, those students most passionate about their new craft started clustering together in excited groups, exchanging hushed secrets. Someone started using the name 'rook', and it stuck.

Shard herself became the first rook to ever crack the farcry of a foreign nation, one belonging to a minion within the Alhazii Caliphate. Together with her friends she listened in on everything being said. Shard was also the inventor of the thought-worm, which after months of effort she was finally able to smuggle into a Mannian farcry and have it transmitted as speech. Her lover Tabor Seech, notoriously, became the first to show that minds could be damaged in the Black Dream through another's force of will, making him the first to introduce violence into the rooking craft.

*

Still no response from the young woman, not even now.

Shard approached the white orb that was Sholene, trying to gain a sense of her but failing.

She said she was listening in on General Mokabi?

One of her tags went off. She went for a look before we could get prepped. Said the Brambles were worse than before, but she got in. By the time we arrived she was poking around in someone's memories and saying it was Mokabi himself talking to someone in Serat. Said she'd found something you would want to see. Then she went quiet.

I'll engage first. Don't come in unless I tell you it's safe. And keep scanning the Black, I don't want any surprises.

I hear that.

Shard willed herself towards Sholene until white light filled her vision. She hoped she could still find a loose thread of the girl's mind that remained untangled, something to lead her back to safety.

There was a flicker of light as they connected, then all at once Shard was in a different place entirely.

A room with arched windows of white gala lace blowing in from a sea breeze. Gulls shrieking outside and the azure blue of a placid harbour. Shard was sitting in a chair, and a white-haired man was standing behind her shaving her face with a straight-edged razor, for she caught a glimpse of him in a mirror on the wall and then she saw her own lathered face; a nose poking out from the white froth that was tattooed fully black, the highest military ranking of Mann.

Staring out from a pair of dark eyes like gashes, Shard took in the old and unmistakable features of General Mokabi, famed ex-Archgeneral of the Mannian Empire, despised conqueror of Pathia and the rest of the southern continent.

Coya had remarked that General Mokabi was marching from Sheaf with an army larger than any ever seen, intent on taking the Shield of Bar-Khos from the south where the siege had been raging for ten long years. Which meant this had already happened, and what she saw was some kind of memory. Sholene was caught in one of Mokabi's recollections, no older than a matter of days.

With growing unease Shard called up her profiling glyph and ignited it with a spark of will, calling to life the habits she had ingrained within it. The glyph vanished, and in its place sequences of running dashes or solid lines appeared wherever she looked, seemingly chaotic for the most part, rippling with patterns wherever there was something to be seen. Raw bindee, the underlying language of the Black Dream; the underlying language of everything.

No one could decode the bindee save for that rare individual, a Dreamer; it was the very thing that gave them their power in the waking world. Within the Black Dream of the farcrys, rooks made do with more generalized manipulations using will and trickery, usually performed through collections of habits enshrined in easily recallable glyphs; a visual method that Shard had naturally carried on into her Dreaming.

Now she studied the immediate bindee of the Black Dream, and saw the shape of what she was inside.

I'm in some kind of memory construct wrapped in a loop. It's what she got herself trapped inside.

Can you reach her?

I don't know yet. I've never seen this before.

Let me see, said Blame.

No! Stay back, both of you.

Well who did this to her? demanded Remedy.

It was a sound question. And the instant she reflected upon it, an image appeared in the mirror over the shoulder of the barber; a head writhing with what looked like many snakes; a sharp face glistening with the sheen of a glimmersuit.

Shard, what is it? You just flared up like a grenade.

What a day this was turning out to be.

It's Seech, she thought with loathing. *Seech did this to her.*

Tabor? He's working for the Mannians now?

It would appear so, though she could barely believe it. To think that her ex-lover – the only other Dreamer from the Free Ports before he had fled to work for the Caliphate – would fall so low as to join their fated enemy. Shard had grown used to thinking of Tabor as a murderer, a thief and a mercenary. Now she would have to think of him as a traitor against his own people too.

Perhaps the Empire had offered him more riches than the Caliphate, or perhaps the Caliphate had simply grown tired of his services, for the Alhazii had Dreamers of their own, and little need to put up with the man's usual provocations, for even as a young student, Tabor had always delighted in shooting off his mouth and puncturing the certainties of others.

Shard was aware of General Mokabi wondering just then how the man had appeared as though from nowhere. He didn't suspect that the image was created and projected by his own mind – just as every-thing else was, ultimately – and that Tabor Seech was not really there at all, but spoke to him through thought alone. The old general knew only enough to fear the Dreamer's powers. His ageing heart was beating faster now.

'You wished to speak with me?' Seech asked in his strange, scratch-ing voice, always spoken in a slow monotone, and General Mokabi cleared his throat, his body tensing as the Dreamer took another step closer behind him to leer over the barber's shoulder, a few of his writhing dreadlocks snapping out at roaming motes of dust.

Mokabi squinted into the mirror, peering at the rainbow sheen of Seech's glimmersuit made bright by the light of day. His second skin was identical to Shard's. They had gained them together three years earlier, during an expedition into the Alhazii deep desert as lovers and star students of the Academy. A journey which had led them to the holy men in their tower of mud bricks and to the ancient secrets of Dreaming: of how to lucid dream in the waking world – and all other degrees of reality – by playing with the living bindee of the cosmos.

'You took your time,' the general barked aloud, and his barber jerked backwards with the blade in his hand, startled that the general was talking to himself.

'Well now I am here, so talk.'

'My message was clear enough, Dreamer. And the price well beyond generous. Just tell me you will do it.'

'Ah, but generous is such a relative term, don't you think?'

The general waved the barber away with a flourish of temper, wiping his face clean with a towel. With the coolness of an old dog, Mokabi stared up at the figure in the mirror, dressed in a suit of wine-red silk beneath a cloak of darkest night, a lean and wiry fellow swaying with an inner dynamism; a man burning up with great desires and passions.

Shard's old lover looked much the same as he had done three years ago when last she'd seen him, though his eyes were bloodshot and his face had grown a little leaner. She'd heard how he imbibed regular infusions of Royal Milk these days, not as an anti-ageing remedy but purely for the kick of vitality it offered him, so rich had he become, selling his services.

Back in the higher reality of the waking world, where Shard sat in her storm-battered eyrie with her eyes closed, the badly scarred portion of her face was itching beneath her silvered mask, and throbbing with a dull pain. Beneath her glimmersuit, her goosebumps had arisen in a rash of emotions.

'You have a problem now in aiding us against your own people, the Free Ports?' asked Mokabi's level voice.

'It isn't a deal breaker, no.'

Tentatively, as a test, Shard tried to will herself away from this loop of memory, to jump to a different reference point outside of it. Nothing happened and so she tried harder, as hard as she was able, until she sensed a measure of panic rising within herself and cut back.

I could be in trouble here.

I'm coming in, Remedy declared. *I can't help from out here.*

What? Stay clear, you hear me?

But it was too late. She felt her rook's presence in the same loop of reality that held her so fiercely, and cursed to herself in Contrarè.

It's tight all right, Remedy remarked, studying his own profiling glyph in action, its output much less sophisticated than Shard's, not raw bindee but ghostly shapes and impressions. *Can't see any feedbacks though. Maybe if we run some dampeners and yank out from the Black, it won't be so bad.*

You're welcome to try it first.

You think maybe—

Sshhh!

By the window Seech was talking again, and his brittle voice held all the general's attention.

'You're asking me to openly go to war against my own people. Needless to say, such a thing should warrant a higher price than usual. Let's say your offer is enough, at least to pay for my coterie of rooks while they run communications security on your assault. It might be enough, even, to entice them into running some offensive actions against your enemy's communications too. But if it is *me* that you are after, one of only half a dozen Dreamers in all the Midèrēs and the only one that will work with you, then I'll need much more than that. Otherwise you're wasting my time here, old man, and my time is more valuable that most.'

The general crunched his false teeth together hard. Peeved as he was his voice remained detached of feeling. He had larger needs than the sating of his own annoyance.

'How much for it all?'

'For it all? Five times as much.'

'Agreed.'

It was the turn of Seech to hide his surprise.

'Perhaps I should have asked for even more.'

'Don't push me, Dreamer. Taking Bar-Khos means everything to me. That doesn't equate to my purse being infinite. Just tell me where I need to deliver the gold.'

'No need, you can give it to me in full when I arrive at the siege.'

I don't believe it, she thought with a start.

Shard?

Ssshhhh!

'And when should we expect the honour of your presence?'

'Soon. I have some business to finish off first. An old lover to contact, in fact.'

Who is he talking about? Is he talking about you?

Seech spun around to face the seated Mokabi fully. The Dreamer's expression had changed in some subtle way, and his eyes were bright while the lower part of his face lay in shadow.

Shard had the sudden unnerving sensation that Tabor was staring not at the general now, but directly at her.

With two strides he was before her and clamping his hands to either side of her head, his fingernails digging in sharply. Shard tried to reel away from a sudden wave of pain, but she was pinned there by his glare.

Sabo! she called out in her mind, a single panic-word that popped protection glyphs into action all around her.

'I thought you might want to know,' Seech said down to her, and she could smell his breath and the perfumed scent of him just like the real thing. 'I'm coming to the Shield very soon. If you want to settle our old score once and for all, you can seek me out there.'

Feedback, Shard. We're being hit by feedback.

Shard was too busy to respond for a moment, for she was igniting every glyph in her dampening suite one after the other, knowing now that Remedy was right and that pulling the connection was their only chance.

Blame, can you hear me?

Yes.

Get out and slap some shock-patches on our necks, we're going to need them.

White light blinded her, flooded her with a howling wilderness of agony, a stunning assault of feedback that would have blown her mind had she been unprepared for it. Her dampening glyphs started buckling one by one.

Blame, hurry!

*

Following the initial successes of their home-grown imitation far-crys, the student rooks had refined their replicas while the practice had spread fully to the other Academies, where others had taken up the craft too.

These days, the Academy of Salina treated rooking as an official pastime of much of its student membership, admittedly a dangerous pastime now that they were engaged directly in the war, their efforts concentrated against the larger network of enemy farcrys in the empire surrounding them. The League had become interested in these developments, and was directing what aid it could their way, including new fully sized farcrys shipped all the way from Zanzahar, large fortunes each one of them, in return for their sustained work against the Empire of Mann.

In response, the Mannians and the Alhazii Caliphate had begun to train and recruit their own small cadres of rooks, including a few from the students of the Free Ports, bribed by riches to pass on the secrets of their trickery. As a further consequence, the inner security of farcrys – an aspect long ignored by those institutions who used them for distant communications – was tightening further every day, and becoming rapidly more violent too. Now minds were torn when caught in Tumbler traps or blasted away entirely by the latest enemy Mirrors.

The Black Dream was becoming ever more a place of war.

*

Shard jerked her eyes open, her vision swimming with the same nausea that came with the worst migraines, sagging back in the chair in her log house that was still shaking with the thunder and wind of the storm.

On the opposite side of the oval worktable, Remedy's head lolled back on his neck, eyes staring emptily at the ceiling. His hand twitched on the wooden surface, still clutching the end of the farcry's fleshy tether.

'He's dead,' Blame said flatly, standing next to him holding a shock-patch in his hand, peeling back Remedy's eyelids to reveal their glassy stare.

Shard felt the sting of the shock-patch on her own neck, feeding a concoction of medicines that helped prevent her heart from stopping and her brain from being scrambled in a seizure, though it came with its own risks every time one was used.

'I didn't have time to get to him,' Blame said quietly. 'Sorry.'

Anger rose in her gullet, became a silent scream directed at Tabor Seech, wherever he may be. She stifled it with a clenching of her jaw, feedback still pulsing through her.

'You got to me first. That's what I expect you to do.'

The young man was shaking. She couldn't tell if it was fear or excitement or both.

'Why do I get this horrible sense that now wasn't the best time to have joined your team?'

What team? she thought, taking in her two fallen rooks.

Hail was clattering hard against the shingled roof of the house, though the wind had died down outside. Shard pinched the bridge of her nose against jagged pains in her brow, watching Blame cross to a window and stare out with open-mouthed wonder.

'What is it?' she gasped.

'I'm not sure. Maybe you should come and see.'

She sighed, then made a careful effort to rise to her feet. Shaky. Her sense of balance all over the place. Shard trod slowly to join him by the window, steadying herself against its frame.

At first she thought it was more hail falling, but no, these things raining from the storm clouds were oddly dark.

'What do we do about Moon?' Blame asked.

'What we always do. Bring her down to the infirmary. Wait for her body to die.'

'It was really Tabor Seech in there?'

Awe in his young voice; speaking of a legend that every rook had heard of.

The storm was Seech's doing, she realized now, and she was as impressed by the feat as much as she was shocked by it. To have created a weather phenomenon of such scale . . . Tabor would have needed to set it up weeks ago, tipping small and delicate factors in intentional ways. He had planned this from the beginning, waiting for the storm to hit today before springing his trap within the Black Dream, sating his vain need to show off his brilliance with a touch of the dramatic.

He was goading her. Challenging her to face him in Bar-Khos.

Lightning crashed within the clouds. It provoked images in her mind; Shard left for dead in the desert sands by Tabor Seech, half her face contorted in burning agony, blood flowing from between her legs.

'What *are* those things?' Blame wanted to know, leaning close enough to the window to mist the glass. His voice was near lost in the deafening clatter of the shingles.

Shard staggered to the front door and yanked it open, gazed in both horror and fascination at what she saw outside.

'Get ready to leave,' she cast over her shoulder. 'Pack what travel gear you can find.'

'We're going somewhere?'

In her dripping cloak, the Dreamer stared hard through the doorway with her seething eyes taking it all in.

They were snails, those things falling from the sky. Hundreds of snails with their shells smashing across the flat stones of the path.

CHAPTER SIX

Killing Truth

They were arguing with each other, gently at first, though their voices were rising with the heat of the words; two men who lounged in comfort on the upper deck of a rocking warwagon, rumbling onwards towards the siege of Bar-Khos.

It was religion they quarrelled over, of all things. Philosophy and the underlying assumptions of life, while they were tended with chee and sweetmeats by mute servants who were the slaves of recent conquests. Like many people of fame, both men feigned not to notice the attentions of those around them, though it was impossible not to, for the air sizzled with raw hostility. Within earshot, the Mannian priests, bodyguards and officers of staff held their tongues in silence but glanced with dangerous eyes at the strangely garbed figure who spoke blasphemy to their general, hatred coiling within them.

No doubt they would have killed this man, had General Mokabi not been paying him so generously for his unique abilities, and had they not known enough of this Dreamer to fear him.

In the waning afternoon daylight, Tabor Seech's skin shone like water and snakedreads writhed on his head. The cloak that he wore, made from layers of hanging cloth strips, soaked up the light with its eternal blackness, blotting him out from the world save for his lean face and his scowling, bloodshot eyes. Stiffly he sat, bedecked with a curious brace around his neck; a gold contour of skin that rose out of the collar of his fine silk shirt, and flowed up around his chin and jawline in curving flames which gripped his face lightly, flexing when he moved.

In his drawn-out tones, the Dreamer pressed on without challenge, his words a calmly measured violence wrought upon them all, so much so that one of Mokabi's nearby bodyguards began to stir nearby, the blades sliding from his lowered scratch-glove.

Tabor Seech pretended not to notice this too.

'Truth you say?' he exclaimed, his nasal singsong of a voice rising so all would be sure to hear him, recklessly enjoying himself. 'And what could you Mannians know about such a slippery thing as that, when you regard truth – *reality*, in other words – as a fixed position to be wholly objectified?'

General Mokabi, ex-Archgeneral of Mann, shifted his weight in the chair uncomfortably, his body gone to fat in these years of retirement. Against the winter chill he wore a hat of grey wool upon his bald dome, beneath which his nose was a prominent wedge blackened with ink. In a face made puffy with age, his eyes were nonetheless alert, inquisitive, challenging.

So far, the general had remained composed in the gale of this man's provocations, though privately Mokabi was appalled, wishing he had never begun this discussion in earshot of his people. Clearly there was no telling how far this Dreamer from the Free Ports might go, how much heresy he was willing to stir for the sake of making his point, and Mokabi could think of no way of stopping him. Not without losing face.

Furtively, he glanced towards a figure sitting hunched on a nearby chair, the Mannian historian and writer Sheldin Ting, bundled in layers of wool and scribbling away in a notebook lying open on a table. Ting was his official biographer for this campaign. A civilian, chosen because he had long been a trusted mouthpiece for the Empire's official narratives, and because he had agreed to write only what Mokabi allowed him to write. Still, he remained a loose set of ears nonetheless.

It was Mokabi's own fault, he knew. In his buoyant spirits he'd somehow thought he was his younger self again; a youth with a reputation for fiery debate, when really he was an ageing general brought out of retirement for his final campaign. He was rusty now at this kind of conversation, too many years spent commanding the obedience of those around him.

'And how else would you have us regard *truth*, then?' he asked with a rougher voice than he would have liked.

'As a gamble of course. A gamble of perception.'

'Hardly a practical suggestion, that. Or is this why the peoples of the south call life the Great Dream, because you are so uncertain all the time of everything?'

In reply the Dreamer threw up his hand before letting it drop into his lap again. His dreadlocks were writhing about his head like snakes, and a few lashed out at the hostile stares around him. 'Surely it must be a matter of degrees and educated guesses rather than absolutes? More than simplified dualities of either *this* or *that*? A combination of the two, or a myriad of different perspectives, or a deeper paradox entirely, unknowable through reason alone?'

The Dreamer inspected Mokabi with his dark eyes; searching for his elusive truth perhaps. 'Take the order of Mann for example. You people are so filled with self-importance and certainty that your minds are closed off from anything beyond your beliefs. If anyone is in need of more doubt in their lives, it is you Mannians most of all. Doubt allows you to stay open to new evidence, new ways of thinking. Doubt keeps us human, allows us to shine a questioning light upon our predicament.'

'So we cannot be certain of anything,' grumbled Mokabi. 'Is that what you're really proposing here?'

A chuckle from one of the priests nearby. His bodyguards pursed their lips together in silence. 'That our actions should be riddled with doubts? *Pish and nonsense I say!* You offer a religion for old women and do-nothings. We did not build an empire on such humbling sentiments. We did not become great on the backs of our indecisions.'

General Mokabi threw a winning grin to his people then composed himself with a sip of chee, observing the man from where he lounged on the sedan: the Dreamer smiling thinly now, dangerously. A chill ran down Mokabi's spine as the warwagon rumbled onwards along the road.

He's like a child, thought the general to himself. *A spoilt child lacking restraint or any respect for authority. I've enlisted the aid of a dangerous fool.*
Yet if I am to take Bar-Khos, I may need him.

Seech was still smiling when he next spoke. 'Indeed the whole world knows of your growing mastery over machinery and nature,' countered the man. 'Yet it is interesting how there are no Dreamers amongst you, no mystics either, not even any real sense of spirit in your daily lives. Only an order of priests spreading dogmas that deny the vitality of life, whilst proclaiming your own selves as a chosen people. And such people! You talk as though you have no beliefs at all, only truths, only the *way it really is*. To listen to your words, you would think it is everyone else who is blinded by their own ideology. Not you.'

General Mokabi caught the eye of his cleverest priest, Anastaza, his religious and legal adviser, swaying back and forth amongst her white-robed companions. They were all glaring at the Dreamer now with naked intent.

Not yet, Mokabi thought. *Not while he still holds the advantage.*

'And you,' chuckled Mokabi with genuine mirth, feeling somehow freed now by the ferociousness of the man's statements, by the open insults of his words, 'you are such a paragon of selfless virtue. Ethical lessons from Tabor Seech, of all people!' And the old general tossed back his head and laughed aloud to press home his point, for he knew the Dreamer's reputation only too well, knew what things he had done for the gain of fame and riches.

Seech's hands were as dirty as the rest of them, for all that he liked to speak like a monk of the Way.

What was this, a sudden withdrawal? The Dreamer had turned his face towards the afternoon sky, and was gazing out without expression over the nearest wooden crenellations that surrounded the deck of the warwagon, silenced at last.

The unexpected cessation of words was like the empty howl after a storm.

Relieved, Mokabi held his cup out for more chee, squinting ahead as the warwagon was pulled along the road by a swaying line of massive, shaggy mammoots. The general's vision had grown poor in his old age, though he steadfastly refused to wear spectacles while on campaign. Squinting a little, he took in the paved military road running before them straight and true, filled as far as he could see with the marching ranks of his mercenary army.

A road that even now led them northwards towards the Lansway, that bridge of land between Pathia and Khos, and the besieged walls of Bar-Khos known as the Shield.

'Look at you all now,' returned the Dreamer's relentless voice in the wind. 'Wishing to take out your knives and gut me for what

I'm saying – for mere words. Are your foundations so insecure you cannot talk about them openly?'

'I suspect it is more your lack of respect.'

Seech raised his voice again for all to hear. 'I have little respect for anyone in this world. You people hardly stand alone in that.'

A truce then, not a withdrawal after all.

'Anastaza!' Mokabi called over to the priest at last, huddled with the others around a smoking brazier. The woman bustled over in her white robe, her eager eyes blinking amongst a face of silver piercings.

'Anastaza. Our guest has expressed some misunderstandings concerning the ways of our creed. Perhaps you would care to enlighten him a little further.'

'*Please*,' drawled the Dreamer in disgust, waving her away.

With a bow, Anastaza began to chant one of the wordbindings relating to the nature of ultimate truth. Her words tumbled out in a fast patter that could only just be followed, a structured argument that had first been used by Nihilis himself, legendary first Patriarch of Mann, as written in his Book of Truths before his untimely death. It was impossible to lose a discourse if the priest was skilled enough in the use of wordbindings, and he knew that Anastaza studied and recited them night and day.

'This is what you offer me?' Seech protested, and Mokabi wondered if he had discovered his weak spot at last, an hysterical loathing of boredom. Even Mokabi could barely stand the droning of wordbindings, had always hated having to learn them as a youth in the Mannian order.

He was surprised when Anastaza abruptly fell silent in mid-sentence, and he saw her hands reaching for her throat and her lips suddenly flapping without sound.

Seech was blinking at the woman's rising horror without expression.

What has he done? Mokabi wondered, as Anastaza glanced at him for support but saw only his annoyed curiosity.

'Enough,' Mokabi sighed, and waved the voiceless priest away.

'A neat trick. What did you do, make her think she couldn't talk?'

'Perhaps she simply realized the emptiness of her own words.'

There was laughter in the man's wretched stare.

Possessed with a need to assert himself, Mokabi lifted his hand to the serving boy by his side, and stroked his thick mop of hair with longing. The youth tensed, not meeting his eye.

He knew the boy still had a tongue in that mouth of his, not yet a mute.

Tonight, Mokabi thought with a throb of his cock. *Some dross and hazii weed to relax you, then we'll see how shy you really are.*

A clatter of porcelain. A sudden searing heat in his lap.

Mokabi leapt up from his sedan chair, yanking at his sodden, scalded crotch as Tabor Seech watched on with quiet bemusement. The boy had clearly knocked the cup over in feigned accident. Now he was apologizing in his stuttered backwoods Pathian while his face drained of blood, eyeing one of the bodyguards raising a scratch-glove with its poisoned blades extended from each finger.

'No,' Mokabi snapped at the guard, and glared at the youth until he caught his frightened eye, saw the glint of defiance still burning there. 'Put a slave collar back on him. Have him sent to one of the pleasure houses when we reach the camp. Maybe he'll be less clumsy with his hands after a hundred soldiers have had their way with him.'

The boy's expression flared red as he was led away.

A shame, in a way, but there were a thousand more where he had come from amongst the slaves accompanying the army.

'Oh father and mother, forgive me,' the Dreamer beseeched to the sky, mockingly. 'For your seed has fallen far, far from the tree.'

General Mokabi stared at him, perplexed. Once more he wondered how much he could rely on this man who had fled the Free Ports, and once more decided not at all, not beyond the fortune in gold he was paying for his services. A traitor working against his own people? Mokabi trusted him even less than his own peers.

Seech frowned and pinned Mokabi with a fierce glare, as though he had heard his thoughts.

'I just erased two rooks from my old Academy for you,' the Dreamer said thickly. 'Not to mention rolling a storm across the Free Ports.'

'You read thoughts too?'

'No need. I have eyes.'

Then I hope you become food for the crows after this is done. I hope I get to spit on your grave, you arrogant self-righteous piece of dung.

The Dreamer inclined his head, saying nothing, staring instead along the road they followed north towards the Lansway and the city of Bar-Khos.

CHAPTER SEVEN

The Cats of Istafari

The old man was so focused on his task that it was a surprise when he glanced up and saw the cat crouched there on the edge of the desk, its round green eyes staring at him as though in provocation. It was one of the hostile ones, one of the big scarred fighters that seemed to bully the rest of the feral cats living here in the ancient sea-cliff Hermitage of Istafari, and which were now sizing up even the newly arrived Rōshun.

Ash stared back at the grey-haired animal's gaze. These creatures had indomitable wills, he knew by now, and they were fearless too. They'd been getting into everything since the Rōshun had inhabited the chambers and passageways of the Hermitage a handful of days earlier, the deserted spaces carved through the rock of the sea cliff, draughty with the fluid breezes from the sea.

'I'm not your enemy, you fool,' he told the cat perched on the edge of the desk. It was clearly willing to stare at him all day.

Maybe it didn't speak Honshu, because it only growled at him softly. Ash raised a single eyebrow. Without warning, he hissed at the animal fiercely enough that it bounded from the desk and fled through the flap in the door.

With a smile Ash sat down again, gladdened that he felt only a twinge in his lower back today. He'd been suffering from back pains on and off for weeks now, though this morning Meer the hedge-monk had administered his hot needles and stones again, while reciting more recollections of the Isles of Sky, which Ash had barely registered amongst his own grunts of satisfaction. Afterwards, he'd found that the shooting pains had mostly gone at last. A miracle worker, no doubt about it.

Relaxed and feeling good, Ash picked up the stylus once more and waited until he had regained the thread of his thoughts.

It was so long since he had written anything down – a letter, a poem that he had heard, a list of things to aid his memory. Ash had trouble crafting the words he needed now while he still had a chance to write them. With the stylus held stiffly in his inky fingers, he muttered and scratched away at the sheet of paper as best he could.

When he was finished, he peered down at the words scrawled upon the page and saw how they were little more than a short and simple list of instructions.

Upon the event of my death:

Return half my shares to the coffers of the Rōshun order. Give the remaining half to Reese Calvone, mother of my late apprentice, Nico Calvone, who resides near the city of Bar-Khos. If she cannot be found then see that it is given to someone else belonging to his surviving family. Burn my body.
Ash

Such words of testament should contain some flair in them, Ash thought as he read them over; some sense of who had written them. For a while he reflected on what words he might use to convey some sense of spirit or sentiment to those who would read them after he was gone, but he discarded them all quickly with a shake of his head.

Such pretensions in your old age. Who will care what it says? Who will even remember this sheet of paper after the shares are divvied up and you are gone and their lives carry on?

Still, even so . . . Ash snatched up the stylus with a flourish, and using the last of the ink on its nib he wrote, beneath his name:

With heart.

Finished, Ash stared down at the ink glistening in the morning light, then leaned forward and blew across it lightly, watching the gleam fade as the ink cured.

Death, his eyes read.

Body.

The farlander chewed on the leaves even harder and noticed the stylus shaking in his hand. He set it down, and lay his trembling hand on the desk too. Another symptom of his illness.

He rose and approached the thin tall window where the new

shutter was still to be fixed into place. A soft sea breeze played across his face. Far below, the blue-green sea of the Sargassi filled his eyes, its surface blown about by the winds into a wintry froth.

The view faced south in the direction of his forthcoming voyage. From here it was easy to imagine the Sargassi extending all the way beyond the horizon to the lands of the southern continent, now under the heel of the Empire. And then to push beyond those lands, on to the Aradèrēs mountains, the Broken Spine of the World, over which they would pass into the emptiness of the Great Hush in hopes of gaining enough Milk for his later task in the Isles. If he did not die first. If he did not get them all killed.

The swells were still rough down there from the winter storm that had just passed over this small island of goats and overhanging cliffs. With pounding force the waves crashed against the rocks at the foot of the cliff, releasing their foamy tangy hiss into the air.

Further out towards the horizon, he spotted one of the mammoth coral trees standing like a tower in the water, topped by what looked like a tangled crown, hints of white at its base where the swells broke upon it. Another tree was barely visible further to the west. Living things seeded a thousand years ago or more, old enough for corals to mass against their submerged flanks, even for certain unique species to clad the trunks which rose into the air, seeming to feed off them. Vertical reefs then, some grown intentionally to support lighthouses in the shallow sea of the Sargassi, the richest waters in all the Midèrēs. Ash could just make out a triangle of sails approaching the most distant of the trees. Perhaps it was one of the great rafts of the sea gypsies, who sometimes used the coral trees for homes during the wilder months of winter.

He had once spent a month living on one of those rafts in his fortieth year, rescued from the waters of the Sargassi near-dead and raving by a clan of sea gypsies who called the shallow sea their home. Traders in pearl and shark skin, Ash had listened with keen ears to the stories of their hallowed ancestors, people who sounded much like the travelling Tuchoni, having fled from the pressures of growing states all around them by adapting to a nomadic lifestyle; though instead of roaming the roads they had taken to the sea, never to return to land again.

In the morning light Ash breathed it all in, allowing the moment to engage his senses entirely. He wondered if he would have liked it here in this Hermitage that was to be the new home of the Rōshun order, this little islet known as Breaker's Island, now that their old monastery of Sato was gone.

A log cracked in the fireplace. A wave thundered far beneath his feet. Ash blinked and leaned a fraction closer towards the view beyond the window. There was something in the sky out there; wings sweeping alongside a great bulbous form. A skyship was approaching.

Lightly, Ash slapped his palm against the sill.

At last.

*

Turning from the window, Ash surveyed all the things he intended to take with him in one easy glance, for they were already piled against a wall. He inclined his head, hearing the sound of footsteps stamping towards his room.

Ash knew who it was even as the door thudded open and Baracha strode in snorting anger.

The first thing he took in was the wooden training sword gripped in the man's hand, and then he met Baracha's hostile glare with an eyebrow raised in curiosity. The skin under the man's lower lip was extended by the pressure of his tongue, something he did when the heat of rage was upon him. Ash looked into the Alhazii's brooding black eyes amongst all the swirls of tattooed script, and was reminded of the touch of insanity in Baracha whenever his temper was flown.

'You mean to do something with that stick, Baracha?' Ash enquired of his fellow Rōshun quietly, nodding to the wooden sword in the Alhazii's grasp.

More footsteps in the corridor outside.

'*Father!*' he heard Serèse call out, Baracha's sharp-tongued daughter. But the big man slammed the newly fashioned door closed behind him without taking his eyes from Ash, and threw across the bolt.

'Beat some sense into you, I was thinking.'

Ah, Ash thought, stepping over to face the man, knowing what this was about.

'They're not going with you. My daughter nor my apprentice. Not on some fool's notion of bringing back the dead.'

'Your daughter is a grown woman. Aléas a grown man. I will not stop them if they wish to travel with me. Will you?'

'You know that I will.'

'Nonsense. It is out of your hands.'

'I tell you I won't allow it. This whole scheme of yours is insane. You've finally cracked, Ash, and I don't mind saying it to your face. Grief has broken you in two.'

Ash took a step closer, close enough to see the bloodshot flecks in the Alhazii's eyes, and Baracha rocked on the balls of his feet, an animal readying to strike. Would he do it this time? Ash wondered. Would he finally step over the line and attack?

'Baracha,' Ash tried, for he had no wish to harm this man. 'You are the new leader of the order, all have agreed on it. And you must lead now by listening to the voices of others. Not as a hot-headed father, nor as a tyrant. You know they will not stand for anything less. Now put the stave away. This is no way to hold a conversation between us.'

'You selfish old bastard,' Baracha grumbled. 'We need you here while we rebuild the order, not traipsing off to your death on some suicide mission into the Hush. *The Hush*, by all that is Holy. And after that the Isles of Sky, where my people will flay you alive with hot sand if they catch you. I'd laugh if you hadn't involved my daughter in all of this. Well no, I say, no!'

'It is her decision. I will not stop her.'

'She barely knew the boy!'

'Yet they were friends, in their own way.'

Baracha stared for a long moment and then sighed in a release of tensions.

'You know my daughter. She's hot-headed is all. Aye, just like her father, before you say it. And she has a habit of forgetting what world she's really living in. A young woman who ignores her father's guidance will end up as nothing but a harlot or a slave in this life.'

'You told her that?'

'Why do you think she's banging on the door?'

'*Father!*' Serèse screamed from outside with the wood clattering in its frame. Baracha rolled his tired eyes; a man who killed for a living, yet out of his depth as a father.

'Come, put the stave down,' Ash tried again. 'Let us sit by the fire and talk a while, as comrades.' And without waiting for a response, he pulled another chair across to the one already before the fire, and sat himself upon it.

The big man sat with a creak of straining wood and rested the training sword across his lap, as though he might still need it. He was wearing a heavy cassock the same deep black as his curled hair, which was tied back from his dark features in a knot. He looked neater this morning than he usually did, his beard trimmed and his hair freshly oiled, the stubble gone from his hawkish, sharp-boned expression. Perhaps he was attempting to set an example in his new role.

Ash thought of how he had once resisted the idea of this man leading the Rōshun order. Yet he had agreed with the others when the vote had been taken, if only because Baracha was the most realistic and cautious of the candidates available. He would keep them alive and safe after he was gone.

With sincerity, over the snaps of the flames in the fire, he said aloud, 'Oshō spoke well of you. He thought you would make a fine choice. He liked the realist in you.'

A grunt. The man was uncomfortable with words of compliment. 'Oshō was a realist too. If he was here now, he would say the same as I and disallow this whole venture of yours.'

'Yet still I would defy him. And still he would understand.'

The anger in the man's eyes faded, buried once more deep within himself for another day, another hour.

'Ash. She's my only child in this world. I tell you, one father to another . . . It would break me to lose her.'

The farlander said nothing, for he was stung to silence by the man's words. His tongue had become a sudden lumpen thing in his mouth.

'She'll listen to you,' Baracha pressed on. 'If you tell her it's too dangerous she will listen to you, you know that. With a few words you can stop her from getting herself killed.'

Ash's sigh was a heavy one. He disliked this burden of responsibility. It was enough that he would be carrying the lives of an entire ship's crew on his back, men who would live or die because of his decisions.

'Fine,' he relented with a clearing of his throat. 'She stays then.'

'And you tell her.'

All at once the tension drained from the room. Together they sat listening to the rude music coming through the door, Serèse's temper fully flown. She was swearing blindly now, in between her threats and insults; a young woman who would not be told by any man what to do.

Ah, Serèse, he thought to himself. *I hope you find your place in this world.*

'If she stays,' Ash spoke up loudly, 'you must agree to cast aside any notions of arranged marriages for the girl. I mean it now. I know how you think and I know Serèse. You will only lose her if you try to dictate her life for her.'

'If you think I'll just—'

'Swear it, swear it now, otherwise she comes with us and takes her chances in the Hush.'

'Fine, I swear it!'

'Good. And Aléas still comes with me. I can use him.'

'So he can get himself killed for nothing?'

'I may need his skills, Baracha.'

Again Baracha's chair creaked as his heavy frame shifted to study the room. He observed the few possessions Ash had propped against the wall ready to take with him; his sheathed sword and his backpack stuffed with clothing, a few books and mementos, nothing else remaining save for the items on the desk.

'You're taking everything?'

A gust from the chimney drove a belch of smoke into the room. The flames flattened out, and then regathered greater than before.

'I will not be returning, Baracha,' Ash replied quietly, and he glanced to the window for a sign of the ship, but could not see it from here. 'I owe this world a body, and my path comes to an end.'

'You're certain then?'

'Soon the pain will be bad enough that I cannot see from it. After that, the end will be swift.'

His words prompted Baracha to swing his arm and cast the wooden sword into the fire. Sparks flared around it.

'You old fool,' he told the dancing flames.

Ash was silent. It wasn't enough though, to say nothing in this moment which was likely their last alone together. He thought back to the testament on the table, its need for some flair in it, some spirit. 'I have left my last testament on the table there. Will you take care of it for me?'

'No,' answered Baracha, and Ash looked to him sharply. 'Better ask someone else for such a favour. If you leave, I'm leaving too.'

'Bar-Khos?'

'With some of the others. We'll establish a forward base in the city. And then we'll turn our skills to striking back at the Empire. I would welcome a chance at that. We all would.' Baracha's voice was grim as he spoke, thickened by passion and memories. He stroked his beard and swept it into the nape of his neck, needing to shape some kind of order in this moment of his thoughts.

'We enter into war against the Empire with barely half of our numbers still remaining, many of them apprentices. We need you here, Ash. I need my daughter and Aléas here.'

'I know.'

'You know, yet still you do it.'

'Yet still I do it.'

He watched Baracha rub the stump of his missing hand where it was banded in strips of leather. The man stared at it long and hard as though recalling the moment the injury had happened, their desperate fight through the Temple of Whispers to kill the son of the Holy Matriarch of Mann.

'Well, you will be missed, you old bastard,' he confided at last, surprising Ash with his sentiment.

They fell to silence. Nothing left to be said.

It seemed as good a time as any to leave. Smoothly Ash rose to gather his bag and his sword, then crossed to the door.

'You had better tell her the bad news then,' he said, and grasped the wooden handle and heard Serèse panting from the other side.

He took a deep breath and flung open the door.

*

Smartly Ash's boots rapped across the flagging of the open gallery, the sounds preceding him through the length of the Hermitage. His eyes narrowed by a sea breeze, he searched for his old friend Kosh amongst all the Rōshun there, his sword in hand and pack hanging from one shoulder. The pack was heavy with the urn of his apprentice's ashes it now carried, removed from the alcove below in the cave of the Terravana. Meer had insisted they would need them if they ever made it to the Isles of Sky.

Ash walked fast to outpace the footsteps behind him, those of Aléas and Baracha who were still arguing bitterly, and the Alhazii's sullen daughter Serèse, who had at least accepted the news from Ash better than she had from her own father.

'Kosh!' he called out, causing the nearest Rōshun to look in his direction. Ash scanned the faces of old companions and younger apprentices alike, slapping a few backs in farewell, shaking hands, exchanging words of good fortune; all of it in a passing hurry, for he disliked farewells as much as anyone else.

None of them had seen his old friend either.

On the southern side the gallery was open to the elements save for a waist-high parapet of stone, where all manner of cats lounged in the weak sunlight, curled in furry balls or watching the comings and goings of the men, many of whom were returning already from their breakfast to tasks of carpentry or the moving of stores and equipment. A whistle of a song threaded its way through the chatter; a sudden peal of laughter. It seemed their spirits had returned now that they were gone from the ruins of their old monastery, where comrades had been left buried in the ground; now that they had a new place to call home.

No sign of Kosh anywhere, which was uncommon of him during meal times, when usually his presence could be guaranteed. Perhaps he had eaten earlier, had taken himself up above to sketch some more of the small island; anything to avoid the dusty, sweaty work of making the place habitable.

Ash stopped before a wooden door at the end of a short passageway, the sound of gulls and his Rōshun companions echoing at his back.

'Look it up yourself!' he heard the voice of young Aléas saying from the gallery behind. 'The early Rōshun of Honshu spelled it out plain as day. The use of master by an apprentice is a sign of respect for his mastery of the Rōshun craft – *not as a sign that he's his bloody master!*'

'Show me,' boomed the big Alhazii voice of Baracha to his apprentice. 'Show me where it says such a thing.'

'I will!'

Ash stilled himself with an exhalation, waiting for their footsteps to pass by. When he raised a hand to rap the door lightly it suddenly swung inwards, and the hedgemonk Meer stepped out with a brief greeting. Meer was dressed in his usual robe of black like Ash and many of the other Rōshun, but really he was a member of the Few.

'The ship is here?' the monk asked him, seeing Ash's pack on his back. The old farlander nodded.

'I'll join you shortly then,' he replied on his way past, and for a moment Ash watched him walking away with his light-footed gait.

'Find Kosh too,' he called after him. 'He would be sore if we left him behind.'

Ash looked down, drawn by the sudden chill that was infiltrating his boots, and saw a white vapour drifting out across the sill of the open doorway and across his feet. He stepped inside, closing the door firmly behind him.

Inside the long windowless room, the old Seer of the Rōshun order shuffled around amongst newly crafted workbenches strewn with boxes of equipment, scratching at himself absently through his heavy robe and poking around in things, shooing the occasional cat out of the way, seemingly content enough in his new setting.

At a workbench near the door, a handsome young man sat hunched beneath an array of reflective lanterns, his face obscured by a pair of yellow-tinted goggles, his hand gripping the fleshy connection of a farcry pulsating on the surface of the bench. His eyes were closed. His body swayed where he sat wrapped in thick travel clothes of wool and canvas.

Rooks, they called themselves in the Free Ports, these rebel youths who dabbled with farcrys in new and mysterious ways. A rising phenomenon according to the Seer, who in the past had expressed an interest in their exploits, though had always failed to explain their importance in a way that Ash could understand.

'Blame, give it another shot,' came a woman's voice from somewhere beneath the workbench.

'Huh,' said the man absently. 'Sounds like that storm Seech brewed up is still tracking across the Ports. It just dumped a shower of flying fish onto Al-Coraxa.'

'Blame. Another shot please.'

The young rook snapped open his eyes behind his goggles, and leaned across to squeeze a soft tube protruding from the bottom half of the device. The farcry looked like a monstrous scaled egg covered with pinkish orifices. It reminded Ash of one of the Rōshun seals, in the way that it seemed to breathe in and out like a lung.

'Got it.'

'Keep it coming.'

He hung back a moment, interested in what they were doing and in the presence of so many exotics around the room, brought here by the pair in the previous day: tanks of grey goo with living things in them; objects like severed scorpion's tails flexing from a line; lamps that glowed without any visible flame. He saw that the icy vapour across the floor was oozing from the closed lid of a tiq casket, and wondered what could be inside. It all had the air of one of those Tales of the Fish set far into the future, where animals were able to talk and men had travelled to the two moons and back, declaring life to be there.

Across the chamber the ancient Seer was shaking his head emphatically with his back to the door, causing the stretched, dangling lobes of his ears to swing above his shoulders.

'These farcrys make a nonsense of secure communications,' he complained. 'And the cost of one alone! I had a look at them when those cheaper replicas began emerging from the Academies of the Free Ports, but you rooks had already rendered the whole business anything but secure. What use are codes when people like you can use rookery to eavesdrop on their leaking thoughts?'

'Times change, grandfather,' drawled the young man at the bench. 'And we know how to make them more secure now.'

'*More* secure,' the Seer cackled as he rooted around in another crate.

A faint smile curled the corner of Ash's mouth. He would miss this old rascal of a Seer, over thirty years together in exile.

'Listen,' came the woman's sharp tone from beneath the worktop, a breathy exertion to her words. 'That was good work you did back then, coming up with those Rōshun seals of yours. And I know what you can do without any exotics at all. You're an old-style shaman and I respect that. You have gone deep. But you've fallen behind the times, and that's the truth of the matter. You Rōshun could be using all kinds of exotics for your vendetta work. But here you are, still using carrier birds and infused dreams to communicate, still running around with swords and crossbows and doing everything the old-fashioned way. Again, Blame, another shot please.'

The old Seer was chuckling to himself as he listened to her words, tugging open more crates to look inside. 'In our game, we favour reliability over innovation,' came his withered voice across the room, and his squinting eyes were bright as he peered down into the box, privately delighted by what he had found there. 'That hardly means we are ignorant of all things new.'

'Good. Then this delivery should get you started at least.'

A hand appeared and slapped down on the workbench, and then a young Contrarè woman rose into Ash's view, wearing a tightly fitted suit of red silk and brown velvet. Fascinated, he stared at the subtle sheen of the Dreamer's skin. Like watching soapy water in sunlight, its surface disturbed by the odd ripple of colours.

A glimmersuit, the Seer had called the second skin she wore. Something that magnified her powers exponentially, allowing her, supposedly, to dream lucidly in the waking world. To perform what seemed like miracles.

Hard to believe it, even when he knew that the Alhazii Caliphate had been using glimmersuits for centuries, for their own few rare miracle men who worked for them in shrouds of secrecy.

While Ash wondered what that shining skin would feel like to wear, whether it hampered her feelings of touch or enhanced them, the woman wiped her hands on a cloth and threw a lingering glance his way, then returned her gaze to the device before her. 'It's running clear now. Let's hope that's the last of it. Better follow the same procedure once we install the new farcry in Bar-Khos, in case they're both infected with the same thing.'

Ash blinked when she turned to acknowledge him at last. He saw the silver half-mask worn on her Contrarè features, his own warped face reflected across it. Sensed the energy coming off the woman, like the crackle and buzz before a storm, causing the hairs on his arms to rise erect.

'Ah,' she said, recognizing him from the previous evening's intro-ductions. 'The man who's flying all the way to the Isles of Sky. I'm sorry, I seem to have forgotten your name.'

'Call me—'

'Ash!' cried the Seer on his way over, spotting him at last. The black skin of his face fell slack as he saw Ash standing with his pack and sword. 'You are leaving, so soon?'

'I am,' Ash answered in Honshu.

'And Kosh. You agreed to let him go with you?'

'He left me little choice in the matter.'

The old Seer dropped his shaven head for a moment. Sighed. When he looked up once more his eyes were large within his black features. He embraced Ash paternally, patting his back, smelling as he always smelled, of woodsmoke and herbs and the dark earth. 'I'm to be the last one standing, eh?' the Seer whispered in their native tongue.

'Who would have believed it,' Ash answered with a lump in his throat, and for a moment he was startled by the thought of the Seer being the last of them, last of the old Honshu exiles amongst the Rōshun order.

A slap of his shoulders. The Seer held him out before him for one last look. Intuitive as always, he seemed to know that Ash was not returning from this voyage, and a sheen of light filled his gaze. 'I was never any good at farewells, I'm afraid.'

'Nor I, Quinsun.'

'Well go out brightly, Ash. Return to the world as I'm certain you first arose from her. With a mighty *roar*!'

CHAPTER EIGHT

Tatters and Frays

Ash was hardly a man prone to worry. Yet from the first day of leaving the Hermitage of Istafari aboard the skyship known as the *Falcon*, heading high and fast over the pale Sargassi towards the southern continent, he observed the erratic, exhausted condition of the skyship's crew, and became increasingly concerned about what he was leading them into.

He knew when a group of men were close to their breaking point. Half the crew seemed as battered and weather-worn as the skyship itself, and the other half bore faces he failed to recognize, fresh recruits by the nervous looks of them, a few clearly still terrified at being aloft in the sky. For the veterans, their hair tied back in knots from tanned faces buried in beards, it had been six months of running through thick and thin without any proper relief from the action, without a chance to experience normal life on the ground long enough for it to matter.

And so the skymen of the *Falcon* stared at their new passengers with stupefied eyes that were coldly silent in their judgements, unhappy in the extreme that they had been coerced into taking this flight into enemy territory and beyond. Mostly they refused to speak to their supercargo, instead hawking in their presence and shoving past with barging elbows, or simply observing with their blasted stares from a distance far greater than the physical space between them.

'I thought you said these people had volunteered for this job?' his old friend Kosh asked in the privacy of their cramped cabin, his Honshu features as old and dark as Ash's.

Aléas and Meer had crowded themselves into the room too, both standing with their backs pressed hard against the door.

'So I was told,' Ash answered quietly, glancing round at the bald monk Meer. The man frowned and looked to the floor. 'They hardly seem the willing volunteers that Coya promised though.'

Kosh straightened in his travel clothes with his hands cupping his portly stomach, eyes opened wide in chubby features that always made him look younger than he really was. 'Well, I think they'd be happy to throw us off this ship,' said Ash's old Rōshun companion in earnest.

*

Trench, the captain, was barely any more civilized towards them, Ash was soon to discover. The captain's dark hair lay scraggly and wild about his head, and his normally shaven face sprouted an unkempt thicket of growth. A padded bandage covered his missing eye, made yellow with the seepage of an infection. Muttering to himself darkly, he prowled the decks for a while, glaring at Ash and the others with his surviving eye, before he shut himself in his cabin and was seen no more.

Only Dalas, the second-in-command, and the ship's boy Berl, hobbling about one-legged with a crutch, acted with any kind of civility towards them. The big, dreadlocked Corician took to shoving men back to work whenever they stared too long at the passengers, his hands signing in frustration, for Dalas was mute, his tongue taken from him long ago as a Mannian slave. The second-in-command seemed the same indomitable spirit he had always been, a great brooding cliff of a man, barely hampered by his missing tongue. For ship-wide commands he wore a horn about his chest, and he also wore a pouch at his belt filled with pea-sized pebbles, which he would throw at individual skymen to catch their attention, curling it into the wind as he did so, up into the rigging to strike the backside of a man smartly.

The ship's boy, young, earnest Berl, was clearly relieved to have Ash and the others join them on board. Berl insisted they come to the captain's quarters that evening for a meal.

'Never mind his foul mood,' he said against their protests, gathered there in the corridor outside their cabins. 'It's traditional on the first evening. Besides, the company will do the captain good.' And he made certain they had agreed before he hobbled away on his wooden leg.

'Wonderful,' piped Aléas. 'Dinner with the captain.'

'After that look he gave us earlier, we'd better go armed,' suggested Kosh.

*

That evening, they left their cabins and made their way to the captain's quarters while the rest of the off-watch crew filled the mess room for their evening meal. Under a starry sky on the swaying windy weatherdeck of the ship, Ash rapped the door and waited.

'Kush,' swore Kosh by his side, holding the girth of his belly with both hands queasily. 'Why didn't you remind me how much I hate to fly?'

'I did.'

'*Hmf.*'

Ash observed his old friend in the gloom of the deck. Kosh had retired years ago as an active Rōshun in the field. He spent his days training the apprentices in archery and old Rōshun bush lore passed down from Oshō himself, deceased leader of the order. The rest of the time Kosh cooked and brewed and sketched whatever caught his eye, living in what peace he could like a man slowly winding down.

Yet Kosh had insisted on coming along on this voyage into the unknown, with his oldest friend from their days in the Honshu revolution together. A matter of friendship and loyalty at first, then a matter of pride when Ash had refused him by saying that Kosh was too out of shape. When it came to pride, or friendship and loyalty for that matter, few could best the heart of this man.

His thoughts were interrupted when the ship's boy, Berl, opened the door and smiled, happy to see them there. He hobbled aside on his crutch so they could enter.

Shadows shivered around the walls of the low-ceilinged cabin. They were cast by the backs of the table's chairs partly blocking the light from half a dozen candles stuck into empty wine bottles, filling the air with their cloying smoke. Aléas and Meer were already there. At the end of the table slouched the captain himself, a flagon close to his mouth and his remaining eye staring at Ash through a flickering array of flames. He pulled a face then tipped the flagon to drink from it. Banged it back on the table again so that Berl jerked where he stood.

'Please, sit wherever you like,' the young lad beseeched them. 'Help yourselves to wine and bread. I'll see if the meal is ready yet.'

Ash sat down more heavily than he had intended, leaning back for balance. He was feeling light-headed again, a little giddy. Chewing too many of the dulce leaves these days, so that they were acting as an intoxicant now as much as a reliever of pain.

'Captain,' he tried by way of breaking the ice, and nodded towards Trench.

A blink of the captain's eye, red-rimmed from exhaustion. There was a sadness in his gaze that went deeper than anger. The sadness of someone who has had enough of the fight, who wants to quit while they still can. Trench allowed his head to loll forwards in a drunken gesture of a nod. 'Ash,' he half-belched. Then he drowned the rest of his flagon and refilled it to the brim from a bottle of wine.

Dalas, the second-in-command, seated at the opposite end of the table, watched them settle with awkward glances between themselves, his thick dreadlocks hanging about his shoulders and his shirt unbuttoned to the waist, so that his broad chest was bare. Ash raised a questioning eyebrow at him, and the big Corician twisted his head by way of a shrug. *Deal with it.*

'Shin,' offered a middle-aged woman seated next to the big man, quickly taming her wild hair with her hand. 'You must be Ash, head of this expedition?' The warmth of her voice was enough to restore some civility to the room.

'Yes. And you?'

'The ship's new medico.'

He didn't ask what had happened to the previous medico. Instead he introduced the others, and they offered nods and platitudes, relieved to have company besides the captain.

The woman Shin never took her eyes from Ash.

'Sorry, I'm staring,' she admitted with a smile. 'It's just . . . I've heard so much about you, these last few days.'

'Oh?' he replied, observing her unkempt black hair and her honey complexion, seeing something of Honshu in her features. But the rest of the gathering were now pouring wine for each other, and she looked away to say her thanks, and did not respond.

Ash held a hand over his own empty goblet when Kosh tried to pour him some, and Kosh frowned. Alcohol only worsened Ash's head pains these days when he mixed it with the effects of the dulce leaf.

'Yes,' Shin replied at last to him. 'Some of the crew tell me they once took you to the southern ice and back on some business of yours. They speak of you as though you're something of a marvel.'

The captain snorted but she ignored him, her eyes taking in every detail of the old farlander sitting across from her. She was obviously aware of what he did for a living, and he could tell that it intrigued her.

'Did you hear?' exclaimed young Berl to Ash, the lad returned without them noticing.

'Hear what?' asked Kosh from around a mouthful of bread. Perhaps his appetite was returning after all. 'And close that door will you?'

'In Zanzahar, we ran across a longtrader just returned from the southern ice. He said they're all talking about the black-skinned Rōshun who came in on a blizzard to strike down their tyrant. They think you're some kind of god of retribution.'

Captain Trench banged his flagon onto the table again, spilling wine everywhere. 'The food, Berl,' rumbled the man. 'Where's our damned food, boy?'

'It's coming!' snapped the boy, on his way out of the door again.

'I want it hot this time, not cold, you hear me?'

Trench glowered and drank from behind the candles, and big Dalas watched him from the other end. Ash wondered where the captain's pet kerido was hiding, until he spotted the creature curled up beneath a leather armchair, its glassy eyes partly opened and watching them. The silence lengthened.

Leaning back, he turned to the nearest window, as he often did in awkward social situations, seeking something of interest beyond the four walls. The window was at the very back of the cabin and made from diamonds of stained glass. The sky was a black swathe out there over the frothy surface of the sea. A lonely light shone from the Sargassi; a lighthouse on a coral tree or an island habitation, he could not tell.

In relief the diners turned to see Berl returning with another crewman carrying a tray of bowls. The meal was laid out on the table, fresh cetch and a steaming spiced stew with sweet potatoes. The smell was enough to make Ash's stomach growl aloud, recalling suddenly that he had skipped breakfast that morning.

'I have to admit,' the medico Shin said to him from across the table, between sips of her stew. 'I was expecting someone a little younger.'

Kosh chuckled softly, dabbed his mouth with a napkin. 'And how old do you think he is? Either of us?'

She stared at Ash but he only looked down into his stew. 'Fifty?' she tried. 'Maybe a touch over?'

'Try adding another decade,' Kosh prompted.

'Surely not.'

His continuing mirth drew a glance from Ash at last. But Kosh pretended not to notice.

'Where we are from, in the northern highlands of Honshu, the men are renowned for remaining vital right up until their sixth decade. And then, without warning, they usually just keel over and . . .' His voice trailed away, realizing what he was saying in front of Ash, the old fool.

'It's the hair we have to sacrifice early,' Kosh went on with an awkward smile, while he ran a hand over his own smooth scalp. 'You should have seen us when we were young. A highlander's hair is fine and straight right down to his waist.'

She smiled as though seeing the image of it in her mind.

'My grandfather was from Honshu,' Shin offered. 'Though he lasted well into his eighties.'

'Your grandfather was an exile?' Ash asked.

'No, he was on the other side of the war. A silk merchant from the lowlands.'

Ash and Kosh exchanged a sidelong glance.

'Right,' she drawled. 'You two must have been People's Army.'

No reply from either of them. A stony silence in fact.

It only seemed to spur her curiosity further.

'Were you there at the final battle in the Sea of Wind and Grasses?'

Ash looked to Kosh, but his friend was stuffing his mouth with food so he wouldn't be expected to answer. They rarely spoke of those times now, least of all with strangers.

'We were Shining Way,' he said, 'pinning Oshō's left flank while we bought time for the kill. Aye, we were there.'

Kosh cleared his throat, then took another drink to help the food down. 'Come and join us,' he told Berl suddenly, standing there in attendance while the rest of them tucked into the stew, which was warming though somewhat bland.

'I've eaten already. Please, enjoy your meal.'

Shin knew well enough when a subject had been changed deliberately, and so she asked some polite questions instead about what they normally ate within the Rōshun order. The lad Berl seemed to brighten whenever they chattered; a family of strangers getting to know each other. Perhaps they all picked up on this, or perhaps it was only the heady wine, for they began to speak more freely after that, so that even Trench added the occasional word to the fray; a comment of scorn, a few muttered curses; enough to remind everyone that he was there. Ash for his part remained silent, relying on others to ask the questions he wanted to ask himself, as was his way.

Across from him, Meer suddenly exchanged a few hand gestures with Dalas, the mute Corician.

'It seems to be based on Contrarè sign language,' the hedgemonk explained when he saw their interest. 'I picked up a little on my travels.'

'I see that you eat meat,' said the woman Shin. 'I thought Ash introduced you as a monk of the Way?'

Meer looked to Ash for a moment then back again, a delicate smile twitching on his full lips. 'Well, he misled you, which was wrong of him. Sometimes I have reason to pass myself off as a monk. But as you can see, I'm not dressed as one now.'

She shook her head to show her confusion.

'Ash is only being kind to a wayward fool who rescued him one night in the Shoals of Bar-Khos, not so long ago.'

'Rescued?'

'He fell asleep drunk in falling sleet. I carried him to shelter, and when he awoke he saw me dressed as a monk and assumed the rest.'

Ash nodded at the recollection. 'A shrine. He was living in a cave where a statue of the Great Fool had once sat. But someone had stolen it, and Meer sat in its place. Pay no heed to his protests, I have seen him sit in meditation for hours. I saw him help the people of the Shoals like any other hedgemonk of the Way would have done. Meer is a cloudman at heart as much as a traveller.'

'Again, he is being overly kind.'

'Have you really been to the Isles of Sky,' the captain interjected, 'or is that flight course you gave me earlier another fiction for us to unravel?'

Meer straightened in his chair. 'Does it matter? You hardly believe we'll make it over the Aradērēs.'

'I made no such claim.'

'You told me the name of every skyship that has tried crossing the mountains and failed.'

'Well the *Falcon* will make it, if any ship can. It's afterwards that concerns me. The Great Hush, land of the kree. You've heard the tales, I'm sure? The massacres? The men who went mad from the air itself?'

A twig broke in two somewhere on the table, but it was only Dalas, snapping his fingers and gesturing quickly; telling him off, it seemed.

With disdain the captain glared back at his second-in-command. He spoke on. 'The worst thing of all? We're flying blind the entire way without a single map to guide us. We're going solely on this man's memory, who, even if he has been to the Isles, claims he took a different route entirely, an established route through the Sea of Doubts. A stowaway, of all cursed things, on board a Zanzahar Guild ship, where he saw precious little along the way. He knows nothing of the Hush, yet he claims we can still reach the Isles if we fly through it for long enough. And this, without charts!'

'I've been to Lucksore too,' Meer insisted gently to the others. 'Perched at the foot of the pass we'll be taking over the mountains. We'll find ourselves a longhunter there to guide us through the Hush all the way to the rift valley of the Edge. After that, it's a simple matter of heading for the eastern coast.'

'Simple!'

Tap, tap, tap. It was the ship's boy limping closer on his wooden leg. Berl refilled Ash's goblet with water then asked if anyone else needed some, keen for the meal to carry on without conflict. At his prompting the chatter arose again around the table.

For an instant, Ash recalled the sky battle in which the boy's injury had happened, flying for Cheem with his new apprentice Nico through an imperial blockade of the Free Ports.

Kosh laughed at something Aléas had said then tried to silence his mirth with a mouthful of wine. With the laughter spreading around the table, Ash took the chance to look across at the captain again, who was poking at his bandaged eye socket with a black-nailed forefinger.

'Damned socket is infected again,' Trench complained as he saw Ash watching him. 'Always goes this way during winter. Must be the damp.'

'Too much stress and worry is what it is,' Berl snapped. 'You need rest. We all do.'

'Well plenty of time for that when we're dead. When we go down into the Hush and the kree get a hold of us, we can all sleep then, eh?'

Ash frowned. 'I was led to believe you had volunteered for this mission.'

'Volunteered? You mean Coya Zeziké calling in a favour right when we are about to have a week of shore leave? Aye, we volunteered all right, as people who were left with little choice in the matter always do.'

Dalas was snapping his fingers again, and this time the captain shut his mouth and drowned whatever else he had to say with another upturn of his flagon.

'The rest of the crew, how much do they know?' Ash asked.

A pained expression pinched the captain's sallow features. Trench wiped the back of his hand across his mouth. 'As much as I was allowed to tell them. Apart from Olson the navigator and those of us in this room, they've no idea yet that our ultimate destination is the Isles. Coya insisted it was too dangerous for so many to know in advance. So for now, I must ask you to keep that information to yourselves.'

'When will you tell them?'

'Believe me, not until I have to.' And the man returned his sullen attention to his stew, and the itching behind his bandage.

The others were talking about the kree now that the subject had been broached by the captain.

'We can see a dead kree when we reach Lucksore,' Meer was telling them. 'Their mouths are like lamprey fish, you know. No jaws at all but a great toothy sucker surrounded by barbed lashes, which they use to ensnare and draw in their prey.'

A clink of cutlery as Kosh dropped his spoon into his half-empty bowl, his appetite flown.

'You're really going into the Edge then?' enquired the medico Shin of Ash, leaning towards him over the table. 'You're really venturing into the warrens of the kree?'

Ash shrugged to imply there was no other choice in the matter.

'It is the only way to gain enough Royal Milk for our purposes.'

'And what purpose is that?'

Ash knew how crazy it sounded, but he said it anyway.

'To bring my dead apprentice back to life, once we have reached the Isles. They need Milk, apparently, to perform the procedure.'

Shin frowned, thinking he was playing with her, and so Ash cleared his throat to catch the attention of the monk Meer.

'Tell her,' he said.

'Eh?'

'Tell her what you mean to do in the Isles.'

He smiled to the woman by his side.

'I can tell you would not believe me if I did.'

'Oh, please try me,' she prompted.

'Well, in the Isles of Sky the privileged can live a thousand years by consuming Royal Milk, and by regrowing new bodies for themselves in tanks of the stuff. With the boy's ashes we will try to do the same.'

She looked to Ash with narrowed eyes.

'You're serious.'

Minutely, Ash nodded his head.

CHAPTER NINE

In Flight

The *Falcon*'s crew treated them as coldly as ever over the following days, while the passengers settled into their cramped cabins and did what they could to pass the time. Ash spent most of his mornings up on the foredeck of the flying ship, meditating or loosening his body with *hathaga* stretching and breathing exercises, good for the back and his joints, along with Meer's daily sessions with his needles and hot rocks.

Soon an eerie silence had fallen upon the ship, the crew all too aware that they were nearing the Mannian territory of Pathia, and the sky blockade which surrounded the Free Ports. They knew that a single skyship should have little trouble breaching the imperial blockade, which in reality was stretched thin enough around the islands to be mostly porous, but you could never tell.

The skyship's colours were changed to those of neutral Cheem, and when at last they spotted the coastline of Pathia in the distance, where the Sargassi sea became a line of white against the rocky coastline, the hush of the nervous crew became complete. The bell rang out, and the lookouts doubled and then tripled around the ship and began to call out what they saw; a few harbour towns, a river delta, a squadron of enemy warships in the water to the west, beyond a small island.

Slowly, shifting and creaking, the *Falcon* adjusted course so they were headed for a river delta, which from the scale of it Ash supposed to be the mouth of the Elba, the mighty river that served as a border between Pathia and neighbouring Tilana to the west. Maintaining their high altitude, they crossed over the coastline unchallenged and left the sea to their stern where their flag of convenience trailed and snapped in the thin air. With the thrusters roaring they sped above scattered banks of clouds that were trailing rain, and then the over-cast cleared before them and old Stones the pilot followed a course along the river, wide enough here that it looked like a flood spilled across the land. On both far banks the many towns were dull smudges obscured by smoke, and to either side the plains rolled away into the horizon, mottled greens and yellows and reds. Snakes wound their way across the plains: roads and side-rivers like the arteries of leaves. It was the sky which the crew watched most of all, vigilant of patrolling birds-of-war. Only merchant skyships could be seen though, bearing trade from east or west, usually some distance below them.

They were in the Empire of Mann now, and the creaking of the sculls and spars and the growl of the thrusters was all that could be heard from the ship, for the men's silence lingered save for the odd joke of bravado.

Some of the newer members of the crew began to mutter in prayer.

*

'You're thinking about him, aren't you?' inquired Aléas by his side, as they stood by the forward rail flying through another shower of rain.

Him, Ash reflected. Aléas did not use his name. They never used his name in conversation, too powerful a thing to utter aloud in the plain light of day; like a swear word in front of children, or a blasphemy in the face of believers.

'In a way. I was thinking of his mother back in Khos,' replied Ash. 'Why, were you?'

The Rōshun apprentice nodded.

'I can't seem to shake it, how he died.'

Aléas and Nico had been friends, close even though the pair had barely known each other. But that was all it ever mostly took, Ash knew. An easy connection with someone and you could be friends for life.

'Just breathe until it passes.'

Aléas gripped the rail and inhaled the oncoming breeze, his blond locks flowing backwards in the stirrings of air.

'If this works, I hope he doesn't remember any of it.'

'That still remains a big if.'

The young man shrugged, as though dismissing such cautions.

'Remember what Meer has said,' Ash advised him. 'The process can be unpredictable. Even if we succeed in bringing him back, he may not be the same person that we remember. He may not even be in possession of his mind.'

'Still. I've a feeling we'll be seeing him again. Don't you sense it?'

Ash glanced across at his companion, saying nothing. *You sense the hope in your own heart*, he thought, like the old man that he was. Expectations were for the young, for those who hadn't yet learned that the nature of life was surprise.

Yet he had no wish to crush the hopes of others, and instead he slapped the rail lightly, saying, 'You recall the time you both had to compete in fishing to settle that score with Baracha?'

Aléas laughed. 'Yes. After Baracha sent Serèse away, thinking they were sleeping together.'

Together they chuckled at the memories.

On the foredeck the rain had lessened, and without a strong wind to drive it sidewise they were well enough sheltered by the huge envelope of gas hanging above their heads. To the south the sky was clearing in breaks of white and blue.

'When you return to the Hermitage,' Ash said aloud, 'Baracha intends to challenge you.'

The apprentice replied soberly. 'An interesting time to become Rōshun.'

Unspoken in his tone lay the ruins of Sato and the dead amongst his companions, Oshō and all the rest of the Rōshun who had fallen in the attack against their order. Aléas had been quieter in his ways since they had left behind their home in the mountains of Cheem. As though he had left something of himself behind.

'We are at war now with the Empire, your own people. You should make sure you are straight with that in your head, and quickly.'

A stiff nod. The young man's gaze fell away to the land far below.

Ash looked over the rail too at the chasm of space below their feet. Nico would have hated these heights. The boy had popped his eyes for most of the trip to Cheem, every time he had caught sight of land or sea.

Far below, the land was creased by the rush of the Red Elba, which despite its name looked grey today, a thin ribbon running through lands of green towards distant highlands. Beyond the highlands lay the Untamed Plateau, that high wilderness where they would find the frontier town of Lucksore and hopefully a longhunter to guide their way through the Hush.

Through the clearing sky ahead, Ash caught a glimpse of a bright whiteness up on the high plateau, and when he squinted he could just about see them, the rising flanks of the Broken Spine of the World, topped with snow and ice.

Beyond them, he knew, ranged the vast expanse of the Great Hush.

Once more, Ash's thoughts returned to the boy's mother back in Khos, Reese Calvone, with her red hair and her fierce protectiveness over her son, her only child.

He had promised the woman he would keep Nico safe, just as he had written and promised his own wife all those decades ago concerning Lin, their own son. But Ash had returned to Reese Calvone with nothing but a clay vial of ashes held in his grasp, a monstrosity which she had slapped away in her furious grief before setting herself upon him.

Even now he could hear the dull fleshy sounds of the woman's palms striking his face, could almost feel the hot sting of her blows burning his cheeks. Though perhaps rather than memory, it was only the sudden heat from his regrets that he felt, and his desire to put them right.

CHAPTER TEN

Reese

East of the city of Bar-Khos, in a downpour of rain thrashing through the bare limbs of trees overhead, Reese Calvone stopped beneath the shelter of a juniper to catch her breath and to wipe a strand of lank red hair from her eyes, and noticed that the palms of her hands were suddenly smarting. Curious, she stared down to see the redness of their skin, stinging now as though she had been slapping something with force.

Just like the day she had struck out at the old farlander in fury, for returning her son in a small clay vial.

Nico.

Not a day or an hour passed without Reese thinking of her son and feeling the loss of him renewed. And with the recollections came the same incriminations; why had he left her and why had she let him go? But the answer was there even as she asked for it.

Her son had left home because she had taken in Los as her lover, a man whom Nico had loathed. Because, in a way, she had chosen Los and her own needs over those of her son.

Reese flexed her tingling hands until the sensation passed, both hands shaking now. She shuddered with barely controlled emotions and looked about for the dog again, the golden-haired animal she had seen from the kitchen window and which had first drawn her out into the bad weather, hoping that it was their dog Boon, after all this time, a living trace of her son returned to their cottage.

No sign of him now though, and the wind and rain were so fierce that she stayed where she was beneath the green boughs of the tree, waiting until the worst had passed. It was only the tail of the winter storm remaining now, having spent the worst of its fury during the previous days.

86

In Bar-Khos, her neighbour Hira had told her incredulously, they were still cleaning up after the high winds had dropped entire vineyards of winterberries onto the city, smearing the streets and buildings with their crimson juices like a downpour of blood.

Hard to believe such a story, yet she had never known Hira tell a lie. Now some were hailing it as a portent for the approaching imperial forces of General Mokabi, which were only days away from the Lansway and the Shield, where they would join those already besieging the city.

The war seemed to be entering yet another desperate phase.

When the gusts and rain finally lessened, so that the drips from the overhanging boughs were more apparent than the thinning drizzle itself, Reese heard again the heavy rumbles in the sky towards the west, not from the rain clouds but from the cannon on the far Shield, where the siege of Bar-Khos was now into its tenth year. She loathed the sounds of those guns, loud enough to hear all this way along the coast. They were worse than a constant intrusion into the peace of her surroundings; a reminder that such peace was an illusion and little more.

People had started to flee the area of the Running Hills, this rugged coastal region between the Chilos delta to the west and the mountains of the High Tell to the east, where the land was a rolling corrugation of humps and depressions much like the neighbouring storm-swollen sea. They fled in fright of those imperial forces now holed up around Tume far to the north; the Mannian Expeditionary Force that had invaded Khos from the sea. So far, the Imperials had been contained in the north to this side of the Chilos river, though they were probing ever further along it towards the southern coast.

People heard one story too many of how far the Mannian slaver parties were now ranging beyond the main imperial forces, and then they were gone the next day, all of their possessions loaded onto a cart to make their way to the relative safety of the city.

Yet still Reese Calvone remained behind like many of her more stubborn neighbours. She would never leave this place that was her home, not even now. All that she knew was here, most of all the memories of her son.

'Boon!' she called out once more, and stepped out from beneath the tree to continue her search for the dog, the fallen leaves hard and slick against her bare feet, for she had forgotten to put on her boots.

Maybe I imagined him after all, Reese thought, recalling too the odd glimpses of Nico that she had been seeing lately, ghosts of movement in her peripheral vision, her head turning in habit towards a son no longer there.

Onwards along the path she trod, listening to the sounds of the forest in the rain, rustles in the undergrowth and the calls of unseen birds. Above her head a pair of striped chirups glided between two trees, webbed arms and legs extended to catch the air, animals that hadn't touched the ground their entire lives.

Sometimes Reese felt like a girl again when she wandered alone through the trees like this. As a youth she had roamed the hill forests around her family farm, at first with her older sister Terl, before Terl had passed away from a coughing sickness, and then later by herself, following the tracks of spotted fox, deer, even the odd solitary wolf, ever deeper through the trails of the Running Hills in search of the unknown, the untamed.

It was on such a walk that she had first met Cole, a young man out hunting with a homemade crossbow, bent down as he drank from a racing torrent. Seeing her approach, the young man had stood with an easy grace and dropped his wet hands to his sides, eyes and mouth open wide.

'Hello,' he'd said at last over the crashing water, observing her gently with his animal eyes.

The next week they had met again in an illicit rendezvous in the depths of the forest. Reese's small closed world had opened up like the blazing full moons of the night sky, in the end leading to a son in her belly and a new home, a new life, which she could call her own.

Her love had only deepened for Cole during those early years as a husband and father, this tall lean man who liked to sit on the porch for hours on end watching the rain and the distant mountains; who made the world seem just right every time she laughed at his dry and easy humour; who liked to smoke and drink then dance and whirl whenever the spirit was upon him.

Before the Empire had come with its tidings of war, and the siege had drawn her husband Cole into it, eventually as a leather-clad Special fighting down in the tunnels beneath the Shield. Without a doubt those years had changed Cole. Each time he returned on home leave he bore even more wounds and scars than before, and brooded with deepening anger and guilt over the companions he had lost, clearly a man who did not expect to survive for long himself. So entirely was he scarred by his years fighting in the tunnels, both inside and out, that finally Reese had barely recognized him any more for the man that she had once adored.

Another memory flashed through her mind. The last night she had ever seen her husband, his drunken features bloated with fury, dragging her across the floor by her hair while their young son watched on in horror.

A monster, where once had stood her man.

Yet still, for all that she resented his actions, even now she felt that burning ache for him, for the person he had once been. Even now she felt that terrifying sense of emptiness, now deepened a thousand times following the death of her son. All that she cherished, gone save for this cottage and farm.

She was never going to see them again, either one.

*

The forest garden looked bare in this month of early winter, though there was still plenty to forage if you knew what to look for. The pigs knew too, for they were snuffling through the grasses and wild crops not far from the trail she followed, looking for ponyon roots and tumbler bulbs, fallen berries and nuts.

Her husband Cole had designed the forest garden to provide a bounty even in the dark season, following the principles of natural farming which he had embraced so passionately before the war. Techniques which been passed to him serendipitously by a travelling Greengrass who was also a monk of the Way, one of many who walked the islands spreading the knowledge of how to farm most naturally, and most bountifully – going with the grain of the land rather than against it.

Cole had planted many of these trees himself, choosing those that would bear nuts and fruits for harvest, and others that would complement each other by attracting or repelling certain insects, or adding specific qualities into the soil. Just like many of the plants he had sown between the trees too, perennial crops that needed little tending once established, and which taken altogether provided a bounty all year round.

A work of love, of intimate trial and error, her husband wishing to create an abundance of life around the small cottage where he and Reese had first settled to start their family. Though he had hoped too, in his own way, to show the other farmers of the area how they could embrace a different way, a way that had been flourishing throughout the other islands ever since the revolution of the democras, with the exception of here in Khos.

Wild farming, some called it. Methods of cultivation first inspired by certain monks of the Way, who had learned how to sow rice without tilling the ground first, simply by coating the seeds in clay, and how to grow abundantly at altitude using rocks for heat and windbreaks, and how to make the most of small lowland farms using trees and perennials. All sustainable methods of farming which added to the soil over time rather than depleted it, allowing land previously made barren to green itself once again, so that over the decades the Free Ports had become one of the most richly abundant lands in all the Midèrēs.

'For Mercy's sake we could stop our endless toil now,' Cole had often declared to his peers in the local taverna, still young enough to fully give voice to his passions.

'Look at how Erēs does it all without effort!' he would say with his lopsided grin. 'We should be copying her ways and using them to our advantage, I tell you, so we can farm without much of this drudgery and without depleting the land too. We can allow nature to do half the work for us instead of always wrestling her, always trying to dominate and exploit!'

Scorn was the reply to such fervour, of course, though as scorn goes it was gentle enough, for it was generally accepted that diplomacy was never going to be Cole's strong point in life. And so, for those early years, many of their neighbours saw only a growing eyesore around the couple's homestead, a wildness of growth when they were used to straight lines and clear separations of crops. A man too lazy to cut down weeds.

In truth she had barely believed them herself, these things Cole spoke of. But for Reese, her husband's need to follow his own path in life according to his inner vision – his wildly unbounded soul – had always been the great attraction. The reason she knew him to be the love of her life.

So Reese had supported her husband's efforts despite her own doubts on the matter, raising their only child Nico by herself much of the time while he laboured to create his unkempt paradise. And over the years, Cole had proven the truth of his own words.

Here it was, all around her in the beating rain. What had once been bare and treeless farmland of tilled fields and stone walls, now a bountiful forest garden, thriving in such natural balance that it hardly needed tending at all, would carry on thriving in a hundred years' time whether anyone worked on it or not.

Cole, a man drawn to wilderness like herself, had created a vibrant pocket of wilful nature around their very home. Though not entirely wild, of course, for they had bellies to feed and a living to earn.

A cultivated wildness then, much as the rest of the Free Ports were said to be.

All of this bounty when people went hungry in the city and across the whole Free Ports. It remained the greatest irony of this war, how people went hungry while the islands produced an abundance of crops all year round. Yet the democras needed to defend itself, and so it needed black powder, which was supplied solely by the Alhazii Caliphate in return for the majority of their harvests.

'There you are,' came a voice from behind, and Reese swung about in alarm, shocked at the sound of another human voice. But it was only Los, her lover, hurrying along the trail with a coat over his head, frowning in that bemused way of his.

'What are you doing out here, woman?' he asked as though she was mad. 'You'll catch your death!' And indeed as he spoke his breaths were spurts of steam in the drizzle, and she felt the cold on her skin at last, and clutched her arms about her sodden shawl. She realized that she was shivering.

In the shadows of the forest Los glanced about as though for wolves or Mannians – a man of the city even now.

'Boon,' she told him. 'I thought I saw Boon out here.'

'The dog? But the dog's dead, remember? Nico told you he buried him in the city.'

'Oh.'

'I think all that hazii weed's making you crazy,' he quipped, placing a hand on her arm, but she flinched clear of his touch.

'It's the death of my son that's making me crazy. The weed's about the only thing stopping me from losing it.' Panting, she turned away and looked about her one last time.

Boon wasn't here.

Nothing was here but the wild farm and her own stubborn memories.

CHAPTER ELEVEN

Return of the King

Stiffly the old general climbed the steps to the upper deck of the warwagon, his knees having grown stiff in the chill air flowing over the deck. His suit of armour still felt too heavy on him, even though it was mostly decorative, splendidly so, a replacement for his old warsuit that no longer fitted his spreading bulk. Too long out of the field, Mokabi knew. Too many years growing soft and living the pampered life of a retired Archgeneral.

On the open deck, Mokabi ignored the movements of his body-guards and the glances of those already there, and turned instinctively to the north. His gaze swept along the road that carried his army along the Lansway, that narrow bridge of land connecting the southern continent with the island of Khos – a bridge that would take them all the way to Camp Liberty, and beyond that to the siege of Bar-Khos.

Across the creaking deck, Mokabi approached the forward crenellations, where one of his officers was squinting through an eyeglass fixed to a stand.

The rolling paved road seemed a long way below them from up here, for the warwagon was a mammoth affair, each of its eight wheels taller than a zel, its height more than a two-storey house. Like a wooden fort rolling across the land.

To the left of him, the Sargassi sea washed against the rocky shore of the Lansway in ribbons of froth, bearing the flotsam and jetsam of a recent storm. To his right swelled the greater body of the Midèrēs, its deep waters made brazen for a moment by a low sun peeking through the clouds.

It was early winter in the southern continent, a season of rain and winds and mud, and indeed coals in a nearby brazier hissed with a few spits of rain.

A poor day for his historic return to the Shield, Mokabi reflected. No doubt his biographer could spice it up a little, adding some sunshine and the songs of forthcoming victory rising from a hundred thousand throats leading the way, casting heroes of all of them. But still, the general's good mood receded in those moments of dreary rain, watching his army trudging in weariness along the road between the two seas.

A quarter of a million mercenaries had so far answered his call, more by far than he had been expecting; drawn here from every corner of the known world by the promise of gold and booty. More people than lived in all of Khos. Just feeding them was going to consume a good portion of his wealth, and Mokabi possessed much of the spoils of the southern continent; a mountain of coins lay in the armoured vault in the belly of this rolling fort.

But they had come, and he could hardly complain now at their numbers or their expense. What did it matter so long as the city fell?

'Quite a sight, Fenetti, eh?' he quipped to the old officer peering through the eyeglass near him, the man's nose tattooed with three stripes of rank.

'Reminds me of when we first arrived here with the Fourth Army.'

'Better than that, man. Look at them!'

Far ahead, a coastline spread away on either side into the haze. It was the island of Khos, breadbasket of the Free Ports here at their easternmost limits, that chain of islands standing alone in defiance of the Empire now that all nations around them had fallen.

Without Khos, how long could the Free Ports survive, surrounded and with only the Alhazii Caliphate to openly trade with? Not long, his strategos had surmised, unless the Caliphate chose to weigh in on the side of the Free Ports at last, which no one considered likely. The Caliph preferred to remain neutral in this war, enjoying his monopoly with the Isles of Sky and all the profits – and protection – that came with it. No, with the fall of Khos the rest of the Free Ports would soon follow, and Mokabi wholly intended for the glory to be his alone.

Over the tramp of the army's boots he heard cannon fire in the distance now. Fenetti the officer straightened from the eyeglass.

'I see them.'

Mouth agape and one eye shut tightly, General Mokabi peered through the eyeglass and adjusted the focus to his poorer vision.

There, quivering and shaking to the movements of the wagon, the low buildings of Camp Liberty surrounded by earthworks and tents, and beyond them the Shield itself. Through the haze he saw first the ruins of the old walls which Mokabi himself had long ago taken, and then past them, wreathed in smoke, the first of the four surviving walls: a cliff of black stone spanning the entire width of the Lansway.

A decade had passed since he had first seen those defences with his own eyes, back when he had expected them to fall after a brief and bloody siege. Yet the Imperial Fourth Army still assaulted them even now, an army he had once led here himself.

Two years into the siege, bogged down in a campaign that seemed to be making little further headway against the surviving walls of the Shield, Mokabi had found himself unexpectedly ousted from his position through machinations back in the capital. Without warning he'd been forced to step down as Archgeneral in whispered disgrace, relinquishing the reins on a loyal army he had planned to do much more with, including trying for the throne. Even with his colossal successes in conquering the southern continent, the general's reputation had been tarnished by his failure to take Bar-Khos in the end. The man who could not be beaten in the field, who never failed at conquest, had been trumped after all by the Empire's most despised enemies, the Free Ports.

Now, at long last, he had a chance to redeem what was otherwise a glorious career.

It had been Mokabi's devising, this newest grand scheme to take the island of Khos once and for all. His idea alone to land an Expeditionary Force on the far coast of the island, with the intention of taking Bar-Khos from its weaker northern side, while Mokabi himself led his own forces against the city from the south, smashing it in between the two before the onset of winter made travel and siege a logistical nightmare.

But of course, Sparus the Little Eagle – present Archgeneral of Mann and commander of the Expeditionary Force – had made his usual mess of things in his invasion of the island, even worse than Mokabi had been anticipating. Now, by all accounts, the present

Archgeneral was holed up in the floating city of Tume vying for control of his forces with General Romano, young contender for the Empire's throne.

It was clear the Expeditionary Force was stalled entirely, and here in the south Mokabi himself was weeks late arriving at the party, having tarried in Sheaf for as long as he could get away with it. This having been his plan all along, to arrive late; for unlike Sparus, Mokabi had no fear of winter's onset. He had a paved Mannian military road to take his army all the way to the siege, never mind how bad the conditions became.

The general had supposed from the onset that any Expeditionary Force would be unable to take the city alone. All along, Mokabi had anticipated their slaughter as they threw themselves upon the lesser northern walls of Bar-Khos, and had intended to postpone his own assault until both sides had weakened themselves against each other. With the defenders adequately thinned, Mokabi would then storm Bar-Khos and without delay this time, taking the city for himself. And all would see that it was he who had finally conquered the Shield; that he had never been beaten in his ambitions, merely delayed.

Yet with the death of the Holy Matriarch during the Khosian campaign, this venture had become more than a simple matter of pride.

Back in the capital of Q'os they still mourned the death of Sasheen. Flags of white flew across the great city even as the plots and scheming were accelerated by all who wished to fill the now empty throne. Pointless posturing, all of it, for Mokabi's best strategos were now clear on this – the throne of the Empire would be decided here, at Bar-Khos.

Whoever took the city was certain to become the next Patriarch of the Holy Mannian Empire.

Mokabi fully intended to be the one.

Just then the old general inclined his head to the side, thinking his ears were deceiving him. For he thought he heard the sounds of battle coming from Camp Liberty ahead, clashes of shields, gunshots, the roar of thousands of throats.

But then he saw the huge banners waving from the distant camp, bearing what seemed to be his own personal motif of a lion, and he heard the sound of his name carried by their ragged voices.

Mokabi realized that it was only his beloved Fourth Army, raising a din in celebration at his return.

'Well they remember you, at least,' Fenetti the officer remarked.

'Aye. Some of the old dogs are still around.'

Excited, feeling the enormity of the moment, General Mokabi peered through the rain over the swaying bulks of the wagon's mammoots and their drivers, taking in the host of fighters squeezed along the confines of the road all the way to the far camp.

In a warmth of satisfaction, he took in the lines of Seration hill skirmishers with their slings and their composite bows. The chain-mailed heavy infantry of the Private Military Companies. The Pathian light cavalry flying streamers from their lances. Longshanks from the Untamed Plateau. Painted wild men and women from the High Pass. Feathered banghori fanatics from the far east walking in step to the wails of their bagpipes, having travelled all this way along the Spice Road . . .

And behind him, in the wake of the rumbling warwagon, the line stretched back south as far as he could see. Amongst them, dwarfing them, rumbled the great wagons carrying the components of the siege towers, drawn by more lines of war mammoots, their long trunks snaking through the air, pointing to the waves of birds-of-war flying overhead.

They scented blood, these men and women on the road to Bar-Khos. Just as Mokabi himself scented blood. They knew that with their numbers the city was ripe for the plucking, and that they could be made rich from the spoils of booty and slaves. It was what he had promised them. It was what they were going to have.

This time, Bar-Khos was destined to fall.

CHAPTER TWELVE

Cities Burning

Down in the hold of a fast skud, Shard the Dreamer and her rook assistant sat alone amongst crates of cargo on a sheet of stained tarpaulin, wrapped in shadows cast by the blue light of the algae lamps they had brought with them all the way from the Academy.

It was quiet in the cramped space of the hold, though hardly silent. They could hear the thruster tubes of the small skyship burning on either side of the hull and the occasional scuffle of footsteps on the deck above their heads. On the floor lay a small open, padded case, next to a clear glass jar partly filled with sand, its lid removed.

'Careful,' Shard whispered to her young assistant, watching closely.

Before him, the sandworm wriggled on the end of a dangling thread like an over-sized maggot, its body glistening white in the soft glow of the algae lamps, plump and probing upwards towards the shaking fingers of the young rook, who held the thread aloft, impatiently, between their nervous stares.

'You okay?' she asked, for his pupils were dilating fast, his forehead clammy.

'I think I touched it,' young Blame admitted. He glanced at her with widened eyes, offered a snort of disbelief. He was swaying a little. 'It works fast.'

'Yes,' she said frowning, deeply unimpressed by his carelessness. 'Which is why I told you to wear gloves.'

Shard was relying on the young rook to help her through this, to be her anchor while she sped through the initial, debilitating rush. Now the man might be more of a hindrance than a help.

'Sorry. I thought you were exaggerating.'

The Dreamer sighed, expelling what annoyance she could. He was all she had right now, this last remaining rook who had only just joined her team. They both had to find a way to work together, just as they'd both found a way into the same bed.

For a long moment Shard studied him, feeling a thrill of memory at their previous nights of reckless play, charged with the recent deaths of the other rooks and the heightened danger of their circumstances – both headed to siege and war.

'I suppose you're wondering what you've gotten yourself into with all this,' she remarked, which were kinder words than those in her mind: *this is the last time I choose a rook because I want to sleep with him.*

'Actually, I'm wondering how much longer I have to hold on to this worm.'

The sandworm's mouth was getting close to his fingers now. Clumsily, he unwound more thread for it to climb. Sweat beaded his forehead, dripped past shadowed eyes. 'How long will these effects last, you think?'

'Brief contact by skin? I'd say you have a few days of interesting times ahead of you.'

'A few days!'

'Maybe less.'

He chewed it over with his teeth.

'Stronger than moon dust, you said?'

'Stronger than anything. It will blow your mind.'

He was starting to experience The Fear, she could see, but he was practised enough in narcotics to gain a grip on it, and to calm himself. Together they gazed at the worm again.

Tiny quills adorned the creature's sides and around its probing mouth, and Shard recalled the slimy bitter sensation that came from putting one of these things in her mouth.

'I really don't think you should do this,' he said once more.

'Can you hold it together or not?'

He considered her question, nodded his head in a judder.

'Then shut up and get ready.'

With care Shard plucked the end of the glistening thread from his fingers, held the worm up in the light so that she could study it more closely.

'This is how we cracked the bindee code of the Great Dream,' she said almost to herself, and in her mind's eye a leaning mud tower stood in a deep desert oasis.

'To become Dreamers, you mean?' he rasped. 'Is this the only worm you have?'

Eagerness in his questions. Perhaps Blame nurtured ambitions beyond the limited realm of rookery. She nodded.

'Seech brought a dozen back with him from the deep desert, though he had to leave them at the Academy when he fled. They died off, wouldn't reproduce. This is the last one that still lives.'

A fine dust was blowing through her mind, stirred by the remembered winds of the Alhazii deep desert six hundred laqs to the east, where the two star student rooks of the Salina Academy had ventured three years earlier on an expedition gone tragically wrong, almost killing themselves in pursuit of rumours of magic in the sands, of shamans who could Dream.

A desperate time, an almost hopeless one, before they had finally struck upon the solitary oasis of Zini, where they had discovered the obliterating juice of the sandworms and the pool of liquid from which the glimmersuits were born. Before Seech had betrayed them all and left her for dead.

Blame was chuckling at something softly.

'If you go ahead with this, you're going to lose your kushing mind, Shard.'

'Maybe. Though there's more chance of it killing me through toxic shock first.'

'Still. If it doesn't. If it takes hold in you. That's going to be some ride.'

He wasn't helping. She could think of a dozen reasons not to swallow this writhing sandworm in her grasp. In the oasis of Zini, in their ancient mud tower, the desert shamans had placed the worms upon their tongues for only short amounts of time, using the narcotic excretions to propel their minds beyond their bodies. From regular uses, a few of them had even become capable of reading the raw code of the bindee.

The desert shaman had spoken of an extreme practice, largely frowned upon, of swallowing the entire sandworm for the strongest effects of all; though it was something rarely undertaken, for few had ever survived the experience.

If it didn't kill you first, they had said, if the worm survived long inside you, then it would fasten itself to your intestines.

Shard would be shockingly high for as long as it remained inside her.

'How will you even get it out again?' asked Blame now, still feigning his concerns for her while he tried to hide his excitement at what they were doing here, his eagerness to see what would happen when she took it.

'I have some ideas.'

'You mean you don't know yet?'

Shard tutted, lowering the worm on the thread so she could scowl at him again.

'You saw that storm he threw at us. You saw what Seech is capable of doing now.'

'Well you're capable of a few things yourself,' he said, grinning.

Flirting with her, now of all times.

She had no choice in this, Shard reminded herself. For the last three years, Seech had been exploring his powers without care or caution, no doubt pushing the limits as far he could. While Shard, at the Academy, had been experimenting with the usual patience and rigour of an Observer, carefully recording everything that she discovered. Seech had a lead on her. He was the stronger Dreamer by far.

'This worm is the only chance I have of matching him. It will heighten my grasp of the bindee. If there was another way, believe me, I'd take it instead.'

There, at last. She had talked herself into going through with this.

Shard dangled the writhing worm over her open mouth and Blame gasped. She dropped it inside and tasted its slimy bitterness on her tongue before she swallowed as fast as she was able, gagging as she grasped for the cup of water on the floor, drinking deeply to help it down. Between pants she took another drink, rinsing the taste from her mouth with the flavour of the water, infused with jinyin and hazii weed to help control the nausea.

A hiccup squeaked from her throat, and she held a hand to her lips feeling a sudden urge to giggle.

Sweet kush, it was having an effect on her already.

A sudden sharp pain in her belly bent the Dreamer in two with a groan. She felt Blame's hand on her back, heard him say something through the red mist in her mind. It felt like she had swallowed a red-hot stone that was trying to burn its way through her abdomen.

Shard rolled onto the tarpaulin holding her belly tightly; nothing else she could risk taking now for fear of killing the thing before it had established itself within her.

Welcome softness beneath her as Blame placed a cushion under her head. Sudden warmth as he draped a blanket over her shivering form.

'Milk,' she gasped. She could at least risk some day-old goat's milk.

Perhaps he was not so useless after all, for Blame was there a moment later, lifting her head as he helped her drink it down, the cool goat's milk soothing the fire in her stomach.

The Dreamer lay back with her mind swirling, seeing patterns in the air that were like the outlines of trees repeating forever within themselves. The more she looked the more she felt like she was flying through them, so fast it was sickening. But when she closed her eyes there was no escape, for she saw the same dazzling shapes leading her off into infinity.

Shard dived head first into it.

*

Hours passed. Perhaps only the stretching of moments.

Someone was peeling her eyelids open. It was Blame. He looked like a dog just then with his open panting mouth and his pupils dilated hugely, the tip of his pink tongue poking from the corner of his lips.

'What are you seeing?' came his voice like an echo from the past.

No words for him. Shard had forgotten how to speak.

'I'm seeing the craziest things here,' he whispered. 'People I haven't seen for years, because they're dead.'

The Dreamer was flying. She was lifting off from her body on the floor and drifting towards the ceiling, which was not a ceiling at all but the closed hatchway of the hold. She rose through it as though it wasn't there, and found herself hovering above the small deck of the flying skud in the starlight of a clear night sky.

Shard had lost all sense of herself. The night air swirled with trails of coloured light. She stared upwards at the rippling canopy of gas that held the small skyboat aloft, then ahead along the short deck, her attention drawn like a firemoth towards the distant lights gathered like constellations beyond the prow; the besieged city of Bar-Khos.

Figures stood gathered at the rail taking in the nearing city. She moved towards them, seeing the Rōshun talking amongst themselves quietly, including the huge Alhazii man known as Baracha. Coya was there too, next to his lifelong bodyguard Marsh, gripping both the rail and his cane in subdued silence.

All of them were silhouettes of blackness, yet colours surrounded each one, auras pulsing around their bodies as though in play. Shard stopped just behind Coya's shoulders, his bright aura shaded with the various crimsons of pain.

Together, they were flying across a black mirror of starry sea contained within the arms of the Gulf, aiming for the Shield of Khos.

From afar the city pulsed like a brazier of burning coals, flooding the night with an impish glow. Bar-Khos was burning, and as the speeding skud flew across the water towards it a silence filled the deck save for the skud's roaring thrusters. Scents of smoke and rumbles of explosions came to her on the wind, fading away just as quickly. In the sky above the city she caught the glitter of flashes from sky battles raging fiercely, and along the coast and above the Lansway, clustershells bursting in the air.

'They said it was bad,' Coya muttered under his breath to his bodyguard Marsh, 'but this?'

Marsh said nothing, only tightened his lips and cast his frown towards the distant explosions, their reflections smeared across the dark waters of the bay and sparkling in his eyes.

'You didn't tell us the city was about to fall,' came Baracha's growl from where he towered above the gathering of Rōshun volunteers.

'It's worse than it looks,' Coya reassured the big Alhazii. 'Mokabi has been hitting the city with sky raids, but they'll weather them as they've always weathered them before.'

Coya gripped the rail hard, for the deck suddenly pitched forwards as the skud dove fast towards the city. Shard witnessed the sudden pains shooting through his crippled body as glimmers of purple across his aura. Flying along behind his shoulder, her mind filled with the sounds of the loft rippling above their heads and the creaking of the rigging and spars, it wasn't any press of wind that she experienced just then but instead the passionate flow of the man's thoughts. Shard sensed his affection for these islands of the Free Ports, strung out in a chain across the Midèrēs though joined in mutual support, where the seeds of the democras, these people without rulers, flourished like wild flowers.

His thoughts pattered against her mind.

Of all the Free Ports . . . Khos, pseudo-democras, where the bastard Michinè aristocracy still linger . . . where we either stop the Empire or are overrun by them . . . Most of all we cannot lose Khos.

Descendant of the famed Zeziké himself, philosopher of the democras, Shard had known this young man Coya Zeziké for half a decade now, long enough to have nurtured a deep though private respect for him. She knew how much he was committed to the cause of the Free Ports.

Years ago, Coya had visited the Academy of Salina where Shard had lived as a burgeoning student rook. A man in his twenties, stooped over his cane yet shining with an inner vitality, impressed, he had claimed, by what the students were doing in their spare time within the Black Dream of the farcrys.

Amongst all the young rooks of the Academy, he had spoken with Shard first. By then she had long cast aside her Contrarè name of Walks With Herself, and had cut her hair short to create even more distance from her heritage, not liking the prejudice it drew to her.

'They tell me you're the best rook they have here,' Coya had said when they were alone and the office door closed.

Shard had said nothing. No sense in denying it.

'Tell me then about the Black Dream. I'm not sure I understand it fully yet.'

'It's a construct dreamed up by the farcrys. Fundamentally, much the same as any other construct.'

'What do you mean?'

She had waved her hand about as though it was obvious, a young rook who already knew it all. 'The Veiled Dream of sleep. The Black Dream of farcrys. The Great Dream that encompasses it all. They're all reality constructs. Some are simply more subjective than others.'

He had sat back and blinked like an owl for some moments.

'Interesting. My ancestor wrote of such things when he wrote of his spiritual highs. How he transcended his own perspective. How he became one with everything within the Great Dream and felt nothing but love, nothing but an eternal bliss.'

Shard had only shrugged, hardly finding his comments relevant to the discussion. Coya had chuckled at that.

In his usual friendly manner, Coya had recruited her in the war against the Empire, enlisting her skills as a rook along with those of her peers deemed most capable, Tabor Seech included. And so as students they had intensified their efforts against the Mannian Empire, which by then had surrounded the Free Ports, and many of her peers had fallen along the way, their minds wrecked or lost entirely, cast senile before their years. Yet Coya had only ever asked for more.

Three years ago, Shard had returned from the Academy's disastrous expedition into the Alhazii deep desert, the only survivor along with Seech. Covered in her gleaming glimmersuit and with half her face mauled by fresh scars, she was suddenly able to do things that few others could barely believe.

These powers had drawn Coya to her once again.

'So you're a Dreamer now,' he had said with a smile and a disbelieving, almost sorrowful shake of his head.

With suspicious glances at the walls about them, Coya had asked if she would join him for an amble on the slopes of the Painted Mountain. In the summer heat, he had told her breathlessly about the network he secretly belonged to, an organization known as the Few. For an hour she had listened as he opened her eyes to a hidden world she had never known existed before, layers within layers within layers.

The Few, he had explained, were an organization founded in the early days of the democras, and given the perpetual mission of guarding against counter-coups and silent takeovers of the revolution, while privately promoting the spirit of liberty and solidarity both at home and abroad. The Few were funded by the League itself, which in turn was funded largely by anonymous public donations. Though barely anyone had ever heard of them.

There was no pay involved. Barely even travel expenses. And travel seemed like a large part of the deal, at least for Coya, who sounded more and more like some kind of troubleshooter, asked to go off to one flashpoint after another.

'We need your help,' Coya had claimed. 'We need what you can do for the Free Ports. We've been trying for years to enlist the services of a Dreamer from Zanzahar, but without luck.'

'I barely know what I can do yet myself.'

'Then keep at it. And help us out whenever you can, no strings attached. That's normally how we work anyway.'

'I'm not even from the Free Ports. You know this. How can you possibly be certain I'd be loyal to this . . . *cause* of yours?'

'Please, Shard. *Walks With Herself.* Your parents were driven from Pathia by the Mannian purges. Those who remained behind still suffer under the heels of the Empire. And now, the people who took you in as refugees in your hour of need, the people of the Free Ports – now we ask of you something in return. Now we ask for your help in our survival.'

Impossible to say no to such a sentiment, especially when it was expressed by this young man with his cane and his glittering, soulful eyes. Coya was a charismatic, there was no doubting it. In a way he reminded her of the Sky Writers back home when she had been a girl; urbanized Contrarè folk like herself – the lowest caste of the low – yet these splendid men in all their colours standing on the rooftops of their city quarter, shaking sticks at the sky while they chanted poems of life and death from the source of the Great Spirit.

All gone now. The Sky Writers wiped out in the first purges.

The very thing that Coya was fighting to prevent in the Free Ports.

*

Shard?

Roars and bangs in the world around her, soft concussions that pulsed through her consciousness like pebbles plopping into a lake. They were explosions in the dark sky over there, pretty blossoms of fire. Bar-Khos swung below them. The siege. The war.

Shard?

It was her own mind calling for her return.

Black sea not that far below them, she saw. Over the skyboat's starboard rail lay the dark hills of the southern continent; over the port rail, the steep and rugged coastline of Khos. In between ranged the skinny bridge of land known as the Lansway, a thin strip connecting the two and covered in a rash of lights, where the might of the Empire had been assaulting the walls of the Shield for years now, slowly taking one wall after the other. Four were still standing, though even now it was clear that the foremost wall was under heavy assault, torchlights swarming over it in a wave as though it had already fallen to the enemy.

The skud was nearing the burning city, and Shard could make out that it was mainly the southern quarters of Bar-Khos on fire, those nearest to the Lansway and the Shield spanning its breadth. Sheets of flames rose brilliant in the eyes, swathes of buildings glowing red amongst areas of black calm. Everywhere she looked, clouds of smoke filled the air.

It was like the end of the world down there, mythic in its proportions, like something from those old Lagosian legends about the Fall of Ages – legends that had come true enough for the people of Lagos, at least in the form of the Empire. A fate that could still happen here.

Coya was pointing at something over the rail, and Shard looked to see a wave of skyships coming in from the south over the open waters of the Gulf. Mannian birds-of-war in their scores.

'I've never seen them in such numbers,' said Marsh.

'It's as well our reinforcements arrived in time.'

He spoke of the thousands of fighting Volunteers that had lately flooded the city from the rest of the Free Ports to shore up its defences, along with squadrons of skyships.

On the deck a voice was calling out for a full burn. The thrusters of the skud roared even louder and the spars strained against the sudden increase of drag from the envelope, and then they were diving straight for the blazing city in a race to reach it before the enemy formations.

Coya had asked to see the action on the Shield upon their arrival. Now because of his curiosity they were arriving right in the thick of it. Starry explosions of clustershells lit the skies to their right. A bang sounded somewhere beneath the boat, debris spattering against the hull.

Amongst the bursts of light the enemy skyships were tumbling now, falling from the sky trailing ribbons of fire and blue streaks from their thrusters. A trio of them, four, five. She followed one that looked like an imperial flagship from the huge banner fluttering in its wake, burning like a wick in a falling candle. She watched it all the way down with its bag rippling empty and its twisting deck spilling debris and human figures, suddenly bringing to life the waters of the bay with a splash of white water; suddenly bringing to life the war and the spent lives that were its fuel.

Beyond the fading splash, the dark Lansway stretched before them, filled with the lights of the vast army brought here by General Mokabi himself. The largest army ever assembled in the history of the world.

Just then the silence of the Rōshun caught her ear. It drew Shard's attention as she watched them now, nine figures standing together along the rail, the glints of their stares fixed on the vast Mannian forces ranged against the Shield. Their enemy too. The people they had come here to take on.

All at once a mood had overcome the cramped and swaying deck like the promise before a storm. With little effort, the Dreamer willed their auras into the visible range once again, and saw that each individual halo had merged into a greater one shared by them all.

The Rōshun shone with a violet intensity of rage.

CHAPTER THIRTEEN

Sore Luck

'Holy kush, it's cold up here,' remarked Aléas, rubbing his long-fingered hands together and blowing into them, stamping his feet in the snow.

'Harder to breathe,' complained Kosh, his fleshy face snug within the fur lining of his hood.

Ash was squinting even with the smoky goggles he wore, for the light here was stronger too, bouncing off the snow which covered the field of the skyport and the pale rock of the mountains above their heads. Inside his leather gloves the tips of his fingers were throbbing, reminders of frostbite during his recent venture to the southern ice. He flexed his hands, trying to get some blood into them.

The Untamed Plateau was as wild and remote as its name suggested, a high tableland of pale mesas standing proud and lonesome amongst the greens and scarlet of ancient forest, the silver of lakes and rushing rivers. Perched in the arms of the Aradèrēs, it was almost surrounded by snow-capped mountains save for a northern horizon of twisted-ribbon clouds, which gathered most thickly where the beginnings of the Red Elba toppled unseen over the brink of the plateau; a heart-stopping waterfall when seen from the lowlands, a pilgrimage for Pathians seeking wonders.

From the deck of the *Falcon*, it had looked as though no human had ever set foot within this vast wilderness, until his eyes had squinted ahead to their destination, the smoky smudge of Lucksore nestled at the foot of the mountains, surrounded by swathes of recently cleared forest like a rash on the rump of the land.

The frontier town lay on the southernmost point of the plateau at the foot of the Aradèrēs mountains, which rose above the settlement and the line of frosted trees as muscular slopes so tall their snowy upper limits were lost in an obscurity of clouds, up there where a crease between peaks marked the high pass that had spawned this settlement centuries earlier.

'When were you last here in Lucksore?' he asked now of Meer the hedgemonk.

'Fourteen years ago. One of my earliest travels. I joined some pilgrims to see the Falls, but I fell so in love with these ranges that I strayed up onto the plateau, and then into the mountains themselves. There are many people living in the Aradères you know, deep inside them, surviving in sheltered valleys. Escaped slaves and tribes of natives driven centuries ago from their homelands. A remarkable mishmash of people with a thousand languages between them. Hostile to strangers, mostly. Fiercely proud of their independence. Very creative!'

They all peered up at the mountains as though they would see who he spoke of.

'Looks quiet,' he remarked, scanning about him.

'Yes,' said Meer. 'Not much business in winter, I imagine.'

The sleepy skyport seemed well equipped for a town the size of Lucksore, with hangars and towers and areas of warehouses, though most of it appeared closed for the winter, and snow had drifted up around the sides of the buildings and the wooden fence surrounding the field. A few hulks lay in a large open hangar, repair crews working over them slowly. They kept glancing across at the newly arrived *Falcon* and making remarks to each other, perhaps gauging how fast and high she could fly. Beyond the hangar, a row of merchant skyships sat on their flat-bottom hulls with their envelopes and rigging removed for the season.

The shore party's boots made crunching noises as they approached a customs shack next to the gate, where smoke rose from a stone chimney.

Meer entered with their wallet of papers and a purse of gold in his hand, and while the rest of them waited outside they exchanged glances with the imperial soldier standing guard at the gate, a tall man wrapped in one of the local tartan blankets as red as his cheeks and nose. When Meer returned the guard allowed them to pass through the gate, and then they were outside the skyport, marching down the cobbled road that led into town.

For all its renown, Lucksore was smaller than Ash had been expecting. Below them, the settlement curled around the southern slopes of a large bowl-like depression half filled with the mirror waters of a lake, so that the space resembled an amphitheatre floored with vividly blue sky. Three white torrents tumbled into the lake in clouds of spray, one roaring down through the town itself loud enough to be heard from far above. The fingers of jetties poked out into the water where small rowboats were moored. Vineyards grew on the opposite slopes of the depression, flecked white by the winterberries that would be used for the famed spiced wine of Lucksore. Streamers of red and purple flowed from every rooftop.

To the east of Lucksore, a massif of cliffs stood like the walls of some demigod's fortress, stark white in the daylight. Their surface seemed smooth as slate, yet when Ash squinted hard he could see that trees had managed to grow stunted and warped from the odd crevice and ledge, and he was able to follow them upwards as solitary blurs of green that became smaller and smaller the higher he looked, until they became mere specks against all the seams in the rock, and then he could see them no further, for none could live any higher. Yet still – craning his neck back as far as he could – still the rock face soared upwards beyond that zone of life to the bright blue of the sky.

Impossible, was the response of his mind taking in the sight, even though he had seen this mountain range up close before.

Once, in neighbouring Tilana, the Aradèrēs had soared over him for a week during a difficult vendetta, their peaks throwing ice crystals and sundogs into the sky. In Nathal he had even taken refuge on their slopes, pursued by a dozen bounty hunters and their trained birds of prey; until a storm had saved him in one of the high passes, a white-out in a blizzard giving him the chance to get in amongst the hunters with his blade, his white cloak and hood rendering him near invisible.

Yet still, as familiar as they were to him, their scale still remained impossible to his eyes – for the cliffs of Lucksore were only a minor flank of the great barrier known as the Aradèrēs, the Broken Spine of the World, that range of peaks standing between the world of man and the Great Hush beyond.

These cliffs were merely a hint of what was still to come.

On the road ahead a pair of tall and pale-skinned women

approached, wearing heavy dresses of cream wool that reached down to their ankles, burdened with heavy baskets perched on their heads, climbing the road in long-legged strides while they held their necks and heads perfectly steady. As they went past, the women stared at the two farlanders and whispered to each other, and Ash heard them giggle.

'The people here are known as Longshanks,' Meer explained as the group ambled downwards, singling out Aléas as though his youth demanded special attention. 'A mixed blood of highland natives and fairer Rorshach from the Lost Coast, descendants of King Haarlan's people, that old lunatic who tried to sack Bairat in his time.'

With a sly eye he noted the absence of interest from Aléas, who preferred to keep his attention on where he was placing his feet next.

'Tell me, Aléas, do they teach you any history, these Rōshun? Or only how to swing your sword about in an efficient way?'

He glanced to Ash to show that he was joking.

'We had a library in Sato for learning. I seldom used it though.'

'And before that, when you were a boy in Q'os?'

'I was schooled for a while, if that's what you mean. Mostly they taught us to follow orders and to fear their authority. I still recall some of the history they taught us. It was a list of dead rulers we were supposed to admire, and famous conquerors hailed as heroes, and a lot of wars.'

Ahead, Meer was chuckling to himself as he listened. 'No wonder you have little interest in the subject then. You speak of indoctrination, Aléas, not education. Real education guides us towards truth, towards the reality of our lives. It is *radical*, meaning the *root* of things, the *source* of them. In Khos, where I'm from, the community schools teach children the arts of critical thinking and self-awareness from an early age. Even classes in consciousness studies for those who show an interest. Real education teaches us that history has been written for the sake of the powerful and perpetuated by the powerful. That the majority of our species have lived ordinary, peaceful lives without even a whiff of war. And more than that. It teaches us where we have been and where we may yet be going.'

'Yet I know where I am from,' drawled Aléas. 'And for all I care, the future can take care of itself.'

Laughter burbled from Kosh and he slapped Aléas on the back in agreement, like the old fool that he was.

Ash inhaled the pungency of pine resin in the air, strong enough to taste on his tongue, and felt something of the old country in these highlands of the Pathian plateau, reminding him of his birthplace in the mountainous region of northern Honshu.

He had always marvelled at the similarities between the uplands of the world, no matter how far apart they might be; how it seemed that no matter where you travelled, if you went high enough you could see the same types of hardy shrubs and dwarf trees hugging the ground, the same tiny-petalled flowers that were always a surprise to the eyes; altitude forming its own common regions as much as latitude and longitude.

He pinched his nose to relieve the tension behind his strained eyes; another headache this morning, made worse by the thinness of the chill air.

Never mind. His spirits soared to be here at last, one step closer to his goal.

'Up there!' Meer suddenly declared, jabbing a finger into the air. 'The Pass of the Snow Monkeys. Our route into the range.'

They all looked up to follow his finger pointing at a break in the clouds. Saw the cleft in the wall of mountains hanging over the town, the high icy pass filled with rivers of mists.

Ash thought of the *Falcon* flying through that high pass, and saw that Kosh's face had grown stiff at the sight of it.

Downwards, the air growing rich with birdsong here, the sudden cry of a buzzard echoing from the slopes. At the bottom of the hill they stopped at a crossroads where a signpost pointed off in four directions: Lucksore Town, the Skyport, the Farrier Road, and the High Trail leading off towards the mountains.

'You are confident you can find a longhunter here to act as our guide?' Ash asked after Meer as the hedgemonk chose the High Trail, leading the way.

'Of course,' Meer cast over his shoulder in a ribbon of breath. 'If we can't find a longhunter here, we can't find one anywhere.'

'Good enough,' answered Ash, and they followed behind.

*

The road to the High Trail ran through a busy district on the outskirts of town, where wooden signs hung everywhere and craftsmen could be seen busy at work: blacksmiths and leather-crafters, fur traders and goldsmiths, timber yards, stables, general stores. The footing on the road here was less slippery, the snow flat and churned to slush as it was, and Ash marched onwards with his feet nimble in their hobnailed boots, a man born of highlands just like Kosh, comfortable in the snow and ice of hard winters.

The people here wore all sorts of hats, from tall bearskins to widebrimmed rancheros. Men favoured beards and heavy coats and the women thick, figure-hugging gowns reaching down to the ground in trailing fringes of fur. A hairy breed of hill zel was common, their stripes brown rather than black upon their white coats. Lean hunting dogs lay out of the way watching the world go by. Spotted maws too were everywhere, the clever white snow monkeys of the region, sitting on verandas or sloping rooftops, speaking to each other in a whistling chatter with their long tails curving around them for warmth while they squatted in the sunlight.

Ash spotted one of the creatures jumping out of an open window with a round of bread in its clawed hand. It leapt up onto the roof and sat there eating it amongst its whistling companions, fending them off with bared teeth, until it relented and shared out a few handfuls too.

'There's so many of them,' Aléas exclaimed. 'Don't they get under people's feet?'

'They do,' Meer answered. 'But the locals believe that some of them are the spirits of their dead ancestors, and so they treat them with reverence. They seem to live quite happily together most of the time.'

As if to prove his point, their attention was drawn to the laughter and flute music of an open courtyard, where people feasted and danced beneath a canopy of red strings that crisscrossed above their heads. A wedding celebration it seemed, for all the singing and dancing involved, and the young couple at the centre of it all.

Spotted maws sat congregated on an outer table enjoying their own feast. One of them watched Ash as he passed by, and he saw how its eyes were strangely human.

'How far are we going?' Kosh asked breathlessly with a strain in his voice. Perhaps his gout was playing up again this morning, though he would never admit as much.

'Not far. There's a taverna on the High Trail called the Last Chance. Popular with longhunters and hangers on.'

'And you say this town is the capital of Royal Milk?' Aléas wanted to know.

'Yes, outside of Zanzahar anyway. The Alhazii have their own operations along the Sea of Doubts, but much of their Milk is used to trade with the Isle of Sky in return for exotics. The people of the Isles fear the Great Hush you see, and refuse to enter it themselves, believing it to contain all manner of diseases that could wipe them out. Much as they fear the wider world. So they buy their Milk from the Alhazii.

'Here, though,' he said with a wave of his hand, 'is where most of the Milk that makes it into the Midèrēs comes from. It's a boom town, right on the frontier, though you might not think it. Every year the longhunting expeditions return from the Hush and the Edge through the high passes, bringing with them their loads. Their stories are just about all we know of what lies on the other side of the mountains.'

They knew enough to fall silent as they clumped past the scrutiny of a pair of imperial guards, stationed beside an archway that led beyond the district onto the High Trail. Past it, the road narrowed into a cobbled path and began to climb upwards into the hills that led to the high pass of the Snow Monkeys.

Directly ahead, the path bent around a building perched on a prominence of rock, its shingled roof covered in yellow hanging mosses above walls of old, sun-bleached redwood. As they rounded on it, they could see how the structure leaned to the side a little, in the same direction as the few scraggly windblown trees around it, which people had tied old rags to in their hundreds; wishful prayers, perhaps, of those leaving on an expedition, or those watching them go.

'The Last Chance,' Meer panted beneath the sign above its front door, which was entirely bare. Whatever had once been painted on it was now washed clean by wind and sunshine.

'First round is on me,' Kosh declared, rubbing his gloved hands in anticipation of a drink. 'I have a mind to try this chappa that Meer has been going on about.'

'Let me do the talking,' Meer told them all. 'It's a hanging offence to obtain Royal Milk without a licence, and the trading families here have many spies in the town. We must be subtle, and cautious, if we are to find a guide without raising suspicions.'

It was warm inside. A small fire crackled in a hearth at the back of the long taproom. The air was humid from a kettle steaming above the flames. Before it sat an elderly woman in a shawl, rocking in a chair as she finger-knitted with a bundle of purple wool. She glanced up briefly at the new arrivals before looking away again, one eye milky white with cataract. Chairs creaked, three men just as old looking over their shoulders from whatever they were playing, the table covered by small blocks of white wood. In a corner, a solitary man sat staring at them from within the shadows of a cowl.

'I thought you said this place was popular with longhunters?' Ash muttered in Meer's ear.

Meer winced.

'Give it time,' he replied without much confidence.

Behind the bar, a thin tall youth with a shock of yellow hair stood reading a news-sheet from the Pathian capital of far Bairat.

'Quiet day,' Meer remarked to him, but the young man only grunted, then looked up from the paper and blinked at the group standing before him, drawn to the black skin of the farlanders.

Before he could start asking questions, they ordered the local drink of custom, chappa, a blend of hot goat's milk and stiff spirits, and took a table by the window furthest from the bar, their skin tingling in the heat. Ash glanced across at the man seated alone in the corner, and knew that he was watching them from within his hood. Around their own far table, the players carried on with their game in the easy silence of old companions.

Sipping on his own hot drink of chee, Ash blinked through the watery glass of the window at the wintry world outside.

'Will you look at that,' breathed Aléas by his side, taking in the sight of what was mounted in the high space above the bar. Ash followed his gaze, and allowed his mouth to drop open.

'Ah, I'd all but forgotten about that,' remarked Meer.

Kosh shifted uneasily in his chair, the wood creaking under his weight. 'Is that what I think it is?'

'A real kree,' breathed Aléas, rising to his feet with a scrape of his chair to study the thing more closely: a fully grown kree, big as a zel.

Ash leaned back with his lips pursing. *What a monster*, he thought, taking in the black sheen of its carapace where sharp spines ran across its peak. The floorboards creaked as Aléas stepped forwards to stand beneath the creature, where he stood with his head craned back and eyes gazing up in wonder. Above him, the massive bulk of the kree hung in the shadows beneath the rafters, its carapace shaped like the stubby kite-shields of Markesh, the six legs hanging limp just beneath its edges; all of it black in this light, though the creatures were said to be a shade of velvety blue. From this angle, the whole thing resembled a monstrous crab.

'That's only a little one,' remarked one of the old game players at the next table, a match poking from between his rotting teeth. 'It's a scout, not a full-grown warrior. Old Tennesey and his men found it dead on the other side of the Spine just below the snowline. Dragged it all the way here.' The match between his lips bobbed once in a nonchalant shrug. 'So they say.'

Ash set down his chee.

'How do you kill them?' he asked across the room.

'Kill them?'

'Aye.'

'People usually just run. Not many have stood their ground and lived to tell of it.'

'Have you seen it done?'

'Hold, and release two,' the man said, and there was a clink of wooden blocks on the table. 'I've seen scouts killed after they were caught in nets. Only ever saw one warrior killed in the open though, and that was from the safety of a warwagon. Took a lucky shot under its maw. That's where they're vulnerable. Damned hard to hit when they're coming at you, though.'

'What about eyes?' Aléas asked him, still studying the creature from his chair. 'Can they see?'

'They can see motion, if it's close enough to them.'

'Hear, smell?' asked Ash.

'They seem to be deaf. Smell is their primary sense.'

'They can smell far?'

'Hard to say exactly. Far enough though. If you're upwind of them they'll know you're there for certain. Downwind, and you can breathe in those scents they release and find a whole lot of strange things starting to happen. Can even cause paralysis if you're close enough and they're hunting you.'

They sobered as he spoke the words, and even Ash grew cold in his bones. Seeing it on their faces, the man offered them more.

'They wage war as a species, that's why they have warriors born and bred for killing. Always move in packs. Sometimes whole armies. That carapace of theirs, on the warriors it's like two-inch-thick plate armour, except they can move as fast as a wolf when they need to.'

'More chappa, if you please,' Kosh called over to the bartender, holding up his empty cup.

Another click of wood from the players, the game carrying on.

'What about those fellows?' Kosh whispered. 'That talkative one sounds like he knows his business.'

'To lead you into a kree warren?' Meer retorted as he took in the old fellows. 'He must be in his sixth decade.'

'And your point?' demanded Kosh with a scowl.

'You want to get in and out of there alive, don't you?'

When the young bartender came over to refill their mugs, Meer leaned towards him over the table and spoke in a lowered tone, feigning a casual manner. 'Last time I was here the room was packed to the rafters with longhunters.'

'Must have been a different season then. All the big expeditions are in the Hush now. Best time to be there. You'll not see them again until the passes reopen in early spring, when they return with their loads.'

Ash and the others all glared at Meer in silence.

'They can't all be there, surely?'

The barman glanced over at the man sitting in the corner with his face hidden. Leaned over the table in a pretence of wiping the surface with a rag. 'You're looking for a longhunter?'

'Yes. Someone still active.'

'If you carry on from here, follow the first track you come to on your left. The cabin's about an hour out of town but it's an easy hike. Cole's his name. Not from around here. Interesting fellow. Likes to go into the Hush alone which makes him crazier than most, but they say he's a good longhunter.'

'You think he'll be interested in some work?'

CHAPTER FOURTEEN

The Longhunter

The air up there was cold enough to chill his fingers to the bone, yet the man was sweating from his efforts, and droplets were shaking loose from every sudden motion he made, so that as he climbed his body rained into the gulf of space.

Occasionally, Cole would pause spreadeagled in his precarious ascent of the cliff, with his leather-bound toes perched on a knob or sill of rock and his calf muscles straining, and he would ram a hand into a crack in the wall and make a fist of it, locking him in place there. Without hesitation he would release the grip of his other slick hand to dip it into the leather bag at his waist, filled with powdered chalk.

Blinking his eyes clear of sweat, he would catch his bearings on his route up the face, gasping in the high rarefied air of the Untamed Plateau, trying to think of nothing but what he was doing.

Cole wasn't certain how much further he could make it today, nor how much he should push his weakened body still recovering from the long journey back from the Great Hush; an experience he was now coming to terms with in his usual manner, by trying to forget about it entirely.

He should have died out there, he knew only too well. After the kree attack on his night camp, after he'd lost everything but his rifle and cat and his last saddle-less zel . . . Well, it was what you got when you ventured early-season into the Hush all on your lonesome, then found yourself asleep in the midst of a grisly kree attack. You died.

Yet miracles had saved him, one after the other. Waking when he had done from his delirium, just in time to flee. Then finding his nearest supply cache without his compass, and every one after that all the way back to the northern highlands. And there, stumbling across the friendly Inchita in their winter camp during a storm. A string of unlikely chances.

The rock face was all he could see before him now. Already Cole's muscles were verging on numbness from the strains he was putting on them. But he needed to keep going, to push it further; climb and keep on climbing without thoughts of return, away from the call of memories altogether, up into the limitless sky.

Clarity; he could see it up there in the bleached sky when he leaned back and squinted past the vertical world he clung to like a fly.

Cole was high now, though still the lone trees sprouted from the rock here and there to the left and right of him. Of all the climbs he had made of this cliff, he was yet to reach the line where they ceased to grow. He doubted if today would be any different.

Below and behind him, the gulf of air was a windy nothingness that waited to claim him body and soul. It was waiting there for the first and last mistake that he made, the slightest shave with bad luck, but more than that – for he was culpable in this – it was waiting for his own surrender to it.

Maybe there was a name for his condition, or maybe he was crazy after all; for whenever Cole looked down from any real kind of height, he was prone not to shiver with fear from it but instead to feel drawn to the empty abyss it offered him.

Down there in the world, down in Lucksore and most of all in the Last Chance taverna – one of the few places in town that he frequented other than the brothel – they did indeed call him crazy, and right to his face too. Cole the crazy foreigner who ventures into the Hush alone. Who throws away the fortunes he makes from Milk on gambling and women. Who climbs rock faces for the sport of it. The crazy longhunter with a face that looks like a dog has been chewing over it for the better course of a day.

And now, the man who had somehow made it back across the Aradèrēs passes in winter and lived to tell the tale. Not that he would be telling it. Not unless he wanted to risk getting strung up for his previous dealings in Milk without a licence.

Smoke rose through the canopy far to the east of him. The Selak Contrarè most likely, holed up in their wintering campground. Even now the forest remained home to scattered tribes of Contrarè living and dying in the old ways, taking only what would be restored to the land in the turning of a year.

Cole was climbing again, pushing himself harder as memories returned unwanted, panting ragged breaths from the effort.

On the other side of the Aradèrēs, living there on the edge of the Great Hush, the highland natives had thought him crazy too for wanting to cross back over the Broken Spine in winter. Wait for spring, they'd advised him. Wait until you're recovered and the passes are clear again. You will die of exposure if you try it now.

But they were wrong, he'd known. Too many unlikely events had brought him here for it all to end in the high frozen passes of the Spine.

Something calls me back to my world, he had tried to explain to the highland natives one night around a high-banked fire. *Something wants me to return to the life I once fled from. Ever since I awoke beneath a tree with the kree attacking me, I've felt it guiding me every step of the way.*

They had sensed it too, for the natives were Contrarè in their own ways and they knew of these things. Relenting to his vision, they gave Cole thick furs and stout snow shoes and blessed charms to aid his way; the crazy man following the path of the Great Spirit.

Later, up in the high passes, Cole and the cat had indeed walked into an unseasonable spell of remarkably fine weather. Still damnably cold at night, enough to frostnip his nose and cheeks, but survivable if they huddled together, and with the snow hard packed and easy to traverse the entire way. Another miraculous window of good fortune.

So much good luck, yet a King's ransom remained behind in the Hush, the entire venture for nothing.

Had it meant anything, really, that sense of being guided homewards – home to the family he had so long ago deserted? Or had it been the simple cravings of his desperate mind?

Returned at last to the sanctuary of his remote cabin, the question had lingered on without answer, while his desire to return home to Khos diminished by the day. It was only the Hush, he began to tell himself. The Hush did strange things to a man's mind, that was all.

Cole grunted. Kept on climbing hard.

'Hello!'

Glancing down, he instantly lost his toehold on the rock. Cole hung there staring at the figure far below him, scrambling up the rock face so fast that even Cole was impressed by it.

A bounty hunter, perhaps? Cole was still wanted in Dasun for that road robbery after all. But that couldn't be it, he'd gone by a different surname in those days. Had he given himself away somehow? Loose pillow talk with one of the girls in town?

Regaining his toeholds, he relaxed the strain on his arms by leaning outwards, then cast a look over his shoulder.

'What do you want?' he hollered.

The figure glanced up just then, and Cole saw his black skin, the black skin of an old farlander no less, all the way here in the mountains of Pathia. One of the old exiles. Interesting.

'Can we talk?'

'We're talking now, aren't we?'

'Can we talk below? I have some friends waiting.'

'What is it you want?'

'We need a guide. A guide into the Hush.'

'Then you're a little late in the year!' Cole called back, and started to climb again, aiming for a ledge he knew was wide enough to sit upon. When he reached it at last, he settled himself against the rock with his legs dangling over the edge.

The climbing farlander was still a long way below.

A guide. Why in Erēs would he need a guide into the Hush?

For the first time since fleeing Khos, Cole felt the same sickness in his stomach that he'd carried for all those years he had fought beneath the Shield; a cold and coiled thing living within him. A portent, perhaps.

Waiting, he drank some water and tried not to look down at the climbing figure. Instead he gazed out across the land, filling his eyes with one of the known world's greatest remaining forests, the unspoiled wilderness of the Untamed Plateau. A land of clouds and visions.

Shades of green and red everywhere he looked down there, save for where deciduous trees were prominent, their bare limbs frosted with snow. Ancient highland tiq, featherwood and black pine were the commonest trees in the forest, though the chiminos towered over them all, their trunks of furred bark as wide as some rivers, their diamond leaves broad enough to roof a house. Indeed, tribes of snow monkeys favoured them for their homes, as did the brushtails and the ponderous long-fingered sequat, and countless other species found nowhere else but here.

Once, if the Contrarè were to be believed, forests like this one had covered all the lands around the southern Midèrēs, until the people of the alhuthut had arisen to devour them for farmland and resources, and much later to deprive those who would live free within their protection. Now, native forests survived only across the highlands of the Aradèrēs mountain range, and in the lowlands where pockets remained as tribal lands or unexploited commons, and even right out there in the Midèrēs sea on his homeland of Khos, as the ancient forest of the Windrush.

Westwards Cole's eyes were drawn towards the frontier town of Lucksore and its azure lake reflecting the sky, surrounded by blankets of snow where the land had been turned over to goats and hill zels, pretty against a backdrop of forested slopes. With reluctance he took in the vast swathes of logged land to the north of the town, and in his unwavering gaze held the sight of the bald and stubbled hilltops – laq after laq of them – pushing into the deep forest like an affliction of mange.

The Empire's ever-growing need for prime tiq and other timbers, now reaching even to here on the Untamed Plateau.

With spirit, Cole raised his flask of water to the remaining forest, toasting the trees and sweeping mesas below him before taking another swallow, wondering how many more times he would lay his gaze upon this great sight before it was gone, or he was dead.

A chip of rock came loose against the kicking heels of his bare feet. Cole glanced down as it fell past the old farlander not so far below him now. The old fellow snapped his face up with a scowl, so that Cole saw the small goatee on his chin and the gleam of his shaven head, his eyes hidden by dark goggles. Cole raised a hand by way of apology.

The farlander seemed hesitant as to which way to go next. No wonder. He had reached that difficult final section at last – the section that had caused Cole's recent lather of sweat. No further handholds lay within easy reach of it. In fact the nearest required a leap in which you had to release all contact with the cliff face for an instant, and the distance seemed a touch too far. One mistake and that was the end of it.

If he goes for it, I'll listen to what he has to say.

The farlander leapt, grabbed the protrusion of rock he'd been aiming for with a grunt and hung there for a moment while he found purchase for his bare feet. He flashed a grin at Cole.

Soon he was pulling up to the ledge and swinging himself onto its thin relief.

'Drink?' Cole asked casually and offered his flask to the old man, who heaved himself further onto the rocky shelf clearly out of breath, his tunic clinging wet to his skin. The fellow pulled up the goggles with trembling fingers to reveal dark eyes bloodshot and tired, as though he was ill. He accepted the offering with a nod.

'Cold day for a climb,' the farlander gasped as he tossed back the flask, and up close there was a curious humour in his expression which somewhat disarmed Cole just then – something in his eyes that he recognized from his own mirror; a certain recklessness of spirit.

'I've felt colder.'

The farlander craned his head to look directly up the cliff. 'You are trying for the top?' he asked, incredulous.

'Yes,' said Cole, then shook his head. 'No. Not today.'

'You climb for the thrill of it then?'

'Do we always need a reason for what we do?'

'I suspect so, even if we do not know what it is.'

Fair words, and spoken openly enough that Cole could not help but feel relaxed in this fellow's presence. They sat there studying each other in silence, until a gust came that made them press their bodies against the cliff.

'Who are you?' Cole asked through the rush of wind.

'Call me Ash. Will you come down and speak with us? My companions are waiting below.'

'What is it you really want?'

'I told you. We need a guide for the Hush. We were told you might be interested in the work.'

'Well unless you're damn well planning on flying over those mountains, there's not much point in us talking, old man.'

For some reasons his words caused the farlander to grin.

'You coming?' the fellow asked brightly, and slid himself over the ledge.

*

'You want to do what?'

The man who called himself Meer sat back in his chair and smiled apologetically.

'We need Royal Milk. A great deal of it. Much more than we can afford to buy at market value.'

Cole was fetching the cat some supper while he listened, strips of jerky hanging from the beams of his cramped cabin. He offered some to the rest of the group but the strangers politely declined. Their minds were set on business.

'You're crazy, all of you,' he decided as he marched through the open doorway, where the farlander was sitting on the rail of the veranda, and filled a bucket from the stream that ran not far from the cabin.

'Maybe,' replied the farlander as Cole returned. 'But crazy or not, we will pay well.'

Inside, the other three were waiting in silence. The young man with the blond hair took a step out of the way as Cole banged the bucket on the floor and water splashed over the sides. With all of them looking on, Cole removed his sodden tunic to wash his face and neck and bald head with soap leaves and shockingly cold splashes of water.

'Pay me how well?' he gasped.

'A fifth of the haul.'

'And how much Milk are you after?'

'Five rhuls, at the minimum.'

'Five rhuls!' Cole stood upright so that water cascaded from his head. 'And you can't tell me what it's for?'

'No.'

Instinctively, Cole looked back at the bearded farlander through the open doorway, which framed Ash in the fading twilight, the crows coming home to roost loud and boisterous behind him. The man was watching Cole from his perch on the veranda rail, his arms crossed together, one booted foot swinging back and forth above the fascinated eyes of the cat, which had gulped down her jerky and now lay there beneath him, her tail lolling in lazy excitement.

'There aren't five rhuls of Milk in all of Lucksore, old man.'

'We know that,' said Meer, trying to catch his eye again. 'That's hardly the point.'

'But why do you need so much of it? Is this a commercial venture?'

The second farlander, the fleshier one called Kosh, leaned forward in his own chair, and his gaze was a spear that tried to pin Cole where he stood. Cole held it steadily, feeling the past rushing through him once again today. It was the gaze of a hardened military man, a man who had killed many times in his life; yet otherwise there was little whiff of soldiering in any of them. The two farlanders were an enigma. The fellow called Meer might as well be a monk, with his shaved head and easy smiles. And the young blond man carried himself with the self-assuredness of a street prince, afraid of no one.

Who were these people?

'No,' Meer told him. 'This is a private matter, not a commercial one. What we need to know is whether it can be done.'

It needed some thinking, that question. So Cole stood and stripped off his filthy trousers and started washing down his body while he worked the matter over in his mind. They all fell quiet once more.

'There's a good reason why I go into the kree warrens alone,' he said as he scrubbed beneath his arms, looking up into a cobwebbed corner as he spoke. 'It's a simple equation, and a sound one. The more people who go down into the tunnels with you, the more chance of the kree finding you out. And then you're all dead.'

'Yes, I understand that,' said the man Meer. 'Tell me. How many trips have you made so far?'

Cole flashed him four fingers, and the man was clearly surprised by that. Meer looked about at the cold and bare room he sat within. 'Four hauls of Milk, yet this is how you live?'

'Three hauls. I lost the last one. And what's wrong with how I live?'

'Nothing at all. You should see how I normally live. But you should be a wealthy man by now. Where has it all gone?'

Cole tucked a fist into his hip and looked up at the far corner again in contemplation.

'Whores and gambling mostly. The rest I squandered.'

Through the doorway the decking of the veranda creaked minutely. It was the farlander, standing up straight with his arms still crossed and the crows calling behind him.

'Can it be done?' the old man rasped.

'You'd be testing your luck, is what I'm trying to tell you all. And that's assuming your ship is able to cross the Spine in the first place. Which is the other part of this plan of yours I'm having a problem with.' He shrugged, shedding water. 'Good odds to gamble on, though.'

'So you will do it, you will guide us in?'

Five rhuls of Milk at least, and they were offering him one fifth of the load. It was more than he had left behind in the Hush. He should be jumping at the chance to join them. Yet still, that worm of dread in his belly was coiling itself even tighter.

'Where did you say you folks have come from?' he asked, drying himself with a fresh shirt.

'Khos,' answered Meer. 'And I wouldn't admit that to anyone right now but a fellow Khosian.'

Cole stiffened. He took a deep breath of the mountain air. Started tugging on clothes over his goosebumped flesh.

'How can you tell?'

'Your accent has been slipping ever since we started to talk.'

So here it was then, after all. The meaning of his survival in the Great Hush and the high passes. The reason all those turns of fate had led him to here, now, this moment. The calling from home again.

From a pail on the table Cole poured himself a mug of water, thirsty as a desert all of a sudden. His hands were shaking, and he was certain they all could see it.

In the cooling air the cat wandered in and lay down before the empty hearth, waiting for him to light it; complacent these days of the miracles he provided her.

For a precious moment Cole remembered a different life entirely, back at the cottage and the farm. A wife and son he never thought he would see again, and their family dog Boon.

'Will you help us?' asked the farlander once more.

He felt an urge to be gone from these people, but his feet were clamped to the floor. All he could do was swallow around the lump in his throat as he tried to speak.

'On one condition.'

'Go on.'

Resignation thickened his voice as he spoke.

'You take me back to Khos with you when we're done.'

CHAPTER FIFTEEN

Future's Ghosts

Beneath a sky hidden by the dull overcast, they hiked up one of the many paths on the gentle eastern slope of the Mount of Truth, a broad low-shouldered hill covered in trees and parkland, named for its vicinity to the Shield and the view from its flattened back to the Lansway beyond, where the siege of the city continued after ten long years and where now an even greater force was assaulting them, Mokabi's newly arrived army.

Indeed horns were calling from the Shield as they climbed, echoing across the rooftops of Bar-Khos like wild obors in heat. Calls of retreat, Marsh the bodyguard told them grimly, making official what they had already heard in the streets below, rumours that Kharnost's Wall had finally fallen, even with the reinforcements of Volunteers from the League, overwhelmed by a hundred thousand of Mokabi's mercenaries.

In the grey skies over the city, squadrons of recently arrived sky-ships patrolled against further enemy air raids. Squinting, Shard could see them clustered most heavily to the south over the foremost battlements of the Shield; small marrow-shaped blobs twinkling with the yellow specks of cannon fire, circling over a bank of smoke that obscured the mighty Kharnost's Wall below them and much of the remaining three walls behind it, smoke that was being pushed inland on the breeze. Concussions rattled the stillness of the cool air. Every so often a scream or the snap of rifle fire carried on the wind to her ears, snatched from the distant retreat.

She blinked hard, wondering for the briefest of moments if any of this was real.

'Creed will be in a foul mood,' remarked Coya to himself, looking up through the trees of the hill for a glimpse of the Ministry at the very top. And then louder, to the others: 'Confined to bed rest while Mokabi's forces take Kharnost's Wall. I hope he will agree to see us.'

Marsh glanced back from where he led the way, the bodyguard's eyes twinkling through his goggles. 'That heart attack of his. I hear it broke old Bearcoat's spirits in two.'

Coya's response was almost lost in a renewed roar of cannon fire from the Shield. 'That will be the day. Marsalas Creed, a broken man!'

His bodyguard shrugged and looked ahead again, alert for trouble. 'It's what they're saying.'

'Then it must be true, eh?'

'Just repeating what I heard.'

Shard was barely listening as they walked, for her gaze was fixed on the Lansway and the action at the walls, seeking glimpses of the Mannian forces beyond the smoke.

Tabor Seech would be out there somewhere.

'I suppose you believe everything the enemy claims too? That Creed is really dead? And this move of theirs is actually a *defensive siege*?'

'What?' Shard said by his side, finally registering the words between them.

'It's true!' exclaimed Coya, pausing to wave his cane at the smoke of the Shield. 'They're calling this a defensive siege now in the Empire's news-sheets. A defensive siege! Can you believe it? They're saying that the people of the democras are *extremists*. A baying mob made crazy by their worship of disorder. They say we're bent on the destruction of Mann, whom we hate most of all because we envy their achievements. To read what they say would have you thinking *they* were the victims here, and *we* the aggressors.'

Shard was hardly surprised, knowing what she did by now of the Empire's ways. She tried to focus, tried to hold on to what they were discussing. But people were dying down there, she realized in her fugue condition. Dying even as the trio ambled along this path talking of war. Those horns called over the heads of men running for their lives.

No wonder Coya was shaking.

'Sounds just like their conquest of the southern continent,' she heard herself say, her tongue thick and lazy in her mouth. 'When they claimed it was a noble gesture in the toppling of tyrants.'

'Indeed,' said Coya. 'And their people believed it too!'

'Or wanted to believe it,' drawled Marsh.

Coya grew sombre, shaking his head as he watched the siege. 'Mercy help those people down there.'

Shard shivered, for it was getting colder now. Across the slope of the hill the shadows were deepening, the sun sinking below the far side.

This war was too much to handle today. Her body was an over-sensitized bag of skin that flinched from every stimulus, even the flow of the breeze against her glimmersuit. Her emotions were the same, fiercely open to everything.

All effects of the worm juice now coursing through her blood, making a dream of the waking world. Her abdomen throbbed dully, reminding her always that the sandworm was inside her. A coppery taste filled her dry mouth no matter what she drank to replace it.

Shard hadn't slept during the night in their temporary quarters in a nearby taverna, too high on the sandworm's juices coursing inside her, wondering in her less frantic moments whether taking the worm had been a sound judgement after all.

For a time, young Blame had rallied from his own delirious con-dition, caused by simply touching the worm. He had marvelled at the potency of the worm's juices while offering her shaking cups of tannis tea to take the edge off the worst of the rushes. But even that hadn't been enough for sleep, and eventually Blame had curled him-self in a corner unable to cope with his own ordeal, and Shard, lost too in strong winds blowing Contrarè greening-songs through her mind along with images from her earlier life – gripping the spinning bed as though she might otherwise take off into flight – had been in no condition to do anything for the young man as the endless night held them in its maw.

Days later, weeks even, the first rays of daylight had at last forced their way through the shutters of the room like rescuers' fingers scrabbling through rubble, slowly unearthing her to sunlight, the food of life.

Rousing herself, she'd found that Blame was gone from their room and missing from the taverna. Run off into the surrounding streets, yelling about bats chasing him, one of the Rōshun had said with some bemusement.

It would teach him to wear gloves next time, as she'd instructed. Or so she told herself, though Shard asked a few of the men to search for him anyway, and to make sure that he was safe.

Barely able to move, Shard had wished only to return to her bed for the rest of the day. But Coya had been insistent he needed her with him, and Coya was a man skilled at getting his way. So she had infused herself with massive doses of tannis tea to coax her mind down from the ceiling, and had allowed him to drag her for hours around the city's limits to appraise its situation, even though she could barely stand straight, could barely even speak.

Down in the cobbled streets the crowds round her had seemed like a raging babbling torrent trying to sweep her mind away. Soldiers were everywhere, along with Volunteers from the rest of the League packed into the city. Down in the southern quarters amongst the press of traffic, a constant trickle of reinforcements had been hurrying for the Lansway while carts filled with the wounded trundled back in the opposite direction, sights of blood-soaked bandages and gaping wounds, the hospitals of the Shield filled by then, fresh casualties overflowing into the city.

Nothing for ordinary citizens to do though but spread the word and carry on with another day in Bar-Khos, city of eternal siege. Or so she had thought, until she noticed the many citizens covered from head to foot by dirt and sweat, people returning from work shifts on the Shield or from the smaller northern walls of the city, where they were erecting great earthworks as fast as they could.

All the while, Shard was trying to block out the growing mood of inevitability she could sense gathering like the clouds over the city, this place that was surely doomed to fall without some miraculous overturning of fate. Usually known for her optimism in hard situations, Shard had witnessed the ghosts of the future in the streets she had just been walking through, drifting through; shadows or impressions of a city falling before her eyes; the mayhem of mass murders and rapes, families slaughtered in front of each other and children's heads dashed against walls or under boots, the desperate panic of ordinary citizenry trapped and with no way out.

The worst of all evils in this world, a city sacked.

Nothing is fated but the Laws themselves, Shard reminded herself again. *All else is only probability.*

It was a thought she tried hard to hold on to now: this city still had a chance at survival, no matter how remote. And perhaps she and Coya could help improve the odds a little further yet.

'You okay?' Marsh asked from ahead without turning round, and she saw his magnified eyes blinking at her in the extra lenses on the back of his head.

'Fine,' she panted, soothed a little by the humanness of his concern. Though he tainted the moment somewhat by eyeing a buxom maiden hurrying past them on her way down the hill, Marsh turning his head to watch her blonde hair and curves from behind; like a dog in heat as usual, even here overlooking the fall of a wall.

By the Dreamer's side, picking his way carefully along with his cane, Coya Zeziké spoke his thoughts out loud again, as he was wont to do. 'I still don't see why you had to take that worm thing now, of all times, when I need you the most. Yes, yes, Tabor Seech. Well I'm sure you'll make a fine adversary in your present condition, eh?'

'Maybe you should concern yourself with your own business, and I with with mine.'

'Yet this is my business, Shard. I hope you can still help me in the Windrush, before your fated reunion with Seech?'

'Of course. It will take time to control the effects of the worm. Weeks maybe. The longer I can put off confronting Seech the better.'

He nodded, satisfied enough, focusing once more on his awkward steps and the placement of his cane on the stony path. She was glad of Coya's slow pace. Control of her body seemed a shaky gamble today, each step forwards one of faith. She even gripped a fallen branch by way of her own rudimentary cane, using it to maintain her balance, so that she and Coya resembled a pair of walking wounded, shambling along to the distant percussions of war.

It had been years since Shard had last stood in Bar-Khos as a girl, fleeing Pathia with her parents. Hardly a city she had wished to return to, though their present destination, it had to be said, was an intriguing one.

She could see it now, the Ministry of War on the very peak of the hill, surrounded by hedgerows and batteries of guns pointing to the overcast sky; home to the Lord Protector, General Creed.

'Why is it,' huffed Shard as they walked along, 'that for as long as I've known you, whenever you ask something of me I usually find myself doing it?'

'Because,' puffed Coya, 'I always ask you as a friend.'

By the pinch of his smile she could tell that Coya was in trouble too, even now that the path had levelled off through one of the narrow, tree-filled tiers of the park. Ahead of them the bodyguard Marsh was pushing the pace as best he could, though the tall figure in his stiffened longcoat had stopped for a moment beneath a withered jupe tree, where an equally withered old monk sat perched on a bench talking to a dog that was watching Marsh instead.

The bodyguard frowned back at the state of her and Coya hobbling along. Marsh was Shanteel, one of the lifelong protectors of the noble Zeziké bloodline, a companion of Coya since they had been boys. Never one to take it easy on his charge, always pushing Coya to his limits.

The Minosian wore goggles that wrapped around his head and allowed him to look behind him at the same time, goggles which Shard herself had provided from the Academy. She knew that he was observing the hedgemonk through the rear lenses in case he might leap up with a knife or a pistol at any moment, but the old man looked harmless enough, clearly drunk on a bottle of wine he cradled in his arms.

'Coya?' exclaimed the monk as they shambled past the figure. 'Coya Zeziké, is that really you?'

Coya stopped, and looked down at the old fellow kindly enough. 'Have we met, brother?'

'No, but I've seen your likeness. It hangs in the library. A spectralgraph, I think they called it. Very real. Though also unreal, in a way. Strange.'

'Ah. That was my wife's idea. Several hours of tedium I wouldn't care to repeat.'

The old hedgemonk nodded, chewing his toothless gums. At his feet the black dog watched them both, its ears pressing back at every rumble of gunfire.

'You come to us now even as a wall is falling,' said the man. 'Yet I see no trace of despair in your eyes, Coya Zeziké. Only hope and clever scheming!'

Coya smiled, leaning closer to press a Khosian coin into the man's hand.

'For your blessings,' Coya said, nodding in farewell.

'Coya Zeziké, blood of the blessed Zeziké!' the hedgemonk called after them drunkenly, standing now with the bottle held high. 'Saviour of the Free Ports, heh!'

'I told you we should have come up by cart,' Marsh growled unhappily, and Shard followed his gaze as he scanned the nearest trees for likely assassins. Seeing Mannian Diplomats everywhere, no doubt, though no wonder, for they had tried to kill Coya many times now, and would no doubt try again. 'And I warned you about that damned spectralgraph too. Let the whole world know what you look like, why don't you?'

Compelled to look over her shoulder, Shard saw the old hedgemonk still standing on the path, though he was pressing his hands together in sami now, pressing them against his forehead in respect, and then against his heart in hope.

Below them in the city, wailing horns continued to lament the falling wall.

CHAPTER SIXTEEN

The Crossing of Storms

'Stones, you idiot, can't you see the rocks? The wind's pushing us into the mountain!'

On the quarterdeck of the *Falcon*, Captain Trench was hollering through sleet that lashed at them through the blackness of a howling gale, causing Ash to marvel that he could shout loud enough to be heard in these conditions, never mind catch a breath in the rarefied chill that passed for air up here.

Ash stood with his back pressed against the port rail and his arms hooked around it to stop the wind from plucking him off his feet. The decking of the *Falcon* was heaving like the bed of a drunk. He rode it with his heart hammering and his head filling with a different storm in a different time entirely: the sea voyage from Honshu, the faces of his fellow exiles looming out of the darkness as though he was there again – young Baso whooping at the thrill of it and General Oshō grimly silent, the rest of them convinced that this was their end.

Now, over thirty years later, Ash grimaced and wiped his eyes clear with numb fingers and tried to shake the recollections from his mind, all too aware that life was somehow repeating itself here, that he was leaving his home behind again never to return.

Through frozen lashes he squinted over the opposite side of the ship and saw the two-tone slope of the mountain growing nearer, its coating of snow a dim paleness studded by black rocks, all of it obscured by rushing sleet and clouds.

'Full ahead starboard, full reverse port!' Trench shouted into the speaking tube mounted near the wheel, where the two pilots, Stones and Lomax, were fighting to change course by turning the starboard side-skuls into the following wind.

Around the wheel, heavy storm-canvasses had been erected to ward off the worst of the icy blasts, though the entrance flap facing Ash had come loose, and it was snapping in the gusts like gunfire. Aiming for it, Ash released his grip on the rail, and was shoved by the wind as his feet scuttled down the slope of the deck. He snatched an edge of the soaking canvas on the way past, stopped himself with his other hand grasped around one of the humming guidelines above his head. Gasping for breath and light-headed for lack of air, he felt someone grab the front of his cloak and yank him in behind the covers.

In the partial shelter, Captain Trench stared at him with his desperate red-rimmed eye, his bearded face underlit by a sickly yellow glow. The space within was a small cell of light and noise amidst the greater blasts of the storm, though it remained gusty enough with three of the viewing slits open so that they could see out, and all around them the canvas sheets heaved against their ropes in a rage to be free. Ash wiped clear the frozen icicles hanging from his nostrils and took in the eyes of the pilots, glimpsing the fear in them, the sickness of panic.

A storm during the crossing had been their greatest fear all along, and now here it was – falling upon them with a ferocity and speed that was beyond anything they had ever encountered.

'That's it,' Trench shouted, peering through the side opening, and he placed his hands on the pilots' shoulders and gripped hard, as though trying to transmit his strength and urgency through the two men and into the wheel. 'She's turning!'

Through the flapping entrance, Ash glimpsed the mountain flashing by their starboard side, no longer growing closer. He swayed for balance as the ship tilted back again, righting itself beneath the great bulk of the silk loft.

'We must land this ship before we are wrecked!' he called out.

'And what do you think we've been trying to do?' Trench yelled back at him, and the captain swept his long sodden hair from his forehead. 'We can't get a purchase with the drag anchors, the wind's too strong. No choice for it now but to ride out the storm.'

'Can I help?'

'No. Get below, man. You're nothing but a hindrance to us up here.'

Ash had no intention of climbing below to huddle out of the way like the others. If this was going to be the end of them, he wanted to be staring it in the face.

'There's a side-valley ahead, branching off from the western side of this one,' shouted a voice at their feet. Looking down at the decking, Ash saw the open hatch of the captain's cabin spilling its soft light and framing the open-mouthed face of their navigator. 'If we can't make the height for the next pass, we should try for the side-valley.'

'Understood,' Trench shouted back, too focused on getting the ship through the next few moments of the storm, still glaring hard at the flashing mountainside. 'Nelson, can you hear me?' he shouted into the speaking tube again, and then he pressed his ear hard against it. 'Nelson!' he yelled down to the powder room in the tail. 'More thrust, do you hear?'

Steeling himself against the elements, Ash pushed his way outside once more. Instantly the sleet blinded him as his hood swept clear from his head and icy needles struck the pain already throbbing in his skull. The force of the wind pushed him towards the steps as though it knew where he wanted to go, his boots slipping on the icy decking. At the top of the steps he grabbed a post and felt his boots scoot out over the weatherdeck below. Ash gasped and regained his footing and struggled down.

On the weatherdeck, Dalas and a gang of skymen were propping each other up in a roped line as they passed items along it to be thrown over the side; non-vital inner parts of the *Falcon* that had been sawn away; barrels of water, furniture; anything they could pick up and carry.

Squinting ahead along the length of the deck, Ash saw another group of crewmen trying to make their way along it with their safety lines unhooked, heading for the front of the ship. Time and again the gale and the tipping deck were sending them tumbling, though they helped each other up where they fell – huddled figures with their storm hoods blown back from their determined, bearded faces, the spars and rigging creaking as the gas loft twisted above their heads. Beyond the men, their more distant mates up on the prow were barely visible save for the luminous green stripes painted on the sleeves and backs of their oiled coats, ghostly lines seemingly afloat in the swirling night.

Even further than that, the glowing stripes of a repair crew dangled from the underside of the envelope, right out there over nothing but space. For a long moment Ash marvelled at their audacity.

'Give us a hand there,' someone shouted in his ear, and he saw that it was the longhunter Cole, working with the sprawling gang of crewmen making their way towards the prow, trying to drag along a massive coil of cable. So the man had been unable to sit doing nothing either.

A figure fell badly. Ash tried to help him up but the fellow grimaced and waved him away, gestured down at his other hand which now hung from a snapped wrist. Ash took his place, helping to heave the coiled cable along the deck. It was anchor cable made from silkfibre, no thicker than ordinary climbing rope but much stronger and lighter. Slipping and sliding, locked in their own individual efforts to stay on their feet, they struggled with the coil up the steps to the exposed foredeck where the wind screamed even louder, and then they heaved it over to the forward rail of the ship, above the small platform known as the nose, just below where the foredeck ended. He glimpsed two crewmen down there already.

Staggering sideways in a sudden gust, Ash gripped his arms around the prow rail and Cole did the same, so that they clung there gasping like fish while the sleet hammered their heads, and for a moment squinted together through the darkness at the carved figurehead of a falcon, its wings spread in flight, racing through the storm just ahead of the ship.

Down they all scrambled into the nose, falling wherever they could around the cable they'd just dropped there. Quickly the skymen checked that no one was missing. Ash sat on his ass for a moment with his breath wheezing in and out of his burning chest. He felt dizzy and sick now, the thinness of the air hitting him harder than he would have expected.

A slap on his back roused him. It was Cole again, offering a hand to him like the old man that he was. It fuelled Ash with sudden frustration. He slapped the hand aside and forced himself to his feet.

'They lost the anchor head,' Cole shouted in his ear. 'But the winch is jammed so they need to replace the whole line.'

Below their feet the slope of mountainside swept past in a blur of rocks and trees, growing closer again.

Just then he saw that it was young Berl bent over the anchor housing trying to clear it; Berl the ship's boy, all of fourteen years of age and with a length of polished wood for one leg. The man next to him was shouting into his ear as Berl reached into a tool case, and then the ship pitched over sharply, sending Berl skidding on his back. Ash's heart leapt, for none of the crew here were bothering with safety lines. The others steadied each other and someone dragged the boy back to the housing, where Berl passed a wrench to his companion and clung on for dear life as they continued to shout back and forth over their task. Ash leaned forward to try and hear what the two were yelling about, and snatched a few words about botched repairs back in Bar-Khos, and someone's name being cursed blackly.

Griping, at a time like this.

It brought a smile to his face.

Without warning the ship pitched over again in a blasting cross-wind. Men went scattering across the planking.

Like a concerned father he looked to young Berl first, and saw that the boy was no longer there.

Ash blinked. Berl's companion with the wrench was clutching the starboard rail and looking out over it. The skyman's horrified face turned to the rest of them, and he shouted: '*Man overboard!*'

In an instant the old farlander was at the rail, leaning out to take in the rolling snowy slopes rushing past not that far below them. A shrill whistle sounded from the crewmen. Within moments the thrusters were turning to full reverse in an attempt to slow the vessel's speed.

Dread nestled in his belly. This was why he worked alone, why he'd always refused to take on an apprentice over the years. A boy lost to the storm on this voyage which Ash was entirely responsible for. A death amongst the crew, and so soon.

Yet through the darkness he saw how the slopes were close and thick with snow. Hope flashed through him that Berl might still be alive down there.

Ash rounded on the men and snatched the frayed end of the cable from their grips. 'Tie off the end to something!' he shouted at Cole's startled expression before he scrambled up the ladder with it.

Hauling the silkfibre rope over his shoulder he ran across the foredeck and jumped off the end of it, landing at a run while he eased the jolts of pain from his body with great whooshes of air. Men tumbled backwards out of his way, and Ash jumped over the last one sprawled on the deck and vaulted up the steps of the quarterdeck, already feeling the strain of the cable dragging behind him, and the hot coals flaring to life in his chest.

'Buy me some time!' he shouted to Trench's startled face through a slit in the canvas wheelhouse, then grabbed hold of the starboard rail. With a quick glance downwards, the old Rōshun launched himself over the edge.

Ash fell, his legs kicking through the air to keep himself upright, still gripping the cable that fell with him.

'*Whuff!*'

He landed waist deep in a bank of snow, the storm howling over bare rocks just above him. Daggers shot from his lower back.

You old fool, what are you doing?

For a precious moment Ash wiped his eyes clear so he could blink through the dark skies towards the *Falcon*. Her storm lanterns were barely visible through the sleet, though it was clear the ship was fighting now against the push of the gale.

Before him on the snow lay the end of the cable. He hoped Cole had followed his directions and tied it off.

Move, said his mind, and he followed its instruction, scrambling out of the snow and crouching down in the storm with the end of the cable wrapped about his forearm.

'*Berl!*'

It was like screaming into the mouth of an angry god. Around him the few hardy pine trees shook and bent over in the gale. Ash leaned into it and struggled along the slope as fast as he dared with his legs sinking deep in the snowdrift, hauling the cable after him, his single lifeline back to the ship. The farlander squinted through eyes that could barely see ten feet ahead.

'*Boy!*'

Something moved out there, lighter than the darkness around it.

A hand raised up with fingers splayed.

Ash staggered towards it and spotted the boy lying there in the snow. Berl was huddled over his broken wooden leg. He went to take another step closer and felt the cable grow heavier in his grasp, losing its slack.

Out of time.

Ash sprang to the nearest mature tree and wrapped the end of the cable around the trunk and looped it through itself, hoping it would be enough. Then he turned and fought his way over to the boy.

'It's all right, I've got you,' he told the lad, not realizing he spoke in his native Honshu as he gathered Berl up and hung him on his protesting back. Ash turned around just in time to glimpse the tree tearing loose from the ground in a small eruption of snow and dirt; saw the tautened cable dragging the uprooted trunk across the slope, spinning and leaping over rocks and catching on other trees.

For a sliver of time all he could do was stare at it.

'Run!' the boy Berl screamed in his ear.

Ash growled and sped across the packed surface as lightly as he could, breathing the fast rhythm of onwi and picturing in his mind the dancing leaps of the snow leopard.

He sprang just behind the spasms of the racing tree trunk, showered with chunks of churned-up snow and propelled along by the wind at their backs, trying desperately to catch up with it. He was running out of footsteps though. Ahead the slope seemed to end in an upthrust of rocks and then the swirling darkness of a great drop.

Ash reached out to grab at one of the roots, but they were just beyond his grasp. He scrambled after it as the tree bounced once over the outcrop of rocks then clear into the gulf of air.

Ash leapt for it.

*

'Cup of chee?' one of the crewmen asked as Ash slid down the steps into the relative heat and silence below decks, dripping wet and with a furnace roar in his ears.

All he could do was stare at the crewman addressing him. 'It's on the brew, if you want some,' said the man as he thumbed towards the mess room where others were congregated, then shuffled off towards the head.

Ash collapsed on the steps and rested his forehead on the back of his hand, his other hand shaking in his lap. He listened to Shin in her nearby infirmary talking soothingly to Berl, the boy as sombre and self-contained as ever.

For an instant, Shin glanced sideways through the severe angle of the doorway at him, a perspective which framed her face just as she swept the hair from her tense features.

You are a beautiful woman, Shin Moloko.

Ash took all the time he needed to catch his breath while his clothes thawed and dripped onto the steps. At last he stood, slowly unfurling his aching body with a sigh, then made his way stiffly along the passage leading to the cabins with a fist pressed against his lower spine, his mouth chomping on a fresh bundle of dulce leaves.

This is why your back is giving out on you, he scolded himself. *All these falls compacting your spine.*

Hearing voices ahead, he spotted figures sitting on either side of the passageway with their backs to the walls between the open doorways of the cabins. It was Aléas and Cole and the cat.

The longhunter sat in a puddle of water dripping from his cloak. He didn't look up at Ash's approach, the blue eyes within his scarred features staying focused on the cat where she lay with her head in his lap. Cole had helped to carry Berl down below, after grinning and shaking his head at Ash in amazement.

Now the battered Khosian stroked the cat's reddish head, and watched Ash's shadow in the reflection of her eyes as they stared up at him balefully, the animal as miserable as the rest of them.

'Tell me,' Aléas was saying. 'The Hush. Is it truly empty of people?'

Cole looked away from the cat's eyes and the reflection of Ash standing over them, observing him quietly. The longhunter had proven himself a useful pair of hands up above, exactly what they would have hoped for in a guide leading them into the Hush. Yet still, that shadow remained about him – this man who was likely a Khosian deserter, if his military tattoos were anything to go by; that sense of his loyalties lying only with his immediate self.

'Beyond the highlands, aye, it's empty,' the longhunter was saying. 'The highland tribes claim the Hush makes humans and certain other animals infertile, as well as mad. They say it's the serpent god that lies beneath the land, poisoning the water with its bile. I think its the kree myself, and maybe the boli trees. Whatever strange scents they give off.' He ruffled the cat's fur and she flicked her gaze up to him.

'And the kree. All of them live in the Edge?'

'Quite a few million of them, anyway. The Edge runs right down the centre of the continent.'

They all jumped as something thudded into the hull.

'Your cat, what do you call her?' came a voice through an open doorway of one of the cabins – Meer perched on a bunk with an open book.

'Just Cat. And she isn't mine. We travel together.'

'She acts more like a dog than a cat at times.'

'Aye. She was raised with hounds.'

The prairie lynx widened her gaze in alertness, knowing they were talking about her. She growled low and menacing when Aléas reached a hand towards her head.

'Don't mind her,' Cole said, and the way he spoke suggested he had softened towards Aléas in their short time together. 'She doesn't like Mannians overly much, is all.'

'She can tell, can she?'

The longhunter smiled faintly.

What else had Aléas told the man? Ash wondered in annoyance. He'd asked that they keep their business to themselves for now whenever they were in the company of the longhunter; this man who Ash was still uncertain whether to trust at all.

'You have a wife, Cole?' Ash asked abruptly, and studied the longhunter's reaction closely.

Cole looked as though he was rolling a stone around in his mouth. The man gazed down at the cat then made an effort to swallow.

'Once. And you?'

'Long ago.'

The wind howled against the window shutters. The deck pitched forwards more. Ash thought he heard shouts from the distant hatchway. He pressed back against a doorway to maintain his shifting balance.

'How's it going out there?' asked Aléas, as though wishing to change the subject.

'Fine,' he answered, even with the *Falcon* dropping fast enough to make his stomach flutter. Somewhere in the depths of the ship a man was screaming his heart out. 'A few crosswinds is all.'

Someone had the fortitude to chuckle. It was Meer.

'I recall the first time I flew in a skyship,' said the hedgemonk. 'It was an exhibition in Al-Khos when we were visiting my mother's parents there. They were taking people up in one to show it off. When our time came, some of the seals in the envelope split open for some reason . . . I remember they said the sun was too hot for the glue, and then we almost crashed into a hillside.'

'Is this your way of raising our spirits?' remarked Aléas.

'What I mean to say is that in all the years I've flown since then, I've seen how far these ships have come along. The *Falcon* is one of the finest. If any ship can make it through this, it's her.'

'And what if no ship can make it through this?'

Another clatter against the hull. A sudden rending of wood.

'We'll make it,' declared the longhunter over the sounds of the storm, and he sounded certain in his words. As though fate itself had decided the outcome long before now.

CHAPTER SEVENTEEN

Casualties of War

Where am I? Shard wondered from where she sat in a tangle of stupefied thoughts, blinking about at her surroundings.

And then she remembered how they had hiked up the Mount of Truth to the Ministry of War, where they had been told to wait in this draughty hallway on the third floor by a thin man behind a desk.

But that must have been hours ago, she realized now, looking out through one of the many windows at the darkness of night outside.

What are we doing here again?

'Two hours he keeps me waiting,' hissed Coya as he rose from the sedan chair quickened with anger, and rapped his cane on the marble floor for attention; and at last Shard remembered the reason they were here, and realized that Coya had reached the limit of his patience.

'What's he at in there, eh?' he demanded of the spectacled man behind the desk.

'I told you, friend Coya. The Lord Protector won't see you, no matter how long you wait.'

'Creed knows I'm still here?'

'Yes.'

'Well damn him then,' Coya exclaimed and took a step for the door. 'He'll see me whether he wants to or not.'

But the two guards before the door steadfastly blocked his path.

'Marsh,' Coya snapped. 'These men are in my way.'

Shard barely followed what happened next. The bodyguard Marsh stepped up to the two soldiers even as they reached for their swords, and after a swift sequence of moves he held each of them by a hand locked in a position of pain, so that Coya was able to duck around them and open the door.

'Coming?' he said to Shard, then stepped inside.

*

They found the Lord Protector as Marsh had warned they might find him, a hollow shell of his former self.

Creed was seated on the balcony of his private study, his great muscular bulk slumped in a wheeled chair with a blanket spread across his legs, the man withdrawn yet surly-eyed, staring at the disaster still unfolding on the Shield while he was forced to watch from afar.

He failed to stir when Coya and Shard stepped out onto the balcony beside him with their boots scraping against stone.

Coya's eyes widened at his appearance. The general's long hair was tied back in a knot, though it seemed more silver than black now, as though the man had forsaken his rumoured vanity of darkening its appearance. His eyes, normally renowned for their piercing glare, were narrowed and bloodshot from lack of sleep, sunken deep in a face etched with lines of worry and sallow in complexion.

He looked like a man barely returned to life.

'Any word?' Coya asked him casually, gently, his anger seeming to have fled, and General Creed craned his head round until he could see Coya from the corner of his eye. He betrayed no surprise in seeing him there, as though he had no care for human company one way or the other.

'Coya Zeziké,' he grumbled. 'Word on what?'

'On the wall, man,' Coya remarked sharply, jabbing his cane towards the fires burning on the Shield. 'The wall of course.'

A clenching of jaw muscles. A few rapid blinks.

'We've lost it. General Tanserine's last counter-attack was beaten back. Kharnost is theirs.' And his voice was a flat monotone, the voice of a man beyond hope.

It seemed to provoke Coya's ire, for when he slapped the general's shoulder in camaraderie he did it hard like a soldier. 'By all accounts, Kharnost's Wall was barely standing. They'll have a tougher time with the remaining three walls, we can be certain of that.'

'Tell that to the men dying down there, even now.'

Coya glanced at Shard, and she saw the shadow of fear in his eyes. There was something wrong here, his expression said, and she suspected he was right, for Shard could sense it herself.

Time for work. Or at least what work she could manage in her present condition, which likely was not much. Shard tried to call up a glyph in her vision but found her mind still too wildly unfocused to craft it. Closing her eyes she tried again with more care – such effort for a normally trivial thing as this – and managed to call it into life weakly; a searcher glyph which cast a pulse out around them, fading without echoes.

'We're clean,' she told Coya. 'No one's listening.'

'My people sweep the rooms every day,' Creed grumbled, and then he seemed to notice her standing there at last. 'So, the only Dreamer in the Free Ports has finally paid Bar-Khos a visit.'

'Not that I had much choice in the matter.'

Creed grunted and dropped his chin, saying no more.

A letter lay open on his lap; a thick square of paper with graceful handwriting upon it, ending with an elaborate signature. Her vision was swimming too much to read any of it though, and she pulled her gaze away, following his own attentions to the action on the Shield again.

Shard was struck by the moonlit view they had here along the Lansway, like a laq-wide road thrusting out across the sea towards the dim southern continent. From their vantage on the southern side of the Ministry, they could see the three mammoth walls which remained standing in the path of the imperial army; and beyond them to the foremost battlements of the fallen wall, Kharnost, where fire brewed in smoky sections all across it. Occasionally the windows and the bricks of the Ministry shook with distant explosions, huge charges demolishing what was left of the wall, the Mannians wasting no time in reducing it to rubble.

'That bastard Mokabi came back to finish the job,' Creed suddenly growled with his hand clenching feebly around the arm of the chair.

'Yes,' said Coya. 'Who would have thought he still had the stomach for it?'

'My people say he has much of the loot from the southern continent at his disposal. That he has thrown the entire fortune into this effort. And all I can do is sit here, watching our downfall from afar.'

'Marsalas, you shouldn't try to carry these burdens alone. This is the problem with your Khosian ways—' but then Coya stopped, hearing the glibness of what he was saying.

They could see much of the southern portion of the city from here, lit by lanterns and braziers. In the gathering silence between them Shard explored it with her wandering gaze, taking in the wide thoroughfare of the Avenue of Lies and the great tented square of the Grand Bazaar, not far from the Stadium of Arms. Spotter balloons floated in the evening skies. Towards the south, the two harbours on either side of the Lansway's mouth were filled with dark ships of all sizes. To the east, far beyond the city's limits, the mountains of the High Tell stood tall in the moonlight, making her feel colder just looking at their snow-capped heights.

The city itself was much the same as she remembered it. Shard recalled her time here grimly, a time of hunger and alienation. As refugees from southern Pathia they had been treated decently enough by the local Bar-Khosians, though some had openly resented their presence there, seeing them as further drains on the city. Their Contrarè features hadn't helped either. A minority of city-folk had called them barkbeaters or worse, the intensity of the siege seeming to stir ancient prejudices to the surface.

Bar-Khos, a city of noise day and night, with the thousands of windchimes strung across the streets clattering in the breeze, the shouts and yells of drunken soldiers and prostitutes, the repetitive songs of the street hawkers selling their wares, all of it pounded by the regular barrages of cannon fire at the Shield, constant reminders of the war. A city that she'd had little desire ever to return to.

Tabor Seech had known how she felt about this place, yet he had chosen it for their confrontation – this city living right on the edge. More mind games, she supposed. Tabor toying with her in every which way he could.

'We're still getting hit hard across the democras,' she heard Coya's distant voice say in response to something Creed had said. 'Sky raids. Hit and run attacks from their naval fleets. Essentially, with all the reinforcements we've sent you, we're stretched to breaking point and hoping that no one will notice.'

Shard closed her eyes once more and carefully formed another searcher glyph in her mind, struggling to hold it long enough to cast into life, for she needed a stronger version this time, one that required an even greater effort of will. At last it came alive and sent a pulse outwards across the Shield and the Lansway to the far camp of the enemy, which she could see as a distant glimmer of lights. Shard slumped back against the balustrade to catch her breath, weakened by the effort, her glimmersuit warming even further.

The pulse returned as a single faint echo in her mind, lacking any definition. Tabor Seech was out there indeed, perhaps in Camp Liberty, shielded as always, though leaking just enough of his presence for her to detect.

'I can sense him,' she said aloud. 'He's here. And he wants me to know it.'

'Sense who?' asked the general.

'Tabor Seech,' explained Coya. 'The traitor works for the Empire now.'

'You came here personally just to give me bad news?'

'Yes, Marsalas, it's what I live for. Though for balance I've brought some good news too. I may have a solution to your Mokabi problem.'

'Mokabi? You let *us* worry about Mokabi.'

'Oh? You have some way of stopping him?'

'So my people tell me. Or of delaying him, anyway. A young engineer from the Al-Khos Academy has come forward with a plan. It seems the ground behind Singer's Wall has subsided over the centuries. Now we're digging it out further. If Mokabi's horde takes another wall, they may well be in for something of a surprise.'

An image flashed in Shard's mind, leaking from the general's thoughts. Thousands of civilians excavating the killing ground between the foremost two walls, and lines of zel-drawn carts carrying away mounds of red earth. Beyond them, along one of the seawalls that ran along the coastline of the Lansway, crews with cranes were exposing the foundations and digging through them. The scene became dizzying to look at. Shard shook her head to be clear of it.

'Well consider this a bonus then,' Coya replied, smiling a little. 'Right now I have nine Rōshun quartered in the city, all eager to have a crack at the Mannians.'

A startled blink, some life in the old general yet. 'What's this, Coya, getting blood on your hands at last?'

'These are bloody times, Marsalas.'

'The Rōshun though. Truly?'

'It wasn't so hard to persuade them. Not after they lost their home to a Mannian commando attack.'

The general's gaze danced for a moment, considering possibilities. 'Maybe the Few are not so useless after all.'

'Please, we've hardly forsaken you. There are more of us in the city besides myself and Shard. If you do not see their work then that is because you are not meant to see their work, but they are out there, believe me. Now stop griping and listen, man. The Rōshun will remain here to engage in operations against Mokabi and his person-nel. In the meantime, I'll be travelling into the Windrush to speak with the native Contrarè. I intend to enlist their help in this if I can.'

'Save yourself the trouble. We've tried appealing to the Longalla already. They turned down our offers of gold. They aren't interested in helping us, nor even themselves.'

'Then maybe trying to buy their friendship was your mistake? We will see what they make of a Dreamer who is one of their own, for Shard has agreed to come with me into the Windrush. If we are able to, we will call for a council of the Longalla and try to bring them into this war on our side, as I have already brought you the Rōshun. Their help would be invaluable in dealing with the imperial threat to the north.'

Once more the general's attention was upon her, observing her mask and her swarthy skin, her narrow eyes set above sharp cheek bones. Was he one of them, she wondered? One of those Khosians who thought of her kind as savages? There was no way to tell from his gaze.

'What news have you, by the way?' Coya added. 'Are the Imperials still holding fast around Tume?'

Shard didn't hear the answer.

A figure was standing next to her that hadn't been there a moment before. A man, leaning on the balustrade with relaxed poise. For the first instant she thought it was a vision of Tabor Seech, but in the next she saw that it was a handsome Contrarè in tribal clothing, observing her with eyes not dark but strikingly blue.

He smiled as though they were friends. A beautiful man, she saw now, unable to tear her gaze from his own.

'*Walks With Herself,*' he whispered, and his voice sounded far away. *Yes?*

'*We will meet again, can't you sense it?*'

'Shard?'

Coya was watching her as she stared at the empty space by her side.

'Let her dream,' rumbled the Lord Protector. 'It's all any of us have left now.'

'Sweet Mercy,' breathed Coya, taking in her dazed condition and then the state of Creed, shaking his head in dismay.

I need something to keep me grounded, Shard thought to herself. *Something stronger than tannis tea.*

Tentatively, Coya was holding a hand out to place it on the general's broad shoulder. Coya was so stooped that his eyes were almost level with Creed's in his chair.

'What has happened to you, my friend? You seem sick of spirit in a way I've never seen before. Have they no Milk for you to take, none of these damned Michinè of yours?'

Annoyed, the general shrugged Coya's hand from his shoulder, bunched the muscles of his jaws.

'The First Minister provided me with some Milk. Still I sit in this damned chair, too weak to stand.'

By all accounts this man had led the Khosian army at Chey-Wes against the invading imperial forces, attacking them at night even though they were outnumbered and out-gunned. Somehow he had managed to kill the Holy Matriarch herself, buying the city much needed time as the Imperial Expeditionary Force stalled around Tume in civil war.

It hardly sounded like the same person sitting before her now.

Has he been poisoned? The Milk itself perhaps?

But no. It wasn't possible to poison Royal Milk. Something else then, a failing in the security measures around him, poison slipped into his food? It happened all the time to enemies of the Empire.

'Shard, what do you make of it?'

She had a feeling she knew what this was.

'*Tell me,*' she asked of Creed. '*Did your health worsen after the arrival of Mokabi?*'

'Are you implying something?' he asked, glowering.

'Just following a hunch. Is it true?'

He didn't wish to answer, and Shard charged her voice a little, loading it with intent.

'Tell me. It's important that I know.'

Staring out over the balustrade, his voice lowered to a hush, Creed answered her flatly. 'Just before Mokabi arrived, I awoke and everything I looked at was red.'

'And you're still seeing red?'

'Yes. In everything.'

'Let me have a look at you.'

He tensed when she placed a hand upon his own, cool and clammy. Shard closed her eyes and tried her best to run her profiling glyph, seeing a concentration of flowing dashes and lines of bindee where he sat. Poor definition though, and when she saw nothing out of the ordinary it hardly reassured her. If Tabor Seech was responsible, he would have made certain to hide his tracks well.

She squeezed her eyes shut even tighter with effort, and called up a series of tagged vigils, which she lay about General Creed and then hid with the best camouflage she could manage; vigils that would alert her to Seech's presence around Creed. Then she opened her eyes and swayed with dizziness.

'Shard?'

'I'm not certain yet. Give me time and I'll see what I can do.'

'Time, she asks for,' grumbled the Lord Protector, and his hand was squeezing itself white around the arm of his chair, while his other shook the piece of paper above his lap like something soiled. 'She asks for time while the bastard's right at my door!'

Coya bent to pluck the paper from the general's fingers before he could protest. 'You're joking,' he exclaimed, frowning down at it. 'Mokabi sent you a letter?'

Coya held it aloft so he could read it aloud.

'"Marsalas. Wonderful to be here in your neck of the woods again. They tell me you are recovering poorly from your recent bout of illness. Please let me know if there is anything I can do. It would be shame to have you on your knees for our final reckoning.

'"When I was a boy in the order of Mann, we were often instructed in the ways of tactics through the use of models and war games. My favourite was always the Shield of Bar-Khos. So impressive to look at it with a boy's imagination! Even back then, I grew obsessed with the idea of taking those walls. These walls. It has ever remained a lifelong passion.

"'Marsalas, it is my destiny to be your downfall.

"'Good fortune in how you meet your end in this. I will show your corpse the fullest respect it deserves.'"

Coya whistled, and lowered the letter to stare at the general's hand, now wrenching at the arm of his chair. With a sudden pop the arm came loose, and Creed tossed it into the corner of the balcony with a clatter of disgust.

Startled, a bird lifted off from the nearest window ledge. It was a thunderhawk, and as it wheeled away across the summit of the hill it cried out as though to Shard alone, then flew southwards to join a pair of its companions circling high over the smoke of the fallen wall.

CHAPTER EIGHTEEN

Seech

The Dreamer Tabor Seech wheeled high above the Shield with his wingtips flexing delicately against the air, scenting smoke and blood from the killing grounds far below. Hunger brewed in his stomach.

It was a thrill to fly with the thunderhawk like this, to wear her body as his own. For a short time Tabor lingered there, experiencing it all through the distorted senses of the bird of prey.

Sudden weightlessness in his belly, as the hawk swooped downwards after one of her companions, giving chase with tilts of her wings. Below them, even now in the darkness, other birds flocked in their hundreds above the rich pickings on the Shield, the corpses scattered around the fallen wall.

Let her hunt. Let her eat.

With a sigh of release, Tabor Seech forced his own eyes open and broke the connection between them. At once he found himself returned to his earthbound body.

The Dreamer sat in darkness facing the only window of his room, which filled his eyes with the distant fires on the Shield.

A wall fallen already. Mokabi would be full of himself tonight, full of the manifest destiny of his creed. Never mind how the wall was nearly a ruin before he'd got here.

This news might please the old general too: this plan of Coya Zeziké to recruit the Contrarè of the Windrush in defence of Khos. For it was clear that Mokabi hoped those imperial forces tied up in central Khos remained that way, while he took the city for himself.

Seech yawned and stretched his spine against the back of the chair, thinking of Shard and how close she was now, right on the other side of the Shield. Close enough for him to kill her, if he wished it.

But not yet. Not like that. Seech fully intended to give his ex-lover a fighting chance here, however slim. Let Shard head off into the Windrush with Coya if she wanted to delay their reckoning a while longer. And let that fat fool Mokabi wait until morning before he gave him the news.

It's the very least I can do for her.

*

In the morning, rising shamefully late by the standards of the military camp surrounding him – though Seech cared nothing for what these people thought of his relaxed sleeping habits, nor anything else for that matter – the Dreamer sought out General Mokabi, intending to deliver his report from the night before.

But the general was long gone, explained his attendants, departed for a quarry to the south of the camp for reasons unknown. Would he like a zel for the ride down, they asked him, and Seech had said no, firmly, for he hated to ride.

Instead he had taken off on foot, marching through Camp Liberty for the southern road and taking in the morning sights of the imperial encampment, its buildings clustered within earthworks and four squat forts between the two coastlines of the Lansway.

It was strange to walk freely amongst the mortal enemies of his people like this. Most of all to be amongst members of the Mannian order itself, the white-garbed priests with their pierced faces and entitled ways, and the warrior Acolytes made anonymous by their masks, watching him with open hostility as he went by, until he blew up his cloak and saw fear and wonder in their eyes.

Leaving the camp through the southern checkpoint, Tabor Seech strode along the wide military road that had first brought him here, his cloak of thin strips billowing behind him in spectacular fashion in an otherwise windless day, aided by the same glyph he maintained to instil his dreadlocks with seeming life. Smiling beatifically, he relished the startled stares of soldiers and civilians alike as he passed them by, the growls and whines of leashed hunting dogs and the crowds of mercenaries parting at the sight of him.

Seech was thrilled to the ends of his toes by the figure he cut through them all, his cloak snapping like an angry creature of the sea.

All across the open ground of the Lansway ranged tents and the smoking camp fires of Mokabi's mercenary army, half of them gone now to the action of the Shield. The Dreamer passed pens of mammoots, great wooden corrals with sharpened poles pointing inwards. Elsewhere lay fields of newly arrived birds-of-war floating against their tethers.

He came to a side road leading to the western coastline. A slight breeze was blowing now across the flats of the two seas on either side of the Lansway, chilling his flesh. Tabor took the dirt track while he willed to life a glyph which warmed him as he walked and needed little effort to maintain. Birds rose in alarm at his passing, though he barely noticed them now, for he had bedded down with his thoughts at last, orderly and precise monologues of things he was working on, and still needed to do. Neither did he notice the tranquil silence until it was interrupted by an explosion somewhere just ahead.

Tabor peered along the dirt road, seeing smoke rising above a small rise of ground. There was something in the air over there – small skyboats circling.

Rounding a pile of earth and rubble loosely covered in weeds, the Dreamer looked down upon a deep quarry like an amphitheatre in the ground. He widened his eyes in genuine surprise.

Down on the floor of the quarry, a section of a mammoth wall had been built across its width, nearly half as tall and thick as the walls of the Shield themselves. An oily column of smoke rose from a heap of burning wreckage at the foot of the wall.

He found General Mokabi at the rim of the stone pit clad in his ridiculously elaborate armour. On the morning after his forces had taken Kharnost's Wall, the general sat here instead in a field chair beneath a sagging canvas roof, angry at something and taking it out on his gathered officers, while his official biographer, perched nearby, scribbled down the occasional word.

One look at Seech approaching across the gritty rim of the quarry caused Mokabi's scowl to deepen even further.

'I hope it's good news you bring me, Dreamer. I've no patience for your provocations right now. None at all.'

Seech allowed his gusting cloak to deflate around him, and feigned a frown.

'I would have thought to find you in good spirits today, yet here you are, sweating in your fury. Kharnost's Wall is yours, man, or have you not heard yet?'

Too angry for humour, Mokabi barked his reply. 'That was yesterday, against a wall that was barely standing. This is today with three strong ramparts still in our way. The real work begins now, if only these fools would realize it.'

The officers around him looked to their feet, or stared morosely down at the fire still burning at the base of the wall.

'Surely it's only a matter of time with the men you have now?'

'Of course it is,' snarled Mokabi, tossing the cup of water in his hands to the ground. 'But time is money and the clock is ticking. These mercenaries do not come cheap.'

Absently, the Dreamer observed the white-cloaked Acolytes loosely standing guard around the general's position. There had been a handful of assassinations over the previous week, Tabor had heard. A few high-ranking priests and even the general of the Fourth Army permanently stationed here. No one seemed to know how the killings had been achieved so silently and without raising the alarm, a fact which seemed to be making people all the more paranoid.

It was as though the Khosians had recruited their very own Diplomats.

Movement caught his eye. Tabor spotted a soldier standing nearby on the rim of the quarry, waving a yellow flag over his head, and he craned his head back. One of the small skuds circling above had fired its thruster tubes on full, and was now heading for the quarry.

He watched, fascinated, as tiny figures hurried along the rail of the skyboat's deck, even as the front half of its canopy suddenly deflated with a dull pop and the boat began to fall; slowly at first, but picking up speed as the nose dropped and the thrusters burned hard.

Two figures launched themselves from the plummeting vessel, then a third. Their arms and legs waved frantically as they fell, before parachutes opened and yanked them almost to a stop. Slowly the figures drifted downwards as the skud sped in a collision course straight for the wall.

A boot scraped against grit. Seech taking a step forward.

The explosion roared with such intensity that Seech held an arm before his face at the sudden rush of dust and air that enveloped him on the rim. Peeking over the top of his arm, he saw debris and smoke rising in a great fountain that bloomed at its top like the cap of a mushroom. The rock beneath his feet trembled.

He coughed, clearing his lungs. When the black smoke finally subsided he saw that the wall still stood unharmed. The boat had missed it by several lengths of its hull.

There was a clatter behind him as Mokabi kicked his chair away, then roared down at the quarry and the men now landing heavily against the ground, silk sheets burying them like shrouds. Seech thought he heard the crack of breaking legs.

'The wall!' screamed the general down at them, his fury echoed by the confines of the quarry. 'You were meant to hit the bloody wall!'

*

In the end, a red-faced Mokabi rounded on him in disgust.

'You can see I'm busy here, Dreamer. What is it now?'

'You asked for some good news. I may have some.'

'Then tell me it, don't make me ask.'

'Coya Zeziké has arrived in Bar-Khos. He intends to travel to the Windrush to rally the Contrarè against the Expeditionary Force in the north.'

Surprise on the general's face. A quick evaluation of what it meant to him.

'And why would you think this good news to me?'

'Come now. We are both grown men here. I know only too well what this means to you.'

The general looked about quickly, his tongue dabbing at his thin lips. Nearby, Mokabi's biographer turned his head as he feigned an interest in the remaining skuds.

Mokabi took a step closer to the Dreamer, and inclined an ear towards him.

'If the tribes harry Sparus and Romano hard enough,' said Seech, 'it might buy you some more time here.'

His words caused Mokabi to stare in calculation.

'Coya Zeziké, you say?'

'There's more. Their Dreamer accompanies him. Someone I happen to know very well.'

'The Contrarè bitch is here? Tell me she won't hamper our efforts?'

'Not yet. She intends to go with him. No telling how long they will be gone.'

'You can deal with her when she returns?'

'Of course. She's outmatched. I can finish her like—' and Seech snapped his fingers decisively.

'Then do it now, if it is so easy.'

'No. Not yet.'

Displeased, Mokabi's round face began to darken once more. He took a step closer. 'With the fortune you're making out of this, you can damn well do what I'm paying you for. Kill that Dreamer of theirs before she causes us trouble.'

The snakedreads writhing around Seech's bemused expression rose up like cobras flaring to strike.

'Clear your head,' Seech snapped back at the general loud enough to be overheard; a clear warning shot. 'You don't get to say what I do or what I don't do. You get to ask. Now move on.'

There, a fire roaring again under Mokabi's backside. It was so easy to make this man lose his temper.

Tabor would not confront his old lover just yet. There was no rush, after all.

Three years had passed since their last encounter with one another, when Shard had returned from the deep desert still alive, remarkably, to expose Seech for what he had done. Three years since his disgraced flight from the Academy of Salina and his exile from the Free Ports, seeking refuge in the Alhazii city of Zanzahar, where Dreamers had existed secretly for a thousand years and more.

Since those days, Shard had been hunting Tabor within the Black Dream itself, where both knew she held the edge. With relentless patience, she had hounded his work there and that of his rook assistants, until they were forced to operate under the densest of cloaks hampered by second-guessing and paranoia. On a handful of occasions they had engaged in skirmishes, and Shard had won the better of him every time.

But it would hardly matter in the end. It was in the Great Dream, the waking world, where Tabor would finally defeat his ex-lover, for Tabor was the stronger Dreamer by far. Knowing the truth of this,

Shard had grown skilled in the art of cloaking herself, so much so that she had cloaked the entire Painted Mountain from his powers, making it impossible to seek her out; impossible, that was, until he had struck upon the idea of luring her here to the Shield and into the open.

'The Lord Protector,' said Mokabi stiffly. 'I'm assuming you're maintaining your vigil on him?'

'Yes, though I must turn the screws slowly. It's something of an art to make a man lose his mind, especially a man like Creed.'

'Well keep at it. I don't want Bearcoat turning up on the Shield and rallying the Khosians into some heroic last-stand defence here.'

'I rather suspect they do not need the Lord Protector for that.'

'No,' answered Mokabi, looking to the north. 'Perhaps not.'

Another explosion erupted from the floor of the quarry, causing them both to flinch; another boat strike, without them even noticing. Together they looked down and saw the newest crash site on the far side of the wall, debris falling around a smoking crater. Another miss.

'Seems this tactic of yours may need a few adjustments,' Seech mocked.

'Then maybe it's time you shut that trap of yours and proved your worth.'

'Meaning what?'

'Meaning what can you do for me here, eh? All this gold I'm flinging your way and what have you shown for it? Your rooks run security on our communications while you run a number on Creed. Is this it?'

So there it was, Mokabi's ignorance writ large. As though miracles came at the drop of a hat to Dreamers, as though these abilities didn't take years in the making and colossal efforts of will and courage in the face of looming insanity.

As though Tabor Seech really gave a damn whether the Shield fell or did not.

'What would you suggest – I shake the walls from their foundations?'

'Why not – can you do such a thing?'

He almost laughed, but another part of his mind was already

thinking it through with sudden interest. Shaking the walls themselves was out of the question, even for him. But a small portion of a
wall, enough to cause a breach perhaps?

Could it be done?

CHAPTER NINETEEN

The Other Side

Long before dawn the old farlander awoke in a bed that was not his own, pressed against the smooth body of another.

It was Shin, he recalled, the attractive ship's medico with her subtle traces of his homeland, Honshu. On feeling the touch of her limbs against his own he pictured the highlights of the previous evening, and it came to Ash that he might be sixty-two years of age and dying, but he was not entirely out of the dance just yet.

He would have smiled, but the pain that had wakened him pinched his head even further when he tried to. Ash stretched out a bare arm and fumbled amongst his pile of clothes until he reached the pouch of dulce leaves, pulling out a wad of them to shove into his mouth. With a sigh he inhaled through his nose and chewed them fiercely, his head relaxing against the pillow as the headache slowly diminished.

When he finally rose to dress in the dim light of the lantern they had forgotten to snuff out, Shin groaned and rolled onto her back into the heat of the space he had just vacated. The blanket snared around the calf of her leg and his eyes took in the caramel tone of her skin. Suddenly, Ash felt a longing for the women of his homeland, as dark as most women here were pale.

Trying not to waken her, he bent and gently kissed her exposed leg. Shin moaned again and stirred beneath the clinging blanket, forming in his mind more flashbacks of the previous night.

He left before he was tempted to climb back into bed with her.

Rain was drumming against the outer hull as he made his way back to his cabin, where Kosh was snoring fitfully on the top bunk beneath a heavy covering of blankets. Two days had passed without incident since they had made it through the storm.

'Ash?' croaked Kosh's throaty voice from the bundle of blankets. 'What time is it?'

'Nearly dawn. They'll be ringing the watch bell soon.'

His old friend groaned. He had gone drinking with the galley crew the previous evening, against Ash's warnings.

'Hangover?'

'Hangover barely describes it. I haven't felt this bad since landing in Bardo Falls.'

His old friend spoke of a time and a city long gone now, when the fleet of exiles from Honshu had first arrived in the Midèrēs, stopping first at a port city in Markesh that would later be razed to the ground by the Empire, and where many of the exiles had tried to drink themselves to death in the first week of landfall.

'I told you to watch out for that potcheen of theirs.'

'Never again,' rasped Kosh, sounding his age. 'Never, ever, again.' And blankets stirred as he raised a hand to his covered head. 'You were out gallivanting again I take it. Well I'm glad one of us is having a pleasant journey.'

Ash scoffed at his friend's misery this morning. Sure enough, he had warned Kosh about the foul home-brewed potcheen some of the crew were prone to drinking, but Kosh had waved him off and proclaimed in a long list all the champions he had drunk beneath the table over the years, including Ash himself.

'I can leave the bucket by the bed if you need it.'

Kosh groaned even louder. 'Just leave me be. Leave me in peace, will you?'

*

On the open deck of the *Falcon* the rain had cleared from the chill pre-dawn air; a passing shower, it seemed, here on the southern side of the Aradèrēs, the Broken Spine of the World. The mountains lay behind them now, their peaks soaring high into a tarry sky while the ship sped across the highlands that bordered the northern Hush.

Low to the west, one of the moons hung like a lantern as it dropped away from the approach of day. Its light struck a few weary lookouts stationed at the rail of the foredeck watching ahead, and the shadowy form of the pilot far back on the quarterdeck, standing slouched over the wheel with the red coals of his pipe glowing dimly.

Above the deck's stillness, the great gas loft of silk rippled and snapped in the wind, sheathed in a fine netting of ropes and struts of wood. The only thing holding them up; a miracle of faith as much as invention.

Wrapped in a heavy cloak, Ash sat cross-legged on the foredeck of the *Falcon* in his early-morning meditation, thinking of nothing as he mindfully observed the inflow and outflow of his deep breathing, both his belly and chest slowly rising and falling. His right hand lay cradled in the left one and his eyes stayed opened as slits, just enough to allow the light of the remaining fading stars to enter his mind.

Just then it came to him, in that way in which revelations revealed themselves during moments of stillness: he was sitting on the very spot where Nico too had once squatted in meditation, when Ash had first tried to teach him how to be still during their flight to Cheem, not so long ago.

'*What's the point of all this?*' came the young man's voice from the past, and Ash opened his eyes a fraction further to stare down at the stained wooden planking of the deck before him, as though it still contained a trace of his apprentice.

'*A mind that is forever busy is sick. A mind that is still flows with the Dao. When you flow with the Dao, you act in accordance with all things. This is what the Great Fool teaches us.*'

The boy had tried to sit as instructed, attentively and without moving, though it had clearly proven an effort for him, even for the first five minutes. His nose had twitched with an itch. His thumbs had fiddled in his lap. When the ship's bell had rung out Ash had taken pity on him, sensing the turmoil of his inner boredom.

'*How do you feel?*'

'*Calm,*' Nico had replied, nodding with gravitas. '*Very still.*'

Ash's eyes had lit with humour. Once more he had been reminded of his lost son.

The ship's bell was ringing out again in the present moment, calling the turning of the hour. Taking it as a sign, the farlander bowed his head as he made the gesture of sami then rose to his feet, his lower back suddenly protesting.

A few coughs sounded from beneath the decking, the odd clattering of boots; crewmen stirring for their shifts down below. The farlander sniffed and wrapped the cloak tighter about himself. It was the fading moonlight that drew him to the starboard rail, where one of the lookouts straightened from an eyeglass mounted there, that old invention from his native Honshu.

'You mind?' Ash asked him with a nod to the glass.

'Go ahead.'

The lone moon was close to the horizon now, a pale blue orb cupped in darkness. The Sister of Longing, many called her in the Midèrēs. Squinting, Ash adjusted the focus until the moon shone full and clear in the eyepiece, trembling a little as though he held it in his hand.

In marvellous clarity the small world filled his eye. White clouds wrapped the moon hanging there in the sky of *Erēs*, clouds gathering into the swirl of an equatorial storm. Cracks and pools of brilliant blue shone through from the ocean below them, seemed to reflect against a halo of light that girded the entire globe.

With his usual boyish fascination, Ash's gaze flickered to the black sliver of shadow cupping the moon, where in the past, if conditions were just right, he had sometimes been able to spot the lights.

Hard to see though in the increasing auroral glow of the coming sunrise. He looked partly away from the darkened side. Glimpsed two dim dots of white light in his peripheral vision.

Once as a boy Ash had counted five of those tell-tale pinpricks on the moon's nearly complete shadow, peering through an eyeglass owned by Semo, the ancient monk of his village, who had taken pleasure in showing the marvels of the night sky to anyone with interest. There were even more lights than that, old Semo had told them; though the monk had merely shrugged with a smile when they asked him what they were. *Who knows?*

Amazing to think what they might be. Signs of intelligent life even, as Ash sometimes believed; cities beyond his imagining, shining into the night like the gas-lit Mannian capital of Q'os from the air.

Or nothing more than lakes covered with ice and containing glowing algae, as some tried to claim, or crystal mountains which captured the daylight only to emit it again by night, or the perpetually burning fires of volcanoes.

Who knows?

It was growing noticeably brighter now as the sun rose and spilled across the eastern horizon. Below the prow of the ship the highlands rolled onwards, snowy hills sweeping as far as he could see, like white flames bent over by the wind. To the south, somewhere beyond them, lay the beginnings of the Great Hush, a largely uncharted continent where they would find the rift valley known as the Edge, home of the kree.

Footsteps beside him, stirring Ash from his musings. It was the longhunter himself stepping up to the rail. Cole rested his mug of chee on the rail while the cat settled down between them, then he nodded a greeting, something curious in his stare as he studied Ash.

The moon was vanishing now in the flourishing light, early bird-song rising from the hills below. Ash squinted, seeing smoke hanging in the air ahead. Thinking to see a native camp, he took a look through the eyeglass and frowned in puzzlement.

There seemed to be animals running around on fire down there, trailing ribbons of black smoke.

'Fire elk,' the longhunter Cole declared from the scope of the neighbouring lookout position.

'Yes, I have heard of them.'

'Look closer. You see the two bulls clashing on that island of rock?'

Ash peered hard through the lens, discerning more detail the longer he looked. On the rocky crest of a hill, two stags were locking antlers which flamed and smoked above their heads.

'Those two will have been fighting all night in the moonlight. Their antlers cause sparks whenever they strike together. When the antlers are chipped in a fight and a flake comes away, the exposed bone is oily and flammable. A single spark and it's burning.'

'Yes, I can see. Magnificent!'

'You should see it in full darkness, close enough to hear the cracks and crackles. Nothing like it.'

Ash whistled through his teeth while Cole poked a thin roll-up into his mouth. Something sparked in his hand and he held up a flame to light it. A metal lighter, Ash saw.

'Look, over there.' Cole gestured with his mug to another column of smoke rising to the west, a column that blew towards them and obscured whatever lay below. 'Fort Hunger, you see it?'

'I see something.'

'Wildest town in the world. Base camp for every expedition going to the Edge. A big trading hub for the natives too. Lots of Blackscar and Brave Ones strutting around.' The longhunter tapped the rail lightly as though in regret, then smiled down at the cat. 'Not today, eh?'

'You like this work, Cole? Longhunting, I mean?'

'I like to ride.'

Ash thought the man was joking, but Cole's expression remained the same.

'It seems poor country for it.'

'Wait until we're in the Hush. There isn't open country in all the Midèrēs that comes close to it.' And as he spoke, the man gazed south as though his salvation lay that way.

'Those kree warrens though . . .'

A muscle right under the longhunter's eye flinched. Cole inhaled and looked out at the brightening sky, filling his lungs deep like a man who knows what it is to drown. During the crossing of the mountains he had spent little time in his cramped cabin below decks, even during the worst of the storm, preferring instead to stay up above where he was confined by nothing. A man who sought open spaces.

'Seems dangerous, doing it on your own.'

'It's dangerous whatever way you cut it. As dangerous as your own line of work, I'd imagine.'

Inwardly, it was Ash's turn to flinch.

'Who told you, Meer?'

'No, your friend Kosh, last night when he was drinking. That's some line of work you're in, since we're on the subject. You people are Rōshun?'

'That is something I cannot speak about.'

'What, killing people for money?'

'There is a little more to it than that.'

'You mean, how you kill people because you like it?'

Ash frowned in puzzlement.

'Kosh mentioned how they call you *inshasha* in your order, king killer. How you like to wage vendetta against people who rule over others. How you like to kill kings and god emperors most of all.'

Harder still the farlander chewed the dulce leaves in his mouth, his breath visible in the cold air, spurting faster now from his nostrils. The juice was rushing to his head this morning, loosening his tongue and provoking memories of a different life, a different person from the one standing here now.

He found himself trying to resist the effects, and then he wondered why.

Relax, Ash told himself. *Soon you will be gone from all of this, and then what will be left of you but your presence in the minds of others?*

'Let me tell you of one day lived beneath the heel of the overlords back in my homeland. Perhaps then, you will understand what we speak of now.'

'Go on.'

'I come from a mountainous region in northern Honshu, as does your new best friend Kosh. I was fourteen when the soldiers of the overlords' Coalition came to our mountain village. The overlords had sent them into the highlands to pacify a rebellion simmering further to the south, but on the way through they were making an example of every village they passed, peaceful or otherwise.

'When they stopped in our village they raided the meat cellars and the local drinking house for liquor. Their officers became drunk, while outside on the road some of their soldiers forced the village men to erect a new . . . how do I say it? A *Law Pole*, right where the old one had been burned down.' Ash paused, grasping for a better description. 'Think of a column of stained tiq, carved with the images of the overlords and with the laws and castes set below them, and everything that is outlawed at the very bottom. One of the men . . . when they were finished, the soldiers dashed his skull in against the pole, as a random punishment for the destruction of the old one. My cousin, married only a week.

'When the people saw what had happened they started to protest. Wives had to stop their husbands from picking up what weapons they had. But we were outnumbered and surrounded. With impunity the soldiers began to round up the village zels, and whatever young men they could find for conscription, even the boys.

'They were lowlanders, most of them, though I hardly understood it at the time. Worshippers of a newly inspired god that was both King and Judge of a rigid caste system, which happened to place us somewhere near the bottom. While we highlanders followed the Way, treating each other as brethren. They hated our kind, thought we were dogs and vermin, and that day they made it clear to us. Fathers were kicked out of the way. Weeping mothers too. Old Semo the village monk tried to intercede on behalf of the youngest ones they were trying to conscript. He called out for mercy. At first he used words and gestures. When they shoved him away, he grabbed out at the arm of one of the soldiers. That was all it took. They beat the monk to the ground with their batons and they kept on beating him, even as he sat there with his hands over his head and the men of the village shouting for them to stop, my father even, who was near blind by then, who rarely even left his bed.

'I liked old Semo. We all did. He had been kind to me over the years, not like the village monk before him. Kinder than my own father ever was. When the soldiers came for me too, I ran around them and joined the monk where he knelt on the ground, and threw my arms over his head to protect him from the blows. My two younger brothers rushed over to join me. There we huddled together, taking the blows. My head was split open. I heard my brother's arm snap. Old Semo's face was covered in blood. The few teeth he had were bared under his arm like he was riding out a gale.

'And then more soldiers gathered round us in a mob, and they took their time with us. They joked to each other, and with us, even as they struck and kicked out. They enjoyed it. That was the worse thing of all. They got pleasure from what they were doing, from breaking the bones of an old monk and a few boys. I can still remember the stink of them. The scuff of their boots before my face. The chalky lines of grit on the ground from their soles. They were raining sweat on us. Spitting on us. Old Semo tried to put his own arms over our heads but they were both broken by then. I saw death in his eyes, a man who knew he was about to die.

'It was the first time I had ever felt real terror. The first and last time I ever allowed myself to feel it. Too much for a young mind to take in. Too real. When the terror passed all I felt was numbness inside, and the blows of the beating that went on for so long that the numbness grew into a kind of boredom, an impatience for it to be over with. My lips were busted open. My scalp hung in a flap over my ear. The soldiers were shouting. The villagers were shouting. I blinked through the legs around me, saw my father taking them on blindly with his fists. They were carrying my sister Lodi away, carrying her like she was nothing but captured prey.

'But I was gone by then. I just sat there while I felt someone prise an arm away. And then I glimpsed an officer leaning over us with a butcher's knife, working away with it casually, like he was cutting through a steak. But he was cutting through the monk's neck, even as Semo was still blinking and gasping with life. The blade was halfway through his neck. The scent of his blood was on my tongue. I could taste it. I didn't believe what I was seeing. The soldiers were still joking as though nothing was happening. I watched the officer cut off his head and lift it up to them. I looked over the ravaged stump and met the eyes of my brothers Alosh and Grin. They were crying like I'd never seen them cry before. We all were, the whole village.

'After that my brothers were spared because of their broken arms, and I was taken instead as a conscript in their army. I was enslaved, is the truth of it. For the next three years they tried to break me down so I would become what they wanted of me, a monster without compassion, and in this they almost succeeded. I will not speak of that time.

'But I escaped, eventually. I made my way back to my family, and found that they had raped my sister that day, and that later she had taken her own life, and my father too was long gone. When I finally joined the revolution to overthrow the overlords, I was willing to give my life for the cause. With all the justice in the world on our side, I did not believe we could be beaten. Yet here I am.'

'And so they call you *inshasha*,' Cole breathed in the cold air.

Ash stared at him with eyes aflame.

'Because sometimes, when I rid the world of one more bloody tyrant, one more oppressor, it feels good right down in my bones.'

CHAPTER TWENTY

The Great Hush

In a layer of wind they flew southwards off the highlands and out across the open plains of the Great Hush, with the ship's tubes burning brightly the entire way.

As the days rolled on the sun arched noticeably higher in the sky, and soon the air grew warm enough for crewmen and passengers to remove the heaviest of their cold weather gear, so that they worked and lounged in open shirts even as their moods grew more sullen. Colourful bandanas and wide-brimmed hats became common sights, along with sungoggles to shield the eyes from the glare.

Ever vigilant, the lookouts watched the plains of the Great Hush rolling below, where the shadow of the *Falcon* wriggled across endless corrugations of land sporting herds of bison, zels and other creatures they had never seen before, causing bickering over their correct names.

The strange boli trees of the region could be seen everywhere in small isolated stands upon the crowns of hillocks; thick trunks supporting upturned palms of branches fingering skywards. Some stands of boli trees were covered in umber leaves with undersides of silver, so that in sudden gusts they reminded the watcher of sunshine cast across water, but other stands were even more remarkable than that, for their crowns were aflame and smoking like clusters of candles. A natural occurrence, the longhunter Cole explained to them. Shedding their ageing leaves through fire.

All of this, yet still no sign of the kree.

If nothing else, Ash had expected the Great Hush to have been *quiet*. Yet birds screeched and flapped as they always do. Animals bellowed and roared and chattered with abandon.

Perhaps on the ground it might have been a different story, where contours and range would stretch out these noises into unexpected eruptions of an otherwise quiet day, but up here, flying across it all at a tremendous clip, the sounds came varied and often enough that they were a constant backdrop to their journey.

Cole had smiled when Ash had voiced these observations aloud, how noisy it all was in the Great Hush.

'Wait until we get closer to the Edge,' the longhunter had replied, with a crazy glint in his eye.

All the while, through the lengthening days and the shortening nights, the *Falcon*'s tubes roared on full thrust so that the sound was always in their ears too, leaving behind the ship an inky trail that smeared across the sky in the high winds; the *Falcon* eating the laqs as fast as she must have been eating through her supplies of white powder.

They crossed a vast marshland submerged in a recent flood, where lines of animals trekked across the silvery waters. Later came a desert surrounded by a crescent of mountains shining brightly in the sun; peaks which glowed brightly behind them by night. Crystal mountains, Cole had explained, reminding Ash of the lights on the moon again, how some claimed they were only a phenomenon such as this one.

After that they passed on into grasslands where the herds appeared less in size and regularity than before, the land emptier, almost desolate. The land of the kree proper.

A jangled mood began to spark across the ship. Cole assured them it was an effect of their nearing proximity to the Edge and the strange qualities now abundant in the air. Squabbles grew common. At night, shouts punctuated the stillness from minds trapped in feverish nightmares. Black jokes developed whenever dispirited men wandered off on their own wearing their belts. Paranoia brewed.

The roll of the sun marked the slow passing of the days.

*

One morning, deep into the Hush now, the shouts of the lookouts alerted them to a trail of white smoke curling low over the plains to the west, prompting all to rush to the starboard side of the ship for an eager look, tilting the deck with their shifting weight.

'A mullaro wagon,' Cole said next to Ash, who stood with Aléas by the rail.

'*Mullaro*,' he repeated to their dumb expressions. 'It's what the highland natives call longhunters, the ones who go after the Milk.'

'They're moving fast,' Aléas observed.

'Aye, and putting out a lot of smoke to mask their trail. They must have sighted some kree.'

'Are they alone out here?'

'No, lad. It's most likely a supply wagon. Ferrying some supplies down the line.'

'The line?'

'You've got two ways of getting your hands on Royal Milk and making it back alive. The expeditions do it the complicated way. They set up a base camp where kree activity is still minimal – we passed that range many days ago. Some of them hold down the camp while the expedition pushes deeper towards the Edge, setting up a string of supply drops along the way. A few remain at each one. By the time they reach the rift valley the group is small enough to remain undetected. From there, they launch an expedition down into the Edge for the Milk, bring it out again, and have it shipped back along the line by wagons like that one. They do this as many times as they can over the course of the winter.'

'And the other way?'

'You do it like the odd highland native does it. You go in alone with a string of zels loaded with enough supplies to get in and out again.'

'Sounds insane,' came the voice of one of the nearby crewmen.

Onwards the *Falcon* flew, leaving the wagon and its trail of smoke far behind.

*

Ash was dreaming of the dead again, when he awoke with a start and blinked about him in the darkness of his cabin, wondering why the world was being torn asunder by bursts of noise.

But it was only Kosh snoring again in the bunk above his head, his friend who claimed to be having so much trouble sleeping.

Easy, Ash told himself, breathing deeply while the faces slowly faded in his mind and the ship creaked all about him. Strange dreams in this place, the Hush.

Across the tiny cabin the chair creaked. Ash's heart skipped a beat as he looked over and saw a still form sitting there watching him in the darkness.

'Who's there?' he croaked like the old man that he was.

He could hear breathing, whoever the figure was. A slow relaxed breathing as though the person had been sitting there for hours, watching over him in a state of peace.

Like a son watching over a sick father.

'Lin?' he croaked again.

Another creak of the chair, the figure leaning towards him.

Nico?

But then Ash blinked and looked once more, and saw nothing but the empty chair.

A rap sounded through the door of the cabin.

Let it be the ship's boy standing there when I open it, offering a cup of hot chee.

He was almost right, for it was indeed Berl standing in the passageway leaning on his crutch. No chee in the boy's hands, though, only an unimpressed Cole standing by his side, the long-hunter glowing with life as though he had been up for hours.

Cole glanced in at the snoring form of Kosh.

'You old Rōshun sure like to take it easy.'

'What can I do for you,' asked Ash, yanking on his shirt, only then realizing that he had slept late.

'The captain would like you to join him,' Berl answered politely. 'In his cabin.'

*

The captain wasn't alone when they walked into his cabin without knocking. Meer and the ship's navigator, Olson, were also there, and they both looked up from the desk, where charts were spread open and held in place by paperweights, Meer and the navigator each gripping a pencil in their hands.

'Good, you're here,' grumbled Trench as the others returned their attention to the desk.

Ash stifled a yawn and stared down at the table of charts, wondering if it was too late for breakfast.

The largest map on display was something Trench had purchased back in Lucksore, pieced together from the accounts of longhunters and the few explorers who had penetrated the continent. Most of it was empty past the Aradèrēs mountains until it came to the Edge itself, the great rift valley still far to the south of them. Down the middle of the continent, the black lines of the rift ran all the way to the edge of the map, and no doubt beyond.

Ash stared at the charts as the captain stabbed his finger at their present position, marked on the navigator's replica, where Olson had been carefully marking their course in pencil marks and filling in what details he could along the way. 'We're in kree country now though you mightn't think it,' Trench said, and trailed his finger southwards all the way to the upper reaches of the Edge. 'And this is where we're heading. Cole, we need to know where you'll be going in. Assuming you have a particular route you favour.'

Cole pushed the brim of his hat from his eyes, leaned across the table and studied the chart for a few quiet moments. He traced a finger down through the markings of a forest, past the skirts of a tear-shaped lake, all the way to a horizontal line of black, a tributary of the Edge that ran directly eastwards, a thin finger isolated from the main rift for hundreds of laqs.

'This tributary here is my usual route. It's our best bet now. Far enough from the main rift that the kree presence is less concentrated. We'll still need to leave the ship a good distance away before we approach it though. Unless we want to stir them up like a nest of wasps.'

'Any idea how many people you'll need?' Trench asked.

'We have four already. For the amount of Milk we need to carry out, we'll need another four, maybe five able hands with us.'

Olson the navigator tutted with his tongue. 'That's a lot of volunteers, considering what you're asking.' And he spoke with the easiness of a man who had no intention of being one of them.

'Well, I ain't the one who'll be doing the asking,' Cole answered, and the longhunter glanced to Ash.

'How do you get down into the Edge without being detected?' Meer asked from the other side of the table, tapping his pencil lightly.

Cole relaxed in his stance, crossing one boot behind the other, and levelled his hard gaze on the hedgemonk. 'Well for that trick, we need to get our hands on a live kree.'

'You're joking.'

'You're welcome to watch if you like.'

CHAPTER TWENTY-ONE

Signs of Kree

It came out with a squeak, the stopper of the bottle. Cole sniffed the dead sour scent of the amber liquid inside and backed away slowly, glaring from under his brows at the shimmering sea of grasslands around the stand of boli trees.

Crunch, crunch, crunch, as he trod back across the layer of ashes and burned leaves to the edge of the clearing, where he stopped in the shade of one of the strange trees, its bare and blackened limbs reaching to the sky. Cole took off his hat, mopped his forehead with the back of his hand, then flopped the hat back on again.

The plains shimmied and the morning sun crawled a degree westwards on its long course through the day. The longhunter hung a hand from the crook of a low branch, squinting behind his goggles against the day's glare.

'See anything?' he said to the figure perched in the tree above him.

'A herd of zels. Three pineys. A flight of geese.'

The old farlander looked gaunt with tiredness today. He'd probably been poking the woman Shin again, Cole thought. At his age, the old dog.

'You certain? A man your age can miss all kinds of things in that blur he calls his vision.'

A grunt. A rub of cloth against bark. The farlander was twisting around to look at something through the eyeglass. The end of the piece was trembling slightly in his shaking hands.

'Hold on.'

Cole scratched his crotch and belched long and loudly, getting the worst of it out of him. The copse of boli trees stood as usual on a small hillock of land. He scanned the trees around the clearing, checking faces in the branches: Aléas and Meer and the navigator Olson, with his face pinched by fear.

'That scent works fast,' Ash said and lowered the eyeglass. 'Directly west. Heading straight for us.'

'You sure?'

The eyeglass dropped into his hand.

Cole propped it against the low branch and took a look for himself.

That *was* fast. Through the lens he spotted the dark form of the kree easily, bouncing and veering erratically in the sway of his aim, speeding on its six legs across the dusty ground with the spines of its carapace riding high. Big though, he thought, as he narrowed his eyes, and then his heartbeat quickened as he took it in fully.

It was no nimble scout but a full-grown warrior.

What's it doing out here on its own?

Quickly he scanned along the horizon for signs of a warband, but he saw nothing save for a herd of zels, running now as they scented the approaching kree. A stray warrior then. Here to make a hazard of their lives for however long it remained alive.

'It's a full-grown warrior, so stay in the trees,' he called out around the clearing. 'And don't be trying any heroics either. Remember, we want the juices from it before it's dead. Scoop as much into the jars as you can and be quick about it. Once that thing's dead every kree within laqs will know of it. We'll need to be leaving here fast.'

Cole glanced to his rifle then picked up the fuse trigger that was lying against the base of the trunk, the fuse itself trailing off beneath the dead leaves. He stood there waiting with it in his hand as the creature rushed up the slope towards them.

Once more he checked the faces around the trees. Hoped they would keep their heads together if anything went wrong.

The kree was amongst the trunks now, whipping through the undergrowth into the clearing like a charging bull. With a whip of lashes the warrior threw its head forward and charged across the clearing towards the open bottle, the quills on its back thrashing like reeds in a storm, its jaws clacking.

'Come on, you bastard,' the longhunter muttered, and right as the kree rushed across the middle of the clearing he pressed the trigger, igniting the charges that would take off some of its legs.

Except that nothing happened, and he pressed the trigger again, kept on pressing it while the creature reared above the bottle and spilled it over, then swung towards Cole as though it had scented him.

Cole cast the trigger aside and swept his knife from its sheath. With the kree charging him, he swung the blade against the trunk and chopped the rope running up it in two.

Into the air went the kree in an explosion of burned leaves and ashes, kicking and thrashing against the netting.

'Shoot it, you idiots!' Cole shouted, grabbing for his own gun.

They opened fire, but a warrior was more heavily armoured than a scout, and ensnared in the netting it was a tricky shot to make the hood that hung just below its carapace; easier in fact for Cole down on the ground.

Cole hefted up the rifle and took his best crack at it, but the kree was thrashing so violently that he missed. A front leg tore through the netting and suddenly the rest of the kree burst through, the warrior landing amongst another eruption of leaves and ashes. Cole stepped backwards despite himself, breaking open his rifle to reload it. Glimpsed the kree rearing before him, the scent of it making his senses reel.

A flash across the tail of his vision. In an instant, the creature had turned away and was chasing after someone across the clearing.

It was Aléas, sprinting across the ground towards a distant tree.

Shaking his head, Cole grabbed his rifle and scrambled up into the branches next to Ash.

'Your boy,' he told him as Aléas sprang up into a tree just as the kree thrashed its barbed lashes after him. 'He's good.'

'Aye. One of our best.'

A few surviving leaves tumbled to the ground as the kree charged the tree in which Aléas had taken refuge. The young man clung on to one of the swaying branches, riding it out.

'Aléas!'

'What!'

'Lead it back across the clearing. Give me a clear shot at it.'

Cole was expecting a complaint in reply, but no, the young man was working his way around the trunk, and he dropped down on the opposite side to the kree then sped around the creature at a run.

The creature gave chase. In a sprint Aléas led it out across the clearing straight towards his position.

'Left, left!' Cole shouted, squinting now down the sights of his rifle. 'No, *your* left!'

The young man darted sideways.

Cole exhaled and squeezed the trigger, hitting one of the buried mines just as the kree scuttled over them again. Even behind his goggles the flash of the blast forced his eyes closed.

When he looked down into the clearing again, the kree was on its back with its two remaining limbs scrabbling weakly at the air.

Thank you, my cousin, Cole recited to the dying creature for the life that it gave up for him; and then he spotted Aléas a few feet in front of it, the young Rōshun lying sprawled on the ground with his hands over his head.

'All right, my lad. You can get up now!'

CHAPTER TWENTY-TWO

The Little Eagle

Responsibility was the killer of sleep, or so his father had always told him; his father, the lowly commander of a border garrison, a quietly self-contained man content to remain in the same station for the rest of his life, even when it meant eschewing the Mannian creed of self-advancement.

So much different from his son Sparus, who had always yearned to climb higher, as high as he could go. What was life, after all, without advancement and the rewards that flowed as a consequence?

Over the years Sparus the Little Eagle, Archgeneral of the Holy Empire of Mann, had grown to know what it was to carry the weight of responsibility into his bed at night, and had long prided himself on his ability to switch off at the end of a long and troublesome day, to simply lie down and sleep, satisfied to prove his long-dead and small-minded father wrong once again.

Yet now, in his soft bed in his warm chambers in the citadel of Tume, with the spiced scents of sleeping incense drifting in the air and slowly relaxing his body, Archgeneral Sparus was caught in the trap of insomnia again, staring at the blackness of his closed eyelids, his head aflame with the day that had just passed and the next still to come.

It was going badly out there, this squabble with General Romano. Though if he was to be honest, it had been going badly ever since they had first landed their forces on the eastern coast of Khos.

After a forced march towards the Reach and a surprise attack by General Creed's forces, which had resulted in the mortal wounding of Holy Matriarch Sasheen, the Expeditionary Force had lost its narrow window of opportunity, just as he'd always worried they would. Winter had fallen upon them early, before they had even reached the northern walls of Bar-Khos, before they had even made it through the Reach, bringing with it conditions that could cripple an army on the march.

Right from the beginning, Sparus had shown little enthusiasm for this grand plan to invade Khos from the sea while assaults against the Shield were intensified. He hadn't trusted it because he hadn't trusted the plan's creator, Mokabi himself, the ex-Archgeneral, who had promised to come out of retirement to see it through. Too many factors remained unknown, with too little time allowed for the Expeditionary Force to complete its mission. No doubt all of it on purpose, so that Mokabi himself could take Bar-Khos from the south and steal the thunder.

He would have refused outright had Sasheen not ordered him to lead the invasion. And now she was gone and the Expeditionary Force fractured; Sparus holed up in the deserted Khosian city of Tume with those still loyal to him, along with most of the heavy guns, while Romano's forces hunkered down along the southern shore of the lake, both sides vying for outright control.

The floating city of Tume might offer Sparus and his army greater protection against attack, not to mention the bitterest elements of winter, but with their forces now landlocked and supplies cut down to irregular deliveries by air, his opponent, young General Romano, in his own camp along the shore, was reaping the spoils of the Reach – slaves for gold and food for the feeding of his men. Framed by the Windrush to the west of them, where the Contrarè were killing anyone who entered, and to the east by the sparsely populated highlands that ran all the way to the sea, Sparus had been forced into raiding for supplies to the north of the lake, ranging around the lines of the Al-Khosian army now dug in there; constant running skirmishes over towns heavily fortified and willing to fight, and which usually managed to burn their supplies before they could be taken.

In this contest of attrition it was costing more men and more black powder to supply his army than it was for Romano, and often for frustratingly low returns.

Desertions were rising, people going over to the side of Romano, whose star appeared to be on the rise. Disease ran rampant through the ranks. Malnutrition was being reported amongst the civilians who had followed them here as part of the baggage train; cannibalism even. And still, his and Romano's forces remained locked in their stalemate, neither one able to break it.

In his more honest moments of the day, those moments like now, when he was finding himself increasingly unable to sleep, Archgeneral Sparus knew that he was losing this battle with the young pretender Romano.

Tonight, in fact, he was wondering where precisely he had gone wrong.

You took on this fool's campaign against your better judgement. You stayed loyal to Sasheen your ruler, and now you pay the price for it.

A sigh. A smacking of his dry lips.

The old Archgeneral would be home right now if not for this risky campaign behind enemy lines; home in his east-country villa enjoying the slow dark days of winter with his mistresses and their gaggle of children.

Yet here he was in war-torn Khos instead, unable to sleep once again, and with someone rapping on the door of his chamber for his attention.

'Yes?' Sparus asked as he sat up in bed, squinting at the light pouring in from the open doorway, partly blocked by one of his aides.

'A message from the spymaster Alarum, sir. He asks to see you, if you're still up.'

'What? What time is it?'

'Almost midnight, sir.'

Damn the man, calling on him at this time of the night. But then, it was still early by the spymaster's standards. Alarum was a fellow who seemed to do much of his business by night.

'Where is he?'

'Down in communications.'

Sparus sighed, rubbed the stubble on his face and pinched a nose that was tattooed entirely black. The spymaster probably had another useless report to tell him concerning Romano or the Khosians, something that would have little to no bearing on his present predicaments. Still, in all his years of command, Sparus had never turned away a report for the sake of his bed rest. He wasn't about to start now.

'Fine. Send him up.'

'Yes, sir.'

Quickly, Sparus reached for his eye patch from the side table and fixed it over his missing eye. He rose from the bed and slipped into his nightrobe and open sandals, the floor too cold for bare feet, the fire burned down to fading coals.

His mind was still whirling even as he freshened up in the water closet. Young Romano could be the next Holy Patriarch of the Empire, for all that Sparus cared. He had reached the limits of his ambition.

Let them squabble in the distant capital over the politics of the affair, where by the sounds of it the infighting had become all-consuming since the death of the Holy Matriarch, nothing but the usual squabbles of contenders manoeuvring themselves around an empty throne. Hence why no one had ordered Sparus and Romano to stand down yet from their conflict. The lines of power were still in flux back in the imperial capital, factions still vying over who would come out on top, both in Q'os and here on this campaign.

'Sparus, are you there!'

Sparus the Little Eagle emerged into the room to see Alarum standing by the dying fire with his cold hands outstretched. A portly man, this spymaster of theirs. His bulk made the Archgeneral seem even smaller standing there before him.

'What is it, spymaster, that you have to come waking me at this time of the night?'

Alarum observed him for a moment as he might observe an elderly and infirm father.

'Some news from the capital. I thought you might want to hear it.'

'Go on.'

'The Élash have finally given approval for this plan of mine.'

'Which one?'

'Travelling into the Windrush to speak with the Contrarè. Enlisting their neutrality or support.'

'So you're going then?'

'With a few of my people. We'll set off first thing in the morning. I've already made contact with some Contrarè. We'll travel through the forest under truce of the tribe. We should be quite safe.'

Sparus had been right then. The news meant little to his current plight. Alarum's plan was a long shot, if even that.

He clamped down on a yawn and turned to stare at the glowing coals in the fire, his stomach churning as though from bad food.

'Very well then,' he told the spymaster absently. 'Report back to me when you return. Good journey.'

Sparus did not hear the spymaster leave.

CHAPTER TWENTY-THREE

Romano

The young General Romano was laughing when he stepped down from his zel and handed the reins to one of his bodyguards, but then he sobered, straightening his thoughts as he approached the stone building before him, spotting the wolfhounds lying curled in the snow.

'Are the purdahs all here?' he asked one of the soldiers stationed at the door.

'Yes, my lord.'

'And the Contrarè renegades?'

'They arrived a few hours ago. They're inside too.'

General Romano cocked his head towards the door. 'It's a wonder they're not killing each other yet,' he remarked as the soldier opened the door with a tug.

Romano stepped inside.

*

The young general shivered beneath his armour in the frigid air of the room, and then forced his body to be still. It seemed colder in here than outside, as though the stone walls leached whatever heat was generated by the men gathered around the walls in their camouflage cloaks.

Many of the figures were smoking long-stemmed pipes, and their quiet talk faltered as the door closed behind him.

Taking his time, Romano plucked something from a belt pouch, a small silver box of snuff, and took a sharp snort from it while he raised his gaze to the single lantern swaying in the smoky stir of air. Hooks hung from chains on the ceiling, empty now of carcasses. A meat house.

Feet scuffed on the floor as a group of Contrarè renegades rose from a far corner. Romano took another snort of snuff then put the box away again, his mind racing. He was taking the firesnuff day and night now, a potent combination of tarweed soaked in rush oil. It made his eyes dance with an edgy eagerness.

'You men are ready to go?' Romano asked in his hard, ringing voice.

'Just as soon as you tell us our work,' someone spoke out, no telling who in this gloom.

'Gather round then. I do not wish to shout across the room like a classroom priest.'

Boots shuffled as the men took a few steps into the light, thirteen purdahs in total, elite scouts of the Empire. They were named after the cloaks they wore, capable of rendering them near invisible in the field. Hardened veterans every one of them, experienced in every terrain and theatre of the Empire. The very best.

Not so, he suspected, with the smaller group of Contrarè renegades lurking back in the shadows, lean figures staring at him fiercely with faces painted red or black or both, their wild hair and dark feathers soaking up the light. Not the best of their kind, these Contrarè, only the most mercenary; renegades exiled from their tribe and willing to work for the Empire's money.

Here they were, the real thing itself, the truly wild and uncivilized Contrarè.

Romano's nostrils twitched. He thought he could smell them from where he stood on the opposite side of the room, but then he realized that it was his own day-long sweat that he could smell, and the purdah cloaks of the scouts intentionally tainted to mask their human scents.

'You're going into the Windrush,' he told them all. 'Those skins in the corner there will be acting as your guides.'

One of the older scouts bent to spit on the floor, then glanced darkly at the Contrarè. 'We've been in the Windrush. There's nothing there but hostile tribesmen and the corpses of those who didn't make it back. Mostly hanging by their balls from the trees.'

'These skins can guide you safely where you need to go. If they don't, they will gain no payment for their work.'

'And our mission?' asked a younger fellow.

Romano hesitated. He knew that what he was about to do here would aid Sparus the Little Eagle as much as himself. But it would hardly matter in the end, for Sparus was losing this contest between them. Any day now starvation would force the Archgeneral to capitulate, and then the heavy guns that Romano needed to storm Bar-Khos would be his, along with the remaining imperial forces.

Even with Mokabi threatening to take the city from the south, Romano could still beat him to it. Never mind the snow and ice, wind and rain, and roads made impassable by floods . . . With the warmed waters of the Chilos open all winter long, the river would be their highway to the southern coast. And from there he would be within striking distance of the city and its pitiable northern walls. Within reach of his ambitions for the imperial throne.

Romano LeFall, Holy Patriarch of Mann.

Not the time to get carried away on such things though. Romano cleared his throat, forcing his mind back to the matter at hand.

'The order is sending a delegation into the Windrush under flag of truce,' he informed them all. 'The delegation intends to negotiate for the Contrarè's support in the war. To win them over to our side.'

At the back of the room, the renegade Contrarè glanced at each other without expression. So the forest natives spoke Trade after all.

'Now, I have been told that the Khosians too have sent their own delegation with the same intentions, headed by a cripple known as Coya Zeziké.' Romano paused. He thought of his informer in the camp of General Mokabi far to the south on the Lansway, the general's own biographer no less.

'Zeziké will soon be entering the Windrush. What I require is that you track him down. You must make certain he does not reach the heart of the forest alive to speak with the Contrarè elders.'

The general allowed the sound of his words to settle, and their import to sink in. Neither Romano nor Sparus could afford another fighting flank opening up against them now – the Contrarè launching strikes from the border of the forest. Whatever resulted from this Mannian delegation into the forest – led by the spymaster Alarum, he'd been told – Coya Zeziké's own mission to recruit the tribe had to fail.

'There's one other thing you should know. He may or may not have a Dreamer accompanying him.'

A Contrarè laughed across the room at him.

'A what?' said the young scout.

'A Dreamer. A very powerful individual. Watch out for her. When you strike it must be fast and in total surprise.'

They looked unhappy now at this business proposed to them. No fanatics, these men, no warrior Acolytes trained from birth within the order to give their lives in battle; only experienced soldiers trying to survive their dangerous occupation.

Romano studied each of them in turn, using his gaze as a challenge. Grim weatherworn expressions stared back at him. A lonely work, what these scouts did. Always solitary or in small numbers, infiltrating behind enemy lines for weeks on end, no hope of rescue if they were wounded or fell ill. Their risks and isolation from the chain of command made purdahs arrogant in their ways, made them think they could act like equals in the company of their superiors. They would not readily lay their lives down on what sounded, even to Romano's ears, like a suicide run.

But he knew how to deal with their lack of commitment. The same way the order ensured the loyalty of its own Diplomats. He simply had to explain how it was in the best interests of them all.

'I should tell you that your families will be rewarded handsomely upon the event of your deaths. I should also explain that should you fail to undertake this task for me successfully, the lives of your families back in the Empire will be forfeited. I promise you all, I will sell them into indentured bondage myself, every man, woman and child.'

Hands dropped to the hilts of weapons in their belts. These men looked close to killing him.

For a moment the young general swayed backwards in the force of their silent fury. Then he swayed forwards again with a snap of his head. Only malice remained in his voice.

'Touch me, and this building gets burned down around you and your families slain, right down to the last infant bastard.'

Consent at last, for they stayed their weapons, and did not step any closer.

They would do what needed to be done, he could tell.

'Go,' Romano growled and told them all: 'Bring me the head of the cripple, or know that your families' lives are mine.'

CHAPTER TWENTY-FOUR

Juno's Ferry

The night was darkened by cloud cover when they approached the stable beneath the walls of a small fort, one of several dotted around the Khosian encampment of Juno's Ferry.

'Pick out whatever zels you need,' said the Red Guard officer leading the way, this fellow who had warmly greeted them after they had landed in their small skud fresh from the city, quick to help in any way after discovering who had come here in person to the front.

'My thanks for everything,' replied Coya Zeziké. 'I think that will be all, Lieutenant.'

Next to the stable block, zels were snickering in the darkness of a corral. There along the fence a group of figures waited, and Shard spotted the glints of their eyes in the gloom, heard them lift rifles and backpacks at their approach. A squad of Volunteer rangers.

She blinked, trying to clear the backwash of light in her vision. Shard was suffering badly tonight from the effects of the worm. Her mind wanted to soar from the constant rushes, but worse than that now were the sharp cramps developing in her abdomen, her body reacting to the constant presence of the worm's juices. Every so often it felt as though a knife was stabbing through her.

Somewhere beyond the fort's walls a wolf howled into the night, though perhaps it was only another hallucination or the calls of a drunken soldier. Through the gloom, Coya was speaking softly to the group of rangers next to the corral, who remained silent as Coya singled out one of their number, a tall woman with short-cropped hair, dressed in buckskin and brown leathers like the others.

'And you are?'

'Captain Gamorre,' she told him. 'I represent this squad.'

'You have their confidence, Captain?'

'I did on the last count. Eight out of nine hands.'

'Excellent. Captain Gamorre, as you might have been told, my companions and I travel into the Windrush to speak with the Contrarè. We could do with some protection, if your rangers are up for it?'

Shard knew that he asked because they were Volunteers of the democras, not Khosian regulars; soldiers who elected officers themselves from their own ranks, and often contributed to decisions. The captain glanced around for any gestures of disagreement, but no one stirred. 'We're worn thin, truth be told. But yes, we'd be honoured, Coya Zeziké.' And she bowed her head in a gesture of respect.

'Please, none of that now,' Coya said as he swept a red cloak around his own stooped frame. 'No telling who could be watching, eh?'

Quickly the zels were saddled and the group began to mount up, though Shard struggled with the task, reeling like a drunk.

'You okay?' she heard the bodyguard Marsh ask as she finally struggled into the saddle.

'Fine,' replied her dreamy voice. 'Ready when you are.'

'You're pointing the wrong way.'

Shard sighed when she saw that it was true, her zel aimed at a wall.

'Just go,' she snapped. 'Don't worry about me.'

They departed in a column, and the mood of the party was a sombre one as they trotted north in their collective silence along a road that wound through Juno's Ferry, parallel to the river. It was cold and the zels whinnied their complaints and snorted steam into the air, while the figures on their backs huddled beneath heavy cloaks.

The night rang loud with the sounds of the army encamped along the river bank, brightened by the dazzle of countless camp fires reflecting from patches of snow not yet trodden into mud. To their right flowed the black waters of the Chilos, a river worshipped by the Khosians and Contrarè alike, famed for its qualities of healing and spiritual cleansing. Even at this time of the year it remained warm, for its source was not far to the north of here – Simmer Lake they called it, where the waters bubbled with the smell of sulphur and were home to the floating city of Tume, now fallen to the Empire's Imperial Expeditionary Force.

She could see the imperial fires twinkling over there on the far bank, and hear the occasional mocking shout cast across the flow of water in reply to the odd report of a rifle.

'How goes it up here on the front anyway?' she overheard Coya asking one of the Volunteers.

'We still hold the western side of the Chilos. They still hold the east.'

'How goes it on the Shield?' enquired a different voice. 'We've heard reports that a wall just fell.'

'They've lost Kharnost's Wall. Though I hear it was almost a ruin anyway.'

'Any idea when they'll be sending us reinforcements?'

Bobbing along on his zel, Coya expelled a visible breath of air. 'With Mokabi's arrival, the Shield is a mincer of men right now. The bodies come faster than they can bury or burn them. I doubt any more reinforcements will be forthcoming. I'm afraid for the time being you're on your own up here.'

'Then we're shafted. No way we can hold the Chilos with the numbers we have here.'

Shard gazed down at the grimy faces of soldiers on the road, and saw how the gazes they returned were vague and distant, as though they stared through her very substance by the fact of having no substance themselves, everything blasted away from having lived and fought too long at the front. They were young and old alike, Khosians and Volunteers, though mostly they looked the same grubby age in the light of the camp fires, hands buried in their cloaks and heads wrapped in bundles of cloth, sallow faces etched with creases of dirt. Like the faces of the dead, she reflected. Everything human gone from them but the flesh itself.

The silence of the riders followed them as they left the road and crossed a line of earthwork defences, before cantering out across the pristine snow beyond the encampment, heading for the distant trees. The Windrush stood darkly across their path, ranging from the banks of the Chilos into the shrouded lowlands of the west.

Ahead, the night swallowed up the riders as they entered the ancient forest one by one.

CHAPTER TWENTY-FIVE

Badlands

It was barely noon in the Great Hush, yet already complaints were starting to filter back and forth along the line of riders, mixed with calls for a rest.

Ignoring them all the longhunter pushed onwards, unconcerned by their lesser stamina in the saddle. Ash too ignored his own body's complaints, the numbness of his limbs and the growing twinges in his lower back.

Ahead of them to the south a fearsome thunderhead bloomed darkly in an otherwise blue sky. Ash listened to the fading report of the thunder echoing across the empty badlands all around, and watched the grey skirts of rain trailing in the distance. Somewhere in that direction, beyond the unseen horizon, lay the rift valley of the Edge, location of the kree warrens – where they hoped to find enough Royal Milk for the Isles of Sky; enough to bring a boy back to life.

At their backs and far beyond sight by now, the *Falcon* and the rest of the crew waited for their return.

Ash rode at the very rear of the column, responsible for the tail while the longhunter Cole took the lead. Chewing on a long stalk of grass, he looked along the line of riders sauntering casually towards the distant thunderstorm to the south. Four skymen had volunteered for the mission, tempted by Ash's offer of gold, including Dalas the second-in-command, oversized on his mount and a poor rider at that, glancing back over his shoulder. Beyond the crewmen rode Meer, staring up at the massif of clouds ahead; Kosh chomping on an apple; Aléas just riding; Cole at the front chatting down to the cat.

The badlands here were rugged corrugations filled with gulleys and dry stream beds. Cole turned them so that they would skirt the edges of the rainfall instead of going through it. Even so the wind picked up as they grew closer, warm and humid against their sweating faces. It tussled the white flag that flew from a pole fixed to the longhunter's saddle, which Cole used often to gauge the prevailing direction of the wind, flowing now east to west across their line of travel.

Ash plucked the fabric of the damp greasy robe he wore from his chest, if only to relieve himself of the unpleasant sensation of its cloying touch against his skin for a moment. Like the rest of them, his clothes had been left to marinate overnight in a barrel of olive oil mixed with kree juice. In the dark hours before the rising of the sun, down in the hold of the skyship amongst its packed supplies, the party had cursed and grimaced as they'd pulled the heavy and sodden garments onto their naked frames, and then had set about the awful business of moving around in them. With the same stinking solution they had rubbed down their zels while the animals reared and fought against their ropes and flared their nostrils against the reek of it, the party bickering at each other all the while, tempers shortened by what they had to wear and what they were about to do next.

'Make certain you are still here when we return,' Ash had told the captain before they left, though Trench had only nodded and glanced away, something angry and morose in his expression, as moody as the sky.

On the move Ash ate a quick lunch of jerky and bread, one leg crossed casually over the saddle, and gazed through his sungoggles at the badlands shimmering in the fierce daylight, searching for signs of life. He was about to take a gulp from his waterskin when the line stopped ahead, and Ash saw that everyone was gazing eastwards, hands shielding their eyes.

The old farlander leaned forward in his saddle.

Movement flashed out there. With nostrils flaring Ash reached for his eyeglass and quickly focused its rocking field of view on a band of kree, ten of them raising dust, scooting fast towards the north in the direction of the ship.

When he lowered the glass he turned to the longhunter at the head of the line. The man was checking the little flag flying on his zel for the direction of the wind. He seemed satisfied with what he saw, for he kicked his mount onwards without concern and the others followed behind, watching the black specks of the kree until they could see them no more.

No one suggested stopping for a rest after that.

*

A wind from the Edge could send men insane, Cole had warned them in earnest, for such winds carried the narcotic scents of a million kree risen on the thermals of the rift valley.

Now, with his white flag suddenly fluttering in a different direction, the longhunter's expression darkened as the breeze began to flow against their faces, heady with the odours of the kree.

The longhunter quickened their pace, his occasional glance back along the line betraying his concern. He told them to tie scarves over their faces and to breathe slowly, and to keep an eye on each other. Soon a potent stench had filled the air, causing Ash's head to feel giddy with every breath he inhaled.

The zels grew harder to control, a condition which only worsened with every new sighting or scent of kree. It seemed the kree were all about them now, and despite Cole's insistence that the creatures' vision was poor and that they could not see far, he kept the party out of sight anyway, using slopes and twisting ravines where no large animals were to be seen anywhere. No birds even.

At last the Great Hush was truly, deathly silent.

Swaying in his saddle, Ash stooped down and snatched up another long blade of yellowed grass and placed it between his teeth. He felt a fat drop of rain splash onto the back of his hand, then another on his shaved head. Thunder resonated overhead, and then a grey deluge was pouring down on the land slanting in the wind, cutting their visibility to almost nothing.

A line of huddled riders. Cole in the lead, little more than a vague suggestion of form.

Off to their left, the cat was spinning in a circle after her tail.

Ahead, Kosh started to sing at the top of his voice.

These scarves over their faces, he reflected, seemed to be helping not at all. In front of him the skyman Jarad was rocking back and forth now in his saddle. Aléas was bunched down beneath his cloak. Dalas played with a knife and glared about for something to use it on. The column picked up pace again, the zels cantering now.

It was a bad idea giving the zels their head like this over rough ground. They were too close to panic as it was, too likely to snap a leg. Yet faster they rode, galloping now through the rain-slashed air with clods of mud flying from their hooves. 'Why are we running?' he called ahead, but no one would answer him.

'Yah!' Ash shouted and kicked his zel up the line, glancing at each face as he passed by. It was as though they were all in a trance, their eyes fixed on the rider directly ahead.

He came up alongside Cole, and yelled at him through the gusting rain.

'Why are we galloping, man?'

At last the longhunter noticed him. Cole shook his head, looking dazed.

'*What?*'

Ash reached out, grabbing the zel's bridle to slow the animal down. In moments he had slowed their pace again. Their mounts snorted hotly.

'How long until we can make camp?' he asked the longhunter.

Cole blinked at him from under the dripping brim of his hat.

'A few hours, I'd guess. Hard to tell in all this rain.'

'Can you make it?'

'Of course I can make it. Get back in line, old man, we're losing daylight here.'

*

Evening. The rain a steady thin drizzle, the gloomy twilight deepening on the cusp of darkness. The line stopped. Ash blinked through his fatigue and saw how the world ended not a throw beyond his nose.

It was the Edge, a ragged lip across the surface of the world; a haze of rain falling into the gulf of space beyond.

Quickly they headed for a nearby hillock right on the rim of the rift, a low flat-topped outcrop with a copse of stunted boli trees standing upon it. Cole sent in the cat to check that it was clear, then spurred his mount up the slope after hearing her call out.

At the top, amongst the cover of shrubs beneath the trees, they dismounted in a small clearing, where a pool of water shimmered in the rain. Soaked to the skin they stretched and moaned in relief before dragging out their tarps, which they were quick to string up between the trees for shelter. Only after that did they see to the zels.

'Can't remember the last time we rode like that,' Kosh said as he rubbed his sore backside.

'There was a time,' Ash remarked stiffly, referring to the days of revolution, 'when we used to ride all day for the pure joy of it.'

'Aye. We must have had backsides of leather.'

The others looked little better. Few seemed able to speak.

'Careful here,' Cole called back, squatting down at the edge of the dripping undergrowth along the rim. One by one the others hunkered beside him, the breath catching in their throats.

Cole had described this stretch of the valley system as a mere finger, yet here, now, it was the deepest valley Ash had ever laid eyes upon, like something from the realm of imagination. In the fading light the far side was obscured by the shifting sweeps of rain. Directly beneath them, over the crumbled rocky lip they lay along, slopes covered in lush jungle seemed to fall forever into clouds of mists.

'How long will the descent take us?' he asked with his mouth suddenly dry.

'A day at least if we set off at sunrise. Maybe twice that getting back up.'

'It's big,' came Aléas's voice along the line.

No one spoke after that, each pair of eyes reflecting the gulf of space below them that was the legendary homeland of the kree.

'Better get what sleep we can,' announced the longhunter as he stood again. 'We've a long day ahead of us.'

'Sleep,' retorted one of the Caffey brothers, the young crewman rising to his own feet. 'As though I could even close my eyes in this forsaken place.'

'Then you get first watch,' snapped Cole. 'And if I catch you sleeping, I'll kill you myself.'

*

Beneath a tarpaulin strung between trees, the three Rōshun lay with their heads propped against the saddles of their zels, trying to sleep in the humid night air while the endless rain drummed above their heads.

Aléas breathed lightly where he slept, undisturbed by the fitful snores of Kosh, who had finally drifted off at last, or by the awful layer of grease soaking his clothes and skin. Only Ash remained awake, troubled by the pains in his head and the pulses of colour in his vision, worsened by the kree scents laden in the air. He leaned against a saddle chewing chunks from a strip of jerky, thinking of home, his real home, back in far Honshu; perhaps because here in the deep Hush, perched on the very rim of the Edge and his life, he felt more distant to that time and place than he ever had before.

It had been a good life back then, raising his hunting dogs and supporting his young family. Yet Ash had longed for more than that, yearning to see the wider world for himself, to travel and explore, and so at times his family had seemed like a burden to him, something to be freed from.

What a young fool I was.

Footsteps were approaching in the darkness, crunching through charred fallen leaves. Ash reached for the hilt of his sword, but it was only the longhunter Cole in his dripping hat, bending down beneath their tarp to peer at their forms through the gloom. Next to him the cat snuffled at Ash's bare feet, not minding the rain.

'Wake him up,' the longhunter growled, and shook Kosh roughly until he spluttered and opened his eyes. 'You're snoring loud enough to wake the dead,' Cole told him in annoyance. 'You want to bring the kree down on our heads?'

'I can hardly help it if I snore,' Kosh complained, rubbing his tired face.

'Then don't sleep,' Cole retorted, and he wasn't joking.

When the longhunter hurried away through the rain the cat lingered behind for a while. Ash could sense her attention focused on the strip of jerky in his hand. He liked these domesticated prairie lynxes of the Midèrēs, especially this one, who reminded him of the springers he had bred and raised back in the old country, dogs that could run and run forever.

'Who needs sleep anyway?' croaked Kosh after the retreating form of Cole.

Ash observed him in the darkness, reminded once more that years had passed since his old friend had pursued vendetta in the field, that he was out of shape both physically and mentally.

'You're certain you are up to this?' he asked his old friend once more. 'You could stay here and hold the camp with Meer until we return.'

'If you ask me that one more time, I'm going to bust open your chops. I'm fine. You need everyone you can get down there.'

Ash bit off another chunk from the jerky then threw the rest to the cat, who caught it with a snap of her teeth and chewed it down. A gentle pleasure flowed through him as he watched her eat; the simple delight of providing sustenance to another.

'Just there,' mumbled the sleeping Aléas aloud, rolling onto his side. '*Mmm*. Just there.'

The two old farlanders chuckled despite their weariness. Kosh shook his head in wonder.

'Dreaming of women, even now.'

'How do you know it's a woman he dreams of?'

A moment of startled silence.

'You think?'

Ash shrugged, knowing that the kree scents were loosening their tongues.

A voice cried out into the night, the skyman Jarad still locked in the grip of his nightmares beneath one of the other tarpaulins strung between the trees. A figure crossed the clearing. Cole's hushed tones sounded out to quieten the man down.

'I was thinking of home just now,' Ash confided.

'Funny. You say *home* and instantly I know you don't mean Cheem, nor that rock in the sea that Coya brought us to. The old country always remained in our hearts, no matter how far we travelled from it.'

Ash exhaled in acknowledgement.

'You recall the seasons in the highlands, how fast they would turn, always somehow a surprise?' he asked his old friend. 'The herds of wild zels on the ridges? The migrations of featherscrapes blackening the skies for days? The red hooks spawning in the rivers, thick enough you could almost walk across their backs? You remember?'

'I remember the challo festivals,' Kosh told him. 'Dancing and feasting and rutting with pretty girls for weeks on end. Happiest times in all my life.'

Both fell into an introspective silence.

'I wonder if my wife and children are still alive,' Kosh mused to himself. 'I wonder if they even remember me.'

Don't go there my friend, thought Ash, and just then he realized how few times they had ever spoken of these things in their thirty years of exile.

Over the decades, news of the old country had reached them from silk merchants who had crossed the ocean, and always the news had been bad. Since the defeat of the revolution and the capitulation of the rebel lowland provinces, many of the highland clans had been pacified once more by the civilized war machine of the overlords. Those things they had been fighting to stop had happened anyway.

Massacres had left thousands dead. Hundreds of thousands more had been cleared from their lands and driven down into the lowland cities in indentured servitude. For many of those highlanders fortunate enough to remain, their land had been seized and rents forced upon them for living on what was previously their own. Now they paid taxes for everything in their lives, even the fiery spirits they distilled in their homes, even the water that sprang freely from the ground.

Only the most cunning of clans still lived with their freedoms in the vastness of the mountains. They continued to resist what others had found to be irresistible, and hoped some day to inspire another uprising – for there would always be other uprisings, so long as the overlords ruled over the people.

'We could have gone back,' Ash heard himself say. 'We could have joined those still living free. Who would have known us after all these years?'

But Kosh only scoffed at that.

'To live amongst strangers? To see with our own eyes how much has been lost?'

'They are still our people. Our kind. And the mountains will still be there. The birds and the sky and the spirit of the place.'

'Yes,' agreed Kosh. 'I'll give you that.'

Ash knew that he was high on the soupy air, but he didn't care.

'At least we fought for them,' he declared with passion. 'When the overlords tried to enslave us like the lowlanders, at least we stood up and fought back.'

'We did, didn't we? And we gave those bastards a bloody good hiding too, never mind the odds against us.'

'More than that. We almost won.'

'Aye, almost,' said Kosh with a grimace.

But Ash shook his head in defiance. 'We lit a fire under the backsides of the overlords. And the fire still burns. Next time we shall win.'

Kosh chuffed through his nose.

'Aye, old friend. Next time.'

His sober tone stilled Ash's tongue.

Other voices drifted softly through the camp, the two Caffey brothers, arguing over zels again. It was all the two Coraxian skymen ever seemed to talk about, that and the family stud ranch they were one day going to run together.

'I'll be glad to be gone from this place,' Kosh grumbled, rubbing his face again in weariness. 'I miss my sleep.'

'Bad dreams?'

'Every time I drift off in the Hush they're waiting for me.'

'Your victims,' Ash said.

'Yes, how did you know?'

'I've been having the same dreams myself.'

The rain hammered down above their heads. Ash peered out from the tarp, regretting that he had spoken. He could just about see the dim shapes of the others, sitting or lying beneath their tarps around the small clearing.

'I see my victims of vendetta,' he spoke at last. 'Not the High Priests and Beggar Kings and all the other wretches drunk on power. I see the women who killed their wealthy husbands in self-defence, too enraged to be deflected by the husband's seal. I see the young ones who barely even knew what they had done. I see the desperate driven to murder by their need for coin. I see all the people who acted out of a sense of justice, seeking retribution for what happened to their sisters, their daughters, their sons. I see everyone who never deserved it.'

'You never had these dreams before the Hush?'

He shook his head, and it was only a partial lie. 'I thought I was at peace with this business of ours. Yet clearly not.'

'It's because you're nearing your end, Ash. You face up to what lies behind you at long last.'

It was the first time Kosh had openly acknowledged the truth of his worsening condition, and his friend's words surprised Ash enough that he was rendered speechless by them.

'You know,' Kosh went on, 'I always thought I would be the one to go first. Somehow it feels wrong any other way.'

'Maybe you still will,' he quipped around the lump in his throat, but then he thought of the Edge of the world they were camped beside, and the warrens of the kree at the very bottom which they would soon be entering, and he regretted the joke bitterly. He was only tempting fate.

Something wet and cold settled on his shoulder. It was Kosh's hand, squeezing hard to show how much he meant to him.

Please, enough!

Perhaps Kosh sensed his tension, or simply knew him well enough after all these long years, for he took his hand away and fell to silence.

A crack rang out in the darkness of the night like a branch breaking, though it came from far beyond the hillock of their camp. The zels shifted uneasily and the voices of the Caffey brothers ceased for a moment. Another crack sounded, this time even further away.

'Do you ever dream of your apprentice?'

Ash winced in the darkness, gripping his hands together even tighter.

'Every single night,' he admitted in a whisper. 'Nico is one of my victims.'

CHAPTER TWENTY-SIX

Into the Edge

Next morning, the looks in their eyes said it all.

'Is this really necessary?' asked Jarad, oldest of the skymen, putting words to their incredulous silence.

Naked now and smearing himself down with a fresh coat of kree oil, the longhunter Cole scowled but did not look up from what he was doing. 'No clothing beyond this point. They'll scent the sweat in them even soaked like that.'

Across the small clearing, Dalas signed something quickly with his hands.

'Aye, what about that cat of yours then?'

Cole threw a jar of oil into the man's hands in reply.

'Cats only sweat through their feet. Now strip.'

By the time they were all undressed, Cole was already slinging a bandoleer of cartridges over his slick torso and the longrifle over his shoulder. He strapped a wet belt across his torso, crisscrossing it with the bandoleer, and hung his glistening machete from it and a netted bag of food, then as many empty water skins as he could fit. At last he fastened on his bundled pair of hooryas, weapons from his old days as a Special, designed for fighting in the close confines of the tunnels beneath the Shield; wide scythes which curved around the knuckles of his hands, with a punch-blade protruding from each of them.

Meer the monk watched on in glum silence, knowing he would be left here alone with the zels when they were gone.

'Each of you take as many empty water skins as you can,' Cole instructed. 'And bring all your weaponry. Those grenades too.'

Aléas chuckled incongruously to himself, drawing curious looks from Ash and Kosh.

'I can't help it,' claimed the apprentice. 'I feel giddy.'

While the men donned scarves over their mouths and noses, Cole dipped his fingers into an open jar and painted numbers on the skin of their backs in vivid green dye he had borrowed from the ship, filled with a luminous living algae that would glow in the darkness. After a final inspection, he nodded that they were ready.

At last the party gathered along the lip of the rift valley. Early mists swirled beneath their feet, as though they were high in the mountains looking down upon the clouds. In the silence of dawn, under a sky flourishing with light though still scattered with diamond stars overhead, they glanced at one another for reassurance, nine naked, frightened, mortal figures standing over the precipice that was the Edge.

There was still time, many of them were thinking. Still time for sanity, time to turn around and return to the world of man.

Their gazes questioned each other and lips twitched into nervous smiles, each waiting for another to speak sense at last, to voice aloud what was rushing through each of their beating hearts: that this was madness.

But no one did.

*

'Tiring work,' Kosh remarked, and dabbed the back of a hand against his right eye, squinting as though in pain. 'This damned grease,' he complained. 'I can't abide it. I'll lose my mind if I don't get this stuff off me soon.'

Tension stretched out his voice. The kree scent was strong here on the steep forested slopes of the Edge, borne on the rising up-draughts. Even behind the scarf over his mouth and nose Ash could smell little else but the heavy stench of it. He felt his stomach begin to cramp and growl with nausea. Strange moods and thoughts were riding through him in waves now. It would only get worse, Cole had told them.

'Best not to dwell on it,' Ash suggested, stepping ahead of his old friend on the trail, and even as he spoke he was surprised to hear the annoyance in his own voice. 'Try to remember when you were not always so old and soft. How once upon a time you were Rōshun.'

'I should knock you off your feet for saying such a bloody thing!'

'Thirty years ago maybe, when you were not so fat.'

Kosh's strangled breath of anger was broken by a sudden curse. He had trodden on another thorn with his bare foot.

Too long from the field, Ash thought sourly, for his head was split in two today, and his temper evidently as short as the rest of them. Without looking back he continued walking down the trail along the fast-running stream they were following, focused on placing his footfalls carefully so as to negate the shocks shooting up into his skull with every jolt.

The air had been growing thicker, hotter, more potent as they descended the great slope of the valley. Vegetation was lush here, and at times they had to hack through it with machetes, panting and sweating in their greasy nakedness. Insects swarmed in clouds amongst the trees, but at least the oil covering their skins held their bites at bay. Brightly striped snakes writhed through the long grasses. Frogs croaked beyond sight. Still no birds to be seen or heard anywhere though.

Down below, their longhunter guide had stopped to hunker next to the stream with one hand resting on the hilt of his machete, his other motioning for the party to stop. He was watching a pair of kree pass by on the opposite bank, loaded down with their inflated sacs of amber juices, near hidden by the undergrowth. Upstream from Cole, the two Caffey brothers were arguing fiercely as though they didn't see them, or didn't care. Aléas too used their halt to hop onto a flat rock in the midst of the flow, where he stood precariously with one foot raised like a crane, his arms outstretched for balance, seeking equilibrium. A whimsical smile creased his handsome features, and for a moment Ash thought that he looked like one of the naked blissed-out holy men of the far east, save that his skin was too light, and the colour of his blond hair was wrong, tussling about in the cool breeze of air over the water.

The cat bounded past Aléas, leaping gracefully from rock to rock as though she wanted to be closer to the pair of kree on the other side. Cole whistled almost inaudibly across the burbling flow and she stopped, hunkering down, trembling and alert.

Suddenly the undergrowth right next to the longhunter snapped apart as another kree stepped out onto the trail they were on. Ash paused six feet from the man, who had frozen where he knelt and was now turning his head slowly to watch the creature tread past him.

'Nobody move!' Cole warned as the creature made its way along their line. 'It won't notice you if you don't move!'

Striped spines lifted slightly along the creature's back, rattling softly like cane grasses. On six legs it ambled past Ash where he stood rooted to the ground, gripping the hilt of his sword for reassurance. He inhaled the reek of the creature, glimpsing the hood which Cole had told them to aim low for if it ever came to that, where the open mouth could be seen with its pink lining, barbed tendrils floating all around it in a cloud.

Across the top of the hood, sets of glassy eyes reflected the light like those of something dead.

A longing filled him to reach out and touch the creature. Even as Cole hissed a warning at him, Ash raised a hand just enough to brush its carapace as it went past. A jolt ran through his body at the contact, something of fear and awe in it. He felt the sharkskin roughness of the carapace sliding beneath his fingertips, the great weight of the animal shifting through its lumbering strides.

Slowly the kree ambled up the trail while the men stood motionless in terror.

'We need to turn back,' the skyman Jarad said aloud as it neared him. The man was visibly trembling now. His reddened, puffy face glanced over his shoulder, back up the slope past the great bulk of Dalas. 'We need to turn back, all of us, while we still can. This isn't worth all the riches in the world.'

'Jarad, stay where you are!'

But Cole's words had the opposite effect on the skyman. Jarad took another glance at the nearing kree then ran from the trail towards the thicker undergrowth, croaking with panic. Instantly the kree swung its head towards him with its spines rising erect. It surged after the skyman, rearing up to knock the shambling man to the ground, flailing its barbed lashes at him. Jarad screamed.

'No one move, damn it!' Cole yelled as Ash swept his blade free from its sheath, saw others doing the same. 'If you attack it now we're all dead!'

Frozen in horror, they watched Jarad screeching as the kree shook its maw over his prone form, its barbed lashes rending his flesh. Ash felt sickness boiling in his stomach. Guilt washed through him as he looked away, unable to watch the man's fate. He met Kosh's wide-eyed gaze and locked onto it fiercely.

With a final chilling cry the skyman fell silent and moved no more. Ash looked back at last, and saw the kree slowly working over him, nuzzling their mouths against his cooling body, sucking out his insides.

In anger or grief, Dalas broke a branch off a tree and smashed it to pieces against the trunk while his dreadlocks flew about him wildly, grunting in his mute silence while the cat jumped in excitement next to him, trying to snatch the branch in her teeth in play. A retching sound carried through their stunned silence, one of the Caffey brothers bending to be sick.

'Anyone else feel like ignoring what I tell them?' Cole demanded to know.

*

They continued descending the slopes throughout the short night, using the light of the stars and the milky glow from the unseen moons to see ahead. As weary as they all were Ash was relieved not to be stopping, knowing it would spare them another night filled with nightmares. The kree were less active too in the cooler darkness, and the party only heard a few from a distance as they carried on downwards. Cole pushed them hard, wanting to make the most of it before sunrise.

In the first rays of dawn they reapplied more kree oil in silence, too tired to speak, and then stumbled on down through the mists and the brightening light of the new day. Deep in the valley, the air was a reeking heady brew, thick with moisture, hot against the skin and in the lungs, upon which they grew ever more intoxicated. Their moods reeled from one moment to the next, and men mumbled darkly or laughed out in sudden humour.

Colours swamped Ash's vision this morning, leering around with a life of their own. He stumbled often, grazing himself a few times, until at last he swallowed his pride and cut himself a stick to walk with, ignoring the raised eyebrow of Kosh behind.

'Old blind man with his walking stick,' muttered Kosh from behind.

Ash let him have that one, knowing he deserved it.

Right now his mood had flattened into a single focused desire to keep going. For a long time he simply stared at the ground before his tired feet as he walked, chewing on some dulce leaves and using the stick for balance. So intent was he on his footfalls that he hardly noticed how the slope was beginning to level off at long last, and that they were nearing the valley floor; not until he almost collided into the back of Aléas.

They had stopped. Cole stood at the tree line looking out through an eyeglass, perched on the low limb of a tree. By his side the cat stared too.

Swallowing down his nausea, Ash leaned against a trunk to catch his breath. Out there beyond the tree line, the plain of the valley floor lay shrouded in thinning morning mists. A river meandered through it as brown as dark chee.

Everywhere he looked the black forms of kree scrambled back and forth in their thousands, like a massive army in disarray. To see the creatures in such numbers was enough to steal his breath away, just as their bitter scents made his blinking eyes sting. Every man stared hard with reddened eyes, sobered by what they saw; save for Aléas, who gazed with fascination and flicked his sheathed sword minutely, whipping the tip against a frond of grass.

They were right all along, Ash suddenly realized with a grim certainty. *This scheme of mine is insane.*

One by one the others were turning away from the sight of the kree with their eyes wide and round, a huddle of owls blinking at their guide Cole for reassurance. But dread seemed to have fixed the muscles of the longhunter's face into a rigid mask. Cole was clearly unnerved by what he saw out there, or by what still lay ahead.

This work was a kind of penance to the man, Ash saw now. Yet there was something of longing in his stare too, a lure he could not break free from. A deathwish perhaps.

*

The scents were almost overwhelming here, enough to bring tears to the eyes. They flowed from the holes in the face of the cliff, where kree came and went from their subterranean hive.

From the base of the steep earthen slope, Cole slowly climbed up to the mouth of one of the smaller entrances with the cat at his side, flapping his hand for the rest of them to follow. He had assured them that the kree would pay them no heed so long as they moved without sudden motions.

Climbing up after him, Ash stopped by the side of the tunnel mouth and gasped for air, trying to clear his head. The dirt cliff rose above them higher still, and he saw how the earth here seemed to be bonded together with some kind of silky white substance.

A kree worker emerged from one of the higher tunnels and scuttled down the slope without noticing them.

'The natives say the kree use murmur worms to craft their warrens,' Cole was telling Aléas as he lit the end of his torch with his metal lighter. 'Probably bullshit, though.'

Deep, deep darkness in there. A flutter of anticipation ran through Ash's spine.

Big Dalas looked dubious at the size of the hole they were studying. The cat sniffed around the entrance.

'Rope up,' Cole told them, and while they tied themselves to the rope they had brought with them he described what they should expect.

'We'll be looking for the main shaft to lead us down into the Royal chamber. That's where we get the Milk. Remember the route, all of you, and stay together no matter what. The cat will lead the way for us.' He paused as one of the skymen retched from the reek tumbling out of the hole.

'We go in fast and you follow my lead. Whatever you do, no matter how desperate it gets, *do not* cut yourself free from this rope. If you get lost down there, you're dead. Ready?'

No one said a word.

He clicked his tongue. The cat took one last look back before scampering inside.

'And remember,' Cole declared hotly, 'no one kill any bloody kree in here, or we'll have the whole hive down on us!'

CHAPTER TWENTY-SEVEN

Descent

'You do this alone?' Ash asked in wonder, grunting each word over the snap and crackle of the torches they held, which were loud in the tomb-like silence of the hive, their brilliant smoking flames leaving a blackened trail along the roof of the tunnel just above their heads as they descended ever deeper into the earth.

'It's a living,' acknowledged the longhunter Cole ahead of him, treading carefully with his gleaming head stooped beneath the low roof. 'Wouldn't want my son to be doing it, mind.'

'You have a son?'

'Aye.'

The man's attention was fixed on the darkness ahead just past their circle of light, where the cat had disappeared moments earlier. From behind, his bare body glistened with the oil and sweat that coated his skin, and Ash could see the scars on his back rippling in his own watery vision, red slashes and the puckered puncture marks of stabbings. Old wounds, Cole had admitted, from his time as a soldier.

Ash blinked to clear his sight, eyes stinging from the smoke and the harsh concentrated scents of the kree that wafted in the subtle movements of air; like holding his face over a bowl of onion juice and pepper and a heady dose of something rancid. The scarf over his face seemed to make no difference at all. He had already pulled it down so that he could better breathe.

The motes of pain in his head had coalesced into a single blade that hefted through the middle of his skull from between his eyebrows to the nape of his neck. Ash chomped on the leaves and concentrated on the feel of the dusty hard earth against the soles of his feet, the rub of the sides against the prints of his fingertips. He was thirsty all of a sudden, but they had left their water up on the surface.

Behind scraped the feet of the others. He felt the tug of the rope tied around his waist, turned his head to see Kosh's face etched deep in the torchlight and set into a grimace of fear, his scarf pulled down around his neck like his own.

Suddenly, they heard the cat crying out from somewhere ahead.

'Clear a way!' Cole declared and pressed himself hard against the side of the passage. Ash did the same, just as a small kree scuttled past them heading up to the surface. 'Clear a way!' Kosh passed on, and back along the line the men swore and shoved each other to one side roughly.

The small kree paused, probing out with its lashes. It studied Dalas's torch for a moment before touching his chest with its tendrils, but the man held his nerve, incredibly, until the creature passed onwards.

They uttered a collective sigh of relief and then continued downwards, deeper and deeper until the stench of the kree grew thick enough to gag on. The cat growled once from the darkness ahead. An opening revealed itself where she stood waiting for them, her gaze fixed on movement beyond.

One by one the party straightened as they emerged from the tunnel. Gloom swallowed the light of their torches in every direction save for down, where at the bottom of an earthen slope the floor heaved with the forms of kree. The air was hotter now, more humid. They were in some kind of chamber too large to fully take in.

'The ones without spines are the workers,' Cole told them. 'The rest are scouts and warriors. Stay away from either.'

Squinting down through the gloom, Ash studied a nest of yellow eggs on the floor to their left, each one larger than a barrel, tended by small workers that cleaned the shells with their maws and the curved tips of their limbs. At the outer limits of the flickering torchlight, others were emerging carrying more eggs or nothing at all from a wide opening in the floor.

He scanned right, taking in the lower ceiling there. Out of the darkness kree hung with their abdomens extended many times their original size; big dangling balloons stretched thin enough to be transparent, holding the same amber liquid the party had seem them carrying in the field.

'What are they?' Aléas asked, and their guide took a moment to follow the young man's gaze.

'Their food stores. What they mostly war over.'

Cole made a soft whistle of air with his lips and the cat stopped at the bottom of the slope, her sleek hair standing straight up on her back like the spines of the kree. Carefully, the longhunter trod down to join her, tugging Ash after him with the connecting rope.

'They can sense us,' Kosh remarked, venturing further out next to Cole and Ash.

He was right. The nearest kree were surrounding the group and probing towards their smeared skin. The cat backed away, hunkered against Cole's legs.

'There's too many of us,' Cole muttered.

Ash spoke in a hush. 'Can we risk going further?'

'Maybe. If we push the pace.'

Again the longhunter whistled softly. The cat looked up at him, then looked out across the floor of kree.

'Go on now,' he urged, and she picked herself up and ventured out amongst the kree and the eggs, carefully weaving a path through them towards the central tunnel in the floor. While she did so, Cole turned back towards the tunnel mouth above and lowered his torch to the slope, dribbling a line of sap across it that burned with a tiny blue flame.

'Follow me closely,' he said, leading the way out across the floor.

It was getting hard to think straight. Ash's mind was sluggish, unfocused, like the slow creep of hypothermia. He trod between two kree and leaned away from the exploring forelegs of the nearest one. Pricks against his bare feet made him look down at the ground. It was littered with detritus beyond his recognition. He swept the torch around to see how the others were faring. They threaded their way along the same route he was taking, Dalas towering above their heads, the blade of his machete resting on his shoulder. Like the rest of them he had eyes only for the kree. The two Caffey brothers followed behind him, and at the back came Aléas, holding a small double crossbow loaded and ready.

In a tight group they gathered around the opening in the floor, staring down into the gulf of it where kree were coming and going. The entrance was large enough to swallow a wagon, and it fell vertically for some feet before curving steeply into a slope until they could see no further, though a warm press of air flowed upwards, carrying the scent of something new now, like bile. The men glanced at each other uneasily. No one moved. The cat was standing at the very edge, and she looked to Cole and Cole stared back at her, puckering his lips in an unhappy knot. When the tunnel was momentarily clear he exhaled sharply then hopped down into it with the lynx.

Their show of bravery seemed to spur the others into matching it. With curses and black jokes they helped each other down into the hole, passing torches and weapons from grimy hand to grimy hand.

'Can we get back up?' Kosh was eager to know, and his face looked up at the opening above them like a man treading water at the bottom of a deep well.

It had been a mistake to bring him here, Ash thought grimly.

'Of course. It isn't that steep,' he reassured his old friend. 'Come on, you old fool.'

The slope was slick like the rest of the floors of the warren. The hardened strands of bile that covered it held a sticky residue which plucked ever so slightly at the soles of his feet. Below, the arching passage swallowed itself in a blackness deeper than night, into which the longhunter was following his cat.

There was something unhinged about a person who would choose to do this alone for a living, and only now was Ash starting to fully appreciate that fact. What twist in a man's life drove him towards such a lonely death as this one?

He followed after the longhunter with a worsening feeling of dread in his belly, the men hushed behind him. Ash had offered each of them an advance in gold and a promised small fortune in Milk for their aid in this, but right now that hardly seemed enough.

'I can't breathe,' the younger Caffey brother was saying over and over. 'This stench is sucking the life from me.'

'Go back then if it's too much for you,' said the older brother.

The air was even hotter now, unlike any cave system he had ever known. Ash could feel the heat pulsing into his bare soles from the floor as though it was rising up through the earth. The walls were sweating with humidity. He stumbled as Kosh bumped into his back, the man mumbling words of apology in a slurred voice.

Ash was little better. His senses reeled from the thick brew he was breathing in. Through his eyelashes, the flutters of the longhunter's torchlight swam and took on a life of their own; a fiery winged creature trying to rise free from the wooden stake that ensnared it, snapping out towards his face. From his own torch a drop of burning sap fell on his arm and he held the flames further away, not daring to look up at the other fire creature struggling in his grasp.

'Hallucinations,' he said to Cole quietly. 'Coming on strong.'

'Aye,' replied the longhunter, and when he spoke on there was a tremor in his voice. 'I keep seeing a wild native youth lurking in the side tunnels.'

'What does he want?' Ash whispered hotly, and he found his gaze flickering to the passage they were passing, caught by the tussles of shadows within.

'I think he wants us to turn back.' Cole deigned to look around at him, and his face leered in the ugly light of his torch like the mask of a demon. 'We're deep now. It only gets worse from here in. You think you can handle it?'

Ash responded with a snort of derision.

Echoes of movement sounded out as they emerged into a wide, low-slung chamber where kree scuttled one way and another into the many tunnels around the walls. Cole dribbled another line of burning sap on the ground from where they had just emerged. He jerked his head at the cat and the animal sniffed out the tunnels on the other side, careless now as she darted around the scuttling kree.

The group threaded their way across with dashes and sidesteps, and watched the cat choose one of the tunnels on the far side before disappearing into it, their breaths loud and ragged against the clicks and scratches of the kree.

What was that along the passage she had chosen? Ash wondered, and peered closer, seeing a faint glow of light eerily red beyond the black silhouette of the cat. Following after her, they found themselves emerging into another chamber, this one filled with a species of giant fungi growing on the floor, which glowed red then slowly purple, then red again. More tunnels led away from this one, all of them exactly the same.

Easy to get lost here, Ash thought, if you panicked and lost your head. But the cat knew where she was going, and she went straight for a large passage at the back. Ash stumbled into it after Cole, tugging Kosh on the rope behind him. The pain in his head was making it almost unbearable to keep his eyes open in the torchlight now. Squinting, he had to grope the wall to keep his balance and feel out the way.

'Easy now,' someone was saying.

'There's a bloody mountain over our heads,' rasped the youngest skyman of the group. 'Can't you feel it?'

A flame danced before Ash's face. He recoiled from it, raising a hand to shield his eyes, but a stranger's grip shook his shoulder and he saw that it was only Cole, stopped now in a high space as massive as the first one they had entered, lit by more of the strangely glowing mushrooms around the walls.

Ash gazed out across the heaving space to the absurd form that lay across its breadth. Open-mouthed, they all gazed in awe.

The queen kree was the colour and translucency of amber; a great, pulsing worm of a thing with liquid-filled sacs for a body, lit from within by a string of glowing golden pearls.

'Huh,' exclaimed Kosh in Honshu. 'A slug the size of a galleon.'

So they had reached their goal at last. The source of Royal Milk.

Turning to face them all, the longhunter said breathlessly, 'Your heads are probably reeling by now but I need you to keep it together, understand? We need to be careful here.' And then he led the way towards the queen kree, waiting long moments for workers to clear a way for them to pass through. Ahead, the queen rose high towards the vaulted space of the ceiling, where more mushrooms glowed upside down, pulsing red and purple, a suitably nightmarish hue for this scene they trod through with heavy feet.

The creature lay in a shallow depression in the earth, lubricated by its own fragrant juices frothed into white foam along the sides of its body. There was a head somewhere at the end of it, lost beyond the angle of their perspective, though they could see the rear end well enough. It reminded Ash of a wasp, even as he saw a yellow egg sliding out from a stretching sphincter. Milk dribbled out around the shell of the egg as it slid out and fell into a puddle of juices. Warm, bad air wafted over them and they all staggered at the passing affront of it.

'Whoah,' Aléas said. 'I thought Baracha was bad.'

Quickly, workers scrambled in to take away the egg, but Cole was faster, sprinkling something from a vial along their path, stopping them in frantic confusion. Other workers, their abdomens engorged with amber liquid, waddled around to the head of the queen kree, where they fed food into her mouth.

Ash felt another splash of hot sap against his forearm. Noticed that the torch in his hand was well past the halfway mark already.

Cole had noticed too. 'We need to hurry,' their guide told them all, and he took the empty bladders from his belt and hurried down to the egg, which was larger than a wine barrel.

'Quickly,' said Ash to the others as he saw what Cole was doing. 'Get as much as you can.' But just then he gasped at a sudden piercing skewer through his temples and clenched a hand to his forehead. He almost toppled over.

'You all right?'

It was Kosh, watching Ash sway while his balance reeled around his feet.

'I'm fine. Stop wasting time.'

'You don't look fine.'

'Go!'

Through a grey fog he saw the men down in the pool of juices. Cole had rolled the egg on end and had cut a hole in the top of it. One by one the men were dunking their bladders into it, filling them full with fresh Royal Milk, while Cole swung his torch about at the kree workers gathering around them in interest.

'Make it quick!' he shouted and his voice echoed loudly around the chamber.

One by one they staggered back up to where Ash was trying to gather himself together, their sputtering, shortening torches spurring them onwards. He stumbled down with his own empty skins and filled them with the last of the Milk pooled at the bottom of the egg. The others were licking their fingers and grinning despite the kree looming around them. He did the same and thought he felt the pain recede a little, his vision starting to clear.

'Tastes vile,' he said to Cole.

'Needs to ferment first,' the man answered. 'It isn't potent yet. Is this enough for you?'

'I reckon so.'

'Good, I doubt we have the time to wait around for another egg to pop out.'

Ash nodded and took in the excited faces of the men, knew that he owed them more than he could ever repay them for their courage here.

Some workers followed them as they retreated back across the floor burdened with their bulging skins. It was the Milk they carried, Cole told them, and the scent of it on their skins. Unconcerned, he told Aléas to take the lead. 'Just follow the cat, she'll take us straight out.'

Behind them, in their wake, Cole sprinkled droplets from the vial to slow and confuse the following workers, and in a low tense voice urged the men to move faster.

*

Upwards they hurried, all of them moving along a sloping tunnel as fast as their heavy burdens of Milk would allow them, the rope tight between their waists and everyone panting hard now, the painted numbers on the skin of their backs glowing a pale green in the dimness.

Faces turned back occasionally along the line of torches; white beacons lit by the sputtering dripping flames above their heads. Big Dalas seemed as though he was trying to run for it, surging up even against the resistance of the rope, pulling Kosh and Ash and Cole behind him with all the power of a work zel.

'Clear a way!' they heard Aléas shout ahead, and in a rush they pressed themselves against the side of the tunnel, though in his lather, Dalas stepped to the wrong side so that the rope stretched tight across the passage, right in the way of a scuttling kree.

It was a large warrior, and the creature crashed into the rope then reared up on its six legs. Its jaws snapped the line in two.

'Leave it be!' Cole shouted, surging forwards as Dalas grabbed for the long-shafted axe he carried on his back.

But he was too late. With dreadlocks flying the big Corician swung the axehead and chopped through the nearest limb of the creature, causing it to swing round at him.

Steel sang as Ash and Kosh drew their blades too, both acting from instinct. Right next to the kree, Kosh whooped like the young man he had once been, shouting the fear from him.

'*No!*' screamed Cole.

Again the axehead swung. The winged blade sank deep into the kree's hood but failed to kill the creature outright, and in the next moment Dalas's fist was punching frantically as he went down beneath its frenzied attack, spines rattling across its back as though in a gale. Men were yelling now. Cole was still shouting, still telling them not to kill it. But Dalas was down there on the floor getting his flesh torn away.

In a rush, Ash and Kosh leapt in and tried to stab at the kree's vital underhood, a tricky feat while it was moving so fast, thrashing its maw over the prone man and stabbing at him with its tapered legs.

Teeth gritted, Ash clutched the edge of its carapace for leverage and felt the animal strength of it pushing and pulling him. Dalas was using the shaft of his axe to hold its jaws from his bloody throat, but the barbed lashes were doing their work on his face, and awfully so. Amongst all the pink and crimson, Ash caught a flash of the mute's manic white eyes, and saw the fight in them even now.

With a growl of intent Ash ducked low and skewered the kree's underhood with the best thrust he had in him, twisting the blade as it sank deep. The creature reared around to face him, the two still connected by the length of steel. Lashes whipped at his forearm, stripping the flesh from it, and Ash threw himself against the hilt to shove the blade even deeper until the kree's legs gave out on one side, and then the other.

The creature lay dead before him, its dark juices oozing out onto the floor.

Somewhere up ahead the cat was roaring.

'You bloody fools, you've gone and killed us all!' Cole shouted and surged past Ash to see what they had done. The longhunter had cut himself free from the rope. 'That kree blood will have the whole nest down on our heads!'

The ground seemed to be trembling, or did Ash only imagine

that, the thousands of kree converging on them from every direction?

Dalas gasped for a breath, though it came out as a bloody bubble which broke upon his ruined face. He made a strangled sound as though he was trying to speak, but then he was still. His eyes glazed over.

Dalas was gone, and what was left of him was enough to make Ash avert his veteran eyes.

From the tunnel behind them they heard the scrabbles of running kree.

'Run!' Cole yelled at the rest of the men staring at the still form of Dalas, and his voice broke the spell so that suddenly they were all moving, running up the tunnel as fast as they could.

Not wanting to slow them down, Ash cut through his own portion of rope then snatched up Dalas's bulging skins and threw them over his shoulder. He took a moment to unfasten the belt of grenades from the man's torso too, and with a final flourish he grabbed up the fallen torch and turned and cast it down the tunnel behind him, feeling the rush of air being pushed along it before he glimpsed the frantic glistening forms of kree warriors scrambling up towards him.

CHAPTER TWENTY-EIGHT

Survival

'Which way? Where are we going?'

'There – ahead of you – are you blind?'

'It's blocked by kree, you bloody fool.'

'*Then wave your torches at them!*'

'Where's Ash? Where's the longhunter?'

'Behind us I think.'

'Where's the cat gone then?'

'*I don't know!*'

Cole could hear their shouts echoing down the passageway as the skymen ran ahead, though his mind was too flown with the wildness of the moment to take it all in, the frantic last few seconds in which he had been hacking with his machete at a kree scout until it lay still. Fear was squirting through his guts.

Another muffled explosion shook the ground. A sudden wash of hot air rushed along the passage from behind, stabbing his ears with pressure. The old farlanders were tossing grenades back there, throwing them like firecrackers at the warriors giving chase.

He stumbled into a chamber filled with giant mushrooms, only to find the rest of the men waving their torches at the surrounding kree, trying to create a path through them, while young Aléas whistled for the cat.

Cole tried to remember precisely where they were within the warren, and shook his head to clear it. They were still deep, still far beneath the level that would take them upwards to the first main chamber of the nest. Workers pressed closer on all sides. Behind him, Ash and Kosh staggered out of the tunnel to rejoin them and to wave the group onwards.

Where's that damned cat, Cole wondered again, but then at the foot of one of the far tunnels he finally spotted a line of sap glowing like the fungi in the darkness.

'That way,' he gasped, pointing towards it.

With Ash tossing another grenade behind them, Cole surged across the chamber after the others' reckless haste, driving the kree workers back with his torch. He glimpsed more warriors converging on them as they hurried into the mouth of the tunnel, and then he noticed that the slope of this passage was taking them blessedly upwards.

Up he scrambled after the men's bobbing torches, as keen as the rest of them to seek the surface. But now he could hear more fighting behind him, and as Cole hurried onwards a debate was flashing through his head, whether to stop and help the old farlanders or to push on while they held the warriors at bay.

Images from the past flashed in Cole's mind, as though they had happened only yesterday: fighting retreats in the passages beneath the walls of the Shield, studded with the wild grimy faces of his comrades from the Specials, men and women alike, near-buried in collapsed tunnels with the nightmare of violence all around him. Blades and pistols flashing in the darkness, explosions rocking everything; sobbing as he fell back, sobbing as he left them to their fates.

Cursing to himself, Cole swung around with a whoosh of his torch and spotted the two old Rōshun not all that far back from him – a pair of naked figures dancing in the torchlight with their blades flashing faster than he would have ever believed, faster even than the kree.

Holy kush, look at them fight.

They were holding the kree back, those two old farlanders – with swords alone they were holding off a tunnel full of kree, filling it from side to side with bodies. But now a warrior was rearing up against the roof with its limbs scrabbling at Kosh, dislodging chunks of earth onto their heads while they fought it off, and Kosh tumbled backwards from an audible strike from one of its limbs.

It was enough to spur Cole downwards, hacking at the creature too, cleaving through one of its legs with his machete. In a rush of air its jaws swung around and knocked him into the wall with his breath and his torch and his machete all flying away from him.

No chance at all to regain his feet in those next desperate moments.

He glimpsed another warrior attacking Ash before the sight of it was blocked by the closer kree rearing over him. On his back, Cole snatched the two hooryas from his belt and used their crescent blades to fend off the kree's silent frenzy, the reek of the creature's attack scents filling his mouth and his head. As it lashed out at him Cole squirmed backwards along the wall, striking back blindly with the smaller punch-blades of the weapons, feeling the pain of every barbed lash against his arms, knowing that he was done for.

But not quite, not yet. Blinking through sweat, Cole glanced up to see the warrior turning on Kosh again, who was staggering about in the shadows thrashing his blade at its limbs. Kosh hacked through another limb, but the warrior side-swiped him with its jaws and caught his thigh. A crunch of bone and Kosh went tumbling one way and his leg another.

Cole scrambled to his feet in the precious moments it bought him. The warrior pounced, and he bent low and stabbed and stabbed again at its underhood, aiming for its eyes before he was smashed aside once more.

He glimpsed Kosh next to him. The Rōshun was yelling without sound at the sight of his missing leg, half gone now. Above them, the warrior thrashed blindly into the side of the passage.

Cole grabbed the fallen man and dragged him away from the creature. He fumbled to untie the loop of rope still fixed around his waist so he could tie off the wound, though it was difficult just then, for he was seeing images of war again in his mind, companions dying of shock from severed limbs just like this one, and they were making him shake.

'Ash!' he roared out with all his fury. '*Ash!*'

Backwards the old farlander danced, with his torch describing wild roaring arcs through the air, no chance yet to notice his friend bleeding to death behind him.

'I've got you,' Cole said down to the prone man, who gasped and squeezed his eyes shut in pain. He tightened the rope as a tourniquet but the blood kept spurting from Kosh's wound.

'Go,' Kosh told him through gritted teeth, and Cole saw that his lips were turning blue already. 'Get out of here.'

Another grenade exploded along the tunnel, another rush of hot air.

'Ash!'

At last the farlander saw Kosh lying there, and dropped to his fallen companion with rapid blinks of surprise.

'He's dying,' said Cole, then rose to the sound of screaming ahead, where the torches of the skymen were distant specks in the blackness. More damned trouble.

In that moment of pressure, the longhunter felt something brush against his side and turned to see that it was the cat, returned to him in those moments. His spirits soared just to see her alive.

Ash was already hauling Kosh onto his back, almost buckling from the weight of him. The farlander's expression was a mask of grim determination. Cole turned away from them, drawn by the sound of the cat growling down the sloping passage filled with kree carcasses.

Quickly he scooped up a fallen torch and threw it as far back as he could.

Suddenly Cole laughed aloud – a crazy, half-second laugh of hopelessness – for he saw the movements of kree massing behind the fallen bodies, trying to get past the dead warriors with their flailing limbs, dragging at them to clear the way. They were moments away from flooding the passage.

The longhunter took a step backwards.

'Ash. Your grenades there.'

*

Kosh's blood was spilling all over him.

'Let me down, let me down,' Kosh kept saying across his back, and each time he did so his voice grew a little fainter, a little closer to death.

Ash knew that he needed to staunch the wound of the severed leg somehow and that he needed to do it now, but there was no time.

'Save your breath,' he gasped at his failing friend on his back, truly frightened at last. He knew that he was losing him.

'Put me down,' panted Kosh again, and this time his wish was fulfilled. An explosion rumbled through the earth from behind, and then a sudden rush of hot air slapped Ash from his feet, spilling Kosh to the floor.

He crawled to Kosh and breathed down fast into his friend's sweaty features. Kosh's eyelids were flickering fast.

'I'm going down,' came his feeble voice from where he lay.

'No!' Ash commanded and slapped Kosh hard. 'Stay with me now. Stay awake!'

'I'm going down, Ash. I can feel it.'

'Kosh!' shouted Ash, and he yanked free one of the bulging skins of Milk from his belt, intending to pour some into Kosh's mouth, never mind that it had not fermented yet . . . But through his blurring vision he saw the fading pallor of Kosh's skin and the slowing rhythm of his shallow breaths, and knew that it was true, that it was too late.

Dripping sudden tears, Ash lay a hand on Kosh's bare, fluttering chest. In the torchlight he saw the tattoo there from their days in the revolution, the same design which adorned his own chest: the lines of a path converging into the distance towards a shining star.

'Kosh,' he said again with his voice breaking.

'My children,' Kosh's lips were mumbling. 'Where are my children?'

His eyes flared for a moment and seemed to focus on Ash. A hand rose without the strength to reach him. Ash gripped the sweaty hand and squeezed it with force, his own hand trembling.

'I'm going,' whispered Kosh with the last wisp of his breath.

His old friend lay still.

CHAPTER TWENTY-NINE

A Purging in Q'os

Kira dul Dubois, mother of the recently deceased Holy Matriarch, stared through clouds of steam at the shrunken figure splayed on the floor before her in his manacles and chains, and reflected on how easy it would be to stamp on his skull until there was nothing left but shattered bone and brain matter; this man who long, long ago, had been her first true lover.

But they remained only thoughts. Outwardly Kira was composed as she settled herself gently on the bench along the sweating wall of the vault and clasped her hands in her lap, waiting for the man to speak.

'You took your time,' the ancient sack of flesh and bones croaked to her from the floor, straining weakly against his bonds.

'Yes,' Kira rasped. 'In fact I took all the time that I could.'

In response he offered a dry retching sound; the man's closest approximation to laughter.

Nihilis had never laughed in those early days of the Empire, back when he had ruled as the first Holy Patriarch of Mann. Nor before then, when Mann had been nothing more than an urban cult with fingers reaching into every aspect of Q'osian life. Such things as laughter and smiles, he had told his worshipful followers, were for fools and the weak only, and they had all believed him, for of course it was true.

Yet now, all these decades later – that awful cough of laughter churning in her ears, a habit which Nihilis seemed to have developed only in his extreme old age. Perhaps living down here in seclusion had softened him over the years, these secret vaults that were a tomb for the still-living deep beneath the Empire's capital city of Q'os, where Nihilis had retreated over forty years ago after faking his own death – easier to rule a people, an empire, he had explained at the time, when no one knew you were ruling it at all, or that you were even still alive.

'Are you sore at me, little Kira?'

The words were a trap, and hovering in the tread of the snare Kira realized fully what she had just said to this man. She clenched her own withered hands together even harder, telling herself to be calm, to keep her mouth shut, to control her anger before it betrayed her entirely.

'You catch me in a foul mood tonight, my Patriarch, that is all.'

'You're always in a foul mood these days, Kira,' he replied, and she blinked at the naked hypocrisy of his words. But that was Nihilis for as long as she had known him. Always he had thrown at people the barbs which came most from his own unrecognized failings. 'Where have you been then, that I can smell smoke clinging to your robes so fiercely?'

She was amazed he could smell anything here amongst all the steam. It was a result of the Milk he supped upon endlessly to keep himself alive, heightening his senses.

'I was down visiting the Shambles. Some unrest has broken out in the streets. I thought I should see it for myself.'

'Oh?' he replied, though he seemed to be barely listening now.

She shut her false teeth with a crocodile clack, saying no more.

Nihilis, first Patriarch of Mann, screwed up his withered features and blew three fast pants of breath in an effort to maintain his focus of will. The man lay with his head clamped securely by wooden blocks, which trapped his forehead directly beneath the spout of a six-foot metal cone hanging from the ceiling. From the end of the cone dropped a slow steady drip of water, falling onto a furrowed brow that flinched involuntarily from each successive strike. Kira knew from her own experience that the water would be bitterly chilled and his head a maddening agony by now.

'Ah, the Shambles, the place of your birth,' he croaked aloud. 'I remember now. You came to us as little more than a street runner, a girl with barbs in her eyes willing to do anything.' A wet noise as he smacked his toothless gums together, and then the man opened his eyes against the droplets bursting against his head. 'Are the Bastards up to no good again?'

He referred to the recent strikes during the Augere du Mann, sparked by the burning down of one of the almshouses in the Shambles, where a gathering of the Bastards of Saint Charlos had been locked inside while the flames had consumed them all; an act which Kira herself had suggested to her daughter, the Holy Matriarch, in order to cower their organization.

'Yes. They appear to have occupied my family's mills.'

'What are their demands?'

'The usual fare. They complain that fourteen-hour working days are too much for them. That they should have two days off in every week. That they should be paid compensation even when they are too ill or injured to work.'

'Kill the ringleaders along with their families. Divide the rest with the usual methods. And do it quickly, before they raise an example for others to follow.'

He was quoting from his own writings, as he was wont to do in his more self-engorged moments, for Nihilis had written the manual on how to control unruly populations. Several of them, in fact.

Kira bit her tongue, trying to ignore how he stated the obvious as though she were a simpleton, trying to remind herself that it was only another technique of his to belittle and provoke, yet another method of control.

The city's Regulators were already setting into plan what Nihilis was advocating. Already they had moved snatch squads into position who would arrest those ringleaders still refusing to be swayed by gold or blackmail; prepared the chattēros of the city's newspapers with suitable briefs to reprint as stories in the morning, explaining why the bloody actions had been necessary. Fermented trouble and division amongst the Bastards themselves through the use of agitators and spies. Further afield, amongst the general population of the city, the Regulators would spread the official narrative wherever people met together socially, using agents paid to speak out as though they were only citizens enraged by these collective actions of the Bastards, which were clearly selfish and unpatriotic, and bad for them all.

Like a sickness, the Bastards would be isolated as much as was possible from the rest of the population, and then extinguished for good.

Yet care still needed to be taken. Push too hard at the wrong moment and you could have even worse on your hands, a full-scale uprising, as had happened in other cities of the Empire. Push too selectively, and suddenly you could have martyrs strengthening the very cause you were trying to crush.

Still, they would be dealt with. And quickly too, before her family's cartel lost even more desperately needed revenue flow than they already had. The Dubois clan was stretched to the limits as it was in terms of liquidity. Following the death of her daughter Sasheen, the Holy Matriarch, they had been forced to watch their shares in the family cartel plummeting in value even deeper than the rest of the markets now falling into decline, profits and confidence driven downwards by the unexpected collapse of crops in Ghazni.

'Kira?'

'Of course, the matter is being dealt with.'

A scream sounded through the open doorway of the steamy vault, long and frenzied in its torment before it faded to a sobbing voice that pleaded to be released; a woman who could take no more of her self-inflicted torture. Kira heard chains rattling from outside in the larger chamber beyond, where members of Nihilis's coterie were Purging themselves too – people buried alive with him down in these bright, subterranean vaults beneath the city, lit by strips of gaslights and reflective walls that made Kira's eyes hurt just to look at them.

Nihilis gritted his teeth fiercely. How many hours had he been doing this? How many days?

His one and only redeeming feature. He still puts himself through the Purgings, even now.

The man growled for the strength that it gave him, then spoke loudly to the roiling drifts of steam in the air. 'Mann is the faith of reason, of madness, of human desires,' he recited loudly. It was a passage from his Book of Truths, the Hidden Book. His favourite source when under extreme duress, when reaching the height of his Purging. 'Know only one thing of the divine flesh and you will know it all: life is the will to power and nothing more.'

What of love? Kira found herself asking in silence, and outwardly she blinked, startled at herself, as though some intruder had leaned close to her ear and whispered the words from nowhere.

Nihilis grinned, chewing his teeth in his madness, flinching from each collision of water against his skull. His gaunt face glistened wet from the tiny splashes. His small and narrowed eyes glowered at the cone hanging over him.

Perhaps he wasn't the only one who was insane, Kira considered, recalling the hours behind her now, the desire she had seized upon of crossing the river with her ageing Diplomat Quito for protection, hoping to return to the Shambles and her family home to make certain that her mother was safe.

Only to recall, in a startling moment of confusion in a smoky side street, that the house was gone and her mother long dead; decades dead.

Maybe we're all mad, she suddenly thought; another intruder whispering into her ear.

Kira dabbed the moisture from her face with a sleeve of her white robe, noticing how sodden the garment was becoming, and tried to calm the sudden distress in her mind. She wondered if she was in need of another Purging herself, so soon after the last one.

'Your daughter's death must have been hard on you,' he rasped across the chamber, as though sensing her tensions. 'I know you were both close.'

His words carried a force in them, and they struck tears into her eyes. She shut them forcibly, glad he could not see her from where he lay, that no one could see her.

Gather yourself. This is no place for weakness!

Skilfully, Kira sought out the well of black rage within her and dipped into it for strength.

'I do not wish to discuss my daughter with you, old man.'

A hiss from where he lay shackled.

'Old man is it? Yet you are older than I, at least in terms of your proximity to death. Do not presume to forget that.'

'After all we have been through, you would threaten me so openly?'

'You mean because we used to rut, once upon a time, so long ago now that I hardly recall it, even should I wish to? Or because we went through the Longest Night together, and the early forging of an empire? Perhaps, Kira, I only mean that I have the Milk to keep me vital, whereas you have only your few years remaining to you. Perhaps I only mean you should think of taking the Milk at last, while it may still do you some good?'

'You know why I do not partake of it.'

'I do?' He closed his eyes for a moment. 'Yes. You distrust the euphoria it brings about. You think it softens the divine flesh made sharp by Purgings.' Nihilis coughed, laughing again perhaps. Drool was dribbling from his lower face along with the rivulets of water. 'You think too much in absolutes,' he continued. 'Always too much the fundamentalist. I'm told it is why you and your daughter disagreed so often.'

'I told you I did not wish to discuss Sasheen.'

'I have little time for squeamishness, Kira. Your daughter is the reason our Khosian expedition remains in such a quagmire. She is the reason your family's star is now on the decline. And yet still you wish to think favourably of her, simply because she was your flesh and blood?'

'I will not say it again. Do not speak any more of this to me.'

'Or you will do what? Pounce across this room and strangle me?'

'I will do worse than that.'

Easy, Kira. Easy.

'Indeed? And what of the rest of your family? You know what would become of them if you took such an insane course of action.'

'Then save us both our losses. Do not talk any more of Sasheen.'

'Your grandson then? Cowering under his bed while the Rōshun came to slay him?'

Kira stood more quickly than she had done in years, filled with the roaring rage that wanted to carry her across the room so she could bend down and scoop out his eyes with her thumbnails. But Nihilis hissed again, chuckling, pleased with himself that he had provoked such a reaction in her, and the sound stopped Kira dead before she took a single step.

He could see her from here, if he turned his eyes to the side.

'You are going to Khos, Kira. You are going there to sort out this mess that your daughter so gallantly left behind for us.'

She stood there panting until she had regained some control of her temper, knowing that he had won, that he had got what he wanted from her. All these years and still she was a puppet on his strings. Kira stared down upon his frail body with its pierced and mutilated genitals and the scars from so many Purgings, loathing every fibre of his being.

How could such a creature be the conduit for all that she believed in, all that had given her meaning in this life; the divine flesh of Mann?

Her body trembling like a thing possessed, Kira listened to what he had to say.

'The Expeditionary Force remains divided and at war with itself. Romano should have wrested control of the army from Archgeneral Sparus by now, yet still the squabbles continue over its command. For his own part, the Little Eagle refuses to cut a deal. Since we both know his obstinacy is due to some misguided sense of loyalty to your family, I am sending you there in person to break them from their deadlock, so they may carry on to Bar-Khos.'

Pain in her palms from the bites of her fingernails.

Focus your anger. He's only using it against you!

It was a disaster, this command he was giving her. It offered Romano a chance at the empty throne, a chance at being the next Holy Patriarch of Mann if he was able to take Bar-Khos. It was everything her family had been fighting against, through their support of Sparus in distant Khos and the local contenders here in the capital.

Her old enemy Octas LeFall must have got to him at last, must have found a way to sway him.

'You wish me to be the one to aid the LeFalls in their ambitions for Romano? You must be out of your mind. I will do no such thing.'

'Oh, but you will.'

'Send someone else. The words hardly need to come from me.'

'You try my patience now,' he gasped. 'Quit this childish rebellion and do as you are told, woman. It is the only way you get to leave this room alive.'

I must buy Sparus some time!

Kira folded her hands within the sleeves of her robe and bowed her head in obedience, her stiff joints protesting with shoots of pain.

I must send him a missive. Instruct him to finish Romano before I have arrived.

'What is it, precisely, you would have me do?'

'You are to compel the Archgeneral into agreeing on joint command of the Expeditionary Force with Romano. You are to inform young Romano that if they indeed take the city of Bar-Khos first, his claims to the throne will be respected here in the capital.'

Kira's throat tightened even as she listened to his words. She knew the Archgeneral would rather take his own life than share his command with the young pretender Romano. Nihilis might as well be sending her to kill him.

Yet she was bound here, bound by whatever he told her to do, and her captivity only caused her hatred to boil.

She tried to speak, then had to start again.

'Surely, I could send a missive to achieve the same result?'

'No. When you are finished with Romano and the Little Eagle, you are to oversee our operation in Bar-Khos.'

Kira turned her head to one side in suspicion. 'You wish me to enter the city personally?' echoed her creaking voice.

'I do. It's vital that our operation there be in place by the time we surround the city. The traitors must be made ready. I want Bar-Khos before winter's end.'

Another scream sounded from outside. Nihilis glared at the ceiling, refusing with all his will now to blink at the concussions of water dripping down on him.

She bowed her head again, pulled by his invisible strings.

'I will do as you say, my Patriarch.'

'I know you will. All that matters is the city, Kira. Do this for me and your family will remain in my favour. Make certain that Bar-Khos falls.'

CHAPTER THIRTY

Left for Dead

At first Cole thought he was lying on his hard cot back in his Lucksore cabin, but when he tried to move he found that he could not, and that a great weight pressed down upon him.

Where am I then?

There seemed nothing to go on, no light or sound of any kind, nor memories of how he had got here.

Am I dead? Cole wondered absently, and the notion aroused a conflict of emotions deep within him.

Far away a deep rumble sounded out. He could feel it in his bones, and in doing so some life returned to him. Cole knew where he was now.

The longhunter cracked open his eyes. He was lying on a cot in an underground bunker, a room lit by a few low burning lanterns, with his ears pricking to heavy explosions rumbling through the ground above his head as they dislodged trickles of earth.

He was back in Bar-Khos, deep beneath the walls of the Shield in the stifling confines of the tunnels, where he had been fighting since the second year of the siege as a Special; a husband and father stunned ever deeper into himself by the violence of war.

Specials were snoring away fitfully in bunks stacked around the room. At a table, Ruby and Finch played cards for their usual exchange of minor sexual favours, while the dogs lay curled on the matting of the floor, farting and dozing. All day long the Imperial Fourth Army had been assaulting the walls of the Shield above them, as they had been for three consecutive years now, and everyone expected something to happen down here too – a breach from the enemy tunnels, an enemy mine blowing up close enough to bury all of them alive. Yet all they could do was while away the hours as they waited for whatever awful thing was going to happen.

Such was life for Specials garrisoned in a forward bunker beneath the Shield. Endless boredom and tattered nerves while they anticipated the very worst.

Other ears were pricking as well as his own, those of the guard dogs curled together on the matting, where a single red-coated prairie lynx lay amongst them. When the big cat rose up at a distant sound and listened for a few long moments with ears twitching, Cole was the only one to notice. His eyes tracked the cat as she stretched and padded out through the open doorway, and then he was prompted to rise and follow after her, thinking to relieve himself as the cat herself no doubt intended.

Outside in the main tunnel he saw the heavy metal door that blocked the way ahead, where the tunnel extended even further beyond the city walls, out towards the enemy. To one side of the door the sentry sat on a chair with his chin resting on his breastplate, lightly snoring. Cole couldn't recall the man's name, hadn't bothered to learn it; just another replacement brought in to replace the last. He picked up a shard of gravel from the planking on the floor and tossed it at the soldier's helm with a thunk.

'Next time you fall asleep on watch I'll slit your throat myself,' he declared to the surprised and blinking young man.

Cole followed the cat into a side passage, a dead end where the latrine was to be found. But he found the latrine passage buried in blackness, and he swore at whoever had allowed the lantern to go out and went back for a lit one. The sentry was dozing again where he sat.

This time he picked up a rock the size of his fist, and threw it with all his might at the man's helm.

'Stay awake!' he hissed down at the soldier sprawled on the floor, and for good measure he kicked the chair to pieces so the man could no longer rest in it, and because it felt good.

Panting, Cole returned to the latrine with a lantern held aloft before him, flooding the darkness ahead with its yellow flickering circle of light. The air was fetid here, and dank. He turned a corner and walked on until the edge of light swept across the back of the prairie lynx. The red hair along her spine was standing up in ruffs, and she was fixed to the spot and staring at something while a low, barely audible growl rumbled from her throat. His hand grasped the hilt of one of his hooryas, and he took another cautious step forward to stand beside the cat.

Cole grunted in surprise.

A man was standing in their way with his broad back turned to them. It was another Special, for the creases in his black leathers glistened in the lamplight that Cole held out towards him.

The man stood perfectly still, arms dangling by his sides.

'Mani?' Cole said to the figure ahead. 'Is that you?'

Nothing. No movement or response. Cole could hear a wet noise in the gloom, like something bubbling. His nose flared at the harsh metal scent of blood. The cat growled now, low and menacing.

With careful slowness, Cole pulled the hoorya from his belt, gripping the hilt so that the curved blade fitted around his knuckles and the edge of his hand.

'*Mani!*' he whispered with sudden fear.

Movement. The figure toppled against the side of the tunnel then slid down it. The cat cried out loudly.

The enemy – they were here!

Too late he sensed someone dropping down at his back, and then a pain sliced into Cole's throat as a wire wrapped around his throat.

He dropped the lantern in fright and reached a hand to the wire that was suddenly choking the life from him while the cat snapped at someone ahead. Across the planking of the tunnel floor the lantern rolled and nearly went out, save for a wan glow around the quietly desperate scuffles of their boots.

Panicking now, Cole shoved himself backwards and crushed his attacker against the side of the tunnel, feeling the hotness of blood seeping down his neck. He slashed wildly behind him with his hoorya but hit only thin air, though he managed to loosen the garrotte with his fingers, just enough to gain a desperate sip of breath. The cat was tearing away at someone now with her claws. A third figure came out of the darkness and flashed in front of his vision.

Cole felt a blow to his side, once, twice, three times, before he looked down to see the knife blade darting through his leathers. No pain from the blows but simple shock at what he was witnessing. His own blade lashed out in frantic effort. Cole couldn't breathe. The wire seemed to be cutting his fingers in two. Later, he would be left with a ragged scar across his throat that would cause people to stare in wonder that he hadn't died from such a wound. But that was later, and this was now, and a knife was again being thrust into his side repeatedly while a hand held his own blade at bay.

Die, kushing die, his assailant behind was grunting into his ear in accented Trade, while Cole kicked out with his boot at the man stabbing him from the front. The blind staggering terror was overwhelming. Every fibre of his body sang of its impending death.

But now the cat had a toothy grip on the enemy hand holding the knife, and the shouts of Cole's comrades were sounding along the tunnel blessedly close. The garrotte around his neck loosened a fraction more.

This was the moment, Cole's watching, delirious mind reminded him with calm detachment.

This was it, right here, when you could take no more of the war.

*

Cole tried to mutter something as he came to his senses, something from a time long gone now. But he found that blood and dirt had filled his mouth, and he coughed and spat to clear it.

The longhunter opened his eyes and saw only motes of colour floating in the utter blackness. Fear clamped his insides, for the taste of the dirt reminded him of where he truly was now. Not the tunnels beneath the Shield but deep inside a kree hive. Buried in a collapsed tunnel after the belt of grenades had all exploded behind him.

He'd been left for dead by the others, he realized. Buried alive.

Panic seized him so entirely he shook from it, and for the longest of times Cole simply lay there gasping and quivering from the shock of his predicament, his worst of fears made real. For Cole had lived these moments before in his mind, imagining how his companions had felt before they had suffocated, those he had left trapped in tunnels that had come down on them.

Guilt, that age-old guilt of the survivor. From that one stabbing emotion came other thoughts and feelings, and from those, Cole was slowly able to gather himself together. At last a cool numbness settled over him like a blanket of frost, and in his mind he started to ask the questions most in need of an answer.

How could he get out of here?

When he tried to move, Cole could feel the loose earth and rocks covering much of his body. The longhunter stilled himself for a moment, his panted breaths loud in his ears. He could hear the sound of nearby scrabbling from behind.

It was the kree, busy clearing out the debris that blocked the passage.

Cole groaned as he tugged his arm until it came loose with a spill of earth and rock. Not broken, thank Mercy. Just badly bruised. There was some space around his head, it seemed. Shifting about, he felt something damp pressing against his face – a bladder of Milk split open before him. Cole stretched his neck out and slurped at the puddle of Milk and grit, wetting his lips and tongue with the stuff.

A soft glow filled his belly, and he felt better for it, enough at least that he could think straight.

Get out of here before the kree find you. Get to the surface before the others leave without you.

With a sharp gasp the longhunter pulled himself a tiny fraction forward; the whole earth shifted around his legs, and he found it an easier effort than he'd been expecting. He was near the edge of the collapse where the rubble remained loose, and with renewed hope he dug his elbows into the dirt and pulled again, then repeated the process until he had dragged himself free from the debris which trapped him.

Now there was a foot of clearance above his head. Cole moved faster, scraping his scalp against the top of the tunnel. He slithered forwards until the shifting surface began to slope downwards, hissing at the returning sensation of his limbs.

He was startled when his hand settled on a mound of fur, recoiled back from it.

It's the cat. It's only the cat.

In haste he shoved aside the earth and small rocks until her head was clear of them, and he could cradle it in his filthy hands.

His companion was still warm to the touch. She was barely breathing though. Behind them the sounds of the kree were getting louder now. Summoning his strength, the longhunter dug with his hands, not caring for the skin that he tore loose, digging fast until the cat was clear.

On all fours he scrambled back for the split skin of Milk and returned with it to the cat. Hastily he held it up and dribbled a few drops into the animal's muzzle, praying that it worked.

As he did so he was picturing the tunnels of the Shield again, and that first time she had saved his life in the desperate darkness. And how he had taken her home with him after that to the family farm, rescuing her from a war he could no longer abide – a war for which he had then deserted his wife and young son Nico.

The Milk was too fresh to have much of an effect, but it was enough.

She whimpered. Fluttered her ears. Seemed to breathe a little easier.

'Come on, girl,' he told the cat gratefully and scooped her up into his arms. 'It's all right, I've got you now. We're going *home*.'

CHAPTER THIRTY-ONE

Reese's Worthless Bastard

'Go on now!' the woman called out to the zel straining to haul the wagon up the steepening road.

Her call still echoing across the land, Reese rose from the shaking seat and flicked the reins across Happy's back, clicking her tongue as the animal's shod hooves slipped on the wet stones and the wagon rocked slowly upwards, the empty potcheen bottles in the back tinkling noisily where Los had padded them poorly with hay.

Happy always struggled now on this portion of the coast road on their return journeys from Bar-Khos. The animal was getting too old for this work, but with the ongoing siege and the requirements of the army there was a shortage of heavy zels in Khos. So Reese only snapped the reins across his back more urgently, praying that this would not be the day he was finally unable to make it to the crest of the hill.

'Well don't just sit there!' she scolded Los, lolling in silence beside her, thinking of games of Rash or women or whatever it was he thought about in the sly privacy of his own head. With a scowl her lover snapped from his reverie and jumped down from the cart to lighten the load.

'Help him, will you?' she called down at him, and he made his way up to Happy, where he took the zel's bit to lead the old animal onwards.

'Maybe it's time you thought of buying a new zel,' he called over his shoulder. 'Sell this old nag for meat. I'll find us a new one for the right price.'

Reese scowled too, and in her coat and trouser-dress she jumped down with the reins still in her hands to walk alongside the cart. From there she fixed her stare on Los's back, his oiled blond locks and fine cloak of marine blue ruffling in the sea breeze. 'You'll buy one stolen from the army is what you mean.'

'So?'

Reese shook her head in exasperation. 'Los, I'm not selling Happy for meat. He's been with me since he was a foal. I practically raised him.'

'Well if he doesn't make it up this hill I can't see that you have much choice in the matter.'

'Go on, boy!' she shouted through her teeth, and snapped the reins over the zel's back with a crack. 'Go on!'

Happy snorted steam through the wintry air and jerked his head up, started pulling with a little more certainty and vigour. A few more surging strides brought them to the crest at last where the road levelled off again, and a few more dragged up the wagon behind. Time enough to catch his breath, Reese thought as she tugged him to a stop, and the lathered old zel looked back at her with his brown eyes, snorted some more and flicked his tail as though to enquire what they were waiting for, no problems here. Silently relieved, Reese climbed back onto the seat while Los did likewise, the cart rocking on its suspension.

What did Los know anyway? she thought hotly by his side, not looking at him. A considerate lover he might be, but that was as far as his selflessness seemed to go in this world, no matter how many chances she gave him to show her otherwise. Los had no notion of what she spoke when she talked about Happy, and no way to grasp it. To him, it was a simple matter of money and cold reason.

To Reese, though, if you were going to use animals as your own personal labourers, like your own personal slaves even, then the very least you could do was treat them with the full dignity they deserved, with whatever kindness you could find in your heart for them.

*

'Drink?' Los asked with a grin, and refreshed himself with a sip of wine from his leather flask.

She answered by plucking it from his hand, and sampled some of the cheap, bitter wine with a wince before tossing it back at him.

Quiet today, Reese thought, picking out the isolated farmhouses dotting the rugged coastal landscape, spotting only the occasional wisp of smoke from their chimneys, over which the far mountains rose steep and tall from the sea.

She was glad to be away from the city and on her way home again. Swiping a lock of red hair from her face, Reese twisted on the seat to look back at the broad delta of the Chilos, the sacred river flowing out into the chapped waters of the Bay of Squalls under a haze of thin mist. A flock of white spearbills wheeled over the delta towards the bay, their red-tipped wings curving through the air. Beyond them the city of Bar-Khos was a smudge on the horizon, where smoke rose lazily from the Shield on the Lansway, and rose too from the cremation pyres of the countless thousands who had fallen defending them.

An air of foreboding had filled the streets of the city during their morning spent there selling potcheen. Dirty faces, hungry and desperate, watching the endless lines of wagons carrying the dead from the Shield. Widows wailing in grief. Children dumbfounded and strangely still.

Too much for Reese, she had found. Too many reminders of all she had lost herself.

Bored, Los was tapping his heel against the driving board in rhythm to some taverna song he liked, staring off into nothing, disconnected from it all.

'Rain coming,' she told him, looking off at the dark clouds rolling in from the north.

'Better get moving then,' he said and took another quick drink.

They set off once more at a gentle gait, riding the racket of the cart along the quietness of the coastal road while Los protested that they should hurry, never mind if the zel was tired. It seemed to annoy him, her insistence on going easy on Happy. As though she was choosing the zel's wellbeing over his own.

'If you'd do as I keep saying and move to the city with me, we wouldn't have to travel all this way every time.'

She scowled at this handsome man ten years younger than herself. 'And what would I do for a living? Sit on your lap making you look good while you lose more of our money at Rash?'

'Hey, everyone has their losing streaks,' he protested. 'At least we'd be safe there.'

Safe, she reflected with her shoulders tensing from the distant cannon fire on the Shield, knowing that he only wanted to be close to the tavernas and whores of the city.

'I'm not moving to Bar-Khos, Los, that's final. The cottage is the only home that I know.'

'Suit yourself.'

'I will.'

'Do that then.'

She sighed with resigned sadness, looking out at the empty landscape around them, at another farmhouse boarded up and deserted, its occupants already fled to the city.

'You're ten years too young for me, Los, that's the truth of it.'

'Nonsense, I'm in my prime and so are you.' And as he spoke he lowered the tone of his voice, just enough for it to matter. 'You'll be thinking differently, after we get home and out of these dusty clothes.'

Gently he brushed his fingers down the nape of her neck. Reese wore a cream blouse beneath her winter coat, and it was unbuttoned in her usual fashion to show off her cleavage. Los had been glancing all day long at her curves and grinning when another man did the same, working himself up for what he imagined was to come later. Now, alone at last, he trailed his fingernails over the goosebumped skin on display, then turned the hand and slid it down under the soft cotton, cupping her left breast.

It reminded her of Cole, the way that he touched her. And maybe, when all was accounted for, that was the only reason why she put up with him. That and the fact that she loathed to be alone.

Today she had no passion for her lover, however, felt nothing stirring within her at his touch. She was so indifferent in fact that she allowed him to carry on without responding, for at least she was warmed by the cup of his hand and the close press of his body.

'I want you,' he breathed into the nape of her neck, kissing her gently.

Sighing inwardly, Reese tilted her head back to look up at the darkening sky while he nibbled on her neck and squeezed harder, whispering into her ear as he held her closer. But a sudden whinny from Happy interrupted him, the zel responding to the sound of hoof beats ahead of them on the road.

Startled, they both looked up to see riders approaching, soldiers wearing the red cloaks of Guards. Los muttered and drew his hand away while Reese hastily buttoned up her coat.

With jingles of harnesses and armour the soldiers reigned in next to them, their zels noisily spewing steam.

'Reese,' declared one of the riders with a nod, and she looked closer at the bearded face beneath the helm and saw that it was Anon, an old friend of her husband from his earliest days in the siege. She hadn't seen the man in years. 'You look well,' he told her with his blue eyes glimmering, and shot a glance towards Los.

'Is there news, Anon? You seem in a hurry.'

'Aye lass, we're advising everyone east of the Chilos to evacuate to the city at once.'

'They can't be so close yet, surely?'

'Some advance forces are crossing the Storm river. We're hearing reports of Mannian scouts and slaver parties to the north of here. Looks like they might be pressing for the coast.'

'Sweet Mercy,' she exclaimed and looked about her. Suddenly the mood of the familiar land was a different one, stark and ominous.

'Can you hold them off?'

The jerk of his head said unlikely, but his mouth spoke otherwise. 'We'll certainly try.'

Los was studying the dying light in the western sky. 'We'd better pack what we can and head back to the city tonight.'

'I'd advise it,' Anon told him with a nod, and his zel was jittery beneath him like the rest of them, sniffing and snicking over Happy as Happy did the same.

She saw how tired the riders were, how eager they were to be in from the cold.

'Thank you,' she told Anon and coaxed Happy onwards again, offering a brief smile to the man. 'Stay safe.'

He nodded in farewell then took a final glance at Los. The soldier had been a close friend to Cole, back when they had both been Specials. Perhaps he thought she should live the rest of her life in mourning, pining alone over the husband who had run out on her and their son.

In silence, Los stared back at the departing riders.

He turned to Happy and shouted, 'Come on, boy!' then clicked his tongue even as Reese did the same, setting them off again.

Together they watched the north ridgelines as though a raiding party was about to come over the nearest one at any moment.

'I told you this would happen,' he growled at her more than once.

Reese ignored him, settling her focus on the road ahead. She lashed the reins across Happy's back, not sparing him now. They were going along at a good clip when the sidetrack appeared to their left and Happy took it without guidance, the shod wheels of the wagon sliding out along the dirt before it straightened again, the empty bottles rattling in a chorus of noise as they bounced up the dirt track through the trees and the tall stands of cane grass without slowing. Rounding the bend, Reese saw the cottage and realized she'd been holding her breath all this time, but her home was still there unmolested as they came to a rickety stop in the yard.

Mannians, so close!

Los's face was tight with worry. His brows were knitted together in that way of his whenever he was thinking hard; always as though he was thinking for his life. Over his head the sky was dark with clouds now. Cold drops of sleet were falling all around them, though Reese had jumped from the cart and was unloading the crates of bottles before she realized the fact.

'My sister-in-law will take us in,' she called over her shoulder as her long hair grew wet against her head. 'She already asked if we wanted to stay with them.'

No answer from him. Reese stopped what she was doing and wiped her eyes clear. She turned to see where Los had disappeared to. The front door of the cottage lay open.

'Los!'

For some reason the hairs stiffened on the back of her neck. Reese froze where she stood in the falling sleet, seized by the curious sensation that she knew what was going to happen next. She couldn't move, the feeling was so strong, couldn't think.

Out he came some moments later, scattering the yard's chickens from his stride. His old knapsack was on his back, stuffed too full to tie it closed.

Los threw up the hood of his cloak and strode past her without uttering a word. He didn't even have the decency to meet her eye.

Now the mood of the land was a lonely one too.

'Los?'

He strode for the cart without looking backwards.

He's leaving you, came the dull thud of words in her head, though she already knew it; knew too that she had been waiting for this moment for a long time now. Desertion was always what Reese expected most of all.

'You worthless bastard!' she shouted at his back, rushing to the cottage even as she yelled out. 'You keep your hands off that wagon or I'll shoot you where you stand!' She went in through the door and through the parlour into the kitchen. At once, she saw the floorboard removed in the corner next to the stove, and the small wooden box lying open and empty.

Huffing and puffing Reese rushed back out with her husband's old scattergun in her hands, but Los was already riding away on the back of Happy.

'You lying cheating *bastard*!' she screamed as she broke the gun open and slotted a cartridge into place. 'Bring that money back to me!'

He was trying to kick the zel to go faster, but old Happy was tired and barely trotting down the track towards the bend. She aimed the gun squarely at the man's back.

Reese gritted her teeth together to see the deed through, but at the last moment she growled and swung the barrel straight up into the sky and pulled the trigger. The explosion knocked her back a step, and when she opened her eyes again the track was empty. They were gone.

You could trust no one in this life to stay around when the going got tough. Not your lover nor your husband. Not even your own son.

Reese Calvone screamed at the clouds over her head as the heavy sleet beat down hard against her face.

CHAPTER THIRTY-TWO

This Boy Kills

Far northwards the sleet was falling too in the Windrush forest. It slashed through the canopy loud enough to deaden the ears of the riders hunched in their saddles below, slowly following a track between widely spaced trees and mounds of snow, every one of them as cold and miserable and weary as their mounts.

Wrapped in her heavy feather coat, Shard the Dreamer gazed gloomily from beneath the brim of her travel hat, the same battered leather hat that she had worn all the way to the Alhazii desert and back. In her belt was her trusty Contrarè boneknife, which had once belonged to her father, light yet razor sharp.

Shard was having trouble remembering what they were supposed to be doing here in the great forest of the Windrush, for she was still soaring today despite the copious amount of cold tannis tea she had been throwing down her neck from her flasks. Since entering the forest Shard had been this way, barely able to sit in her saddle without feeling light-headed and dizzy. The rushes from the worm's juices were intensifying. Not to mention the cramps in her abdomen, which had been steadily worsening until now she was almost doubled over by them, waves of pain strong enough that she gritted her teeth while she rode them out, barely able to speak or see through her smarting eyes.

The worm's juices were eating at her insides, she suspected, just as she'd been told could happen by the old shamans of the deep desert if her body continued to reject it. This pain might only grow worse over time, yet there was little she could do about it here in the forest, save for nursing her hopes that the condition would settle down by itself, that the worm would be accepted.

Lightning seemed to flicker through the air of the cold day, coalescing in the corners of her eyes. It was hard to look at the falling sleet, all those streaks of motion dissecting the air. Shard rocked in the saddle with her head down under her hood, eyes nearly closed.

Shard, are you there?

She blinked, wondering if she was hallucinating again, but then the voice of her rook assistant repeated itself, clear and strong through the link of their farcrys.

Blame. Is that you?

Yes. Just checking in. How are you coping with the worm?

His concern brought a crease of a smile to her Contrarè features. For a moment Shard regretted leaving her assistant back in the city to oversee their rooking activities.

Coming on strong now. Nothing I can't handle. Anything to report?

Yes. Some increased activity around our friendly farcrys. I think it's Seech's people. I've enlisted some help from the rooks at the Academy to keep communications open.

Good. Keep me informed.

Will do.

Anything else?

No. Just wanted to make sure you were fine.

Couldn't be better. Speak later.

Yup.

Shard snapped the connection with the Black Dream and the living farcry belted around her waist stopped breathing so rapidly, returning to its dormant phase once more.

At least she could recall now what they were doing here. She tugged her hood back a little so she could see around her through the sleet. The forest seemed empty of human habitation, though she knew that was only an illusion caused by the vast space of the Windrush and the Contrarès' famed skills of stealth. That morning they had come across the remains of a Mannian Purdah scout hanging head first from a tree, his body frozen stiff, including the awful sight of entrails dangling from his open stomach. The man had been hanging there weeks by the look of the carved signs of warning on the tree's trunk.

Later that day with the odd flurry of snow drifting down through the trees, a Contrarè village halted the party in their tracks, a circle of huts on stilts standing in the silence of a clearing. It was obvious the village had been abandoned though, the people no doubt having moved deeper into the forest for safety. Sticks dangled on a rope from one of the platforms, lashed together in a seemingly random fashion, though they told where the people had gone to those who could read them, their own tribe.

Cautiously, the party circled around the stilted structures and carried onwards.

'Where are they?' Coya muttered with concern, ahead of her in the line. 'I thought finding a Contrarè guide to lead us to the elders would have been the easiest thing of all.'

'Give it time,' Shard drawled thickly. 'They're out there.'

When she spotted a stand of mature cane grass, Shard cut down the thickest stem with her boneknife and banged it against the passing trunks of trees. The hollow stick cracked out through the dense forest in a simple rhythm she had learned from her father, who had rapped it out on the door frame every day he returned home, declaring his presence and his peaceful intent. She could only hope that the Windrush Longalla shared the same meanings of rhythm as their southern cousins in Pathia, her own people the Black Hands.

Once we too used to live as a free people, her parents had often told Shard and her sisters around the fire on the darkest nights of the Starving Fox, their eyes shining with emotion, surrounded by the walls of their urban home. *Once we lived without money and greed and the need to sell our labour to survive, for we had our land, and the land supported us as it supports all living things, and we were content.*

Then why don't you go back there? Shard had sometimes scoffed at them, for their sentimental nostalgia had often angered her. Always they talked as though life had once been better than this, as though all the things that dazzled Shard in her youth – the skyships and sea galleons, the fireworks and festivals, the street plays and bazaars selling a thousand colourful things – all were somehow inherently bad.

We did not always live this way, her father had often insisted, as though it meant the world to him that she and her sisters understood. *Once we lived in the forests simple and carefree, where all living things were our kin.*

Shard had barely been able to imagine it, living rough in the forest like a half-naked savage, living like a wild animal amongst all the others. How banal such a life must have been back then. How terrifying in its ignorance.

Still, she had always allowed her father the last word in these things, for despite his backwards ways she loved him deeply, and in the end his tired shining eyes had usually quelled her temper, so that she would nod along with her sisters, pretending to comprehend.

In her memories of those times, and despite all his talk of the Contrarès' relaxed old ways, her father had always seemed a busy man, rarely resting. Back then in Sheaf he had made a living as an independent street crier, plodding the streets of the city calling out the day's news in exchange for random coin, banging hollow sticks of cane grass together in the Contrarè fashion while most other criers used bells. Every day he ranged across the city like that, shouting his voice raw.

Mostly he had told as much good news as he did bad, for the citizens tipped him better that way, and so he was able to feed his family. Besides, he would say, who really wanted to hear endless bad news in their ears day after day and nothing else? Such a life would drive people insane with fear and negativity.

With the fall of Pathia, however, to forces of the Mannian Empire, all of that was to change. Under their new rulers, independent criers were hounded from the streets one by one until all of them were gone. Her father was the very last to go underground.

Soon everything seemed to be changing. Beliefs became ever more uniform. Only the creed of Mann was permissible, *there is no god but thine own self*: a form of self-worship which glorified human beings alone, or certain humans anyway, and gave them dominion over all living things to do as they wished with. Beliefs which ran entirely opposite to those of the urban Contrarè, who continued to worship the world around them in awe, who considered all living things as reflections of the sacred.

Helplessly, the people of the city watched on as the world they had known was dismantled around them by the occupation forces of Mann, their lives essentially looted.

Tolls became the norm for everything, for the drinking water in the city, for the roads they walked on, for the very roofs over their heads, as though their taxes hadn't already been high enough. The people were squeezed for all they were worth, so that they had to work ever harder just to stay in the same place as before.

Worse still was the change of atmosphere in the city, the slow shift in the attitudes of people towards others, promoted by the news-sheets and the official creed, which criticized the voiceless and extolled the powerful. Crimes by those of a certain ethnicity were highlighted over others. The poor and disabled became figures of public mockery, as though their circumstances were all of their own making; as though anyone's ever was in life. In particular, the Contrarè found themselves singled out once again, labelled dangerous extremists whenever their wild cousins in the remaining forests made some kind of stand.

Divide and conquer, her father had explained to Shard and her sisters in their huddles around the evening fire. Driving wedges into cracks that already existed between people. The poor pitted against the lesser poor. The believers against the non-believers. Man against woman and dog against dog. Everything split apart and isolated and individualized so as to be easier to control. Nothing new in this, he had said, except how good the Empire was at it.

When the first purges had begun, word reached her father that he was on the list. As a family, they had fled to the neighbouring Free Ports.

Shard exhaled her memories in a plume of steam and stopped banging the trees on her way past, for her hand had grown sore from it, and still no Longalla had shown themselves.

The Dreamer swayed in her saddle and washed down her thirst with another pull from her flask, swallowing the bitterly cold tannis tea and wondering what her father would make of her now, travelling through the legendary Windrush forest, a place he had spoken of visiting for many years.

She should bring him here, she thought now. Once the war was over, she should coax her father and mother from their peaceful home in the eastern ports and bring them here to meet their Longalla cousins. He would like that. They both would.

That was, if this war ever did end.

And if they somehow managed to win it.

*

Three days of riding through the forest in the bitter cold had sapped the talk from all of them. No one spoke save for when it was neces-sary, not even the usually talkative Coya.

The Dreamer's mind swayed and soared while the cramps in her belly grew even worse. Seeing the pain in her eyes, Coya offered her some of the cakes of hazii weed which he carried with him everywhere, a mixture of oatmeal and honey and strong Minosian bud, a comforting and clear-headed relief that soon soothed the pains in her abdomen and lifted her spirits too.

Onwards they rode in silence, the rangers leading the way.

Shard had taken the measure of the rangers over the previous days, dressed in buckskins personalized with colourful braids and tassels beneath grey cloaks of wool, and sporting hats of all kinds and dark snow-goggles over their eyes.

They were veterans all of them, young and old alike. The oldest was the crop-headed captain known as Gamorre, a woman at ease commanding the men of her squad; the youngest a man called Xeno, armed with a sniper's longrifle, his shaven scalp tattooed with the legend, *This Boy Kills*.

Each of the rangers wore an iron picket pin like a brooch on their cloaks, which could be driven into the ground to tether zels in open country, though she knew they represented much more than that. When facing the enemy in times of action, some of the famed rangers of the Volunteers were known to drive the pins into the ground where they stood, to which they would tether their own selves with a cord of leather, refusing to move from the spot no matter the odds, until killed or relieved by one of their companions. Such was the spirit of these fighting men and women, these highly trained defenders of the democras.

Also assigned to the squad were the two medicos, who cut a different appearance entirely in the black leathers of the Specials, or Special Operations, Khos's own elite volunteers. The older of the pair, Kris, was prone to shooting dark looks in Shard's direction, as though the woman distrusted her very appearance. Her medico apprentice, though, the younger, smaller woman, was more open in Shard's company, more curious about what she was.

Often, whenever they stopped to water and rest the zels, the young woman would share a few words with Shard, a few breathless questions about what she did and how she did it, marvelling at the very notion of a Dreamer or a rook.

Curl was her name, and it seemed that she was a refugee just as

Shard was, escaped from the wasteland that was now the island of Lagos. She was also a survivor of the battle of Chey-Wes.

Curl happened to be strikingly beautiful, so much so that the men often watched her from the corners of their eyes as though entirely unable to stop themselves. Marsh stared openly with longing. She was a woman worthy of envy, just as Shard had once been before her features had been scarred in the deep desert, and she had been forced to wear the half-mask on her face.

'Can't you use your powers to heal your scars?' the young woman asked her now by the side of a rushing stream, where they had stopped once more to refill their canteens, and where Shard poked at an itch beneath her silvered mask. In the daylight Curl's dark hair stood in a crest on her head like a travelling Tuchoni, or indeed like certain Contrarè. She was as small as Shard was tall, a tiny beautiful perfection.

'Believe me, I've tried,' Shard offered in reply, readjusting the mask on her face. 'But flesh is hard to manipulate. Almost as hard as thought. I might just have to live with the scarring for the rest of my life.'

'Maybe we all have to,' replied Curl with feeling.

It was snowing today, and the fat white flakes were tumbling in a flurry through the bare limbs overhead. The snow dusted the cloaks and beards of the men and the striped backs of the zels standing along the bank of the stream, causing Coya beside her to squint from the deep folds of his hood, turning his head round to gaze back at the rare mammoth chimino tree a few hundred feet behind them now, the windchimes of cane grass hanging limp from its boughs. He shielded his eyes, trying to make out the platform at its very top through the tree's huge diamond leaves, hoping perhaps for a sight of the Sky Hermit who Shard had told him would be living up there.

It was dangerous, to be lingering this close to a Sky Hermit. The Contrarè would not take it lightly. But then, as Coya had reminded her, they were hoping to make contact with the people here after all.

Shard was just about to fill her canteen from the stream when the first shot rang out. She froze, seeing Curl dive for cover and Coya's bodyguard bundling him to the snowy ground, everyone else squatting down as more shots rang out. For those first brief moments Shard remained standing, too bewildered to move.

A flock of crows had risen from a nearby tree, squawking and flapping. In their wake, silence fell slowly upon the scene.

'What was that?' the captain called out.

'Man down!' came a voice from behind a tree, where the huge ranger known as the Loaf had plodded off to relieve himself moments before. As a group they hurried to the sound of the voice still calling out.

The Loaf was lying on his back with another ranger kneeling over him, black blood seeping from the front of the big man's buckskins. In a calm rush the two medicos went to work on him, cutting away the skins of his torso with small knives as though they'd done this a hundred times before. The older medico, Kris, slapped his face with a bloody hand and snapped at him to stay awake, to keep his eyes open. Still alive then, still breathing.

'Damn it!' Sergeant Sansun swore as he tugged the ammunition belt clear of the prone man. A handful of rifle cartridges were blackened and smoking in the belt.

'Defective cartridges,' Sansun rasped, and the disgust in his voice suggested that this had happened all too often before. Shard had heard how soldiers hated using guns whenever conditions were damp, for black powder ignited at the merest hint of moisture. 'Must have gotten wet.' And he tossed the belt to one side then pushed himself to his feet.

'Save your efforts,' he said down to the medicos, taking one glance at his companion's wounds. 'He's done for.'

They ignored him, of course, in their professional way. Stunned and with her senses reeling, Shard could only watch as Curl wiped the blood clear to see the wounds better, two dark little holes amidst the hairs of his heaving chest, instantly overflowing again with blood. The young medico wiped once more and sprinkled a bag of powdered coagulants onto them, and then Kris pressed hard with pressure dressings, slapping his face again. 'Stay with us now, you big lug. Stay with us, Loaf!'

But the Loaf had stopped breathing. They thumped his mountain of a chest to restart his heart but to no avail. The Loaf was dead.

*

Sweating in the falling snow, the men hacked away at the frozen ground with sharpened stakes and their single shovel, cutting a grave big enough to take the Loaf's great size.

Shard hung back from the scene, sipping from her flask of cold tannis tea to calm her mind, not wanting to intrude upon this silent ritual of the close-knit rangers. A few birds rose from a distant tree, drawing her attention in their direction.

'Company,' announced the young man Xeno suddenly, squinting through his sniper scope in the same direction.

Heads swung round to see three Contrarè men walking towards them through the undergrowth. Shard's heart skipped with sudden excitement. She found herself taking a step out from beneath the shelter of a tree towards them.

Up close, the Longalla men looked fierce enough in their red and black war paint and their dark hair cast in outlandish styles, each one different from the others. They sported buckskins blackened by fire, bone piercings and tattoos, blankets tied around their torsos; belts holding machetes, hands carrying bows.

Their movements were as graceful as any other animal of the forest.

'Ah, at last,' said Coya with a sparkle in his voice, and he rose and shambled over to greet the approaching figures with Marsh by his side, the bodyguard resting one hand on the hilt of his knife. Shard supposed she should make herself useful and so followed behind, catching the widening eyes of the men as she came nearer.

Solemnly, the oldest of the Contrarè men bent down to scrape away a section of snow, and pinched some of the forest's humus between finger and thumb. Straightening again, he dabbed a little of it onto the end of his tongue, tasting the life and death of the forest, then flicked the rest of the earth into the air above their heads. Worshippers of the earth and the sky and all the vitality in between.

Shard had seen her parents perform the same ritual many times with the dust of the ground, and had even feigned it herself when it seemed expected of her, never truly feeling its meaning. Now, with these wild Contrarè men singling her out for attention, Shard knew they would sense the fakery in her gesture if she tried the same thing in response, and so instead she simply nodded her head in greeting.

Some disappointment in their eyes, though it was hidden quickly.

While the other two studied Shard with interest, taking in her own Contrarè features and the pica feathers sprouting from her collar, the older fellow spoke out in loose Trade, introducing himself and his companions. He blinked his surprise when Coya introduced himself and Shard, for even here they had heard of the famous descendant of Zeziké.

Famed or not, though, the man demanded to know what they were doing here in their forest.

'We must speak with your council of elders,' Coya explained in earnest. 'On a matter of the utmost importance.'

'Hah, then you will need to hurry, Broken Wing. The council is already being attended by other outsiders this full moon.'

'Other outsiders? Who?'

The man shrugged. 'Your enemies. Some people of the Empire. They have asked for a truce while they speak with our tribe. They travel now to Council Grove. There they will speak to the gathering.'

Coya glanced at Shard, shifting uneasily over his cane. 'How long do we have?' growled his voice to the Longalla.

'As I said, until the fullness of the moons.'

'That's only a handful of days away,' observed Shard.

'You will guide us there?' asked Coya in hope.

'No. We must stay here. We must protect the Sky Hermit. Head north-west for the Moth river. Follow it west. It will take you to Council Grove where the elders are gathering. We will send news ahead so you will be safe in your travels there.'

While they talked the other two Contrarè continued to stare at Shard. One of them stepped closer now, and held something out in his hand by way of an offering. It was a black and white pica feather, just like the many others fixed to her collar.

'My young brother, Seldom Speaks, says he dreamed of you last night,' explained the speaker of Trade. 'When he awoke, this feather was lying upon his chest. He says he would like you to have it.'

She accepted it with a nod of thanks. Her delirium was starting to return, for she could feel her head slowly spinning.

'Good hunting,' said the Contrarè man, and for a moment he studied Shard with a certain puzzlement in his gaze, and then together the three men turned and jogged off through the trees until she could see them no more.

Frantic now, Coya snapped at the rangers to hurry. He cursed and snarled under his breath while they rolled the Loaf into the hole and covered him with earth.

'A bloody Mannian delegation,' he spat into the air. 'I should have known it. I should have known the Empire would try to buy out the tribe.'

'Relax,' Shard said, and her tongue felt numb in her mouth. She wanted to lie down just then to still her head, yet here was Coya spurring them to get moving again. 'The Longalla will likely chase them from the forest after they've listened to what they have to say.'

'I hope you're right, Shard. I have a bad feeling about this. A sincerely bad feeling!'

It wasn't like him to express his doubts in this way. As Coya's words echoed in her head, Shard glimpsed the briefest of images flash before her in the untrodden snow, a possible future perhaps: what seemed to be Coya lying in this very forest in the darkness of night, felled by a crossbow bolt poking from his skull.

'Shard?'

It was nothing, she told herself. Just another product of her fevered imagination.

'I'm fine,' said the Dreamer, motioning Coya away, and she glanced once more after the departed Contrarè, and then at the back of Coya.

'Let's go,' Coya insisted, struggling into his saddle.

They wasted no time saying words over the fallen ranger. As the others mounted up, the young man Xeno stood by the unmarked grave finishing his hazii stick, as though even Coya Zeziké could not hurry him.

'The big man will be missed,' said one of the rangers.

'Aye, a dying shame,' said the young man Xeno without feeling, and in his tone of voice hung a single certainty: *life is tough, deal with it*. And then Xeno tossed the remains of his hazii stick onto the mound of earth and climbed into the saddle.

In a single line they rode out from the clearing with the occasional glance backwards, leaving a grave behind marked by nothing more than a smoking roll-up curled upon the dark, upturned earth.

CHAPTER THIRTY-THREE

After Losses

'What do you mean we're heading for the Isles of Sky?'

The cat lifted her gaze from the floor at the tone in the longhunter's voice, while every other face in the mess room turned to Ash for an answer, faces bright in the daylight pouring through the open gun ports. A few shouted out angrily, demanding an explanation from the old farlander, their voices strained by what they had already been through and by the thought of even more lying ahead.

'A straight run into the Hush and back was the deal,' one of the crewmen declared, and others called out their agreement from the many benches and tables about the room.

They're going to mutiny, Ash thought as he held up a hand in an effort to calm them, and he glanced towards Meer and Aléas, who were facing the skymen of the *Falcon* too.

They're going to go crazy, said his glance to the hedgemonk.

I know, Meer replied with a waggle of his brows.

Where was the captain in all of this? Trench was the one supposed to be breaking the news to his crew, not a shattered Ash still stunned from all that had happened in the Edge. He was nothing but a target here, a target for their collective hostility if ever there was one.

He gripped his sheathed sword and held Cole's steady gaze, for the longhunter was the closest to him with a weapon, and he looked just about ready to use it.

Cole had said a handful of words since escaping the kree warren with his cat, having caught up with the rest of the party as they ascended the slopes of the Edge with their hauls of Milk. During their zel-ride back to the skyship the battered longhunter had kept his thoughts to himself, yet upon their return to the *Falcon*, Cole had insisted on knowing when they were heading home and, in front of the others no less, opening up the whole matter while Ash could barely hold his feet or think of anything but his cabin's bunk.

Something had changed in the longhunter down in those tunnels, where he had been left for dead while the survivors fought their way to the surface. Ash could see it in him, the difference in his spirit. He was determined to return to Khos now, whereas before he had seemed merely resigned to the fact.

Yet here he was, being told there was a long way to go yet before that could happen. They were going to the fabled Isles of Sky first.

'If Dalas were here he wouldn't stand for it!' shouted someone else to wide agreement, a lean skyman who pushed off from one of the cannon along the sides to glare across the room at him, and just then Ash wasn't certain if he imagined the crew pressing a fraction closer.

They were sore at the loss of big Dalas, the real backbone of this ship, a man they had all liked. And they were ragged too from the scents of the wind they had all been continuously breathing in while waiting for the party's return from the rift, in no mood for this sudden shifting of plans. Ash could sense the potential of violence in the air, their tensions gathering for an explosive release.

Aware that their anger was wholly justified, Ash struggled for the right words to diffuse the situation. His head was pounding again in great throbs as though someone was jumping upon the side of it, and had been ever since he'd emerged from the kree tunnels barely able to see, carrying the body of Kosh on his back.

Now Ash faltered, his vision dim. Again he glanced to Meer for support, and the hedgemonk opened his mouth to speak, only to be usurped by another voice behind them.

'We couldn't tell you, damn it all,' rumbled the captain, and the gathered crewmen parted to allow Trench to step through their circle, his pet kerido chirping on his back.

Captain Trench stood before them, glaring, with his single eye shot red with alcohol and lack of sleep; a man seldom seen outside his cabin during their voyage, now standing as a brooding presence amongst them all. 'We're at war in case I need to remind you of it. Or maybe you're all too ignorant to know what would happen if word leaked about a ship of the Free Ports heading for the Isles of Sky? Aye, we're going to the Isles, and only after that do we return home.'

'We signed up as a ship's free company,' said another skyman. It was old Stones the chief pilot. 'We deserve to cast a vote on this.'

Captain Trench squared up to the smaller grey-haired man. The pet kerido hung loosely from his shoulders, looking back with its glassy eyes at all the figures surrounding it.

'This is my ship, damn you!'

'Aye, and our lives.'

For a moment Trench appeared to sway on the brink of a great fury, but then he turned his back on the pilot to glower instead at the rest of the crew, and he growled low and menacing. 'Anyone who has a problem with our new course can get off at the coast and take their chances. Is that understood?'

'And what if we all say no?' announced the pilot. 'Will you fly the ship by yourself?'

'Please,' said Ash and raised his hand again. 'There is no need for this. Let me make it worth your while so that we share no hard feelings here.'

'And what are you offering, farlander?'

'We have Milk. Enough that some can be shared out amongst the crew.' And he looked to Meer for confirmation of what he said, but the monk waggled a sly hand uncertainly. 'Plenty of Milk,' he pressed on regardless, for they would make do, somehow. 'Every man who wishes to stay on will earn a portion of Royal Milk for the risk he takes in this venture. Every man who wishes to get off at the coast will earn the same.'

They were stunned into silence by his offer. Even a thimbleful of Milk was a fortune to these skymen.

And so I buy their lives again, he reflected with a narrowing of his eyes, thinking of the skymen Dalas and Jarad lost in the hive of the kree; thinking too of his old friend Kosh, foolish enough to have come with him, buried now on the slopes of the Edge.

Holding his tongue, Ash watched as the crew talked themselves into accepting the offer, while around them the stirred-up dust slowly settled in the late daylight spearing the room and his sensitive eyes. Seeing the change in their mood Captain Trench strode away as though the matter was already settled, neither looking to Ash or any other.

'We had a deal,' snapped Cole, isolated now in his anger.

'We can still take you back to Khos with us. Our deal remains the same.'

The longhunter held his breath for a long moment, considering Ash sharply.

'The Isles of Sky,' he mocked. 'If I'd known you were this crazy, old man . . . If I'd known you were clearly out of your mind . . .'

'Yes,' snapped Ash, turning away with thoughts of his bunk. 'Well now you know.'

*

A figure was sitting in the corner of the dark cabin when he awoke, and Ash knew at once that it was a dream he was having, for he could see that it was his dead apprentice sitting there slouched in the chair with a foot up on the side-table, a shadow with eyes gleaming pale and lively.

'Bad times,' Nico said in a hush, and in the quietness of the night Ash could hear the sounds of snoring from the other cabins, but not from the empty bunk above his head.

A grunt was all that he could manage in response. He couldn't move when he tried to, though the fact did not disturb him much. Rather it was a reason to relax further, for there was nothing else that could be done.

'I was sorry about Kosh,' said his apprentice. 'He was a good man. I think he went bravely, don't you?'

'Yes,' Ash croaked. 'He did.'

'That's all you have to say about it?'

'What else should I say?'

'Some remorse perhaps. Some grief.'

Around them, the ship groaned and creaked as she sped on her course across the night sky. From the ceiling, the unlit lantern rattled minutely to the vibration of the thrusters. All was normal, yet here he was speaking with the dead.

'Kosh is hardly the first good friend I have lost, Nico. We are Rōshun. We live by the sword. It is wise to prepare ourselves for these things long before they happen.'

'That must be a strange way to live.'

'It is the only way to live.'

'Still. To have known someone for that long—'

'*Enough*,' Ash snapped at the boy, and his voice was like the lash of a whip.

Ash sighed and tried to move again. Nico always had a way of unsettling him with his questions. 'What is it you want, boy?'

'Only to talk a while.'

'Fine. Then talk.'

Footsteps padded by the door of the cabin. A shadow crossed the beam of lantern light leaking from beneath the door. For a moment he thought it was the ship's medico Shin come to visit him again for a late-night tumble, but the footsteps carried on.

'I tell you this,' said his dead apprentice. 'Those kree frighten the life out of me. I'm glad I wasn't in those tunnels with the rest of you.'

But Ash barely heard him, for he was thinking of Shin now. Maybe he should go and visit her once Nico was finished goading him here. See if she was up for the company of an old man in the loneliest hours of the night.

The chair creaked and Nico sat forward to settle the front legs lightly on the floor, set his foot down too.

'You really think this is going to work then?'

'What is it you are asking me?'

'The Isles. Do we have enough Milk for the Isles?'

Ash chuckled ruefully at the boy, a sound that emerged like a hacking wheeze.

'So this is why you are here. To see how your chances are faring, eh?'

'You haven't answered my question. Is there enough Milk for the procedure?'

'Barely. Meer thinks we can get by.'

'A shame we can't just water the stuff down a little.'

'Hmf.'

Nico's voice grew serious. 'And you think it will work? That I'll be myself again, not just some vegetable lying there unable to speak?'

'How would I know – am I a seer? We will have to wait, and see what happens.'

'That's easy for you to say,' Nico hissed back at him. There was anger in his voice now. A tone of accusation. 'You're not the one who's dead.'

CHAPTER THIRTY-FOUR

The Isles of Sky

Ash emerged onto the deck with a heavy hood thrown over his head, drawn out from his cabin by the shouts of the lookouts and the excited clatter of feet across the decking.

The old farlander moved with slow deliberation, for truly he could barely see today, the world diminished to dim shadows and nauseating washes of colours. He made his way up to the fore-deck, where the skymen clustered there parted before him, until he clutched a hand around the rail, and faced the figurehead of the falcon and their direction of travel.

The skymen murmured amongst themselves, clearly interested by what lay ahead.

Days ago the ship had reached the eastern coastline of the Great Hush, and the ruffled azure sea that was the Eastern Ocean. From there the *Falcon* had turned due south, following Meer's suggestions and the zigzagging coast as the air grew ever hotter and more humid, all of them glad to be gone from the lands of the kree.

Even from beneath his hood, behind his goggles, he was squinting fiercely against the rays of the sun. Through his sickening vision he glimpsed Aléas standing there at one of the mounted eyeglasses; or at least he glimpsed the sheen of the young man's straw hair and scented his familiar soapy freshness.

'What can you see?' Ash asked him now, surrounded by the press of the skymen. It was the time of midwinter back in Khos, shortest day of the year, yet here on the *Falcon*'s decks the crew were stripped down to short trousers and sweating beneath a blazing equatorial sun.

'A mountain range,' Aléas answered. 'Rising near the coast. Runs from east to west across our path.'

'A big range?'

'Sure is.'

Ash couldn't help but drum his fingers upon the rail in a slowly gathering excitement. Perhaps they were going to make it after all, he thought with sudden wonder, and the relief that he felt right then was like the shedding of thirty years, as though a weight he hadn't known he was carrying all this time slid slowly from his back.

'Tell me everything you see.'

'We're high. To our left lies the Eastern Ocean. Some big clouds floating over it like islands. The sea is sparkling. It looks calm down there. I can see the white wake of a ship in the water. And I can see real islands on the horizon, lots of them.'

'The Shell Islands,' announced Meer's voice from behind. 'The beginnings of them anyway. They say they wrap the girth of the Eastern Ocean.'

'So these mountains will lead us to the Isles of Sky?' Aléas asked.

'No, lad. You're looking at the Isles right now.'

The mounted eyeglass squealed as Aléas turned it sharply back to the sea. 'Which ones?'

'Not out there. *There*. In the mountains.'

Another squeal of the mount.

'You're losing me.'

Ash interrupted. 'The name is a false trail, Aléas. The Isles of Sky are only named so to throw others off the scent. Part of keeping their location a secret.'

'Wait,' said the voice of the longhunter Cole from nearby. 'You're saying the Isles are not islands at all, that they're in those mountains instead?'

'Yes,' cackled Meer. 'The Isles are really a city spread across those peaks we're flying towards, a city known as Mashuppa. And in a way the peaks *are* islands, only instead of water surrounding them, for much of the year they are surrounded by clouds. And their foothills connect to the sea by a river known as the Cocachim. You see the big estuary there on the coast?'

'Yes.'

'The sandbars make for treacherous navigation and help to hide the river mouth. The Guild traders of Zanzahar use it to sail all the way to the foot of the mountains.'

Ash could hear the skymen listening eagerly, and passing along the words in mutters that were spreading back along the ship. There seemed no sign or sound of the captain yet, still holed up in his cabin, even now.

'That's odd,' said Aléas at the eyeglass. 'I swear there's something rising out of those mountains. I can just about see it. A line running right up into the sky.'

'Yes,' chuckled Meer. 'That will be the Sky Bridge.'

'The what?'

'You'll see!'

It was shockingly humid at this latitude. Ash's shirt was open and the sleeves of it rolled up from his tattooed arms. He could feel the warm sough of air tugging at the sweaty hairs of his chest. Something nudged at his leg and he saw that it was the cat. He stroked behind her ears absently as he gazed at their nearing destination.

'How did you come to this place?' asked the longhunter of Meer.

'As a stowaway, on one of the Guild's trading ships.'

'You must like taking chances,' quipped Cole.

'I was young, foolish. It's not something I would care to repeat. Being a stowaway is a miserable way to travel, I can tell you.'

Ash grunted, knowing only too well what he spoke of.

'The natives of the Isles call themselves the Anwi. It means *the lost*, or *the fallen*, or something like that. They believe that they are descended from exiles cast off from one of the moons, people who had to settle here on this world long ago.'

'Hah!'

'It's true, lad. It's what they believe. Anyway, when I was there some friendly Anwi took me in and allowed me to stay with them in the city. A family of artists and intellectuals. I grew close to their daughter, who was in training to be a Crucible, a kind of priestly engineer come Observer. They were pleased because she had never shown any interest in having a lover before then.' He chuckled, thinking back on it. 'Triqy, she's called. If we're lucky, for a share of the Milk she will help us restore Ash's apprentice using the rest of it.'

The mountains hung in the hazy distance, though it hurt Ash to focus on them. He was finding it hard to grasp that they were almost there at last, almost at their final destination; a myth made real.

'Time to get ready,' the monk declared with a slap of the rail. And when those around him stared at him blankly he said, 'Well we can hardly land in the Isles looking like this, can we? We must arrange our disguises.'

'Disguises?'

*

The flowing burnooses were comfortable to wear in the stifling heat, and by the time the ship was nearing the mountains the crew looked splendid in their new Alhazii outfits, many with their heads covered by the deep folds of hoods. Others hung over the sides while they painted a new name on the hull of the ship in Alhazii script. A new flag was run up so that they flew the colours of the Caliphate. For all appearances they looked like a Guild skyship of the Alhazii.

Aléas appeared on deck with his hair and skin dyed darkly like the rest of them, a shocking change in appearance, though the sharp angles of his features remained unmistakable in Ash's watery vision. He stopped to watch the monk applying fine strokes of paint to Ash's features, replicating the tattooed scripts seen on the faces of the more devout Alhazii.

'Good job,' he commented, and Ash grunted without turning his head. 'You look like a half-sized version of Baracha.'

Through his pain, the thought brought a wry smile to Ash's lips.

'Try not to smile until the ink has dried, will you?' admonished the monk. 'Now. Let me hear your best Alhazii accent.'

'*I was born in the razee of Fe'nada oasis, how is that, Blessed Brother?*'

Meer laughed and clapped Ash's shoulder.

'I hope that was a joke, my friend. Otherwise I'm going to insist that no one speaks during our entire stay, save for me.'

At least Ash's sight had improved a little over the course of the afternoon. Ahead, the peaks were close enough that he could see them better now. They seemed wreathed in dark rain clouds that hid any sign of the Isles of Sky, or Mashuppa, or whatever the city of the Anwi was called. Ash could even see the line rising up out of the clouds that Meer had called the Sky Bridge, though it remained faint even as they grew nearer.

Downwards the *Falcon* swooped, approaching the easternmost flanks of the range, where a silver river wound its way towards the coast. A town spread across the foot of the slope, where the mountain torrent first slowed and widened, a settlement obscured by mist and smoke.

'Guallo Town,' Meer declared. '*Guallo* meaning foreigner in the Anwi tongue. It's used as an insult. The Alhazii traders occupy the town. For most purposes it's as far as they can venture, and as far as we can go ourselves.'

'You mean we won't be seeing the city?' exclaimed Aléas.

'Not possible, I'm afraid. I'll be slipping in alone once I send word to my contacts. The crew can run repairs during your stay in the port. Something that keeps you all on board and the ship inactive until my return.'

Disappointment flushed red across Aléas's expression.

'So this is it?' asked Cole into the wind. 'Where all the exotics in the world come from? All the black powder?'

'Yes, this is the place. The Crucible priests create the exotics up in the city, amidst great secrecy.'

'We won't be seeing the city at all?' complained Aléas once more.

This time Meer pretended not to hear him, and turned his voice back to Ash.

'If we're lucky, the Alhazii should leave the ship in peace once they see our Guild port pass.'

'Another fake?' asked Ash.

'Of course.'

'They say such a thing is impossible.'

'Not if you're friends with a Dreamer.'

Ash nodded, suitably impressed, and the monk tutted and lifted his brush away until he was still again. 'Let us hope that it works, then.'

'If it doesn't, we're going to have an awful lot of explaining to do. Now hold still will you? This is a tricky bit.'

*

Surrounded by dense jungle, Guallo Town was a settlement of wooden warehouses and buildings of pale stone, flanked on the northern side by the clear-running Mashuppa river winding its way out to sea, and on the eastern side by a canal which led to an area of docks where large sea-going trading ships were moored.

The *Falcon* circled slowly over a high white wall that surrounded the entirety of the settlement. Tall, skinny watchtowers stood around the wall and along the waterways. Within them, figures surveyed the skies as though for incoming skyships, though Meer said otherwise.

'It's the start of the rainy season,' he explained. 'They'll be watching closely for birds.'

They all stared at him.

'Big birds,' he explained.

No one could tell if he was joking.

Over it all rose the mountains, climbing in steep green terraces into the clouds. A white road could be seen winding its way upwards from a building in the wall.

Down came the *Falcon* into an open field that was the town's busy skyport, where windsocks blew and other skyships were tethered. With a bump her flat bottom slid along the ground and crewmen clambered over the side to tie down the ship.

Few heads turned to pay attention to the new arrival in the field, just another vessel amongst many. After some moments the hull door swung open on the starboard side, to reveal Ash and the others of their party gathered there in the hold around Meer, all of them wearing their loose burnooses.

'Here we are then,' said the monk at the top of the ramp being lowered to the ground, squinting out at the fierce sunlight. Meer stood next to a zel that was loaded down with the skins of Royal Milk they had gained from the Hush, breathing in the pungent scents of the surrounding jungle. 'Here we are.'

For a moment Ash regretted not being able to go with him, but the monk had been insistent that he go alone. Meer would have to lie low for a while in Gaullo Town itself, before his Anwi contacts could smuggle him into the city.

Reluctantly, Ash handed the man the urn containing his apprentice's ashes, which he had brought all this way with him at Meer's insistence. The ashes were a physical trace of Nico, supposedly to be used during the process of restoring him to life.

'Look after him,' Ash said, not letting go just yet.

'Of course,' Meer replied with heart, and gently plucked the urn from his grip. 'Remember now, there's no telling how long I will be gone. I'll send for you if I can. At the very least, I'll let you know how the whole process is going with your boy up there.'

'Do that. As soon as you can.'

'Well, wish me luck,' Meer said with an optimistic smile and a wave of the leather wallet that was their fake Guild port pass, then he tugged the zel to follow him down the ramp.

'Luck,' offered Aléas.

Ash gazed after the hedgemonk with narrowed eyes, his chest rising and falling fast.

CHAPTER THIRTY-FIVE

High Times, Low Times

In a sheltered clearing of the Windrush, Shard was relieved when the party stopped to make camp in the falling darkness, where they picketed their zels and built a large fire to warm their chilled bones, weary faces shining in the light of the rising flames.

With snow tumbling down they huddled around the fire beneath sheets of canvas tied between the trees, hands and feet extended to catch the welcome heat of the flames. They ate what dried meals they carried in their bags, and brewed pots of chee so they wouldn't have to stomach the near-frozen water from their flasks.

Armed with their mugs of steaming, soothing chee, the rangers played a round of sticks and bones with their gloved hands and the two losers took first watch around the perimeter of the camp, skulking off into the undergrowth to climb into some nearby trees. Beneath their canvas shelters, the remaining rangers broke out their supplies of hazii weed and started passing sticks amongst themselves, joking and cajoling in a rising mood of smoky banter. None mentioned the dead companion they had left behind, though they placed a mug of chee close to the fire as though he would be wanting it, and there was a sense that their jovial spirits were an effort to honour the fallen man known as the Loaf, a kind of wake in typically Mercian fashion, a celebration of life more than a sombre reflection on his passing.

Shard munched on one of Coya's hazii cakes and relaxed into the easy mood of the camp, glad to be off the hard saddle of the zel at last. It was easier to ignore the whispers in her mind in this cosy circle of life, those breathless voices that had been speaking to her all day in words too soft to properly discern, an effect of the worm juice no doubt, hallucinations of the forest speaking to her, just as her father always claimed forests spoke to those open enough to listen. Now it was human chatter that filled her ears and mind, and she basked in it as much as in the heat from the fire.

By her side, Coya lay back against a saddle and toasted his stockinged feet upon the hot rocks surrounding the blaze. His eyes were glazed as he chewed on another one of his hazii cakes, watching the rangers with keen interest.

'You still soaring?' he asked with his mouth full.

'A little,' she said with a shiver, though she had mixed some tannis with her chee to help subdue her mind, and the weed was helping too.

She peered at him through the glimmering firelight.

'Something on your mind?'

'Hah. Many things. So many I'm having to make an inventory of them in my head.'

'And what's at the top of the list?'

Coya chewed that one over. 'Actually, it isn't a list. I imagine shelves of wooden boxes in my mind, each painted with a number, or sometimes a picture. And inside I place images of whatever I need to hold in my head.'

'Box number three then. What does it hold?'

'Ah, let me see . . . Yes. Box three holds Ash and Meer and the flight of the *Falcon*.'

'You're thinking of them, even here?'

'Wondering how they are faring, yes. Hard not to, considering how important they might be to our cause. That one ship could sway the course of this entire war.'

'If our best hope is that one ship making it to the Isles of Sky and back, then I truly doubt our chances.'

'Nonsense. They'll make it. I can feel it in my guts.'

'More likely you're feeling that stew you just ate.'

Coya chuckled softly in the firelight, a little high on the weed. He surprised Shard by reaching out a finger to poke her lightly on the arm, and then he did it again, provoking a reluctant smile from her. Nothing was so bad if you could still smile, his dancing eyes reminded her.

It was Coya's gift, she had long ago noticed, his gentle use of touch to break through the skin-encapsulated barriers between people. A kind of magic when you saw him connect like that, and people responded to it in kind, with simple openness.

Just then, Shard caught the bodyguard Marsh watching her too, his eyes roaming over her silver half-mask and her leather-sheathed chest exposed beneath the parted cloak, but mostly lingering on her face, drawn to the satin-smooth glimmer of her second skin as though he desired to know what it would feel like against his own. So Marsh was still interested then, even after all these years of unrequited chasing, a chase that had been too much fun to simply end by taking him to bed.

She inclined her head, slowly looking him up and down too. Teasing him.

The bodyguard cleared his throat.

'You seem spooked,' she observed.

'Just a feeling. Can't seem to shake it tonight.'

Suddenly he inclined his head, listening to the faint sound of thumping in the far distance. Contrarè tree signals passing through the forest.

'We'll never catch up that Mannian delegation,' Marsh muttered to Coya quietly, thinking of the most pressing matter at hand, as always. 'They've too much of a head start on us.'

'I know. I just wonder why they think the Contrarè will listen to them in the first place? What compelling case can they make for the Longalla to side with the Empire?'

'Gold. Threats. The usual pleasantries, I reckon.'

'I don't like it,' Coya grumbled to himself. 'I don't like it one bit.'

For all their riding they still hadn't reached the Moth river, which the Contrarè had told them to aim for. From there they would have to find Council Grove by themselves, and before the passing of the full moons when the elders would be meeting in council.

For a time Shard stared at the fire and lost herself in the tumult of the flames. She breathed deeply to anchor herself, knowing that she would likely soar off at any moment if she allowed herself to, and prone to do so even if she didn't.

The flakes of snow were falling on the back of her neck, minor dabs of coldness transmitted through the sheen of her glimmersuit. Coya rose stiffly to refill his mug of chee. Marsh the bodyguard stared out at the surrounding blackness of the forest, as though he could sense something out there. Shard followed his gaze, in no condition to go out and look with her mind's eye.

Shadows danced between the trees like figures stalking closer. Shard huddled closer to the fire, longing for the security of home.

CHAPTER THIRTY-SIX

Aiding the Enemy

From her sleeping furs the Dreamer's eyes snapped open and fixed on a shape swaying close above her face, like a crooked stick somehow animated with life.

It was a crinkleback, Shard realized, spotting the patches of brown skin on the snake's flanks resembling fallen leaves – edges upturned like the real things – and the tiny spines of its hood flaring in alarm.

The snake was gazing at her, its glassy eyes fixed on her own; two diamonds reflecting the glimmers of the camp fire.

By the fire, Marsh glanced over from his vigil with a puff from his cheroot, then turned away again, tossing another stick upon the coals.

Shard? announced a delicate voice in her head.

She stopped breathing for a few heartbeats. Wondered if it was another hallucination.

Shard, can you hear me?

An icy thrill ran down her spine like a drop of water. She knew it was Tabor Seech, talking remotely in some way not related to her farcry.

Tabor? What are you doing in my head?

I'm speaking through the snake. It's been searching all night for you. Listen – there isn't much time, I have to warn you about something.

Really? Last I heard you were working for the Mannians.

Well, yes, I am. But listen. Your position is about to be ambushed.

Shard screwed her face into a frown.

Aren't we beyond pranks by now, Tabor?

You fool, I'm trying to warn you here! General Mokabi himself asked me to contact you. It's complicated, and we don't have time to go into details, but

believe it or not Mokabi wants your mission to succeed. He wants the Contrarè
of the Windrush to wage war against the Imperial Expeditionary Force.

You mean, he wants his rivals bogged down while he takes Bar-Khos for
himself.

Precisely. You always were astute, Shard. Now listen!

Hold on. How did you know where to look for me?

A little birdy told me. It doesn't matter. Now listen! One of your sentries is
already dead. He just had his throat cut while we've been chatting. Imperial
scouts are moving to surround your camp even now. You must waken the
others. You must arm yourselves!

Tabor—

She paused, seeing the bodyguard Marsh suddenly drop his
smoking cheroot by the fire as he peered at the surrounding darkness
through his goggles, which she knew allowed him to see at night, for
they had come from one of the Academies.

Do it now, Shard!

'Up!' she suddenly hollered as though struck by a fork of lightning, though when she jumped free of her skins she found that her
tongue was like a dead thing in her mouth, still asleep. 'Up!'

Marsh was kicking out the fire even as Shard evoked a glyph in
her worm-addled mind, producing an implosion of air above the
camp like a mighty hand clap and sending a rush of wind over them
all. The flames of the fire were extinguished in an instant.

They were quick, these Volunteers. Men and women rose to arm
themselves even as shadows sprang at them from the night.

Sparks flew from the clash of blades. Grunts and curses and bodies
tumbling in the snow. A gunshot spat fire. Something whipped
through the clearing, then something else followed after it; crossbow
bolts zinging back and forth wildly.

The Dreamer willed to life her night vision so she could see the
scene about her more clearly.

Figures were attacking from all around the perimeter of the sheltered hollow they were camped in. Dogs even, great wolfhounds
leaping down through the brush. Most shocking of all was the sight
of Contrarè with their feathers rising from their heads and machetes
swinging high. Renegades by the looks of them, no war paint to be
seen.

Some of the Volunteers had managed to load their rifles and were firing at anything that moved. At the centre of the camp next to the dead fire stood Captain Gamorre, bellowing orders even as she hastily fixed a pair of Owls over her eyes. Next to a tree trunk, young Xeno was kneeling on one knee with the butt of his sniper rifle nestled in his shoulder, scanning through the scope of the weapon calmly, eagerly. He fired once and cracked the rifle open to reload it without looking away from the scene, already choosing his next target. Marsh was pulling a stirring Coya closer to the centre, sleeping skins and all.

Flashes around the perimeter, some gunshots being fired into the camp now. A Volunteer fell to the ground before her. A snarling wolfhound had grabbed another by the arm while a figure yelled and stuck him with a knife. Others were fighting toe-to-toe.

Too many of them, she realized, as anyone would have just then. *They're going to overrun us.*

Captain Gamorre had seen it too.

'Pull back!' the woman started yelling. 'Get to the zels!'

Not much that Shard could do while friend and foe were tangled up together like this. The two medicos were gathering up their field bags in a hurry and so Shard did the same, hauling her travel bag over her shoulder and then the heavy sleeping skins too.

When she turned towards the tethered zels the animals were already loose and scattering through the trees, bounding away up the slopes of the hollow. Some were panicked enough to charge across the camp instead, and one flashed past Shard, almost bowling her over. It carried on and crashed into Coya, who was rising at last from his skins with the help of his cane, knocking him backwards even as a crossbow bolt streaked past his head.

Coya fell and another bolt flashed over his sprawling form. Marsh was swearing over him, grabbing at the animal's reins as he fought to calm it. Over his shoulder the bodyguard shouted something towards Shard, but she couldn't make it out.

A frantic crunch of leaves sounded from behind. Even as Shard swung round she imaged a glyph in her mind and launched it towards the figure charging at her – a Mannian, who instantly stumbled over a tree root and sprawled into the snow. As the man rolled to a stop he tore off his night goggles, momentarily unable to see. Behind him a big wolfhound growled and bared its teeth.

Sweet Holy Mercy!

Fear rooted her to the spot as the animal leapt for her. It was like the sandcrawlers of the deep desert all over again, coming at them over the darkness of the dune. But then Shard flung herself out of the way and threw her hand back in the dog's direction, casting another blindness glyph in its face. Still the creature was on her, tearing at her boots and legs.

A figure fired a pistol and the dog yelped and leapt backwards, retreating into the tree line.

It was Curl, the young medico. A pistol smoked in her grip as she helped Shard to her feet.

'Forget the zels,' the girl shouted. 'We're running for it!'

Shard could barely see for the trails of light smearing across her vision now, barely think for the sensations washing through her mind. She was losing her clarity again, her concentration. For a moment she stood there lost in the brilliance of it all, captivated by every motion of the struggling fighters, every glint of steel, every single glitter on the icy snow lit by gunfire.

And then she forced herself to focus.

With her glimmersuit warming against her skin, the Dreamer swept the sweat from her face and sought out Coya in the scrum of movement around the camp. She wasn't going anywhere until he was by her side.

Over there. Coya was down on his back with Marsh stooped over him, the bodyguard yelling something across the smoking fire – yelling out for a medico.

In a flurry of strides Shard was next to him, bending down to see Coya lying immobile in the snow with a smattering of blood fanning out from his head. It took her a long moment to finally see it, and when she did Shard could barely believe what she was looking at.

A crossbow bolt had gone through Coya's skull from ear to ear. Inspecting it more closely, she saw that it had gone through the rear portion of the skull, right through his brain.

He's dead, came the awful truth in her mind.

It was just as she had seen it, days ago when they had buried the Loaf, this very image flashing through her mind.

'Is he dead?' asked the bodyguard's voice in her ear.

'Not quite,' spluttered Coya, impossibly so, and he blinked and coughed with the crossbow bolt fixed firmly through his head. 'I'm all right,' he gasped. 'I'm all right.'

'You're pretty far from all right, Coya,' she said down to him. But he could say no more in reply, for Marsh was already lifting his charge with a grunt to throw him over his shoulder.

'I don't think we should be moving him like this!'

Marsh ignored her and hurried after the majority of Volunteers who were fighting their way out now, hacking a route through the enemy up the northern side of the hollow. Someone pulled on Shard's arm too; Curl again, still looking out for her. Shard started after them, struggling up the slope on all fours with her pack and sleeping skins gone now, her ears filled with the howls of the fighting.

In the darkness she could see everything as though it was twi-light. Up ahead, a spearhead of Volunteers were pushing hard for the lip of the hollow. Behind her scrambled the rest of the rangers, firing back at enemy fighters rushing through the camp after them. Shard heard Coya's name passing on their lips; word of his injury or that he was dead. Calls to protect him no matter what the cost.

At the very top of the hollow she paused against a tree trunk to catch a proper lungful of breath, and was startled by the sight of one of the rangers turning around to face their pursuers. More from curi-osity than any sense of bravery, Shard turned round too to face them, and saw another Volunteer further down the slope, falling now from the slash of a sword, figures of the enemy clambering over him.

In anger Shard threw a blindness glyph at his attackers, feeling the strain of it now as the figures lurched sideways into the brush. More attackers surged past them though.

Do something, she thought with a surprising calm. When Shard scanned through her glyphs in her mind's eye, she spotted right away what she needed here – a trick she had picked up from Tabor Seech himself. Willing it to life she launched the glyph down the slope at the nearing enemy and a tangle of sparks ignited in the air, and then the whole side of the hollow seemed to burst into a wave of flames, which rolled over the pursuing men.

'Nice,' grunted the ranger by her side, a grizzled Volunteer whose name she had momentarily forgotten. Shard swayed with sudden dizziness. Her glimmersuit was hot now, pulsing with its own heat generated from the casting of the glyphs. With the flames in her eyes she saw the old Volunteer bending down to ram his iron picket pin into the snow, and when he straightened once more there was a leather cord dangling between him and the pin. The man had marked the spot upon which he would make his last stand.

'Better go,' he said to her now, squinting downwards. A hound was yelping in circles with its tail on fire. The screams of men seemed to cut through the bones of her chest. For a moment Shard felt sickened at what she had done, but she hardened herself to it.

Already the rest of the party was disappearing into the dense trees beyond the hollow. She thought she glimpsed the face of Curl turning to look back, but something seemed to pin Shard to the spot, just like the old ranger by her side.

'What's your name?' she asked him as the man lifted his shortsword at the ready.

'Chin Lars of the Inner Isles.'

'I'll remember you, Chin Lars.'

His glance shone at her with a lifetime of meaning. But his voice only said, 'Go. Get out of here.'

The words released her.

She ran for it in her heavy coat, her breath wheezing in and out of her chest, not daring to look back.

Gloom swallowed Shard beneath the dense canopy of the forest. Bushes snagged at her sleeves. The others were just ahead, figures darting along a trail in the snow.

You still alive? came Seech's voice in her head, even more distant than before.

Get out of my head!

You had me worried there. What are you on anyway? Have you taken the worm juice again, is that it?

In response to her silence she heard his dry chuckle in her mind.

It won't help you, you know. I'm still the stronger Dreamer, and we both know it.

Shard snarled as she pushed her way through the undergrowth, weak from the previous glyphs she had cast, reminding her that what he said was true.

Don't think I owe you anything for this. I'm coming for you, Tabor. I'm coming!

Ah, Shard, he said while his voice was fading almost to nothing. *I wouldn't have it any other way.*

CHAPTER THIRTY-SEVEN

Waiting for Word

Days passed without news from Meer. Days of sweltering heat and waiting.

Ash stood on the foredeck of the *Falcon* in the shade beneath the silk loft, which bobbed and swayed minutely above his head in the faint afternoon breeze, the leather bindings of the spars creaking slightly, those flexible lengths of wood which fixed the envelope to the ship. Behind him, relaxing in the heat, Aléas and Cole sat against the rail posts playing a game of head-to-head Rash for matchsticks and pride.

The sunlight speared into his goggled eyes. The insects swerved in a crazy frenzy around their heads. Ash wiped sweat from his forehead, wishing they were in the coolness of the sky again.

Everywhere he looked he saw a million points of white reflecting from the jungle foliage around the settlement, and from the individual blades of grass across the field of the skyport itself, and dancing on the rippling water of the river. The air shimmered between all that he looked at.

It seemed their forged Guild credentials had passed inspection, and so far their disguises too. While many of the crew had stained their skins with the oil of rhuberry nuts, many of the older men hadn't needed to, since they were as swarthy as any Alhazii from so much open-air flying. It helped too that they mostly stayed below decks out of the sun when not working on repairs and maintenance tasks on the ship, the shutters and hull doors flung open wide to relieve them of the stifling heat.

A monkey chattered out from the jungle canopy, and then another replied in what sounded like a burst of derisive laughter. Ash leaned forward to peer through the eyeglass once more, aimed at the top of the nearest mountains.

The clouds were gone today from the high peaks that were the Isles of Sky. Rising from them, Ash took in the arrow-straight line of white which soared straight into the sky, craning back his head until it was swallowed in its own vanishing point.

The Sky Bridge, Meer had called it, without offering any explanation as to what it was.

Through the lens he saw flashes of violet light pulsing up and down it, as alien as anything he had ever seen.

If he looked hard enough he could see the white walls of the Anwi city up there, which appeared curved and bleached like great whale-bones placed on their sides, running along the saddle between two peaks before disappearing in the haze.

Mashuppa, he reflected. City of the Anwi. City of the Lost.

Though he would never have admitted it, Ash was starting to feel the tension of their long wait now. Up there in the city, his apprentice Nico might be stirring in some way with life.

Meer had been vague about the process, knowing little about it himself save for hearsay. Only that it could be done, that certain Anwi were reborn in copies of their bodies grown in artificial wombs, and that the procedure required a great deal of Royal Milk.

Had Meer's contacts arranged it all without trouble? Had there been enough Milk to pay for their help and to undertake the process itself? What was he doing up there – *and why hadn't he sent word?*

With a quiet sigh, Ash followed the winding mountain road from the city walls all the way down to the foot of the slopes and the settlement of Guallo Town, where he caught sight of the cables rising upwards on white pylons carrying boxes up and down the slope, some of them shining with glassed windows.

The cables and the road both ended or began at a large, odd-looking building set into the perimeter wall that surrounded the lower settlement entirely. Meer had called the structure the Clearing House, the only way to get through to the city. Darkened windows wrapped around the upper storey of the structure, which leaned out over the lower half, and metallic cones sprouted from its flat roof. It seemed constructed from some strange material he had never seen before, gleaming white like the perimeter wall itself – a wall with cruel spikes lining the top of it, pointing both outwards and in. A wall intended to keep people inside it.

Watching the scene, Ash suddenly blinked from a flash of violet light nearby. Quickly he panned the eyeglass along the wall. Through the rigging of another skyship he saw something lying motionless on the spikes at the top of the barrier, covered in purple fur. A monkey, he realized.

A puff of dark smoke was drifting upwards through the air above it.

'Huh.'

'What?' asked Aléas.

Ash straightened his back with a wince. 'Tough one to crack if we had to,' he admitted, then frowned in frustration. 'And still no word from Meer.'

Aléas set down the cards in his hand and offered his full attention, though the longhunter Cole carried on as though he heard nothing, squinting out from under his brim at the grassy skyport around them.

'You think he is in trouble?'

'I think it strange he has failed to send us news yet.'

Young Aléas shrugged in that loose way of his, a slow roll of his shoulder. 'Maybe he's sold the Milk for himself, and now he sits up there with his Anwi lover enjoying a life in paradise, laughing at the fools who brought him all this way here on a false pretence.'

'That is a poor joke, Aléas.'

'We're talking about a man who pretends to be a monk when staying in Khos so he can legally beg for food in the streets.'

Ash's frown only deepened.

'Look,' interrupted Cole, nodding towards the distance.

They turned to see a figure walking between the hangars of the skyport towards the ship – a tall Anwi dressed in a one-piece suit of leather, his head covered fully by a mask and hood. He was carrying something under one arm.

'He must be roasting alive in that suit of his,' murmured Aléas.

But Ash barely heard his voice. He stood motionless as a statue, watching closely.

The figure was seven foot tall at least, or so he judged as it approached one of the *Falcon*'s crewmen standing on the ramp leading up to the open hold. Words were exchanged between them and the figure passed the leather wallet he carried under his arm to the crewman. He glanced up at the ship just then, and behind the clear glass of his mask a pair of eyes locked onto those of Ash. The skin looked dark.

Suddenly the figure lifted its fist into the air by way of a salute. When Ash merely stared back in reply, the Anwi turned and strode away.

Moments later the crewman stepped up onto the deck and passed the leather wallet to Ash.

It was Neels, a young man who seemed to scrub his teeth with a covestick every hour of the day. 'Fellow said it was for you,' he said with the white covestick in his mouth even now, handing Ash the thing.

With Aléas leaning over him, Ash opened the wallet and looked down at the paper note that lay within. Next to it was a hard black disc, its outer edge unevenly serrated, with the writing PASS scrawled across its surface. Something else slid into sight as he tilted the wallet for a better look. It was the smallest vial he had ever seen, a needle-like sliver of glass containing what at first he thought was a dose of Royal Milk, though it looked even whiter than the liquid they had obtained from the kree warrens.

Carefully, he read the note aloud.

'"Success. Your boy is now growing in a . . ."' Ash squinted, trying to read the word, '"in a wetwomb. There is a good chance he may be restored fully, body and mind, with a little help. Please find a small amount of properly fermented Milk I was able to obtain for your use. With it I have enclosed one pass for you to come and join me here in the city to help in the process of bringing Nico fully back. I have also enclosed an image you will be eager to see. Good news all round, Ash. You should rejoice!"'

And rejoice he did, inwardly, when he held up the image Meer had included with his letter – an image captured on a thick square of glossy paper that trembled in Ash's hand.

It resembled one of those newly fashionable spectralgraphs that captured a person's likeness with a flash of light. Though this picture was in colour rather than sepia, and the detail was truly remarkable. Like looking through a tiny window onto the real thing.

'What is it?' breathed Aléas, craning to see.

Together, they gazed down at what looked like a human foetus growing in a cloudy tank of liquid.

'Is that him?'

'I think so.'

'He's done it then!' said Aléas.

'Yes,' said Ash, rocking slightly now.

Sudden emotions sparkled in his eyes as he looked up at the city in the clouds. Somewhere in those peaks Nico would soon be reborn. He could finally believe it now, having seen it with his own eyes.

'Damned lot of fuss over one person,' Cole growled and tossed down his cards. 'Does this mean we get to go home soon?'

But they were both too excited to acknowledge Cole, this outsider to their affairs. Aléas was busy reading the note again to himself. When he finished he flicked the page over, and his expression fell.

'Wait a minute,' he said. 'There's another note on the other side here. In different handwriting.' He grimaced.

'What is it?'

'The spelling's terrible.'

'Aléas, what does it say?'

'"Your friend was captured just after he gave me this message to deliver. Authorities are calling him a spy. They say he will be executed like all spies. He has asked for your help in this matter. I suggest you make it quick."'

They all looked to the distant form of the Anwi walking from the skyport, too far to call back. Ash gripped the wallet in his hand, with its vial of Milk and its single pass into the city.

'Aléas,' Ash said with a thoughtful tug of his beard. 'Fetch my sword.'

CHAPTER THIRTY-EIGHT

Infiltrator

Ash waited in line before the door to the Clearing House, trying not to dwell on Meer's capture, or what the hedgemonk might be going through up there in the city at the hands of his interrogators. Captured as a spy, of all things; usually a crime worse than any other.

It was hard to know what could be done about the situation. Nor how they would now retrieve his apprentice, or even whether Nico was still undergoing the strange process of growth.

One step at a time, Ash told himself, as he always told himself when circumstances seemed too much to deal with in their entirety. The Milk was helping in its own way, the tiny sliver of fermented Royal Milk that Meer had gifted him in his Anwi-delivered letter, which Ash had drunk down in the previous hour.

With his head lowered beneath the hood of his burnoose, he listened to the occasional chat of the Alhazii men standing in queue before and behind him, feeling the pulses of the Milk's rejuvenation coursing through his body, his muscles twitching with energy. The pains of his lower back and most noticeably in his head had diminished almost to nothing.

How long would these remarkable effects last? he wondered.

It was early enough that the queue for the Clearing House was still a long one, though he had been waiting here in the rising heat long enough that most of the line was now behind him. The Alhazii waited to pass through so they could take a cable car up the slope of the mountain to the city, shaded from the tropical sun by their loose burnooses and their parasols. The cars were running on the other side of the wall, dark bearded faces peering out from those with open windows, interspersed with freight cars that he assumed were being loaded from the endless wagons rumbling up from the Alhazii docks, bearing cargo from the warehouses into an open bay of the shiny white building.

From the structure's darkened windows above, Ash could sense eyes watching him as he finally stepped up to the metal door and waited his turn to enter. His gaze took in the white surface of the building, smooth and without seams just like the perimeter wall itself. Pearlstone, Meer had remarked before he had set off on his mission. An organic substance grown into the shape that was needed.

He blinked when a male voice squawked from a grille set next to the door, accompanied by a loud crackling hiss. '*Hrmph-maffle-crik!*'

'What?'

The hiss faded away. 'Enter your pass into the slot provided.'

Ash took the serrated disc pass from the leather wallet and slid it into the slot, hoping that he did it right.

'*Maffle-muffle-crik!*'

'Huh?'

'Remove your pass. Do not lose it.'

When the steel door slid open it expelled a sigh of frigid air, wonderfully refreshing. The old farlander hesitated only briefly before he stepped through into the corridor of white walls beyond, and the door slid closed behind him.

Along the ceiling, three rows of glowing orbs illuminated the way, one row of lights blinking on and off in a running sequence so that it seemed they were guiding the route. He followed them around a curving corner into a side-passage, where another door slid open and led him into a windowless chamber with a high vaulted ceiling. Inside, his breath condensed to mist in the air.

Another door slid closed behind him. Ash could see no way of opening it.

'Remove your clothes,' came a disembodied female voice from the ceiling, and his eyebrows rose in surprise when a hatch in one of the walls slid open into darkness. 'Place them in the cubicle provided. Any jewellery and other items too.'

No point in being shy about it. Save that if they were somehow watching him his black skin might spark a few curious stares. No choice in it, he supposed.

Quickly he stripped off and bundled everything into the hole in the wall: the burnoose and boots and gloves, his leather flask of water, his pouches of leaves and gold and silver coins, the sun-goggles, his sword. Without sound the hatch slid closed again and Ash was left standing with nothing more than his naked body for warmth. He wrapped his arms about himself and stamped his feet on the hard tiles of the floor, which were too cold to sit upon even if he'd wanted to. His teeth began to lightly chatter.

Suddenly it was snowing in the chamber. White flakes blew from vents in the arched ceiling and fell all around him. Ash looked up and felt them settle against his skin. They weren't cold like snow, nor did they melt away with his heat. Gradually the flakes covered his entire body and face, and when he rubbed them clear the flakes turned to talc, leaving a chalky smear in their place. A layer of the stuff covered the floor, while the finer dust began to fill the air so that he breathed it in too and started to cough, feeling light-headed.

'Please breathe normally,' the placid voice advised him.

And then, like a sudden change in the weather, it began to rain from the vents overhead instead, and the droplets were so scorching hot that Ash hissed from the burning sting of them. In streams and rivulets the dust of the snow washed away into gutters around the edges. Gasping, Ash cleared his eyes and looked about him through the steady shower of water, wondering how long it would last.

Too much energy in him today, he was finding. He was jittery from it, unable to stand still for long. As the time passed by and the water kept falling Ash began to shadow-spar where he stood, the air whooshing from his lips while he punched and kicked and hopped around the chamber, feeling light on his feet, feeling young again.

'Please remain stationary,' announced the voice, but Ash ignored it. He sparred with a ghost opponent until the shower finally stopped and the last of the water dripped clear. Suddenly warm air was blasting into the room, drying his skin in moments.

A door slid open in the far wall.

'You may now exit the chamber to redeem your belongings.'

*

The cable car swayed about him as it rose into the air, creaking noisily.

Ash stared down through the open window at the slopes of the mountain falling away not that far below. The jungle was receding now, replaced by terraced farms and intricate drainages rushing with water, as the car climbed the cable up the mountain, roughly following the course of a winding road.

From here he could look back and see where vast swathes of the jungle appeared to be turning brown and dying off; all along its upper edges, in fact, wherever water seemed to flow, eating into the deeper canopy lower down. Indeed, the odd solitary tree passed close enough below for Ash to see the mottled sickliness of its leaves. And the crops too, those growing on the terraced farms, seemed blighted in some way.

Clouds were trailing rain up there nearer the peaks. A shower passed over the cable car, soft rain pattering lightly on its metal roof, and Ash leaned out of the window and opened his mouth to taste a sample, just as another car went past in the opposite direction bearing a startled Alhazii face.

Ash winced, for the water was foul and his eyes stung from it.

Bad rain, he thought with a frown, reminded of what fell from the skies in distant Q'os.

It was as though something was poisoning the land and the sky of this place.

*

This high up, the air was starting to grow noticeably thinner. It felt like hours since the cable car had begun its long journey.

Indeed the world below was losing itself now to the gathering dusk, though the trails of jungle mists remained faintly visible in their luminescence. Thanks to the Milk his vision seemed sharper than he had ever known it. To the west the sky was a deepening wash of blue which shone brighter where the sun had so recently set. Over his shoulder to the east, he saw a dark, greyish band arching just above the far horizon; the shadow of the world itself.

Even as he watched, a pink glow brightened the band of shadow across its upper edge and then a star glimmered, two stars, three; a handful wherever he looked.

Such beauty!

Under a dome of stars, Ash saw that he was approaching the walls of the city at long last, and a white building that looked much like the Clearing House down in the town.

The white walls blocked his view of the city beyond. Above them, though, soared a structure which made him blink in wonder. Into the night rose a limb of pearlstone arching impossibly high over the glow of the city, ending in a central hub where other more distant limbs reached up to join it too, all of them covered in thousands of windows lit from within, faintly illuminating what looked like netting draped over the entire structure. Those flat-sided legs of the Sky Bridge glimmered with the same violet light that shot upwards into the sky, following the colossal needle thrusting towards the stars.

For a moment he squinted as a blinding light swept over the walls. Through his splayed fingers he spotted a vessel coming down from the sky with its wings cupping the air like some giant bird, landing somewhere on the other side. And then the car was entering the side of the building and everything fell away from sight, and Ash jerked as it came to a sudden, swaying stop. The door on its side popped open.

'Welcome,' announced a disembodied voice.

Alone, Ash stepped out into the City of the Lost.

CHAPTER THIRTY-NINE

Rubbing with the Enemy

Sunrise found them hunkered down on a lonely outcrop of rocks overlooking the surrounding forest of the Windrush, exchanging the odd rifle shot with the enemy force that had circled their position. There were snipers in the trees below them, betrayed by puffs of smoke drifting to nothing in the grey, though brightening, morning air, and occasionally a flash of movement between the rocks at the foot of the bluff: a Contrarè head ducking down, a Purdah scout rushing between cover, slowly making their way upwards.

'Bastards don't give up, do they?' growled the bodyguard Marsh from where they all lay on their bellies in the dirt, the bodyguard perched on a rock peering through an eyeglass. A shot struck the rock and threw dust against Marsh's grimy cheek, but he didn't flinch from it, merely raised an eyebrow in disdain. For all the lack of sleep in the man, for all the tightness of their present situation, he seemed chirpy enough this morning.

Coya too seemed more lively than he should this morning, considering there was a crossbow bolt sticking through his skull.

'They do seem determined to have at us,' he replied from where he lay on his back, grunting in pain as the medico Kris finished cutting off the ends of the wooden bolt extending from both sides of his head.

Still alive and talking, even now. For the life of her Shard could barely believe it, even though she had worked on him herself during the previous hours of darkness. Exhausted and barely able to talk, she had cradled Coya's head in her hands while she purged the wound clean with her mind, pinching off what internal bleeding she could, slowly realizing that the bolt through his brain was the only thing keeping him alive now. It could not be removed.

Yet Coya had taken the news as calmly as a man being told of placid weather, in stark contrast to Marsh, lifelong bodyguard to the man since they had both been boys, who had sworn loudly in a sudden burst of temper, cursing Coya for these reckless plans of his that made it impossible to protect him.

All the while the enemy fired at them from the trees and tried to get closer to their position, and Shard tried her very best not to fall asleep.

'Maybe they're in a hurry,' Coya ventured now, focused gamely on other things like the enemy forces surrounding them in a tightening ring. 'Maybe they're worried about the local Contrarè turning up.'

'I doubt it,' said the captain of the rangers from further along the lip of the outcrop. 'Most of the Contrarè war bands are in the eastern fringes now, ranged along the Chilos. Far from here anyway.'

Again the bodyguard spoke up, addressing Coya in his angry clipped voice.

'They were after you last night during their attack on the camp, did you notice?'

'Nonsense,' retorted Coya, blinking up at the sky.

But it was true, for Shard had seen it herself.

'Marsh is right,' sounded her own sleepy voice in her ears. 'They were trying to kill you. I saw the bolts flying your way.'

Coya Zeziké considered the news sombrely.

'Perhaps they found out my mission here, and have decided to stop me.'

'*You think?*' mocked Marsh.

Five of the rangers had made it out alive from the ambush of the camp, nearly half their number left behind them as they fled. For the remains of the night the survivors had made a running retreat through the forest, a 'run and reply' as their captain had called it, a routine they had obviously performed many times before. While one group of rangers stopped and fired back at their pursuers to keep the enemy heads down, the rest leapfrogged past their flanks, running onwards for a distance before stopping too, firing back to give the first group cover while they retreated. And so they had leapfrogged like that for what seemed like hours, the sweat running off them in sheets as the enemy tried to outflank them, until they had spotted the outcrop of rock ahead, and had run for the temporary salvation that it offered.

For the last few hours they had hunkered down in the rocks sheltering from the occasional sniper shot, dozing while they could or staring down with blasted eyes into the surrounding darkness, the survivors still in shock at the loss of their comrades. They had huddled together for warmth, for they had been unable to save any zels or food or sleeping skins during the retreat, so they had no way of keeping themselves warm. With the first welcome rays of dawn their professionalism had begun to assert itself once again, sheer necessity overriding their bleak silence. Voices had croaked out in query or suggestion.

'How are you?' came a voice now, and it was Curl the younger medico, her sagging crest of hair cleaving the blue sky in two, come to check on Shard's bandages.

'Fine,' she breathed, and winced as the girl inspected the wound on her calf where the enemy wolfhound had mauled her. Curl looked calm for all that they were in a tight spot here.

These people had witnessed some interesting things during the frenzy of the night attack. Enemy fighters reeling about as though blind. A wave of flames bursting across the enemy-covered slope. This morning they seemed to treat Shard with a new-found defer- ence, even the wild young Volunteer Xeno, who offered her a nod before taking another deafening pop with his rifle, then ducked down quickly as a shot struck the rocks in reply. Shard turned her head to take in the situation below.

The bodies of three renegade Contrarè lay dead amongst the scree and rocks at the foot of their position, where gangs of black birds squabbled over the flesh. They had long stopped fleeing at the occasional gunshot over their heads.

Footsteps scrabbled from behind. It was Sergeant Sansun return- ing from his scouting trip down the other side, a bare open slope with only a few trees and rocks for cover.

'It's clear down there,' he reported to the captain. 'Not a soul any- where.'

Captain Gamorre frowned. 'They must think we're fools.'

'So we stay here then,' said the sergeant. 'Dig in and wait them out.'

'No,' announced Coya, and struggled to sit upright, his pale face etched with lines of dirt. 'We're wasting time here that we no longer have. I must be at the Contrarè council, no matter what the cost. The entire war may hinge on its outcome.'

His stare was an open challenge to the captain, and Shard knew who was going to win this one. Coya, she had long ago decided, was not a man to ever bet against.

The captain looked to Sansun for his opinion, and the sergeant shrugged.

'Looks like there's some marshes to the north of us,' he said. 'We could break out on the north side and head for those. Lose them there.'

Captain Gamorre squeezed her eyes shut tightly, summoning her inner reserves.

'We have any smoke grenades with us?' she asked him.

'Aye.'

'Then get ready to move out,' the captain told the others wearily. 'The man's got somewhere he needs to be.'

*

By the fall of early twilight the party staggered out into a large forest clearing with the remnants of the day darkening behind them, chased by clouds and heavy snow flying sideways in a gale.

Through frozen-lashed eyes they saw the flowing river ahead of them, and the stilted platforms of a Contrarè settlement standing along its banks.

'Must be the Moth river,' one the Volunteers called out. He meant the river that would lead them to the elders of Council Grove.

At least they were no longer lost.

Faces glanced desperately over their shoulders towards the direction they had come from, knowing their pursuers to be close behind. All day they had barely stayed ahead of them.

Quickly they staggered towards the structures in the midst of what was now a worsening blizzard, the dogs of the settlement barking madly. On the outskirts they came upon a roofed corral of zels, and Coya cursed and demanded to be let down from Marsh's back.

'I don't believe it!' Coya exclaimed aloud as he staggered to the corral, and they all caught a glimpse of what he was staring at on the rumps of the zels – the branded miniature hands of Mann.

'They're here,' Coya declared and shook his head in wonder. 'That bastard Mannian delegation is here, tonight!'

The Volunteers didn't like it, pinned by the enemy both behind and ahead. 'We're in no condition to fight,' spoke their captain on behalf of all.

'No need to,' spoke up Shard, stirring from her stupor. 'The delegation travels under truce, just like us. If they cause us any harm, the people here will fall on them.'

'Maybe those sons of bitches behind us will hold off then,' ventured Marsh, 'if they know their people are here.'

The forest was a dim wall around the clearing of the encampment, glimpsed through breaks in the blizzard. Over the feathers and fur of her high collar she peered at the twilight deepening within it, trying to sense how close their pursuers were out there. In this weather, the Purdah scouts might be glad of a respite themselves, a chance to hunker down in their cloaks in conditions of exhaustion that must rival their own. The sergeant too was watching the trees, and the lad Xeno peering through his scope for a sight of the enemy.

Well they couldn't just stand here all night long, freezing to death in the blizzard. Shard peered ahead at the nearest stilted structure. Thought she spotted something flying from its roof, a banner of sky blue. The Contrarè colour for truce.

She tucked down her head and stomped towards it, not waiting to see if the others followed.

*

It was a trading station, the structure they approached, a two-storey log building perched on stilts by the bank of the river, with a sign swinging in the gusts.

There was a lift contraption sitting beneath it, big enough for four people to stand inside. Marsh and the sergeant pulled on a vertical rope, and a felled trunk that was a counterweight began to lower as the lift rose squeaking into the air, bearing them upwards.

'Remember,' Coya called down to the Volunteers awaiting their turn. 'The Mannians are under truce so we can't touch them either. Keep a lid on your tempers, all of you.'

He was as ragged as the rest of them, for all that poor Marsh had carried him all this way.

'Any symptoms yet?' the Dreamer asked Coya, studying the blooms of blood on his bandaged head.

'Not yet, but I've certainly lost some memories. Let's hope they're all bad ones, eh?'

*

Together they stepped through a wooden door into a stifling atmosphere of heat and smoke, and the chatter in the room ceased as the door slammed shut behind them.

Shard took in the tables and piles of bedding about the room, and the fire burning in a stone hearth in the centre beneath a hole in the sloping roof. The room was mostly empty, but a group of four men sitting at a table in the far corner turned to study them, eyes widening in surprise at their non-Contrarè appearances and their stained travel attire much like their own: the Mannian delegation.

Her gaze flickered towards a few hands reaching for weapons at their belts.

'We don't want any trouble here,' called out a man who came rushing from behind the bar to stand between the two groups, wringing his hands in distress. He was Khosian. Coya turned to address the fellow, using Marsh to prop him up.

'Good to be in from the cold, eh? And you are?'

'Mull, the proprietor. We're a family business here. We don't need any trouble.'

'Then I'm surprised you opened your doors to this vermin,' Sergeant Sansun snapped at the man, drawing a sidelong glance from Coya.

A chair scraped; one of the Mannians getting ready to climb to his feet, restrained by a burly fellow with a hood over his head despite the stifling heat of the taproom. They were the only other customers there, save for a few drunk Contrarè sleeping it off against the walls.

'Brother Mull,' announced Coya gently. 'We require shelter for the night, and some hot food if that is possible. It has been a long and tiring day and we are all more than a little spent.'

The proprietor nodded, eager to please if it meant peace for the night. But then the door clattered open once more, and the remaining rangers entered one by one, rifles in their hands, and stopped short when they spotted the Mannians on the far side of the room.

~In return the Mannians stood abruptly around their table, hands now resting on the hilts of their swords, though the burly fellow remained sitting, watching from within his hood, puffing smoke from a long-stemmed pipe in a casual manner.

'No trouble I say!' screeched the proprietor again. 'If you're going to fight then take it outside into the storm!'

In brooding silence the two sides glared across the smoke of the fire at each other, though the Dreamer Shard ignored them all and dropped herself heavily into a chair.

'Stand down,' Coya said quietly. 'All of you.' And with Marsh's aid he took a seat next to her and waited for the Volunteers to settle.

In moments both parties were sitting and exchanging guarded looks through the smoky hostile atmosphere. Satisfied they wouldn't kill each other just yet, the proprietor nodded and hurried away, returning quickly with flagons of hot spiced wine and loaves of warmed bread.

Still, the mood of potential violence remained in the air. Sergeant Sansun's chest was rising and falling fast as he stared hard at the group of Mannians, his hands clamped to the sides of his chair as though to hold himself in place. Young Xeno scratched his neck consciously, drawing attention to the tattooed slashes which symbolized his enemy kills. His gaze was much like Curl's beside him, dark with animosity.

Across the room, the burly fellow threw back his hood to display a bored smile. At once, Coya straightened in surprise.

'Well I live and breathe,' he declared.

'You know him?' whispered Shard.

The fire crackled in the hearth. Outside, the wind of the blizzard blew in a sudden gust, causing the structure to creak around them. The burly man puffed a few perfect rings of smoke as though to mock them in their silence.

'Alarum,' answered Coya in a hush. 'Spymaster for the Imperial Expeditionary Force. Member of the Empire's secret intelligence web, the Élash. I'm surprised to see him leading this delegation into the Windrush himself.'

Once more the door blew open and the blizzard gusted into the room. Kris the medico stepped inside and shut out the blast of the storm with a bang, snowflakes settling around her.

'It's done,' she whispered to Coya as she passed his table.

What was this?

'Well, time to make our introductions, I suppose,' Coya announced as he dabbed his mouth again with a handkerchief then pushed his chair back and rose with a firm grip on the table.

'What?' said Marsh with a start, but Coya only waved him back into his seat. He reached for the stick that had replaced his lost cane, then turned and shuffled over to the Mannians.

All talk ceased again. Chairs creaked as the rangers turned their heads to follow his slow walk. A click sounded from beneath Marsh's dripping cloak and then another; the bodyguard pulling back the hammers of his pistols.

With Coya's approach, the spymaster flicked a finger and his three companions left the table for another beyond earshot. Coya settled opposite his arch-rival.

They both spoke quickly, hunched over the table together, teeth flashing.

Restored a little by the hot wine and bites of food, Shard cast a listening glyph that projected their voices into her ear.

'Coya Zeziké,' Alarum was saying, taking in the man's head wrapped in its sodden bandage. 'Here to enlist the Contrarè.'

'Alarum. No doubt you are here for the same reason.'

'I speak with them tomorrow at the full-moon council. I do hope you can make it.' Alarum paused to take in the party across the room from him. 'Though you all look about ready to lie down and die.'

'Oh, I wouldn't discount us just yet.' Coya leaned closer towards the man. 'What are you thinking here? That you'll turn them against the Khosians? It will never happen, man, the Contrarè of the Windrush hate the Empire even more than they distrust the Khosians. They'll likely dance on your corpses after you've had your say.'

'Yet even so, you seem in a great lather to beat me there.'

'Only because I know what you are, spymaster. I know what it is that you do.'

'Oh? And what is that?'

'You are of the Élash. Notable for blackmail, bribery and torture, subversion and slander, assassinations, the sowing of paranoia, the killing of innocents for leverage, indeed every filthy trick in the book. I've read your field manuals on the subjects. Chilling stuff, I must say.'

'So you know what spies really do in this world. Good for you,' snorted Alarum, enjoying himself or at least pretending to.

'Aye,' said Coya, 'and I also know how the world looks when you get down on all fours like a Mannian. And I tell you now, it will not work here, none of it. The Contrarè will see right through your rotten scheming.'

'Perhaps. Or perhaps you underestimate me, and they will not.'

For a spell they both stared at each other across the table. And then Coya was rising from his chair unsteadily, his body as crooked as ever. A thin sliver of blood had run from his bandages down upon his neck. It looked as though he would leave the discussion without a further word, but then Alarum held up a hand to delay him.

'You know, don't you, that if your people would only cease their struggles against the Empire, none of this would be necessary at all?'

Suddenly Coya straightened with a crack of his spine, anger overriding his pains.

'What did you say to me?' he demanded loud enough for all to hear, and the Volunteers shifted on their chairs, ready for anything, their leathers creaking against straining muscles. Marsh the bodyguard narrowed his eyes, glancing once to Shard.

'Lay down your arms,' advised the plump spymaster. 'Succumb to the inevitable in this war of ours. It will go easier on your people if you do.'

Violence might well have erupted just then, had Coya not surprised them all by stamping his stick upon the planking. A drop of blood shook from his head and fell to the floor.

He raised the stick and pointed it unerringly at Alarum.

'You are uninvited guests here in our lands. Do not provoke a bloodbath tonight, for you will die in it, more surely than anyone else here.'

In the quietness of the room a chair creaked loudly: Alarum, leaning backwards with a mocking grin. 'Such marvellously strong words for a cripple!'

Yet Coya seemed impervious just then. His left hand clutched the back of a chair for balance, but his right pointed his makeshift cane straight at Alarum as though it was some stick of truth, and his expression shone with a fierce certainty.

'We will beat your empire in this war, you know. The ascendency of Mann will come to pass and then you will topple into yourself, as all empires do in the end. And the spark of it will happen here, in Khos, where your forces will be smashed to pieces against our defiance.'

And with that, Coya tossed his stick clattering onto Alarum's table, and hobbled slowly away with all eyes upon him.

'If only it was that easy,' Alarum called after him. 'But we Mannians still have a few surprises up our sleeves yet.'

Coya stopped to look back over his shoulder.

'Aye,' he replied through naked teeth. '*As do we.*'

CHAPTER FORTY

The Yapping Dogs of War

The skyboat was an old trading rig of a style familiar here in the Free Ports, though if a person knew where to look closely enough they would see that the vessel was not so old or raggedy as it first appeared; that it had been recently refitted, and the repairs and replacements had been treated to look weatherworn rather than new.

The small crew stood or sat around the deck while the skyboat hung in the night air over the floating city of Tume, deep in the heart of the island of Khos.

In a gloomy cabin below the rear of the weather deck, centred in a dim circle of light cast by the lantern hanging from the low ceiling, Sparus the Little Eagle, Archgeneral of Mann, and young General Romano, challenger for the throne, both sat tied to chairs facing each other with spite gleaming brightly in their eyes.

A third shape sat in a shadowed corner, clad in the white robe of the priesthood. It had been silent so far but now it spoke aloud, and both men turned their hostile stares in surprise.

'Gentlemen,' Kira croaked through the shadows. 'The words I am about to say will no doubt be as detestable to your ears as they are to my tongue. Listen carefully, nonetheless. This business between you must come to an end. The assault on Bar-Khos happens now.'

The two captives said nothing. Both panted fast through their nostrils. Sparus, though, glared with particular venom from his one good eye, obviously suspecting what was coming.

'Save your scorn, Sparus. I gave you warning. I gave you time to settle this affair. Yet I arrive to find you still locked in this stalemate with the young pretender. Nothing has been achieved.'

The Archgeneral's voice was a rumble of disdain.

'Then what do you suggest we do about it?'

'That you agree to a joint command of the Expeditionary Force with General Romano here. It would seem he is to be the next Holy Patriarch after all, if only you are able to take Bar-Khos.'

'Sense, at last!' hissed Romano, tipping back in his chair in sudden enthusiasm.

In contrast, Sparus the Little Eagle was silent for a moment, his eye fixed to the floor.

'Impossible,' he said at last. 'I cannot agree to such terms.'

'Then my Diplomat has been instructed to throw you over the side.'

In another dark corner the shadow of an old Diplomat shifted his balance, ready to act in the instant. It was the same man who had surprised them both in their sleep, forcing each back to this boat under the noses of their guards. Kira's way of telling them that she meant business.

Young Romano held his tongue now, though his eyes gleamed with triumph. Sparus the Archgeneral could only hang his head.

'Of all the people they could have sent to put the knife in me – I did not expect it to be you, Kira dul Dubois.'

'Nor I, Sparus. But in this instance I must submit to a greater power, as you must submit.'

From beneath his thick brow his one eye glared at her coldly. 'You are fine with this? After your daughter made me swear never to let it happen?'

'No. I am not fine with this. But we must move on. What does it matter anyway, a dying promise to Sasheen? She is gone now. She is no more. What will she know of it?'

'I will know of it. You will know of it. And this piece of dirt here in front of me will know of it.'

'Easy, old boy,' Romano retorted. 'Or do you forget who you are talking to here?'

A delicate sound came from Sparus, the Archgeneral rubbing his molars together in silent fury.

'Young Romano,' declared Kira. 'The Archgeneral has remained a loyal ally of my family for many years now. I will not forget that easily. Even if you do become the next Holy Patriarch, Sparus is to remain Archgeneral of the Empire. Publicly, we will state how he is your personal choice for Archgeneral, and that he has agreed on joint command of this campaign in order to support your claim to the throne. You have become allies, and it will be seen to be so. The Archgeneral's reputation will remain intact in all of this, do you understand me?'

'And what if I said no, old witch?'

Across the room, the Diplomat took a step closer towards the light.

'Then it is you who must be thrown over the side, Romano, not the Little Eagle,' announced Kira with a subtle delight.

Now it was Sparus's turn to glare at Romano.

'Do not mistake me here,' Kira told the young general. 'I come at the urging of the order. Your family has already agreed to this, as has mine. There are no choices here. From this point onwards your hostilities will cease. You and Sparus will both lead the assault on Bar-Khos. I will stay here in Khos to ensure that this is done.'

Her words left a lingering silence in their wake.

'We are settled?' she asked Sparus, and the Archgeneral brooded for a long moment before nodding his head.

'Romano?'

Another nod, the young man refusing to look at her.

'Now get me out of these ropes, you bitch, before I truly lose my temper.'

'You will have to ask me with more decorum than that, child.'

Suddenly Romano jerked his arms against his bonds to be free. *'Get me out of these damned ropes I say!'*

But Kira ignored him now. With a creak of stiff joints, she leaned forward to exchange a meaningful glance with Sparus.

'Who's to say our young general here will even survive the battle of Bar-Khos? Or the diseases running through the army? He should be careful while he is here. He is not the Holy Patriarch yet, hm?'

And all three looked at the man struggling in his chair, enjoying the display of his discomfort.

CHAPTER FORTY-ONE

The Race

In full daylight the figures ran across the gleaming snow, leaving a trail of footprints in their wake, remaining only barely ahead of their pursuers – a pack of wolfhounds with their tails held straight behind them; a loose wedge of renegade Contrarè; and at the very rear a line of Purdahs, last survivors of the imperial scouts.

It was Shard down there running for her life through clouds of her own exhalations, she and the rest of the party, the Volunteers at the front and rear and Marsh the bodyguard jogging along by her side, carrying a jostling Coya on his back.

'They're gaining on us,' noted Coya with a quick appraisal over his shoulder.

'They've been gaining on us for the last hour, you fool,' snarled the sweating, panting Marsh beneath him.

All morning they had maintained this same relentless pace along a trail following the Moth river, ever since setting off from the trading post at daybreak; a pace that was threatening to drop Shard in exhaustion.

Aware that tonight would be the time of the full moons, night of the Longalla council, they had risen as early as the imperial delegation, who had slept in a different room from their own, and had watched the Mannians and their few Contrarè guides gather their zels from the corral before setting off for Council Grove at a fast clip, quickly outdistancing their own march on foot.

No sooner was the delegation out of sight before them, and the Contrarè settlement far behind, than a howl sounded through the trees of the forest, and the enemy rangers who had been waiting all night for them launched their latest attack.

Since then it had been a contest of endurance, firing the odd wild shot backwards as they ran.

Only once had they slowed in their flight, when they had come upon the zels of Alarum and the others of the Mannian delegation on the trail. Some of the animals were lying down in slumber while others circled about in confusion. Doped up with something, she realized. Dosed sometime during the night. Shard recalled the older medico coming in from last night's blizzard after the others, and sharing a few words with Coya.

Coya had grinned mightily when he saw the bewildered animals on the trail. No doubt imagining the spymaster's pinched expression as their mounts had become useless beneath them.

Now, with the winter sunlight slanting sideways more than downwards, the party was scrambling up a snowy slope in ragged desperation, following the bank of the river as it rose into rocky bluffs and cliffs. If Shard had possessed the energy to project her mind just then, to soar like a hawk, she could have seen over the next hill beyond the party, where the bulky form of Alarum and his companions hurried along the trail that would take them to Council Grove, ragged too now that they had lost their zels.

Into the west the sun was falling fast. Rich iron tones struck the trees of the Windrush, casting lengthening shadows across the virgin snow.

They were running above a deep ravine, she saw. Ahead, a face on the rocky trail turned to glance backwards. It was Curl, with the sweat pouring off her as she ran. The young medico caught Shard's eye and then she looked ahead again, where the foremost rangers had thinned into single file as their path became a ledge in a sandstone cliff, falling straight down into the river. Their pace slowed as a consequence, needing more care with their footfalls. For a time it looked as though their pursuers would catch up with them, but then the enemy reached the ledge and slowed down too.

'I think they're flanking us,' rasped Sergeant Sansun.

Sure enough, a short time later a screaming renegade Contrarè leapt down onto the ledge right in the path of the foremost rangers – the captain and the sergeant.

Steel dazzled in the sunlight as more renegades jumped down to join the fight. The party was trapped. Marsh dropped Coya onto the snowy track and turned to face their pursuers behind with his two pistols in hand. Xeno did the same with a wicked-looking blade.

The wolfhounds came in snarling. Marsh shot two of them. Xeno took out the remaining one with his blade. Over the fallen dogs leapt the Purdahs, hacking with their swords.

Reaching for her boneknife, Shard tried to summon a glyph, any glyph, but found her mind too shattered to focus. The action pressed all around her now. Someone bustled against her back. She heard a yell and turned in time to see the medico Curl staggering on the edge of the ravine, her hands grasping out for something to stop her.

Shard tried to reach her in time, but could only watch as the girl fell over the edge with a scream.

She scrambled to the edge and looked over the rocky lip.

Curl was hanging there from a sharp knob of rock, her feet scrambling over the rushing white water of the river far below.

'Take my hand!' Shard shouted down at her, but the girl was clearly terrified, and would not release her precious grip.

'You're going to fall into that river if you don't take my hand!'

Curl gasped and shared a frightened glance with her. The girl's hands were sliding on the smooth rock, her feet kicking for purchase below. With a curse, Shard tore free her heavy coat then carefully climbed down to join the young medico. She had always been a confident climber in her youth, brave too, and it came back to her now with ease. She gripped the same knob of rock so that she hung there facing the frightened medico.

'Hey,' she tried for lack of anything better to say.

Curl blinked the sweat from her eyes.

'Hey,' she gasped back.

'I would help you up – but I seem to have squandered the last of my strength getting down here.'

'Can't you – click your fingers – or something – and make us fly?'

Shard adjusted her grip and glanced up at the action above.

'No need. Look!'

Above them the renegade Contrarè were suddenly retreating along the ledge. War yells were rising from further along the trail, and Shard saw the retreating renegades toppling off the edge one by one, blood smearing their buckskins as they fell.

A great bear of a man stepped into view swinging a shortsword before him like a veteran, dressed as a Contrarè and with his skin striped red like the painted warriors who followed behind. Shard thought she glimpsed the tattoos of horns on either side of the huge fighter's head.

Like a man possessed, the giant was tearing into the enemy Purdahs now, hacking with his blade and fist until the few survivors broke and fled in disarray.

Grit rained on Shard's head. Blinking her eyes clear, she looked up once more to see a handsome Contrarè man looking down at them over the edge, studying her with a pair of brilliantly blue eyes.

'Hey-ho!' he greeted them both warmly. 'Can I help you up?'

*

'You're Bull, the pitfighter from Bar-Khos!' declared the medico Kris in obvious surprise, addressing the big man who had just saved them all, dressed as a native yet bearing the tattoos of a Khosian soldier. A deserter perhaps.

His face was certainly mashed and scarred like that of a professional fighter. His receding hair was growing long at the back, and he indeed had the horns of a bull tattooed on his temples.

'I was,' he answered. 'Now I'm Strutting Bull of the Longalla.'

'I'd heard you had fallen at Chey-Wes,' said Kris.

'I fell, aye. But then I got up again.'

The big man Bull sounded tired. Dark rings circled his eyes as though he had not slept in some time.

'You're Red Path warriors,' the captain realized, addressing the group of red-striped Contrarè. The captain was still shaking like the rest of them, still trying to find her bearings now that the fight was over, the blood cooling. To Coya, she said, 'They protect the tribe and the Windrush from hostiles.'

The blue-eyed Contrarè man nodded, glancing again at Shard. 'We have been tracking those renegades and scouts ever since they entered the forest.' And he glanced back at the group of Contrarè behind him, dispatching those of the enemy still alive, then gazed down at the stooped form of Coya. 'And you must be Coya Zeziké. Here to speak with the elders of the council.'

Coya was using a sword as a crutch now. His face was streaked with dirt and blood, his blond hair sprouting up like the nest of a bird – yet he grinned wildly.

'Ah, you've heard then.'

'Hard not to,' replied the big man Bull. 'They're beating bark all across the forest with the news of it.' He finished wiping the blade of his shortsword clean with a rag of enemy clothing, and he shoved the weapon back into its sheath.

'Come,' he declared, and slapped Coya's shoulder hard enough to make him stagger. 'We'll take you to Council Grove ourselves. We're almost there.'

CHAPTER FORTY-TWO

City of the Lost

'First time in Mashuppa?' asked the young Anwi woman in the tan overall leading the way.

'Is it that obvious?'

The woman shrugged a bony shoulder, disturbing the flow of golden hair that lay upon it. 'Every time I show a new Guildsman the city, their expression is the same.'

Her voice was muffled when she spoke. She wore a white mask over her mouth and nose, just the same as the one that Ash now wore at her insistence. It was to help him breathe better, she had claimed, though it only made it harder to inhale the thin air of the city; a remedy, then, for the foulness of the air here, which seemed to hang like a sickly miasma over the streets, scratching on the back of his throat as he breathed, like the notorious Baal's Mist back in the imperial capital of Q'os.

The Anwi woman had been assigned to Ash in the gate house as some kind of guide, though he was wondering now if something had been lost in translation, for she seemed to be more than that, a minder perhaps.

No Alhazii to be permitted into the city without a guide, she had told him matter-of-factly upon meeting him, before leading the way to the only hotel that foreigners were allowed to stay in, the Guallo's Rest.

And so now she led the way with her long strides eating up the distance, and Ash hurried to keep up with her.

'Nice sword,' she commented briskly.

'Ceremonial, mostly.'

'You Alhazii do seem to love your big knives.'

'A weakness, I know.'

They walked on through the cold night streets with Ash staring around him like the Guallo that he was, realizing how poor Meer's meagre descriptions of the city had truly been.

Between the circle of peaks, the caldera of Mashuppa was huge enough to swallow a city, and indeed it looked as though it had done just that, for it was choked by the illuminated buildings and roads which filled its bowl-like depression entirely, spreading up over its rim and spilling out onto the rounded peaks; a thriving city in the sky.

Over it all the five white limbs of the Sky Bridge met above the centre point of the caldera, where they entwined like fingers which pointed skywards. One of the moons hung up there beside it, blazing in its fullness, almost too bright to look at.

Meer had mentioned that the limbs were home to the Crucible priests and the legislature of the Isles, including the ruler of the city. Ash was looking at the source of all the world's exotics and black powder, and the place where his apprentice was supposedly growing back to life. Right there above him in the sky.

He felt a tingle run up his spine.

'Truly something,' he said to his silent guide. 'Why is it called the Sky Bridge, by the way?'

'Oh, it's just a name.'

She was being evasive, not wishing to tell him more. But Ash needed information, a sense of context, and she was the only source he had.

'This netting. What is it for?'

'Didn't they explain anything to you, Alhazii?'

He blinked innocently like the greenback Guildsman he was pretending to be.

'The nets keep the flaxon out. Soon as the rainy season comes, they'll be upon us.'

'Flaxon?'

'Yes. Another blight we must put up with.'

'You speak good Trade,' he observed.

'Just part of my job. Many people speak it here so they can enjoy the imports. It's a lot easier than Alhazii.'

'Imports?'

'Books and newspapers from the outside world.'

'You people don't leave the city much?'

She did't respond to his question, though she cast him a side-long glance. Meer had already told him how the Anwi were forbidden to leave the city, and that how, if they did, they were forbidden from returning. It seemed that many Anwi were susceptible to the normal diseases of the wider world, and chose to keep themselves in isolation.

A kind of prison then, this city in the clouds.

'They told me you all live forever on the Royal Milk that we Alhazii keep bringing you.'

'Hah, you are thinking of the Elect,' she said, before she caught herself and said no more.

Too many secrets, Ash reflected. These people held a monopoly in this world with their priceless exotics, and clearly it made them as paranoid of spies and infiltrators as the Guildsmen of Zanzahar.

Together, they walked along a wide thoroughfare lit by street lamps blasting a harsh white light across the black paving, through a district which seemed to be mostly warehouses and silos. A few people hurried through the bitterly cold night clad in thick clothing. Riders on long-haired mountain zels clattered by with their heads tucked down into fur collars. Ash was wheezing a little in the high-altitude air but his guide hurried through the streets without slowing, wanting to get in from the cold it seemed. With clipped warnings she kept him on the pavement, for wheeled contraptions occasionally sped along the roads in both directions with their fierce lights stabbing out at him, whining past on six-wheeled legs like splayed kree, people sitting on seats in front of an open wagon. How they moved was a mystery to him, for there were no zels drawing them along.

'Groundcars,' she explained, amused by his stares, though in a semi-bored kind of way, as though she had seen it a hundred times before. 'We grow their bodies like we do our buildings. Run them on flux like everything else here. Charged coils in their bellies.'

She was trying to boggle his mind yet further, he thought.

Some moments ago Ash had noticed that they were being followed, though he was careful not to betray his awareness of the fact. As they crossed the street he chanced a glance from beneath his hood, spotting a figure some distance behind wrapped in a thick cloak. He made no comment to the woman leading the way. Stopped looking before she noticed.

The Guallo's Rest was a brightly lit building rendered in the Alhazii fashion of low columns and archways, with balconies all across its upper storeys. It looked incongruous in its surroundings of rounded white structures that were the houses and stores of the Anwi. His minder marched him inside past the stares of two Anwi guards, and Ash took a single glance in their direction so he could study them a moment later in his mind; black uniforms and torso armour and half-helms of polished metal, their eyes covered in visors of dark glass, their belts laden with batons and holstered pistols. They wore breathing masks like everyone else on the streets.

In the spacious lobby his minder spoke to a narrow-eyed man behind a counter in their native tongue, which seemed to be a series of pops and clicks interspersed with words that had no meaning to him. Watching them talk, it struck Ash how every working Anwi he had seen so far was young of age.

His nostrils twitched and his stomach churned with hunger. Meat was cooking in a nearby kitchen.

Not yet, he told himself sharply. *Get rid of this woman first.*

The narrow-eyed man behind the desk cleared his throat to catch Ash's attention.

'No smoking of tarweed or hazii weed anywhere in the building, or in the city,' he said with a frown as though that was precisely what Ash was about to do just then, spark up a fat cigarillo. 'No drinking of alcohol allowed except in permitted recreational areas. No loitering in the streets unless you intend to buy something. No soliciting. Curfew for Guallos is midnight sharp. No exceptions.'

Three flights of steps and an endless corridor later, Ash finally found himself at his allocated room. His minder showed him how to operate the light by turning a knob on the wall, similar to the gas lights of Q'os, though there was no hiss of a flame, no sign of any fire at all.

She hovered in the open doorway, leaning against it, while he took in the bed and the glass doors of the balcony and the bowl of fruit on the table, waiting for her to leave.

'Please don't think of leaving the hotel premises unescorted,' she said in a bland and hollow tone, and he saw then how tired she was, how much she wanted to get home to her bed.

The Anwi woman glanced at her wrist, where a device was strapped tightly around it. 'If you need anything, my replacement will be right downstairs. See you in the morning.'

At last she closed the door and left him alone.

Ash released a pent-up sigh.

*

He locked the door with a turn of the knob and made his way to the balcony, snatching up one of the fruits in the bowl on his way past the table. With a shove he cast open the glass doors and stepped outside into the crisp night air.

The old Rōshun took a hungry bite from the yellow fruit in his hand and gazed out at the night city, chomping on its bitter flavour. The Guallo's Rest stood in a district right on the northern rim of the caldera, underneath one of the curving legs of the Sky Bridge. Below and around him Mashuppa hummed in all its brilliance, the streets forming strings of light like the arteries of a leaf, the lights of ground-cars crawling along their straight lines. A haze filled the great bowl. Around the opposite rim of the caldera a series of chimney stacks belched smoke and flames into the night sky. Fumes poured from vents in the Sky Bridge limbs too.

Ash tilted his head, hearing the unmistakable snap of gunfire in the far distance. Sirens were wailing somewhere. Several craft circled in the air around one of the limbs of the Sky Bridge, shapes like huge birds with cones of light shooting down from them. He squinted, seeing smoke rising from the district they circled above, and the glimmers of flames from several buildings. Some trouble in the streets, perhaps. Or simply some kind of accident.

His ignorance of this metropolis in the sky was like the shroud of darkness enveloping it all.

As a Rōshun on vendetta, Ash would have spent weeks researching an urban locale he was unfamiliar with before making his move. But he knew next to nothing about this place or its people, the Anwi, and he regretted not pumping Meer for all he was worth.

Ash finished the fruit by swallowing down its core with pips and all, then returned for another, wondering how he went about finding

313

a proper meal in this place. A voice was talking loudly in the neighbouring room. Outside the door something clattered along the
corridor, wheels squeaking. The farlander flopped onto the soft bed
and sighed. Despite the ongoing effects of the Milk, he was tired at
last.

How to find Meer? his mind asked from where it was gently gnaw-
ing away on the problem.

Impossible to know from his present vantage. What he needed
was a source of information.

Ah! he thought as he sat upright on the bed.

What he needed was a guide.

*

Downstairs in the lobby, an Anwi man lowered the newspaper from
his face and squinted up with dour, watery eyes.

'You need what?'

'A *guide*,' Ash snapped back at his new minder, and he knew he cut
a fearsome sight with his dark face inked with Alhazii script. 'That is
what you are, is it not?'

'But for your room? Why would you possibly need a guide for
your room? Are you simple?'

'Not for my room. For my *view*. I have no idea what anything is
out there. A few pointers is all I am asking for.'

Another crazy Guallo, said the man's expression, though he sighed
as he rose and followed Ash to the stairs.

'What's the matter?' asked the man, rallying with a smirk. 'Don't
like elevators?' It was the same question his previous minder had
asked him. Once more Ash recalled the last climbing box he
had found himself trapped within, back in the Temple of Whispers
of the imperial capital. The raging faces of Acolytes squeezing between
the doors.

'Better for your health,' Ash replied as they climbed the stairs
instead.

He was breathing in the rhythm of sensa again, as he had been on
his way down to the lobby, gathering a tension of energy within his
sternum. It was hard to cast his voice effectively these days, his vocal
cords weakened by age. Back in the private menagerie of Bar-Khos he
had managed it, Nico taking cover behind him as he'd frightened off

the banthu like a pack of dogs. In Q'os too, surprised by assailants crashing in through the door he was meditating before, Ash had shouted out so fiercely that his attacker had dropped his weapon like a hot iron. But years ago he had been able to do much more with it, and tonight, with a buzz of youth still about him, he was hoping that was once more the case.

Back in the room, Ash closed the door behind them and watched the Anwi man step through onto the balcony. With a final long exhalation of breath he stilled himself entirely, the force inside him pushing for release.

'So. What is it you want to know?' came the young man's voice from outside.

Ash snatched a pillow from the bed as he crossed to the balcony. He snapped the cloth cover so that the pillow dropped out from it, then stopped two strides behind the man, staring intently at the back of his head, twisting the length of cloth around itself.

The mood in the air suddenly changed, and they both sensed it. His minder turned slowly, flinching as he took in the cloth hanging from Ash's hand and the glare of his eyes.

Without warning Ash lashed his face with the end of the pillow-case. Hardly painful at all but the shock of it opened the man's eyes wide.

Before he could recover his wits, his context, Ash lashed him again but with his voice this time.

'Where is he?'

'What? Who?'

'The spy that was just caught in the city.'

His mouth gasped like a beached fish, and so Ash slapped him again with a snap of the cloth, bringing tears of confusion to his eyes.

Ash threw all the intent he could into it.

'The spy. Where is he?'

'In the hands of the Committee! That's all I know.'

'Have they interrogated him yet?'

'Yes, yes. He's already confessed to being an agent of the Mannian Empire. He's due to be executed as a spy.'

'Where is he?'

'What? On the Sky Bridge of course. Leg Pashak. The next one west of here. But you'll want to avoid that district right now. Some riots have broken out. Very serious.'

'Riots?'

The man raised a clenched fist, as though it was supposed to mean something to Ash.

'*This leg. Leg Pashak. You know it?*'

'Of course, it's where I work.'

'*Describe the layout.*'

'You want to know the layout of where I work?'

Another stinging slap to the face. His pale cheeks had flushed a bright scarlet.

'*Tell me.*'

Lowering his head, the minder started to recite from memory what he could recall. Ash listened attentively, surprised in fact by the ease of it all, by the power he had managed to project into his voice that seemed to grip the fellow so entirely. He'd forgotten how much he disliked using his voice in this way, the bitter taste of forced compliance. Yet he carried on with it, nudging with questions in the right direction until he had assembled a reasonable picture in his mind of a route to Meer's location: a maximum-security cell block belonging to something called the Committee, employers of this young Anwi.

'Good man. Now turn around.'

'Excuse me?'

'*Turn around.*'

'Have you lost your mind, Guallo? Who do you think you are?'

Ash grabbed one wrist and then the other, and while the man blinked, stunned at what he was doing, he tied them tightly together with the pillowcase, in the process glimpsing a timepiece strapped to his arm. He took a moment to inspect it more closely, seeing a tiny dial of symbols slowly rotating around a centre.

'I'm just about to lose my temper here, you hear me?'

'I hear you.'

For all his height the minder weighed little more than Ash did, and with his hands bound he led him easily back inside and across to the bathroom. 'What are you doing?' the Anwi demanded when he saw Ash removing the belt from his trousers.

'Hitching you up,' he answered, then looped the belt around the man's hands and fastened the end to a hooked light fitting in the ceiling, so that the Anwi dangled there on the tips of his toes.

He inspected his work with professional calm.

'*Try to escape,*' he commanded of the man.

A desperate glance below the sweaty pit of his arm, eyes wild.

'*Escape!*'

The Anwi grunted and swung about for a few moments, tugging at his bonds, and when everything held fast he gasped and flung out a foot instead, hopping around in a complete circle for somewhere to perch it on, managing to catch the lip of the steel bathtub.

Should have seen that, Ash thought with a sigh, and he bent and grabbed the curled lip of the bath and began heaving it across the floor, its feet squealing against the tiles and the sound of it echoing off the high ceiling until it seemed loud enough to wake the entire hotel. Only when he had finally dragged it far enough to stop did he realize that the young minder was shouting out for help.

Quickly he stopped him by ramming a yellow fruit into his gaping mouth, then used another pillowcase as a gag to keep it in place.

Ash nodded once to the man hanging there trembling and staring back at him, then closed the door on his confused expression. On his way to the balcony he snatched up the remaining fruits in the bowl and stuffed them into his pockets. Then he plucked up his sword and breathing mask.

Down below in the gardens of the Guallo's Rest he spotted the dark shadow of a guard dog sniffing around some bushes. Ash tilted his head to one side for long moments, and heard a crunch of feet along one of its pathways, the slow and steady tread of a night watchman.

Find a better way out. Try the other side.

And so he glanced upwards, inspecting the balconies and higher storeys above him, plotting the easiest route to climb. He paused for a moment in his deliberations when he saw the constellation of Ninshi's Hood hanging up there in the night sky, a familiar sight in this other-worldly city.

He had until dawn, perhaps, before his guide was discovered and the alarm raised. It would have to be enough time.

A soft exhalation escaped him as he lightly hopped onto the balustrade. Ash looped his sword over his back then began to scramble upwards, hands and feet reaching for easy holds in the stone facade of the building as he climbed past the balconies of other rooms, alive once more in his element.

With a final heave he vanished over the edge of the roof of the hotel, leaving in his wake a blazing star which his foot had obscured only a moment before.

CHAPTER FORTY-THREE

Dark Vapours

Despite the bitter cold, people were partying tonight in the districts built around the northern rim of the city, and Ash found himself walking along bright and busy streets filled with life and noise and drunken revellers, sucking the chill air through his breathing mask just as everyone else did.

By now he'd seen enough Anwi of his own shorter stature to know that he did not stand out in a crowd. He kept the hood of his burnoose over his head, though it was as much for warmth as anything else, for in the brilliantly lit streets his face was visible enough within the folds of cloth, and it hardly seemed to matter. There were plenty of other faces in the streets as dark-skinned as his own, and it was a surprising relief to walk along thoroughfares like any other person, without drawing the usual stares from passers-by, as had happened in Lucksore and in so many other places before that.

So what's the plan? he asked himself casually as he strolled along the pavement, and right away the answer came to him. He didn't have a plan. He had no idea how he was going to free Meer.

You're just going to stroll up to the Sky Bridge and see how it goes, is that it?
But what choice did he have?

A noisy tram rumbled past on rails set into the road, drawing him out from his reflections, people staring out with the breathing masks still on their faces. Everywhere he looked he could see vibrantly coloured images on prominent display: faces with dazzling smiles adorning the sides of buildings or store fronts, next to foreign words and pictures of things that made no sense to him. Advertisements, he realized, like the ones that had taken over every surface of distant Q'os.

So much of this city reminded him of the imperial capital of Q'os, in fact. Was there a connection, he wondered? Indeed, was there a reason the people here had shortened end fingers just like the priests of Mann?

If Ash turned his head he could see his mirrored reflection accompanying him along the street, flashing across store fronts of glass lit brightly from within; a hooded form with a sword slung beneath his burnoose, passing displays of fine jewellery and diamonds, suits and dresses, wines and foods, paper masks and statues, exotics, ground-cars and all sorts of miscellanea he did not remotely recognize. In one instance, which stopped him dead in his tracks, he spotted what looked like a range of phalluses and orifices hanging there in a pulsing red light, though as he stared he grew uncertain, for some of them seemed encrusted with smooth diamonds and gleaming surfaces of gold.

Jewels glittered all around him in the streets too, worn upon the silk dresses and suits of the passers-by. From the upper balconies of tavernas the more hardy talked in loud self-importance, while inside steamy cafes people chatted at tables, dressed in fashions of clothing and hair wilder than any seen even in Q'os. Large feathers seemed to sprout everywhere, perhaps inspired by the Alhazii. White gloves on long-fingered hands. Cosmetics on every face he looked upon, men and women alike.

Time after time though it was the women who made him stare hard. They were goddesses here in this city in the clouds, glorious in their perfections, perched next to men often twice their age or older, erect and as long-necked as delicate flowers. Whenever they caught his eye he felt the thrill of it pulsing through him like the occasional rushes of the Milk, and their faces lingered in his mind like spectral-graphs in colour, their painted lips and powdered complexions, their mysterious glassy stares.

Again in the streets the disparity in ages was apparent. It was the young who were serving tables and manning counters or decorating the arms of their patrons, while it was mostly the old who cavorted around and acted as though they owned it all.

He moved on, slowly gaining a sense of this city, threading a way towards his destination.

Above the glow of the district and almost over his head, one leg of the Sky Bridge soared in a dizzying arch towards the central hub, sparkling with that weird violet light which also flickered across the heavy netting covering them all. Along the underside of the great arch the windows were burning with lights like a river of stars, obscured by plumes of steam and oily smoke that poured steadily from a multitude of vents.

More smoke was rising to the south of the district above the roof-tops. Ash thought he heard a chorus of gunfire coming from that direction, but no one in the streets responded to it in any way.

Nearby, though, a window was suddenly crashing to the ground, and at last heads were turning to look about them with interest. Ash stepped sideways into a doorway, where he could safely observe.

He glimpsed figures running across the street ahead. People wearing suits and dresses like everyone else but with masks covering their faces, leering monkey masks.

Another broken window crashed to the ground in big pieces as one of the group ran past with a hammer in their hand. A woman screamed in horror. Men shouted out in anger. But the figures danced through them, hopping and swinging their arms in a caricature of monkeys, and they screeched at the people in the street before disappearing down an alley.

Ash was almost tempted to follow after them out of curiosity, but he was close to the base of the Sky Bridge limb now. The wide thoroughfare he was following seemed to be leading him right to it. So he carried onwards, and he saw that ahead lay a huge open plaza with the base of the white leg rising up from its centre, starkly lit by floodlights. Glass doors were embedded in its nearest side, from which people were coming and going, guards stationed outside them much like the guards outside his hotel.

More immediate than that though were the double lines of guards stretched right across the end of the thoroughfare, stopping everyone trying to enter the plaza to inspect some kind of identification before allowing them through.

Ash turned away from the scene into a gloomy side street, looking for another way to get closer. He entered a darker district behind the noisy thoroughfare, with less people around, less activity and groundcars. Large blocks of housing rose over poorly lit store fronts, most of them closed and shuttered by metal grilles. The windows of the dwellings above were mostly dark or lit by a brownish light that waxed and waned and never seemed to settle. He heard a baby crying. A man shouting. The faint drums of music. Further along people were hanging out of the windows overhead, watching out for something.

He could hear a roar of voices from somewhere nearby. A battle raging in the streets.

A riot!

Excited now, Ash trod over the rubbish in the gutters and headed uphill towards the soaring limb of the Sky Bridge, keeping the sounds of trouble to his left and looking eagerly along every side street that he passed. Figures ran by him without regard, either away or towards the clamour. The roar of voices was much louder now, creating a strange kinetic energy in the air.

Ash frowned as he saw another double line of guards blocking off the end of this street too, not far from the open plaza and the base of the leg. It would seem the entire plaza was surrounded, then.

He turned away and stepped towards a small park encircled by a waist-high wall and paved with stone. Trees lined the park within, each one girded in its entirety by a metal cage through which limbs continued to grow. Figures shifted next to a few fires smoking in metal barrels, men and women heavily clothed against the cold, talking and coughing, a few turning to watch him as he stopped and peered again along the street at the open plaza and the guards.

'What's that under your burnoose, a weapon?' asked a voice next to one of the fires in rough Trade.

He saw a grimy bearded face behind a filthy breathing mask. Dark eyes shining brightly. Ash stepped into the park towards him.

'Yes,' he said matter-of-factly.

'A sword?'

Ash nodded.

'Can I see it?'

Why not. Ash opened his burnoose and swept the blade from its sheath and held it out before them, the curve of steel reflecting the dancing light of the fires. The man bent over it, fascinated by the rippling watermarks along its surface. Other figures turned to stare and mutter their surprise.

'You can use it then, I take it?'

With a flourish Ash sheathed the blade once more.

'What do you think?'

'Hah, I reckon so,' wheezed the fellow.

Ash looked up from beneath his hood, inclining his head in the direction of the riot. 'Sounds like trouble.'

It was a woman who spoke up in reply from the glow of another fire. 'They just went and sentenced a dozen more saboteurs to exile. Then beat into some resisters outside the prison for good measure. Now it's all kicking off again.'

'Drink?'

The bearded fellow wiped his mouth dry and held out a bottle, but Ash shook his head.

Close up he could see that the man was middle-aged like some of the others, though most of them were young. They all wore dirty breathing masks, and most had their heads bundled in cloth. At last he noticed the heaps of blankets stowed away around the nearest edge of the park. Sleeping rough.

'A cold night to be out,' he remarked as he warmed his hands above the flames.

'I've known worse,' came the fellow's stoic reply.

'Can't wait for the rainy season myself,' spoke the woman again, a grey-haired lady missing her front teeth. 'Nothing like being wet all the time as well as cold.'

In reply another voice called out in their native tongue. They all laughed at what he said.

Ash gazed up at the arching limb of the Sky Bridge, its surface as white and seamless as bone. Impossible to climb, he suspected. He studied the netting stretching out from the leg, not liking the way the violet light flashed across it, reminded of the monkey he'd seen killed trying to climb the wall back in town. His prospects seemed little better on the ground. The guards strung across the end of the street looked like they were there to stay.

Wait and watch, as was the Rōshun way. Hope that something presented itself. Try to get inside and rescue Meer. Never mind that such a plan was recklessly desperate.

Shouts in the distance. A pair of figures emerged from a side street and hurried up the road, scarves tied over their faces. People shouted down from the upper windows and they shouted back at them, waving them out. A soft breeze caused the leaves to rustle in the trees. They looked like a joke to his eyes, those trees encased in their white-painted cages. And sickly too, unless whatever species they happened to be always looked more dead than alive.

'You like trees or something?'

'Just wondering why they all seem to be dying.'

'Dying?'

'Every tree I have seen in the city. The leaves are mottled brown or crinkling with leaf burn around the edges. It means they're sick.'

'Sick trees he says!' laughed the woman from the other fire.

'No, it's true,' said someone else breathlessly, a younger spectacled man wrapped thickly in blankets. His skin was as black as Ash's. 'They *are* dying. Sure it's even in the news now. Though they say it's the bark beetles. Or the fungus. Or is it too long a dry season?'

The young fellow looked up at the Sky Bridge over their heads and tightened the blankets about himself with angry tugs, his eyes red-rimmed and morose above the dirty material of his breathing mask.

'The fools would rather report the symptoms than the real cause. They're pumping out more gases and pollutants than ever before is what it really amounts too, all those Elect trying to finish that Sky Bridge of theirs. But you'll never hear how the poisonous air is making us retch, or how it's so bad now that even the trees are weakening from it, so beetles and fungus and drought can finish them off. Not that anyone would listen.'

'Barely look at them myself,' admitted the bearded drinker, staring at the trees around him as though for the first time.

'No, hardly anyone does, Chappa. And that's why we'll wake up one day and the trees will all be dead and the crops we eat will be dead and the water itself too toxic to drink. And that'll be the end of us, unless they've somehow finished the Sky Bridge by then. In which case the Elect will save themselves – but only themselves. And all of this will be gone.'

Ash shivered at the young man's words and the resigned certainty of his manner, sensing doom in this city of the lost.

CHAPTER FORTY-FOUR

Running with Street Dogs

Suddenly there were footsteps pounding along the side streets and the echoes of shouts coming closer. People were running into the road and spreading outwards, many of them looking over their shoulders.

Goggles and bright scarves covered most of their young faces. Lean street dogs sprinted and leaped amongst their numbers in reckless excitement. From the side streets behind them a few gunshots echoed out and scattered people into cover, chased by bouncing smoke grenades trailing a yellow mist. Quickly the reeking mist thinned the remaining crowds.

Ash could feel it stinging his eyes, but despite that he took a few steps closer, one hand gripping hard around the railing of a dying tree. People flashed past his vision. Through the yellow smoke he could see fallen figures trying desperately to regain their feet, but armoured guards were catching up with them now, and batons were rising and falling, boots kicking and stamping, bones snapping, heads bouncing.

Memories flushed through his mind like freezing water.

'Yoy-yay, Yoy-yay!' shouted the crowd in their anger, coalescing again on the other side of the street to pierce the air with their whistles and taunts. Rubbish and grit blew about their legs in a downrush of air. Some shielded their eyes from the white light shining on them from a winged craft hovering above, a light which shifted onto the figures being beaten on the ground, prone forms in the rolling smoke surrounded by gangs of guards.

Part of Ash was back in his home village again, watching the soldiers beating the life out of his people. But another part of him was watching, thrilled, as one of the park dwellers vaulted over the low wall with a stick in his hands, yelling at the guards to desist. It was the young black fellow with the spectacles – his blankets and glasses gone now, his torso bare – plunging into the mist.

In a heartbeat Ash was over the railing too and running after him, his sheathed sword in his hand.

He saw a pair of guards beating a young woman on the ground. He took down the first guard by sweeping the man's leg out from under him, and the second with a ringing blow to the guard's helm with his still-sheathed sword. The young woman was curled in a ball with her teeth gritted in a bloody face, hands scrunched up for protection. Ash grabbed her coat and dragged her back across the street, his eyes streaming with tears from the yellow smoke.

Around him, goggled figures were scampering amongst the smoking grenades to snatch them up wherever they lay in the street, before hurrying back to drop them into pails of water. The street dogs danced between them in play. Near the walls of the park, more people were busy breaking apart the paving and building mounds of rocks for others to use.

Soon projectiles were flying towards the guards. The fiercest of the crowd surged forwards with sticks in their hands, yelling at the guards to get back and to leave the fallen alone. Like an eddy they formed around the young black man. Roaring their might, they somehow drove the guards back to their ranks and their lines of shields on the far side of the street, jeering them on.

A brief victory then; a resurgence of spirit that Ash felt rushing through the crowds of people and into his own body, entirely sweeping him up in the moment. Wiping at his eyes, he took the chance to look at the faces about him. They were young for the most part behind their scarves, their own bloodshot eyes open wide with excitement, though there were older people there too, some who were helping with the wounded or passing out water, or running milk into people's eyes to clear them. One old man came to Ash and gently tilted his head back so he could wash out his troubled sight, murmuring soft words of gratitude.

Suddenly the air rattled with shots from behind. Right next to Ash someone dropped to the ground. It was the old man who had been treating his eyes, lying there motionless on the paving with his spilled milk spreading out next to his head.

Ash ducked down behind the fallen man and squinted over his still form to the far end of the street and the open plaza, where a cloud of white smoke was rising from the lines of guards stationed there – rifles aimed squarely at the crowds. He gripped his sword fiercely.

They fired another volley of shots, though most of the people were down on the ground by then, protecting their heads with their hands or huddling behind whatever scant cover there was. Three shapes sprinted off the street to join others waving them up from behind a low wall, their legs bouncing loose with fear. In the very middle of the road, amongst the shouting and the gunfire and the shifting haze of smoke, a lone person stood undaunted with legs spread wide, swinging something round and round through the air – a slingshot singing for its release.

It was an old grandmother, Ash glimpsed in surprise. An old white-haired elder with goggled eyes and a white mask covering her features, leaning forwards over her belly to release the shot from its sling – sending it not at the guards themselves but at the limb of the Sky Bridge far, far overhead.

Right in front of Ash, a hatchet-faced man who was sprawled on the paving glanced back over one shoulder and offered a crazed grin. The fellow clutched something in his hands, and when he climbed to his feet Ash saw it was a bottle with a flaming wick of cloth stuffed into the neck, and he knew what would happen next even as the man threw it, even as it sailed through the air in a high arc to burst into flames right at the feet of the massed guards.

A roar rose up from the throats of thousands. More figures were rising now with flaming bottles in their hands.

These people knew what they were doing.

Within moments the bottles were showering towards the shooting guards, so many that it was a sight to behold, dozens exploding in ripples that forced the guards backwards in flaming panic, some beating at their armour and dropping rifles in dismay.

Back in the revolution of Honshu they themselves had used fire-flasks to good effect, but never before like this, not in such numbers. A reckoning of fear it must be for those armoured men trying to hold their line against a wash of fire and the rage of a thousand pressing people.

Those lines could break, he was starting to realize. And if they did it would provide the perfect cover for Ash to seek a way into the plaza beyond, and then the Sky Bridge itself.

It was the opportunity he had been hoping for.

Drawing his sword, Ash rose to his feet and waved the naked steel above his head like a rallying flag, as dramatic as old Oshō in his day, then set off towards the end of the street, joining others likewise, doing the same, gathering more as they went until they were a mass of people rushing for the lines and the roiling black smoke. Even the street dogs were running alongside them, snarling at the nearing forms of the guards behind their black shields; just like the strays from his days in the revolution.

Through the smoke the crowd charged blindly, only to face a sheeting jet of water from a stationary vehicle behind the lines. The raging jet washed back the flames and scooped people off their feet even as the ragged lines of guards were parting in two. Over their helms, Ash spotted a wedge of riders surging across the open plaza towards them, violet sparks flying from their waving batons.

A stranger's hand yanked him to the side of the street clear of the charge, and with an onrush of air the cavalry riders leaped over the flames and into the scattering crowds, hacking with their batons as they went.

It was chaos after that, like the bloody rout at the end of a hard-fought battle. Though rather than defeat it was simply another ebb in the tide, for as the crowds fled from the scene Ash could see them filtering through side streets to gather again elsewhere, perhaps to try the line at a different spot. A running battle which looked like lasting for the whole night.

His chances of breaking through were gone though. Even as he looked towards the plaza he saw guards breaking out to take a crack at anyone sprawled on the road.

Time to go, he realized. Time to find a better plan.

*

Ash looped his sword over his back again and turned about smartly, only to find more guards rushing in from behind. Someone toppled to the ground before him with a shout.

Towards the park he retreated, towards its welcoming shadows beneath the dying trees. Ten strides he'd taken before something struck his back and a paralysing pulse of pain ripped through his body.

When Ash blinked through his swimming vision he found himself sprawled on the paving unable to move or gain a breath. He tore the mask from his mouth, gasping desperately for air.

Through sheets of nausea, Ash saw a baton lying on the ground next to his face, flickering with that violet light – and above it, two pairs of boots approaching. He tried to move but failed. His cheek was pressed against the hard surface of the paving, and a beam of light from the guard washed across it so that he saw a fossil imprinted in the grey surface, something small and oblong and edged by frills.

Get up! he told his body, though when he tried to move again he was only able to roll onto his back.

Helpless, Ash watched as the guard grabbed a hold of his burnoose and hauled him to his feet, seeing random colours flashing. He could barely feel his left leg.

Two guards had a hold of him, and they yanked his hood back and turned his face from side to side for inspection, gabbing away with their pops and clicks and strange words. *Guallo*, they kept saying in their excitement. *Guallo! Guallo!*

His head was just beginning to clear when he felt his hands being clasped roughly behind his back. Felt the cold touch of steel manacles locking around his wrists.

The shock of it jolted Ash back to life.

His foot swung out, planting a boot firmly in the groin of the guard before him. Even as the man bent over he swung round and lashed the armoured kneecap of the other guard with the toe of his boot. The man went down with a snarl.

Ash was off, hopping through the park with his hands locked behind him and his left leg barely working at all. Shouts pursued him in Trade, from people on the ground being manacled by guards.

'Hoy, hoy!' they were yelling. 'Run for it, Guallo!'

He made it to a shadowed alley, reeling against the wall and twisting himself round to look back at last. One of the guards was following him, aiming a pistol right at his head.

Ash could only gasp at the sight of it.

The first shot tore a chunk from the wall above his head. His ears rang from the concussion.

The second shot ricocheted from the space where Ash had pushed away an instant earlier.

*

The old farlander staggered along the alley with the guard behind yelling raggedly in his native tongue, as though the man had breath to spare for it.

It was hard to run with his hands behind his back and only the thin air to sip upon, hard not to wonder how he'd gotten himself into this desperate position. Ahead, Ash could see a wide thoroughfare lively with people and the sounds of music. He staggered into it, almost running into a passing groundcar on the road. Over the passing flash of its bodywork he glimpsed a pair of guards on the far side of the street, uniformed backs turned on their own parked vehicle.

Why not? he asked himself in sudden hopeful mischief and with a quick glance backwards, and then he was staggering across the road towards the vehicle, propelled by his inspiration.

How hard could it be, after all?

The two guards were talking with someone on the pavement as Ash slid himself into the driver's seat, and with a limber writhing manoeuvre looped the manacles over his feet so that his hands were before him once more. He adjusted the sword on his back so it wasn't prodding his spine and took a quick glance to his left, where the pursuing guard was just emerging from the alley, right in time to walk in front of a speeding groundcar.

Ash looked away from the man's flying body and back over his shoulder. The pair of guards were turning now to the scene of the sudden collision. He glanced down at the switches and knobs and dials before him, all of them unintelligible. It was his feet that struck upon something hopeful, touching some kind of pedals down there, one for each foot. The old farlander pressed one of them hard, and then the other. The car whined but failed to move.

There was a mirror on the top of the windshield. He saw one of the guards looking his way.

'Come on, how hard can it be?' Ash snarled and started flicking switches at random.

A pair of squeaking arms swept across the grime of the windscreen.

'*Tchenhey-po!*'

More guards had emerged from the alley and were running towards the groundcar. Ash growled and shook the steering wheel in frustration while his foot stamped on a pedal, and in the process accidentally pushed something on the wheel, just as the nearest guard pointed a pistol at him.

Suddenly the groundcar was lunging forwards down the street, fast enough to push Ash back into the cushioned seat.

He glimpsed a guard gaping at him from the middle of the street and then he was past him, seeing the fellow in the mirror running after the groundcar with the others just behind.

The road pitched downwards and the vehicle picked up speed. The guards slowed and then stopped, giving up the chase.

'Hah!' Ash exclaimed as he leaned around in the seat, jerking his chin at them in the hope they could see him. 'Hah-hah!'

A jolt almost bucked him from his seat as the groundcar bounced off the side of a parked vehicle. With the buildings flashing by on either side Ash twisted the wheel to straighten the machine out. It was harder than it looked, or maybe his arms weren't working right yet. Either way the car wove across the road and clipped another coming in the opposite direction. Metal screeched and then he was past it, head up and grinning like a dazed fool, racing along an ever-steepening street which seemed to lead down the slope of the caldera itself; a sleigh ride in a contraption he had no idea how to stop.

They were giving chase back there. Purple lights flashed in the mirror and sounds wailed in the distance like birthing squatcha; sirens, he realized, waking the whole world to his flight. He knew then that he'd gained himself a little breathing room but nothing more. He still needed to find a way to get clear.

In absence of a way out you must create one, Molari, his old evasion instructor, had always told him.

Ash yanked on the wheel viciously and turned the vehicle into a side road curving off to the right. The groundcar wobbled and he jerked the wheel left, right, left again, getting a faint hang of it now, amazed at how the machine responded to his touch even as he barely held it on the curve of the road; somewhere in his mind wondering why the splayed wheels were screeching like distressed animals.

Teeth bared, he straightened out from the curve and barrelled down the middle of the road with the mirror catching distant flashes of purple. Through the windscreen people were jumping out of the way, cars swerving to one side or the other. Another experiment with his feet showed the other pedal to be a brake. With more confidence he applied speed and hunched forwards over the wheel, on the prowl for a way out of this. He was calm enough, for all that the flashes stayed fixed in the mirror, and for all that he was alone here in this city of strangers.

A dazzling light shone down into his face. Ash held up a hand and saw a pair of massive wings hovering in the sky over his head, a cone of brilliance shooting down from them to pin him to his seat. A downrush of hot air washed over him, scattering litter from the sides of the road.

Blinking, he yanked again on the wheel and negotiated another flying corner with the wheels screeching over the ground, enjoying the subtle art of it now, the flowing control of velocity held loosely on the edge. His sight was swimming again, though he glimpsed greenery to his right: a park flashing by and the silhouettes of tree-tops.

Ash applied the brake and twisted the wheel sharply, heading for the darkness of the park. In the frame of the windscreen the pavement bounced out of sight and a green lawn landed in its place, and then he was crashing back into the seat and the contraption was slewing across slick grass, Ash yanking the wheel one way then the other.

Signs flashed by both left and right of him. All he could see now was the green world whirling past within the cones of light from the front of the groundcar, and the purple lights flashing close behind.

A tree whipped through the glare of his lights.

Another tree.

A bench.

'*Whoah*,' exclaimed Ash as the car headed for a high stone kerb, and before he could react the wheels bounced over it and the vehicle vaulted into the air.

He felt a lurch in his belly then a crunch in his spine as the car landed hard with a splash of water. He was in a pond, it seemed, which explained the cold water flooding in around him.

Ash was out and wading to the edge before the pond's surface had even settled. Shedding water, he hurried off into a line of trees with the sounds of guards on foot close behind, beams of light bouncing around him. No damned way out of this, he was starting to think.

Keep going.

Ash surged onwards, slowed by the sodden burnoose flapping about him, and was startled when the nearest bushes exploded with a charging zel.

He thought it was one of the guards at first, but then he glimpsed the rider on its back, a man wearing a wide-brimmed hat like a ranchero and with a black scarf across his face. Even better, the figure was bending down in the saddle and holding out his hand in offering as the zel charged past.

No hesitation in the matter. Ash clasped the gloved hand and leapt up onto the back of the animal, and then he held on tight while the rider turned them in a circle back from where he had come.

'Keep your head down!' shouted the rider over his shoulder, though the branches whipping past their faces were all the warning Ash needed.

A light glared down through the trees as the flying machine swept over their position, noisily seeking them out. In its passing glare he saw that the rider was another black-skinned Anwi man.

'Who are you?' Ash shouted in his ear.

'Call me Juke!' he boomed back, and then the zel surged beneath Ash as they bounded from the trees onto hard paving, and the man turned the animal and spurred it clattering across an empty street, leaving behind the park and the frantic searchings of the law.

CHAPTER FORTY-FIVE

Council Grove

From the floor of the Windrush forest, Council Grove appeared ahead of them as a wide and shallow hill with steep sides, its flattened top bearing pine trees laden with snow and the drifting smoky columns of camp fires.

With curses of relief the party staggered towards it.

'You were with us before Chey-Wes,' Sergeant Sansun was saying to the big man Bull ahead, clad in Contrarè buckskins. 'What happened to you?'

Shard, stumbling along in her weariness, looked up from her feet in something of a daze, knowing that the sergeant spoke of the recent battle near Tume, in which General Creed's smaller force had slain the Holy Matriarch and stalled the imperial advance.

'They captured me, after the battle,' answered Bull without inflection, and Shard listened on, for it was the first time she'd heard the sergeant speaking to anyone with such obvious deference, even with Coya. They said that Bull had once been a famous Khosian pitfighter, one of the most celebrated of all.

'Kush!' spat the sergeant. 'That must have been rough. How did you escape?'

'You know, I'm still not certain.'

'Mind telling me about it?'

The big man was silent for a while, long enough for Shard to think he would say no more.

'They kept us in a pit in the ground,' he said, 'where we lived like chained dogs for most of the time. For the rest of it, we were taken by the priests for drugged interrogations. One night during a rainstorm I managed to break free from the pit, and we fled the camp together.

The others headed for Juno's Ferry. I headed for the Windrush instead.'

'The priests used drugs on you?' Shard heard herself ask aloud through her own pain, causing the man's great head to swing around, catching her in the tail of his eye, before he turned away again. She knew she looked rather wild-eyed just then. A rush had been overcoming her body and mind ever since she'd sighted the hill of Council Grove, and at the same time the cramps in her belly had returned with a stabbing agony.

'They used a kind of white dust, amongst others. Why do you ask?'

She had heard rumours of the methods employed by the Mannian order against its enemies. Their use of drugs and repeated interrogations to scramble the minds of their victims, secretly conditioning them to act as spies or saboteurs or assassins amongst their own people.

Bull certainly carried the harried look of such a person, his eyes red-raw from lack of sleep.

'You've been sleeping poorly since then?'

He faltered and fell into step beside her, interested now. He was huge, this man. He seemed almost as wide as others were tall.

'Hardly at all,' he admitted. 'I'm plagued with nightmares every time I close my eyes. You know something of this?'

'A little. They were most likely messing with your head when you were their prisoner. Implanting suggestions. Tearing down your identity. Shaping you to their uses.'

Bull was looking directly at her now, hungry for whatever information she might have.

'Is there a way to set things right again then? These nightmares . . .' He shook his head again, and Shard could have sworn there was fear in the warrior's eyes. 'I would like to be free of them, I tell you.'

'Perhaps I can look at you later, if there is time?'

'Yes,' he agreed. 'I would appreciate that.'

They were hiking up the stony path to the ridgeline of the hill now, and Shard put her head down once more in concentration. Reaching the top and gasping for air she saw something entirely unexpected: the hill was actually a great laq-wide crater with inner walls even steeper than the outer ones, cliffs for the most part, surrounding a plateau of small lakes and dense forest echoing with the calls of a great many birds.

Shard felt another rush of lightness entering her head. The air was clear and everything stood out with a fine and solid clarity. She squinted, seeing black and white pica birds wheeling in flocks at the very centre of the crater, soaring above a conical rise of ground upon which a grove of thirteen chimino trees rose like towers above the canopy. A great bonfire burned down there, sparkling in the dull afternoon light beneath a full moon rising from the east. Drums beat out into the evening stillness, figures dancing as silhouettes before the flames.

'Thank Mercy we made it in time,' Coya said from Marsh's back.

'That mean I can put you down now?'

*

Beneath the light of the full moons, hundreds of pica birds were chattering noisily from the trees of the grove like a host of excited night spirits, watching over the council of humans gathered in the clearing below and listening without comprehension to their words rising in the heat of the great fire.

Never before had the Contrarè of the Windrush seen these black and white birds gathered in such numbers. At ease with reading the signs of their forest lives, the Longalla knew that the creatures had been drawn there by the presence of the Dreamer, this woman who had supposedly shed much of her Contrarè ways along with her name, *Walks With Herself*, yet who caused the forest to speak to her through the clacks and ragged calls of the pica. Indeed she had clearly begun to soar the moment she set foot in the grove, just like their own sky hermits.

She was still soaring, even now. She swayed with her eyes closed and her face pointed to the sky, her body an anchor in the surface of the world while her spirit flew ever higher.

No telling what she was seeing as the Dreamer swayed almost imperceptibly to the soft beat of the drums, oblivious to the two figures standing beside her facing the circle of Contrarè elders, all gabbling like the birds above.

'Hear me!' cried one of the figures by her side, though the Dreamer showed no reaction to his outburst. It was Coya, thrusting aloft the stick he was using as a cane before their gleaming, painted faces. 'Still your tongues and open your ears!'

Indeed the elders fell to a sudden hush at his words, for they held this man in high regard, just as they did his companion, the Contrarè Dreamer. Coya Zeziké was a name known to them even here, a man who expressed the spirit of his ancestor through his own powerful oratory. Following another hostile incident between the Longalla and the Khosian landowners around their forest, they had heard of the famous fiery speech he'd given in the distant Meeting House of the League, a place fashioned on the egalitarian council circles of the Longalla themselves. Coya had spoken of the tribe's right to live free as they had always lived, and of their right to defend themselves and the forest with force of arms if needs be.

Heysoo, the Longalla had taken to calling him. Wise Grandfather.

Yet now, standing here before them, he seemed nothing more than a frail youth bent over a stick, his head wrapped in a bleeding bandage.

'It's true,' Coya said, while hushed voices translated for those who spoke no Trade. 'I come here partly as a delegate of the League. But you know too that I am a friend of the Longalla. Just as my ancestor Zeziké was your friend, he who claimed the democras was inspired by the assemblies of your people in the Windrush. And as your friend, I am here to ask for your aid. The people of Khos, the people of the democras, are calling on you to join this war with us. Let us put aside our animosities and unite against the Empire's forces here in Khos. Together we can defeat them. Together we can smash them into the dust so they can never return. Alone, though, we will each fall.'

Voices erupted around the fire, but Coya held up his stick again to draw their silence.

'You doubt they will not come for you here in the Windrush, after they have taken Bar-Khos and Al-Khos? You doubt they will not force their ways upon the tribe and enslave you if you resist? That they will not fell these trees as though they were made of gold until all are gone? You doubt any of this, for even a single heartbeat?'

Next to Coya, a portly figure was shaking his head theatrically and smiling at the foolishness of what he said. Alarum was dressed like some kind of hill bandit rather than a Mannian spymaster, though he bore himself as though he wielded much unspoken power.

Already harsh words had been exchanged between the pair. The Mannian was clearly enjoying himself this evening, and finding it difficult to remain silent while Coya had his turn.

Other figures were enjoying it too, this contest of words between the two men. The Longalla elders stared fascinated from their circle around the fire, men and women alike gathered in council. Also there were younger faces amongst them, youths considered as *shakota* by their peers, 'old souls' mature beyond their years.

A voice spoke up loudly from behind the circle, one of the Red Path warriors with his painted face cast fiercely in the firelight. 'The Longalla are five thousand fighters strong,' he shouted in Trade for Coya's benefit. 'We will kill them all if they set foot in the forest, as we have been killing their scouts to the east!'

But another older Contrarè shook her head sadly while holding up her withered hand for attention, a tiny figure peering out from a heavy wrapping of blankets. She replied in her native tongue while someone nearby translated aloud, speaking over her thin croaking voice. 'We are not in the high forests of the Broken Spine, *Always Speaks Loudest*, where you can travel for a moon without seeing the tracks of another. We are in the Windrush, an island of the great world forest standing alone on an island within the Salt Sea. We are isolated here and with nowhere to run. Wise Grandfather is right in this. It does not matter our numbers or how fiercely we can fight. If the cult of the Red Hand conquers Khos, they will devour the forest around us until there is no more of it, not even this sacred grove we are gathered within. If we declare war on them then it must be by the side of the Khosians, and it must be now while they can still be defeated. Yes, *Heysoo* speaks truth and I support our friend with all my heart, as should we all.'

The old woman nodded at Coya and Coya nodded in reply, while around the circle some grunted agreement and others shook their heads in denial. Several figures rose and carried the skins upon which they had been kneeling to sit instead behind the old woman who had just spoken so eloquently.

'I too agree with Wise Grandfather,' declared a fine-looking fellow with rare eyes of blue, his hair hanging in skinny dreadlocks. It was the same fellow who had guided them here with Bull. 'We must join the Khosians in this. But Oka is wrong to think the cult of the Red

Hand is invincible. Profit is the master of the Empire, no matter their numbers. We can defeat them here in the forest if only we make them pay for every tree and every Contrarè which they fell – if we make them pay enough that they retreat for fear of losing even more.'

'Well spoken, Sky In His Eyes!'

'Ayee!'

Even more figures rose from around the fire to settle behind the younger man.

'Wise words,' spoke out the Mannian Alarum again. 'Though before you judge how much blood must be shed in this cause of yours, perhaps you should listen to what my people have to offer? The order of Mann is prepared to promise you this much at least. Should the Longalla take up arms against the Empire here in Khos, should you help the Khosians in their war against us, then we shall bear our full force against you when we finally conquer this island.'

Shouts barked out in anger, and the spymaster held up his hand to ward them off like angry blows. 'You should all know by now that the cause of the Khosians is a defeated one. That is why the great Coya Zeziké himself is here in the Windrush to beg for your help. It is only in their desperation that the Khosians condescend to speak with the barkbeaters of the Windrush at all, and even then through someone who is not even one of their own. Well I am permitted to tell you this much: if you join with them now you will go down with them. You will turn this forest into a mass grave, even if we have to bomb it from the air and burn the whole lot to the ground to make our point.'

Coya snorted. The circle of Contrarè shook their heads in alarm, feathers bobbing and bone jewellery rattling, while the younger hot-heads gripped their weapons and bared their teeth, restrained only by the banner of truce the Mannian delegation was under and the hands of their companions.

'You threaten these people with their own destruction?' Coya muttered to the man, but Alarum ignored him, holding up both hands now beseechingly.

'I have another promise too which you must consider. If you agree not to side against us in this war, we can sign a treaty here and now promising your autonomy in the forest after we have taken Khos. You will be spared your lives and the Windrush will be protected. We will allow you to live as you have always lived, free and without interference.'

'And what worth is a treaty from a Mannian dog of the Empire?' spat one of the Red Path warriors.

'The Empire may be many things, but we are generous to our friends and allies. Take our hand in friendship now and prosper, or die here with the Khosians.'

Coya Zeziké lowered his head with a frown, one hand kneading the other on top of his walking stick. Some saw him glance to the Dreamer standing by his side, still oblivious to it all it seemed; then he glanced to his bodyguard standing under one of the trees, watching broodingly.

A voice sang across the fire. A narrow face squinted through the glimmer of the coals, his cheekbones like blades.

'I agree with the Mannian. The Khosians' fate is sealed in fate. And if we join them now we will only seal our own fates too. Look at Pathia. Look what happened to the Black Hands and the Long Walkers, when they tried to resist the Empire from the scraps of their lowland forests. Consider what is befalling them even now for their defiance.'

Right then the Dreamer stopped swaying to the beat of the drums and snapped her head erect, suddenly returned to the confines of her body and the awful cramps in her belly. She was startled by the talk around the fire and by the many heads turning now towards her, for these Contrarè knew who she was, and that she came from Pathia too.

Black Hands, Shard thought with a roaring return of her senses. *They're talking of my people here.*

With an arm pressed against her stomach for relief, Shard held up her other palm so she could see it better, as devoid of tattoos as any white-eye's. She and her family had fled to the Free Ports before she had been old enough to gain her tattoos as a woman of the Black Hands. Since then, she had never gotten round to having them done, despite her father's regular protestations.

In the roar of her ears, Coya's voice rose like a rush of waves breaking upon her mind.

'If you do nothing and we win here, the Khosians will never forgive you for your betrayal. How long will the peace last between you then?' The fire spat and sparked in their collective silence. 'Surely it is better to join with us, your brothers and sisters in spirit, the people of all the democras, rather than with these butchers, these bloody conquerors?'

Shard was panting quickly, her heart racing. Now that her eyes were open again she fought to keep them open, for when they were closed her mind sped through lurching geometric flights that seized her entirely.

The sandworm was too much to handle tonight, no matter what she took to dampen its effects. It was as though this grove of chimino trees held some heightened vibration of the forest and she was resonating with it, conducting its full force through her spine and the pulsing cramps in her stomach, feeling sick from the pain of them.

Only the strongest of will held her now to the ground before the shining faces of the Longalla, her tangled thoughts trying to make sense of it all.

The tribe was caught between two mighty rocks, she could tell, and even though she hadn't been following most of what had been spoken, Shard sensed the division rising amongst them. Their auras pulsed faster with shades of uncertainty, shades of anger and fear.

'What is your opinion, Walks With Herself?' asked the handsome Longalla man with the striking blue gaze, Sky In His Eyes, and for a moment she was struck by how he used her Contrarè name, warmed by the sound of it in her ears. 'They say you are a mighty Dreamer of our people. What does your heart tell you now? Who will win this fight, truly now – the democras or the Empire?'

She swayed in her boots and felt Coya's hawk-like gaze watching her intently, this man who was her friend in his own way, and who could well drop dead at any instant despite all she had done for his terrible wound.

Coya had asked her here to add weight to all that he must ask of these Contrarè, but now she had almost forgotten her original purpose, and was instead engorged by the pulse of the forest and the blinking of the stars, all of life and death demanding truth in these moments of decision.

'If you wish to know the outcome of this war,' she answered thickly, obliquely, 'then ask your sky hermits, your seers.'

'Yet I am asking you,' insisted Sky In His Eyes softly.

Too much for her just then, these pressing questions of his, those eyes that stared at her like daylight glinting through clouds. Shard's mind began to spin around the circle of Contrarè, whispers of their thoughts threading with her own until she reeled at their very centre. She staggered back a step, losing her balance. The Contrarè watched her with open mouths.

'The odds will remain with the Empire even if you come to the aid of the Khosians,' she heard her own voice saying aloud, and Shard realized the truth of the words even as she heard them. She had been feeling it ever since she'd arrived in Bar-Khos, deep down inside her: the shifting tide of the war. 'Though the outcome remains uncertain.'

Coya was tugging at her sleeve, muttering, scowling. 'What are you doing? Why are you telling them this?'

'I'm sorry,' she mumbled, but Shard was having trouble even seeing him clearly, for she was spinning faster now, and her vision was once more smearing into chaos.

She gripped Coya's arm hard for balance, for something to keep her on the ground, while the Contrarè gabbled all around her.

Suddenly Shard's head tilted back, and she saw the tops of the trees thrusting into a night sky aswirl with stars and moons and a sudden streaking meteor. And then Coya was looking down at her, and Shard seemed to be lying on her back on the frozen ground, her eyes fluttering and her belly tightening in agony.

The last thing she glimpsed, past Coya's stricken features, were the hundreds of eyes staring down at her from the high trees, the pica birds silently watching her, ruffling their wing feathers as she took off into flight.

CHAPTER FORTY-SIX

Flight

The forest fell away as Shard rose into the night sky high above the Windrush, spinning slowly to take in the world and the war about her.

A knot of lights glimmered through the still night air beyond the eastern edge of the Windrush – the captured city of Tume afloat on the silvery waters of Simmer Lake, matched by a rash of camp fires around the southern shoreline: the Imperial Expeditionary Force.

From the closest corner of Simmer Lake, the glistening waters of the Chilos meandered along the edge of the forest with more lights ranged along the far bank, following it southwards towards the red glimmer of Juno's Ferry, where explosions and cannon fire sparkled in the darkness.

An imperial assault was taking place, it seemed, and a major one at that. It appeared the enemy were no longer content to remain on the eastern side of the river for the duration of winter.

Shard was witnessing a new chapter in the war unfolding, yet it seemed not to matter just then who was fighting who or for what. She felt a clean detachment from it all, freed of all earthly concerns, and in her freedom she rose even higher, slowing her spin yet further.

With a clarity of vision she saw how highlands covered the eastern half of the island of Khos, rugged with impressive snowy peaks, diminishing into foothills that ran down into the wide plateau of the Reach and the valley of the Chilos. She tracked the holy river on its long course all the way to the southern coast of the island, where it emptied into the Bay of Squalls not far from the fiery glow of Bar-Khos and the Lansway, that dark bridge to Pathia and the southern continent, where Mokabi's forces were assaulting the Shield.

Still no telling pricks of sentiment, even when she thought of

Seech and how she would soon need to face him. And so the besieged
city panned away from her sight as she turned westwards to face the
lowland half of the island, where its many towns were strung along
the rivers and roads like faintly shining jewels. At last Shard faced
north and the sight of far Al-Khos perched on the northern coastline, with the Midèrēs sea shining in the moonlight all the way to the
curving horizon.

She was watching it all so closely as she drifted around that it
took a moment before her instincts told her to glance upwards,
startled, at the apparition hovering before her in the air.

A naked woman floated there with the same Contrarè features as
her own, though she was older than Shard, lined about the eyes and
marked by stretches across her belly, and her breasts were fuller,
and her black hair was long and flowed across her shoulders as
though it swayed in invisible currents of water.

'Walks With Herself,' said the woman in a voice of honey, floating
amongst the stars in her fulsome nakedness.

'Yes?'

'I would talk with you, if you will listen to my words.'

For an instant Shard felt the danger of a sudden fall, and she
glanced down at the distant speck of light directly below in the dark
sea of trees, the bonfire of Council Grove, no doubt, where her body
would be lying unconscious to the world while voices argued over
war. When she looked up again, she was still floating there before the
woman.

'Who are you?'

'An expression of the Great Dream, as all things are,' the figure
answered, with the tenderness of a mother. She reached out a hand
to touch the side of Shard's face, the side normally covered in scars,
though not now. 'I'm whoever you need me to be.'

'Then who are you?'

'Call me Elios, if you must call me anything. Elios, Mother of the
Forest. That sandworm in your gut. It's killing you.'

'I know.'

'Then kill it first. You know which concoction will work. Hold as
much of it down as you can and hope the worm dies before you do.'

'But I can't, not yet. I must master it first.'

'You mean you must master this man Seech first.'

344

'Yes.'

'It is that important to you? Important enough to risk your life?'

'Yes!'

'But why?'

'I have my reasons.'

'Then share them with me.'

Heartache surged through Shard suddenly, shattering the detached calmness of her mind.

She saw a bundle in her shaking hands, the size of a miscarried infant wrapped in a shawl. A hole in the drift of sand where she was burying him.

Memories crashed upon her. Recollections of the expedition into the Alhazii deep desert, of the year she had worked so hard to forget.

*

Shard had been nineteen at the time, a student of exotics at the Academy of Salina as well as their leading rook, cocky and self-assured for her age because she was a travelled Contrarè refugee all the way from troubled Pathia, and because she was smart and remarkably good at what she did.

So it was hardly a surprise when she had been one of only two student rooks offered a place in an academic expedition into the Alhazii deep desert, hand-picked by its leader, Feyoon, the Academy's most flamboyant of Observers. They were to search for the fabled sandworm of the Zini oasis, Feyoon had told them with his usual fervour. A sandworm fabled to aid in unlocking the underlying bindee of the cosmos to a special few, the so-called Dreamers of the Alhazii.

Weeks later, a sea voyage on an armed convoy to Zanzahar had cured Shard quickly of her arrogance, attacked as they had been by a gauntlet of imperial men-of-war and hit by foul weather for the rest of the time. From the teeming Alhazii metropolis of Zanzahar, the largest city she had ever seen, the expedition and its local guides had set off east onto the famed Spice Road through the dusty rock of the Sill, hoping to reach a place where they could find guides into the deep desert and the oasis of Zini.

In practice, the Spice Road revealed itself to be more of a route than a road that skirted the northern foothills of the Sill Mountains.

It was dotted with waystations where skyships moored for the night and caravans pitched up with their cargoes: exotics from the Isles of Sky being carried into the far east, and spice brought back in return, that potent narcotic known elsewhere in a refined form as dross, to which many of the Sill Alhazii seemed to be addicted.

Along the way, the copious forts and patrols of the Caliph they encountered offered the impression of safe travel, but on one hot dry day travelling through a pass in the hills, their complacency was shattered by a sudden ambush by hill bandits. The encounter saw the death of Feyoon, the expedition's leader. And everyone else too, save for Shard and Seech, for together they had run at the first instant of trouble.

In her survivor's numbness, Shard was shocked further when she heard that Tabor was of a mind to continue onwards, to travel into the deep desert in search of the sandworm and the secrets of the Dreamers. An insane idea if ever she had heard one.

She would have protested, yet she knew this man well who was her lover. Seech would have taken it as a personal victory over her, perhaps the most important of all their ongoing contests.

So onwards they continued, alone.

*

For weeks they travelled the Sill, stealing and trading what they could for survival, often relying on the kindness of others. Slowly they made their way closer towards the deeper desert, with their travelling clothes becoming rags and their hair growing wild, until they bore the resemblance of beggars.

But good fortune eventually befell them too. In a settlement on the very edge of the Sill they had come across a trading caravan preparing to carry onwards into the sea of dunes that was the Alhazii deep desert, and before she could protest, Seech had talked the caravan captain into allowing them to come along. Too late to turn back now, Shard had gone along with it.

And so it was that Shard and Tabor, after months of travel and personal risk, after weeks of riding through the desert on the backs of swaying sandwalkers, at last found themselves where the expedition had always intended to end up, at the life-giving waters of Zini oasis, a settlement dominated by a mud-brick tower.

Enclosed within the tower, the desert shamans were as Feyoon had said they would be, secretive and protective of their ways. Soon it became clear to Shard that had she not passed herself off as a young man the shaman there would not have spoken with her at all. But given time, they admitted to knowing the secrets of the sandworm, and after a month of careful negotiation and explicitly making a nuisance of themselves, one of the shamans agreed to take them under his wing.

The old man had smiled when Tabor had pumped him for information concerning the Dreamers.

Yes, he had admitted – they had indeed produced a handful of Dreamers over the centuries, though they were more rare than Shard and Tabor had been led to believe. While all the desert shamans took the juice of the sandworm in their rituals, few had ever truly unlocked the code of the bindee. Those rare exceptions who had done so, those whose names were recited as ancient masters, claimed time and again that the process was unique to themselves, how each person must decipher their own code individually; a personal experience that could not be shared with another.

Lovers still, as close as any two people can be who competed on every level of their lives, Shard and Tabor now found their old rivalries blossoming like never before. For years they had tested each other to see who was the best rook between them, a battle which Shard had decisively won. But now it seemed that Tabor had found a way of proving he was the better person after all. To her face he swore he would unlock the bindee before Shard could.

And so it was in a spirit of rivalry that they set out to prove they could do it, even as the shaman laughed with his eyes at the arrogance of their presumptions.

*

Over the following weeks they discovered that Feyoon had been right in his claims concerning the bile of the sandworm, that it was one of the most potent substances in the world.

Obtained from their friendly shaman amongst a litany of warnings, they had surprised him by taking to the worm's juices remarkably well. Perhaps because they were both skilled rooks already versed in the disorientating strangeness of the Black Dream.

Perhaps because they already possessed copious experience of mind-altering substances taken in heroic doses.

Indeed they took to the juice almost too well. Chanting words of intent over and over, a Contrarè trick that Shard had used in her rooking for focusing her mind, they took ever-increasing doses of the juice until even the old shaman began to marvel at it, shaking his head in dismay.

Respect, he tried to tell the pair gently. *You must respect the slow rhythms of the worm and engage upon a relationship with it, a kind of courtship. You should not force it or you will go crazy in the head like Zawooz over there, you understand?*

But they were already half crazy, the pair of them, and so they paid him little heed. Soon paranoia was descending upon them both like a world of echoes and mirrors, so that even when Shard was free of the juice, recovering in between their sessions, she started seeing things that should not be there, could not be there, and Tabor heard meanings in her voice never intended. Sometimes demons racked those endless nights spent voyaging into the unknown together.

One night at the very peak of this inner exploration, they both ventured off for a walk into the dunes as high as they ever had been or ever would be again, and heard a pair of rutting desert foxes screeching out to the sister moons in their mad passions. Somehow even in their delirious conditions Shard and Seech found similar passions surging within them, and on the shifting sands they had rutted like the two animals they were, calling out their chanted words of intent, losing themselves so fully that when they both came together in ecstasy their minds blew away entirely, leaving them both adrift beyond space and time where there was only raw and fundamental information, the binary code of the Great Dream, the bindee.

No satisfying way to share what Shard and Tabor experienced in those moments or hours of silent unravelling, for language was too thin a tool to fully express their awakening.

Blasted of all thoughts, each became aware of the slow dance of vibrations from which everything was made, pure information prompted into existence by nothing more than the focus of their attention, like a beam of lantern-light illuminating things in pitch blackness; a vast and strange existence in which nothing was truly real but their own consciousness; a cosmic illusion, a Great Dream, a seething unconsciousness that was evolving towards higher complexity and a distant unknowable singularity.

The bindee, they realized, formed the underlying web of their seemingly material existence, its binary code presenting the simplest form of discrimination within the All. The first information.

And beyond the cosmos? Outside of the Dream? Too far to see, too deep to fathom, too impossible to grasp. Perhaps nothing lay out there for there was no 'out there' to be comprehended. Or perhaps beyond this cosmic egg of a maturing universe existed countless others, which begged the question – what then held them all?

Did they exist in some creator's mind, and if so, what then held the mind of the creator?

In dawn's prescient light, waking upon the dune and feebly stirring in their bodies and minds once again, Shard and Tabor realized they were no longer the same people as before. Something fundamental had changed within them.

*

Over the forthcoming days the shaman saw it too, this change in them. He came to them with an offering: an invitation to follow him into the tower.

In the dead of night he led them down beneath the leaning tower of mud, where a rock cave sheltered a pool of dark liquid.

It was the source of glimmersuits, the shaman had translated for them. Now that they had unlocked the code of the bindee they could choose to take the next step, to clad themselves in a glimmersuit of their own. Only then would they be able to manipulate the bindee as Dreamers.

Of course Seech was the first to splash into the strange pool, submerging himself entirely in his clothes before he'd even asked if the process was reversible. Only after a long deliberation did Shard step into it herself.

Moments later, upon stepping out again it was as though their skins refused to dry.

It took days for Shard to become remotely at ease with this living second skin now covering the entirety of her body. Her sense of touch was just the same as it had been before, though her sensitive parts seemed even more so now. The suit even sweated like her own skin. When she moved there was no sense of it, no folds or tucks or creases. For long hours she would study herself in the mirror, pulling back the lips of her mouth or the lids of her eyes, trying to see where the glimmersuit ended.

Shard marvelled at what she was now able to perform before her eyes. It was like rooking, her most passionate of passions, though this was rooking in the waking world, with real things she could touch and see. With their new second skins, both Shard and Seech found they could read the bindee whenever they wished to, and more than that, they could reach out with their minds to manipulate it. Soon they had discovered how to see and speak from afar, even into the past. How to tell of a person's illness. How to plant a desire into an animal's mind.

Sometimes she rejoiced at these new-found abilities, and sometimes she trembled late at night in fear of them. She was strongly aware that whatever lay in her future now was vastly different from before, and that there was no turning back.

After a while the people of the oasis began whispering about the two strangers amongst them and their increasingly strange ways. Tensions rose between the pair too. Even now Tabor was annoyed that he hadn't attained the state of Dreaming first, to the point where he claimed it had all been his own doing by rutting so fiercely with her, that he had inadvertently taken her along for the ride. They began to fight more often. Began to separate their experiments and their daily lives.

Began to unravel.

*

When Shard first discovered she was pregnant, she was both surprised and appalled.

Tabor flung himself into a fury at her unexpected news. He claimed she had done it to sabotage his work there, that she wanted to return home and this was the only way she could tear him away. Such hubris, she had thought in her own silent anger.

For a time she even wondered whether she should keep the child or not. There were concoctions she could take, even here in the desert, to rid her of this burden. Seech, of course, was all for the idea.

One night he came to her with a flask of the stuff he had already brewed.

Shard had slapped it out of his hand, resolving there and then to have the child no matter how untimely it might be for this man she had once considered her lover. Whatever feelings she had for him seemed to vanish in that moment.

They spoke even less after that, and Shard's belly began to grow. She dropped hints whenever she could then started saying it straight out. Yes, she told him, she wanted to return home before the child was born. Yes, she wished to be with her family in the safety of their home.

When he still refused to leave she pointed out the obvious. How long do you think it will be before the shamans see this bump beneath my robe? How well do you think they'll take it, their secrets passed on by trickery to a mere woman?

For an instant she was certain Tabor was considering ways of getting rid of her quietly and without fuss – so low had he fallen in her eyes. But with a mighty show of regret he had appeared to relent at last, agreeing that they would leave and soon. A fortnight, he asked her for. No more and no less. Let him procure some zels first so they could travel between oases back to the Sill.

What Tabor spent most of his remaining weeks on, though, seemed to be the acquisition of some sandworms, for the single worm in their possession had been withering away by the day. Tabor grew obsessed with the notion of returning to the Academy with proper living specimens in hand.

On the fateful night before they were due to leave, with a string of zels tethered outside their hut, procured once more through the good faith of the old shaman, Shard was wakened by a single shout in the night, and stumbled to the door to see flames licking from the side of the mud tower, and smoke billowing from its small windows, where figures leaned out calling for help. Even as she watched on someone jumped, burning, from a high ledge and crashed into the sand, not moving.

What has he done? she instantly thought, knowing it was the work of her companion.

And then Seech himself was pounding over the sand towards the hut, and suddenly he was there before her with his panting face leering through the darkness, painted in someone else's blood; clearly high on something, telling her that they had to go, his claws yanking Shard after him towards the zels. Under one arm he clutched a heavy box, and when she asked him what it was, he told her it was some sandworms, of course, what else would it be? And Seech grinned as though it was a good thing he had done here, a victory of some kind, a way out of their predicament; and she saw then that the old shaman had been right after all, that the two of them had been playing with madness all along.

'*You set them on fire?*' Shard had screamed at him in dismay.

His smile had faltered, and he looked to the gathering inferno and then to the people of the oasis flocking to the dreadful scene with pails of water, and he flexed his neck and said, 'No choice in the matter, they found me out. I – I only started a small fire in there to make my escape. Come. We have to go!'

A silent fury possessed her right then. She grabbed Seech as he tried to climb into his saddle and flung him with all the caged hatred she had been fostering for the man, so that his body went spinning before it landed in the sand and rolled through a stand of grasses. She was stepping towards him with her hands held out in claws as he rose unsteadily and turned to face her. Hatred twisted his features too; as though his face was turned inside out with it, displaying his true inner self at last.

Seech glared with intent and roared the air from his lungs, and suddenly flames were searing through her mind and toppling her over with agony and panic; real flames, burning and searing her skin, some kind of Dreaming power he had discovered for himself. Shard clutched at the side of her face as the glimmersuit and her own skin both hissed and smoked where they had fused together, knowing now how he had started such a blaze within the tower.

He came to her and shook her prone body for a while, shouting incoherently, and when he ran out of breath he held her in his arms, sobbing, saying he was sorry, that he didn't know what he had done. The smell of burnt meat filled her nostrils. Suddenly a blade of pain stabbed through her abdomen, then another. Shard cried out from it, knowing that something was terribly wrong with her unborn child. She reached down and felt hotness between her legs, wetness. Blood smeared the palm of her hand when she raised it to her eyes.

Shard shrieked aloud at the night sky filled with flames and tumbling smoke. From where she lay she saw Seech rising with tears in his eyes to cast one final glance down at her. She bit down on another scream as she heard him mount his zel and lead the string of animals out onto the open dunes, leaving her there to pay the consequences of it all, to suffer through the worst night of her life.

Too much to live through again, the pain of those emotions.

Utter blackness.

*

'Walks With Herself,' soothed a woman's voice in her ear.

It was Elios, Mother of the Forest, or whoever she was meant to be, figment of her mind or spirit guide she did not know. Regardless, the woman's arms held her in their embrace while Shard wept with all the loss and anger remaining since that awful night.

'You left a part of yourself behind in the desert,' said the woman softly. 'But your child is one again with the Great Dream, where it will know no suffering, only bliss.'

'It hurts,' she cried aloud.

'I know, I know. You must learn to embrace your heart in the Contrarè way, Shard. You have been fleeing these emotions, hiding in your work for all of this time. Let them out of you, my child. Give them voice.'

'He left me alone out there. He left me alone to deal with it all.'

'I know.'

'He will pay for this. For all of it!'

'Then first you must master the sandworm, as you say.'

'But I don't know how. I fear it's too much for me.'

'Fear not, child of the Dream. It will come to you. It may be on its way even now.'

Shard glimpsed the stars smearing slowly around them, far suns in the black eternity of the cosmos. So much like the Black Dream itself, though here she could not hide from herself or her past, for here was the place where all meaning flowed.

'The child, did you give him a name?'

'A name? No. He was miscarried.'

'Still, he deserves one, don't you think?'

'I hadn't thought of it.'

'You did not wish to think of it. How does *Tippetay* sound?'

Shard drew back from the woman in surprise, blinking through tears at her shining face.

'The Longalla here use the word for certain moments . . . When they see a brief eddy in the river before it folds back into itself . . . a lone cloud forming in the thermals . . . the flowers of the moon orchid. Something precious that does not last for long.'

It was the kind of name her father would have suggested, Shard realized. 'Tippetay,' she repeated, sampling the sound of its syllables on her tongue.

The woman smiled.

*

'Here, take some of this.'

Shard blinked up at a pair of striking blue eyes, two moons shining in an oval of Contrarè face paint, much like the Sisters of Loss and Longing in the night sky overhead.

Cramps were splitting her stomach in two, just like the night in the deep desert. But she was returned to the Windrush now, slouched against a tree just beyond the main circle of the council gathering, clutching her abdomen while her breath hissed through clenched teeth. The pains shot through her as though the worm was chewing its way through her inner flesh, and she started to panic, seized by the belief that it really was eating her from the inside out, the whole world flying through her with the spinning horror of it. She rode on waves of nausea.

A cool breeze fluttered Shard's lashes and soothed her skin. It was the handsome Contrarè man blowing lightly across her face, the one who had helped her up from the ravine. She inhaled the coolness of his breath, seeing that he was crouched over her with the back of his hand held towards her face. A small pile of snuff sat perched on his skin.

'Sensee bark,' he reassured her in smooth Trade, and nodded, urging her to try some. 'It will help you come down from these heights of yours.'

How beguiling, that smooth voice of his. Shard took a quick snort with a finger over one nostril, instantly feeling the rough sting of it in the back of her throat.

Almost at once her skin began to grow numb. The spasms of pain subsided within her. The ground no longer lurched when she looked at it.

In a flash the vision returned of Elios, Mother of the Forest, more real than any dream. Goosebumps rose on the back of her neck.

'More,' she gasped, and he produced another pinch of the snuff for her to snort.

Shard sniffed then leaned her head back with a thunk. The roar in her ears settled down into a gabble of voices, the Contrarè around the coals still divided and talking it through. Coya stood as a bent silhouette against the red glow of the bonfire. Alarum too, larger and straighter, gesturing at them all.

'Good,' said the Contrarè man quietly. 'I can see some colour returning to your face.' He lifted one of her eyelids to better study her pupil. Grunted. 'You were lost in flight for a while. I was beginning to think I would have to lead you back myself.'

So he was a seer of some kind, this handsome Contrarè dressed and painted as a Red Path warrior. He could see beyond the veil of waking. Shard looked at his skinny dreadlocks tied back with a band of cloth, a sign of power amongst the sky hermits of the Contrarè, though she had never known of one who was a warrior too.

Coughs racked her chest when she tried to sit up straighter. Cool skin pressed lightly against the clammy heat of her forehead. 'Easy. You have a slight fever.'

He threw a blanket of wool across her lap and fussed with it for a few moments, tucking it in around her. 'You must rest,' he said with a tap of her knee. '*Hozakay.*' Take it easy.

The quivering firelight washed across the side of his painted face, so that his gaze speared her with its intensity every time he turned his head from the shadows. It was true what they said about glimpsing a person's soul through their eyes – those most exposed and naked parts of a shining mind.

A mind without bounds, she saw now as she held his gaze; a mind that was loose in the sky like her own.

'Who are you?' she asked with sudden curiosity.

'What? I am Sky In His Eyes,' he declared as though she should know him, as though the whole world should know.

'Of course. We spoke at the council.'

Her voice caused him to straighten and to consider her with wry interest. He had seemed familiar to Shard when she'd first seen him around the fire, and now even more so.

Where have I seen you before, my handsome man?

'Well I have heard of you, Walks With Herself,' he declared with some amusement. 'The sky hermits speak highly of the Dreamer who comes from our cousins the Black Hands. They say you are a true daughter of the Contrarè.'

'Wishful thinking, I imagine,' she muttered back at him, making another effort to sit up.

Oh my ... What a luxury it was to move without the cramps doubling her over in pain. Even more so to see straight again, and not fly off the instant she closed her eyes.

She breathed deeply, the tips of her fingers tingling. Felt energy pulsing up from the earth through her spine, blowing the fog from her mind.

It was the first time she had felt centred since taking the worm.

'That sensee bark. Have you more of it?'

As though by magic he flicked his hand and held a bulging pouch before her, a priceless bounty. 'Thought you might want more of it. It works fast, heh?'

Gingerly she accepted the gift. Cradled the pouch in her hands as though it held the most precious thing of all.

Elios had spoken of this. Had said something about help being on its way.

'I'm afraid I have nothing to give you in return.'

But he waved that away like the annoyance it was.

'Thank you then. I'm in your debt.'

For a long moment he studied her features and the metal sheen of her mask.

Around the fire the Contrarè were still huddled in their blankets, talking and shifting from one position to another, the massive leaves of the chimino trees forming a natural roof above their heads. Some of the warriors were dancing now behind the circle of elders, the drums beating faster than before.

They were a close-knit people these Longalla, as all Contrarè were, everyone in the tribe treated as a member of their extended family. She watched them gathered in their circle passing drinks and pipes with their immediate neighbours. Laughter rang out even as other voices argued hotly, the singing of the dancing warriors pulsing through it all in shouts and howls that stirred her blood, made her want to get up and join them in their wildness.

Sky In His Eyes read her desires and spoke to them. 'Feeling up to it?'

But there were more pressing matters on her mind to be dealing with just then.

Footsteps came towards them through the trampled snow. She saw Coya's bent figure hobbling towards her with Marsh by his side.

'Can she talk?' Coya demanded to know.

Shard had never seen the man in such a temper before, not over all the years she had known him. She glanced to Marsh but he only shrugged, not wanting to get involved.

'You're sore at me. I can tell.'

'What do you expect?' exclaimed Coya. 'You told them the Empire is a stronger bet right now than the democras.'

'I only spoke the truth.'

'Well they took to your words, truth or not. Now they say they need to call a Grand Assembly. And consult with their sky hermits. Stalling for time in other words. Seeing which way the wind blows first.'

'You can hardly blame us,' Sky In His Eyes offered. 'The Mannian made a compelling case too. We only ask for more time to consider.'

'That bastard spypriest,' Coya growled and threw his glare at the distant figure of Alarum, now talking amongst his small group of companions. 'We can't afford this delay. We need the help of the Longalla now!'

Fiercely, Shard gripped his wrist as memories came back to her.

'Juno's Ferry,' she gasped.

'What?'

'We need to leave now before we're cut off from the city.' Shard struggled to her feet, using the tree to hold her upright. 'Juno's Ferry is under assault. It looked like a big attack. I think the Expeditionary Force is on the move again.'

Coya hissed through his teeth and scowled at the night around him as though it couldn't get much worse for them. On her feet now, energy flowed across her glimmersuit in ripples of heat and bright colours. She felt strong and alive and ready to take on their cause again – ready even to face Tabor Seech.

'We'll need fresh zels,' Marsh prompted.

'You will have them,' answered Sky In His Eyes, though before he could wheel away Shard reached out a hand to stop him.

'Thank you. For your gift I mean,' she told him breathlessly, and kept her hand pressed against his own. 'I hope I have a chance to repay you some day.'

Marsh rolled his eyes and turned away.

'Ho-ya!' Sky In His Eyes exclaimed, smiling as though they were old friends, old lovers even. 'We will meet again, you and I. Can't you feel it?'

'Yes,' she told him with a smile.

CHAPTER FORTY-SEVEN

High And Dry

The young Anwi man who called himself Juke leaned back against the door and exhaled a lungful of smoke as though it was a release of all the tensions inside of him.

'Shit,' said the man, staring down at the thick hazii stick dangling from his lips. 'I've been needing to cook this one all day.'

With relaxed slowness he tossed the manacles that he'd freed from Ash's wrists onto one of the chairs, then rubbed at the thick black thatch of hair on his head. In a cloud of blue smoke he turned to check through a spyglass in the door.

'Make yourself at home,' offered his blunted voice, and Ash didn't need to be asked twice, for exhaustion was bearing down hard now, the sleep of champions awaiting him. Ash lay down his sword then dropped into a deeply padded armchair near the sole window of the room, embraced by the touch of its warm fleece covering. Here would do just fine.

'Chee?'

The old farlander could only nod. Through the curtained window of the small apartment he could still hear sirens prowling the city streets below. A light swept through the curtains and then was gone. Ash rested his head back and sighed with the last of the strength remaining to him. Squinted up at the white ceiling where a symbol had been painted in sweeps of black; a large circle orbited by two smaller circles, slashes arching between them.

No way was he going to move from this chair. His eyelids were drooping with their own weight, and images flashed behind them, stark scenes playing out from the riot in the streets: people folding under the strikes of batons; pools of blood on the streets crisscrossed with footprints; faces grim with everything on the line.

Noise from the small kitchen caused his eyes to open a fraction. Juke was filling a shining kettle from a faucet above a sink. With the hazii stick hanging from the corner of his mouth he set the kettle down on a counter and turned a knob on the surface, then leaned back with his arms folded and stared down at the floor in smoky silence, thinking to himself.

Shaded lamps dotted the apartment, waxing and waning erratically. Sky-blue paint covered the walls. An oval rug covered much of the floor, woven in geometric designs that were typically Alhazii. Ash observed a bookshelf beside him brimming with books and assorted miscellanea: a woowoo board from the High Pash, a small jade statue of the Great Fool, a collection of miracle sticks from the Green Isles, a tiq incense burner in a style common in the Free Ports.

As for the many books on display, most seemed to have titles written in Trade, and Ash studied them as he always studied books in a room. He spotted scriptures and travel journals from across the known world, including a battered copy of the Book of Lies written by Nihilis, first Patriarch of Mann, perched somewhat incongruously next to the writings of the Great Fool.

No poetry to be seen anywhere, though, the farlander noticed with disappointment.

From the kitchen the kettle was whistling steam already, and without a naked flame in sight. Juke whistled too while he poured the boiled water into a pair of white mugs. He came back into the room and sloppily offered one to Ash.

The chee was hot but not so good. Poorly cured or poorly blended, or maybe it was just old. Still, it felt wonderful to drink it down and fill his empty stomach with something hot before it started to eat itself from hunger.

'Food,' tried Ash. 'Have you something to eat?'

A stick of white bread landed in his lap. Ash bit off a chunk without ceremony.

Still whistling, the young Anwi man crossed the rug and fiddled with a flat box on a side table until it started to squawk with noises; some kind of music, Ash realized with a start. The room's lights flickered then dimmed a little further.

'*All right*,' said Juke with his head nodding to the rhythms.

Drumbeats pounded off the walls as though they were sitting

around a gathering of musicians. A woman's voice sang out in a desperate rhythm that wove itself through the beats, beautiful and haunting. Ash liked it, found the toe of his boot tapping against the floor.

'*All right!*' said Juke with an exhalation of smoke, seeing the old farlander tapping along to the music. Juke turned a dial on the box and the music climbed even higher, pulsing through Ash's head. The Anwi man turned and opened a door to a darkened bedroom, kicked a bundle of clothes away from his feet. With a few popping words he spoke loudly, then slapped the backside of someone lying on the bed. '*Op-guani!*'

That language of theirs. Ash could gain no grasp on it, no sense of patterns that might suggest a syntax, no obvious commonality between the sounds. It seemed little more than a mongrel smattering of words interrupted by those pops of the lips and clicks of the tongue.

Questions formed on his lips, but his voice eluded him when the man returned and flopped down on a settle along the wall. He was too spent for words. Too focused on the bread and the chee. Stupefied, they both blinked at each other across the low table between them, Juke seemingly fascinated by the old farlander sitting in his home. In turn, Ash studied his dark face amongst the plumes of hazii smoke, the man's lean features etched deeply like someone who laughed often. Such a familiar-looking face, Ash thought, realizing how the young Anwi could pass for an unusually tall native of Honshu, save that his eyes were not quite folded in the same way.

'Sorry,' rumbled Juke over the music, remembering his manners, and he leaned forwards with the hazii stick held out towards him. 'You smoke?'

Ash swallowed, cleared his throat.

'Not for years,' he admitted, though it seemed to have been that kind of day, for he found his body leaning forwards in the chair and his hand reaching out for the stick. He took a few draws and held them in his lungs as he passed it back to the man.

'It's good grade, straight from the source,' Juke explained, putting his boots up on the table, the grooved soles indented with dark soil. 'I do a little trade in weed on the blackmarket. Buy it off some Alhazii contacts down in Guallo Town and smuggle it into the city.'

The young man was right, it was strong weed. Ash could feel his body starting to relax into its embrace.

'Your painting on the wall behind you there,' Ash said in surprise, plucking a strand of hazii weed from his lips. 'It comes from Honshu.'

'It's a replica, but yeah, sure. A few Anwi have visited your homeland in the past.'

He stared at Ash's glazed expression. 'The Sparon, the Fallen Leaves? People exiled from the city on political charges or for killing one of the Elect?'

Ash nodded vaguely, recalling what Meer had told him.

'Yeah, most die fast out there in the world. Taken down by some disease they've never been exposed to before. But some make it. And a few write journals of their lives in the wider world, or paint what they see, and copies make their way back to us. Illegal as all hell of course.' He shrugged. 'But then what isn't these days?'

Juke stretched across with his long arm to another smaller bookshelf next to the settle. 'There's a journal in there from an Anwi exile who made it all the way to Honshu, and was a friend and lover of the Great Fool himself.'

'You joke.'

'It's all there in her journal. If you want, you can take it with you.'

'What's this, giving away our books again?'

A young blonde woman padded into the room, scratching her head and dressed in a fleece nightrobe. When she bent down to lower the volume of the music, he saw how her white face was crinkled from sleep.

She rubbed Juke's hair and plucked the remains of the hazii stick from his fingers. In response he grabbed her and pulled her sideways onto his lap, from where she squinted across at the battered, weary, hungry, somewhat high farlander sitting in her living room, gazing back with hooded eyes, sheathed sword perched by his chair.

'Triqy,' she said with a nod.

A fine-looking girl, Ash thought lazily, if you were into exotic, waif-like features.

'Ash,' drawled his heavy reply.

'I'm glad you made it here,' she told him in Trade that was as good as her lover's. 'I wasn't certain if Juke would have a chance to make contact this evening.'

'We had our problems,' Juke admitted with a wolfish grin. 'He decided to take part in a riot then ran from the law in a groundcar. Man has his style, I'll give him that.'

'How did you find him?'

'Had to scan the security channels. Half the guards in the district were after him. Good thing I was on the zel.'

'My hero,' Triqy said with mockery.

She studied Ash with a curious and steady gaze.

'You've taken the Milk that Meer sent down,' she observed of the farlander. 'I can tell.'

'That was yours?'

'Yes, from my family's supply.'

'My thanks.'

'Can I run you a bath? You look like you could use it. I've been heating some water in the tank, should be ready by now.'

A hot bath. The mere thought of it turned his tired muscles to butter.

'If I can stay awake for long enough . . . yes, that would be kind of you.'

While the water rumbled and splashed in a side room, Ash and Juke sat gazing at each other again across the table, inhaling the cloud of smoke that rolled between them, their black faces shining in the softly waning light.

'Saved your ass out there, old man,' Juke muttered with sly humour.

Ash's eyes smiled back at him. He was starting to like this fellow, or maybe it was just the mood-enhancing effects of the hazii smoke.

Indeed the hazii stick had burned out between the Anwi's fingers without notice. Ash pulled a face and looked about him at the strange room in the strange city with the strange man staring so intently at him.

He looked back at Juke with a snap of his teeth.

'Juke. Who *are* you people?'

*

'I used to be Meer's lover,' the young Anwi woman told him in a hush from where she squatted on the white bowl across from the bath. 'Years ago, when I helped hide him in the city. I'd never met a man before so travelled, or who liked to go shopping without ever actually buying anything. Just to look.'

'Shopping?'

'Close the door if you're going to be talking about that stuff!' Juke called from the living room over the din of the music.

'Close the door? So I can be alone in the bathroom with our new naked friend?'

'I doubt he's in any condition to jump you, Triqy.'

Ash submerged his ears beneath the hot soapy water of the bath so that all he could hear were the muffled sounds of their words. He knew he was beyond moving now. They would have to drain the water out and leave him here for the night, like some beached porpoise too spent to save itself.

She was still talking, the Anwi woman, when he raised his ears above the surface once more.

'I was young. He was crazy. I suppose you know how that story goes. Anyway, that was the last time I thought I'd ever see him again. And then last week his letter turns up asking for help. Well, we put him up in a safehouse for a few days – Juke wouldn't have him here, so that was that.' She bit her lip and stared hard at the doorway where Juke was sitting just out of sight, save for the occasional plume of hazii smoke that wafted through the air, swept a twisted strand of blonde hair clear of her eye. 'Not that I blame him. Everyone assured me the safehouse was . . . well . . . *safe*.'

'How was he caught?'

'An informant, most likely. Believe me, the underground is riddled with them. And the authorities watch all communications too. Anyway. We knew you were coming. I was the one who sorted out that pass that got you through. And Juke delivered the letter during one of his pickups.'

'I've been tracking you ever since you entered the city,' Juke declared through the doorway. 'Almost didn't see you sneaking out of the Guallo's Rest.'

Ash stared at the stains of dampness along the top of the wall. The paint was peeling in places, revealing an older coat of blood red. A hideous colour for a room, he thought. Who would choose such a thing?

'And you are part of some . . . resistance?'

'We have friends, people struggling for the same things that we are.'

'Such as?'

He heard her blow her lips out and say, 'Where do I begin? Well, our priority used to be the attainment of full representation for all, not just for the Elect. That would have been a start, at least.'

'I'll say it again like I'm always saying it,' Juke called through the doorway. 'What point is there in gaining token representation for everyone if the system itself is still a rigged sham? If you still only get to vote for those representing the interests of the status quo? Look to the Free Ports and Minos to see how you do it right. Open assemblies. Delegates with recallable mandates. Local and League co-operatives. Sustainable economies fostering diversity instead of monopoly. Wild farming that doesn't tear the heart from the land. All sane. All doable if we were any way sane ourselves as a culture.'

'For a start, I said! For a start!'

She carried on as though her lover hadn't spoken. 'And of course an end to this crazy paranoid nonsense about hiding away from the world and banning anyone's return if they leave us. Some friends of ours run a smuggling operation between here and Zanzahar, getting people in and out. And they try to make sure that news and accounts of the Fallen Leaves make it back here so that people can hear of them.'

The lights dimmed for a moment, then returned to their pale flicker. She stopped to take a deep breath and to look at the open doorway.

'Always the Free Ports with you!' she cast at Juke. 'I swear if that damned Zeziké were alive today you'd be there rather than here.'

'Better believe it,' he said and puffed a series of clouds through the doorway.

Ash heard water rushing in the bowl and realized she was standing, pushing a metal button in the wall. She came and knelt by the lip of the bath. Dipped her hands into the water then perched there rubbing them dry.

'Tell me what you mean when you say Elect?' he asked.

'Meer really didn't tell you anything, did he?' she mused, looking off across the small room at a picture hanging on the wall: a sketch of a ranchero riding with a herd of wild zels, a scene straight from the prairies of Ghazni.

For a moment he thought of Khos, and wondered how the war was going and the ongoing siege. A different world, it felt to him now.

'The Elect are the Anwi elite who get to live forever. Like my family.'

Ash looked at the short nubs of her little fingers. Her large blue eyes in her delicate features and the crease of concentration upon her forehead. Late twenties perhaps, older than Juke certainly. A teacher maybe. Or a dancer.

'People in the cartels and the administration, and Crucible priests, and celebrities, and artists and scholars like my parents. They prolong their lives with Royal Milk, the same Milk the Zanzahar Guildsmen bring here in return for exotics. And when even the Milk isn't enough to hold off death, they have a new body grown in a wetwomb like a new set of clothes to slip into.'

Ash nodded vaguely, recalling what Meer had told him. He listened with eyes closed.

'The Elect of this city are the only ones who get to choose who stands for the positions of Archon and the legislature. They have it all locked down. They run the show, and every decision made is cast in their favour, usually at everyone else's expense, mostly the young.'

'The young?'

'They do all of the labour in the city. A few go on to become Elect themselves, though most end up waiting in the food lines, suffering from some breathing illness or cancer.'

'And this is why they are in the streets?'

'Partly. Though mostly it's because times are changing. Some people can sense it, even if they're not fully aware of why. They see things in the city winding down around them. Brown-outs and the soaring costs of food. Everything getting worse. They hear the hollow talk of the Elect about downturns and recoveries and how everything is fine, and all the lies only make them wonder even more.'

'Tell him the truth now!' shouted Juke.

She sighed. Splashed her hand in the water next to his thigh. Ash could feel the cool motion of the water against his skin, but he was too tired even to be aroused by it.

'Juke believes we're all doomed. He thinks the majority of Anwi don't care enough to change our direction, even if they did know where we were headed. He's wrong though.'

'Tell him!'

A yawn stretched Ash's mouth wide. He was trying to listen, he really was.

'The city's dying,' she said in a hush, as though it truly was a dangerous fact to disclose. 'It's running out of power.'

Triqy propped her arm on the lip of the bath and rested her chin on it, then whispered into the soapy water. 'Everything in Mashuppa is powered from the same ancient sources. Five surviving Flux Lenses from the ships of the exodus. But they need strokestone for the lensing, and it tends to burn out given enough time, especially if overused. We're running low on the stuff, no matter how much we look for more. We passed peak supply of strokestone several years ago. Now there's less and less of it to keep the Lenses running and the lights on.'

On cue, the room's ceiling light dimmed again and then struggled to brighten.

'Yet even now the Elect still dream of returning home, and throw most of the power we have into completing the Sky Bridge, which they never will.'

'And no one speaks of it,' croaked Juke, deadly serious at last. Another plume entered the space of the doorway, and hung there for a moment gathering form like the silence behind it. 'The plants are dying. The people are dying. Ten, fifteen years left of power and then it's all gone, lights out forever. And all we're given are lies and denials which people repeat like sleepwalkers.'

'Make sure you see Mashuppa properly, old farlander! Next time you come this way, we may all be gone save for a ragged band of survivors clawing through the rubble.'

'Nonsense,' retorted Triqy. 'The majority of people will rise up long before that ever happens.'

'*Hah-hah-hah!*'

But by then Ash was falling asleep and three heartbeats away from a snore. He splashed a handful of water over his face to revive himself momentarily, then met her gaze with an easy hazii smile.

'Is he even listening?' asked Juke's voice.

'No. You put him to sleep.'

Ash smacked his lips as his heavy eyelids closed once again.

'How long have you been lovers?' he asked her in a murmur, and she snorted.

'Lovers? I met Juke last year at the stadium when I was installing some lights there. He's a part-time rider for the Treen entertainment cartel. We moved in together to spread out the rent.'

'I heard that!'

'You were meant to!'

'And you,' murmured Ash. 'What is it you do?'

'Didn't Meer say? No, of course he didn't. I'm an apprentice Crucible priest. I work in the Sky Bridge.'

Perhaps he had slipped into a dream, was talking now only to his own mind.

'A priest? Surely not?'

Her lips turned into a thin smile, he saw through his lashes.

'Only an apprentice. I become a proper Crucible priest if I make it another five years.'

'A long time.'

'She'll be fine,' growled Juke. 'Her family will look after her like they always do.'

'At least I like it,' she continued. 'Tinkering and learning how things work.' She shrugged a slender shoulder beneath her fleece robe. 'If you're into crafting or exotics, the priesthood is the best game in Mashuppa.'

'So you are the one who was helping Meer? I mean – the business with my apprentice?'

'The wetwomb? Yes, though I had some help. There are a few Crucibles sympathetic to the underground.'

'You have seen him, my apprentice?'

'I have. He's up on the Sky Bridge, growing fast. The new accelerators just make them bloom right out of the tanks.'

Ash's heart was beating a little faster now. The surface of the water had stilled entirely as his breathing stilled. In his mind Nico took another step closer to the waking world.

'My thanks for your help.'

'You're welcome.'

Interesting that Triqy had yet to mention Meer's pending execution. Perhaps it was too harsh a reality to speak aloud.

'What of Meer? I'm told they will execute him as a spy.'

Her nod was a grim one. 'In two days' time, by order of the Archon.'

Two days' time. It was not much to work with.

'This Archon. He is the ruler of the city?'

Triqy nodded. 'Yes, voted by his peers, the Elect.'

'He's also a Dreamer,' added Juke. 'Like the Alhazii Dreamers. They say he blackmailed the secret from them. A very powerful man. Ruthless to the bone.'

'Tell me,' said Ash, 'can you get me onto the Sky Bridge before the execution?'

'Inside? You really think you can get Meer out from there?'

Ash blinked up at her delicate features, seeing hope in her eyes.

'If we had a week to prepare, maybe. In the two days that we have remaining . . . no, I must find another way to save him.' And even as he heard the weariness in his own voice he realized how much was still left to be done.

'Tell me everything you can that might be of help. For a start, tell me about these birds that everyone seems so afraid of.'

Again the torrent of her words washed over him, and part of Ash listened while another part of him wondered how he was ever going to free Meer.

Once more his gaze observed the ornate hanging on the wall at his feet, a column of symbols brushed in black ink. Triqy had told him what it meant and he tried to recall the words now.

Something about speaking truth to the powerful even if your voice shakes.

Ash sat upright in the bath with the water sloshing out of it, knowing in that moment what he needed to do.

'Ah!' he said aloud.

He had been thinking about this in all the wrong ways.

'I need to take this to the man at the top.'

CHAPTER FORTY-EIGHT

Speaking Half-Truths to Power

This really is the most insane thing I ever heard of. If Juke thinks it's a great idea, doesn't that tell you something?

Are you saying my plan stinks?

What plan? If this is anything at all, it's the absolute lack of a plan.

Ash curled the corner of his mouth into a smile. He liked this spicy woman with her sharpshooting mouth, whose wit somehow reminded him of Nico.

Rumbles and judders as the glass box rose through the air along the sloping underside of the Sky Bridge leg. He stood there jittery with energy, his forehead pressed against the cool glass he was gazing through.

You okay?

Yup.

In fact he was humming a song from the old country, full of life this morning, light on the balls of his feet. Earlier, standing over the bowl that was a latrine in the apartment bathroom of Juke and Triqy, he'd drained the last of the Milk in a frothy jet while wondering again how long the effects would continue, this buzz of energy that was like being a young man once more, ready to take on the world all over again.

Ah, the hopeful rebellion of youth, he reflected. *We should never lose this.*

A faint bloom of moisture spread upon the glass he was leaning his forehead against. Ash rubbed it clear with his hand. At this height, he could see the mountain peaks that surrounded the crater city and the saddlebacks ranging between them, where fingers of the metropolis extended outwards into outlying suburbs.

This morning a layer of white clouds surrounded the crater and peaks, and the sun shone fiercely down on them as far as his eyes could see, so that the city and its outer regions looked like islands in a sea of white froth. It pleased him to see the city in this way at last, a poetic vision of the name given to it by the Alhazii, these so-called islands in the sky, though the image was marred somewhat by the thick mist of pollution sitting upon the caldera, obscuring everything.

Beneath the Alhazii robe he wore, Ash could feel the farcry she had given him hanging against the hairs of his chest, a smooth stone shaped like a kidney, the same breadth and thinness as his hand. Amazing to speak in his head like this with the woman, to know that she was seeing all that he saw.

Damned heavy though, for all the size of it.

Heavy, this farcry of yours.

You must be joking. Those crappy obsolete farcrys we sell the Alhazii are the size of barrels.

Yes, but then you do not have to carry those about with you.

You know, I really can't tell if you're joking or not.

Does everyone here possess such a device?

Mostly. Though the city's network is hidden from the outside world. Our people invented the Black Dream you know, long before their exile.

A bell rattled and the glass climbing box came to a stop with a conclusive clunk.

You're there. Top floor.

*

Left here, I think.

You think?

Yes. Fairly certain.

Then why do I feel lost?

I got you through those security checks, didn't I? Trust me. It's left here.

Ash pulled a face then strode down a corridor identical to the last one, save that it was wider and busier with use. He was in the central hub now, making his way through a labyrinth of spaces that was the administrative heart of the Sky Bridge and the city. The same windows ran along the same cream walls, showing what could be the same people sitting in bright offices at desks; talking, reading from flickering screens, punching their fingers into black contraptions. Along the carpeted corridors, Anwi men and women in fine suits of grey or cream passed him by with quick glances at his hood and burnoose, but nothing more.

My message. Have you sent it to the Falcon *yet?*

Juke's riding down to Guallo Town with it now. Says he has another pickup to make anyway. Turn right here, then left again.

It was warm in these corridors. The light was like crisp daylight though it shone from orbs along the ceilings. The swirling brown carpets gave way a little beneath his treads.

You're there.

Ash turned a corner and found himself approaching a pair of guards in black uniforms, the duo standing on either side of a doorway between blue flags hanging limp on poles. They raised their gazes from the floor at his approach, looked at the pass swinging from his neck, and said nothing as he stepped through into the room beyond.

He found himself in a kind of lobby, oblong in shape and vibrant green with potted plants. A door at the far end was guarded by another pair of bored guards. Assorted Anwi looked up from comfortable settles lining the white walls to take in his sudden Alhazii appearance, before returning their gazes to newspapers or the bland stubble of the cream carpet.

'Name?' inquired a middle-aged woman from behind a high desk, her eyebrows pinched together in a face heavy with cosmetics.

'Call me Ash.'

'How can I help you?'

'The Archon. I must see him.'

'You don't appear to have an appointment with us, Mr Ash.'

'It is very important that I see him.'

She laughed quietly at that, a little chuckle like the twitter of birds. The people waiting around the room were listening with pricked ears.

'Without an appointment that's simply out of the question. His schedule is over-filled for the day as it is, just as it is every day he chooses to hold office. If you leave an enquiry with me, I'll make sure to pass it along.'

She blinked as he swept his hood back from his head. The Alhazii ink markings on his face had faded in the bath the previous night.

Ash flashed his canines for show and spoke with the pent-up force of his will.

'Tell him an old farlander is here to see him. An old Rōshun. *Tell him now.*'

'Well,' she said in a sudden fluster. 'I can't guarantee anything. But I'll let him know.'

'Thank you,' he told her before she could change her mind. His boots rip-ripped across the carpet and took him to an empty chair directly across the desk in her eye-line. He sank down into it deeper than he had been expecting, holding out his hands to steady himself while he floated on its wobbling surface. The woman watched him for a moment, then left the desk and entered the far door between the guards.

It's true then. You're a real life Rōshun?

In the flesh.

This is going right off the scale. Juke will freak when he finds out. He loves you guys.

After a time his body stopped bobbing in the chair, and he looked about for the music he could faintly hear. The sound of musical pipes was coming from a gauze hole in the wall behind him, and he craned his head round to peer through it, but could see only darkness.

From the corners of their eyes, every Anwi in the room was watching him.

They seem nervous.

Little wonder. You should be nervous too. The Archon isn't just the ruler of the city. He's a Dreamer, Ash. He can snuff you out with a pinch of his fingers, and he has the reputation to prove it.

Huh. I've met more kings and self-proclaimed gods than I care to remember, Triqy. Enough to know they are only people like the rest of us.

He'll never see you anyway. Not on the spot like this.

We will see.

The woman returned and glanced at him over her desk but said nothing. She sat down and returned to whatever she had been doing before his arrival, reading it seemed, flicking her gaze towards him occasionally from beneath her thickened lashes.

What followed was an endless time of waiting, just as he'd been expecting would happen. Triqy grew quiet in his mind. People entered the inner door then left a while later with varying expressions. Others replaced them where they had been waiting. He wished that he had his sword with him, if only to grip it reassuringly, stroke the grip with his thumb while he sat there passing the time. His fingers started drumming against the chair to the music coming from the wall, wanting to annoy the woman behind the desk with his presence, to remind her that he was still there.

The old farlander popped his mouth open then closed it again. Craned his neck back and forth and stared up at the arching ceiling overhead. A painting covered the ceiling, depicting a watery landscape: a blue sea crashing white against the coast of an island where a circle of stones stood tall, with an entire world hanging across half the sky.

You people really believe you fell from one of the moons?

We don't believe it. It's an historical fact. We were cast out, and had to settle here on Erēs.

Cast out why?

Because we lost a civil war.

He nodded, understanding at last.

Exiles, Ash thought, looking up at the alien vista again, beautiful in its own strange way. People yearning for their home.

It's what our name means, Anwi.

The Lost?

More than that. Anwi is that mood we sometimes experience when we look up into the sky and see the moon of Mangala shining there in its whiteness, our first home before it was gripped in ice, and Sholo brilliant and blue, knowing we can never return to either. Anwi is the yearning in our hearts for what we have lost and what we long for.

He felt a lump in his throat; a sudden ridiculous burst of sentiment at what he heard.

With a newly found appreciation Ash examined the people around the room dressed in their fine silk outfits, sporting jewels and immaculate hairstyles that seemed to defy their own weight, their faces old yet glowing with vitality.

Are all these people Elect?

Of course.

How long have they been living for?

Some could be five hundred years old. Some might only be a hundred. The

Hort, the truly ancient, are said to live for millennia. They would never have to wait like this to see the Archon.

Let us follow their lead then.

What?

He was tired of waiting. Ash rose as best he could from the shifting embrace of the chair and crossed the carpet, heading for the inner door.

'Excuse me, you can't go in there!'

What are you doing?

Triqy, did you really think I came here to sit and wait all day long?

What? But—

Ahead the guards were yanking out their batons now, and Ash snarled and grabbed an arm and spun the stick around so that it struck the other guard in the chest, shocking him with its violet light. The man dropped and an instant later his partner dropped next to him, jerking and convulsing on the floor.

It happened so fast that the first scream sounded out even as Ash was through the door and hurrying along a corridor, stunstick still in his grasp.

More guards shouted after him. He was stopped by a round door of bronze like a massive coin set on its side, and he flung his weight against it, found that it rotated easily from the centre. Bright daylight shone at him through the opening and Ash stepped through, glancing back at the guards running to catch him. He spotted pistols in their hands.

The room was as spacious as the empty floor of a warehouse, and brightly lit by a wrapping of windows overlooking the city of Mashuppa. On a raised platform on the carpeted floor, a lean and tanned man dressed in a white smock stood above a table, surrounded by a group of children, all of them watching what he was doing.

Ash tossed the stunstick in his hand clattering across the floor, catching their attention, then threw back his hood.

'*Sosay!*' one of the guards shouted from behind, and suddenly two of them were pointing guns at Ash's head. 'Get down now!'

From across the room the man called out in a clipped voice that fully occupied the vast space, speaking in their native tongue. The guards hesitated, exchanging uncertain glances. At last they holstered their pieces and withdrew back through the door, glaring at Ash as they did so.

Once more the figure returned to whatever it was he was doing. Though now the children whispered and studied the old farlander standing in their company.

Again the man's voice rang out, echoing from the glass windows, and the children returned their attentions to his work on the table.

What does he say to them?

What?

Translate!

He says, 'Right there, children. Do you see its heart beating?'

Intrigued, Ash stepped across the floor for a better look at what lay upon the table. The first thing he saw were the bloody cuffs of the Archon's white smock, and then the man's gloved hands smeared red too. A small blade was held delicately in his grasp, above what seemed to be a hairy corpse splayed open to reveal its vivid internals. Ash stopped a few steps from the table, staring down in disbelief at the form strapped upon it.

The creature was still alive, whatever it was. Some kind of ape as large as a human, its oversized teeth fixed in a snarl of pain upon its hairy features. From throat to navel it had been cut open and the flesh peeled back from its ribcage, with the ribcage too sawn through and spread apart. Ash could see its heart beating in the open air.

'One moment,' the Archon said to him in Trade, then cut away at something again, causing the animal to clack its teeth and flinch against the straps that pinned it down. Some of the children gaped in astonishment and leaned forward for a better look. Others glanced away.

Ash took a step closer.

Again the Archon spoke to the children excitedly.

Triqy?

Don't worry, children, translated Triqy's voice. *It doesn't feel the pain, not like us. It's merely an animal after all. A living mechanism, like that clock over there.*

The Archon sounded just like one of the priests of Mann, echoing their belief that only humans were sentient beings.

Ash glared at the scene, feeling a sickness coiling in his stomach. He looked up to take in the lean form of the Archon, standing there in his butcher's smock above his victim. The man's face and hands were long and olive in complexion, and his skin gleamed wetly in the same manner as the Dreamer Shard back in the Free Ports. His eyes were thin and folded just like Ash's. Two streaks of white curved from his temples in what was otherwise a head of jet-black hair formed into a quiff. Likewise his lips were painted black, and his fingernails.

How old is this man, Triqy?

It's something of a secret. Some say a thousand years. Don't play games with him, he'll break you. He's well known for—

Triqy?

'I've broken the connection,' announced the Archon without looking up, and Ash tried to cover his surprise, wondering how much the man had overheard. 'I hope you don't mind. At my age, you will understand when I say my privacy is a serious matter to me.'

The Archon's voice was calm and lyrical, like the voice of a man soothing an animal before he cut its throat, or prising apart its living organs for the satisfaction of his reason.

With a sniff he straightened from his work to inspect it for a moment, then stepped to a sink next to the table to peel off his bloody gloves. Washing his hands and arms his voice sang out to the children, who obediently walked hand in hand for the door without making a sound.

'Now, what can I help you with, old Rōshun from Honshu? Don't tell me I've gotten myself mixed up in some vendetta nonsense without knowing it?'

Again Ash glanced down at the creature strapped to the table and its fevered stare, then back up at the blue eyes of the Archon.

'Not yet,' he answered carefully.

'A threat, so soon. How delightful!'

Their voices echoed through the great empty space, which was bulbous and tall and shaped like a closed tulip, and seemed to bulge from the side of the Sky Bridge so that most of the walls were lined with spotless glass filled with blue sky. Few furnishings of any kind, Ash noted, seeking to learn more of this man through his chosen environment. Little but space and light, a blank frame for the clouds in the sky and the city caldera far below. As though, indeed, the man wished to give nothing of himself away.

He watched the Archon tug off his bloody smock and toss it upon the floor. The man turned to face him, snapping the cuffs of his snug-fitting cream silk suit. His blue eyes danced within his lean face. 'I understand the Rōshun order was recently annihilated by the Empire. Somewhere in Cheem, I'm told.'

'You are well informed.'

'We maintain our sources in the Heart of the World. Idle curiosity more than anything else, it's so easy to grow bored otherwise. Still. Here you are, a living breathing Rōshun. I must say I'm rather thrilled.'

High above the man's head, shapes hung from the curve of the ceiling lit by a lattice of artificial lights. Some forms he couldn't recognize, like the giant bird creature with a great curving bone sweeping from the back of its head and its leathery wings stretched far to either side. But then he spotted a fire elk hanging there on its wires as though running across the thin air, and next to it a kree warrior, poised to rear up and attack.

Ash stood facing the Archon, with a distant clicking clock the only sound in the room. The Archon didn't look a thousand years old; more like fifty, and well maintained at that. Even considering Ash's habitual lack of expectations in anything, he found that he had been expecting something different from this. A withered old crone perhaps, sombre and wise from his aeon of experiences. Not this hawkish wire vibrating before him, carrying himself in such a way as to remind Ash of a coifed Mannian actor and major celebrity he had once slain on vendetta, immaculate in every detail of his presentation.

'You are holding a friend of mine in custody,' Ash declared boldly, wishing there and then to cut to the heart of the matter. 'I would like to discuss the matter of his release.'

'Ah, the *spy*,' replied the Archon and nodded as though a great many things were falling into place. The man spun around and strode across the room in his smart shoes, tugging his cuffs again. 'Come. Let us talk somewhere more fitting than here.'

But Ash remained unmoving, lingering next to the splayed animal on the table. It was looking up at him now with its bloodshot eyes, some hint of a question in its gaze. He found his breath catching in his chest.

The Archon had turned and was reading his expression with a repressed smile.

He flourished his hand through the air and something snapped upon the table too fast to see. Ash saw that a bolt had shot from a metal clamp through the animal's skull. The shadow of life faded from its eyes.

'Satisfied?'

He offered no response.

'Then come.'

*

'A real living Rōshun right here in Mashuppa,' the Archon said, climbing the steps ahead of him. 'It isn't often an Archon is so impressed with his company.'

'You have heard of us then.'

The man's thin face appeared in the hatchway he had just disappeared through, flashing his perfect teeth. 'Stories of the Rōshun's exploits are sold here throughout the four peaks. Exiles, just like us. They are popular amongst the younger generation, as all fanciful things are.'

Ash followed the Archon up through the open hatchway, finding himself buffeted by the wind on an airy platform on the pinnacle of the roof. He saw how the Archon's office was fixed to the side of the superstructure's hub like a blister. From here the vertical span of the Sky Bridge was close, a mammoth spike of white that shot up into the sky before being lost in the haze.

The Anwis' single hope of returning home, whatever that was supposed to mean.

He glanced down at the legs of the Sky Bridge below, arching over the blocks and parks of the city and the specks of groundcars crawling along its roads, and then back up to the vertical Bridge itself. Struck by wonder, his eyes reflected the violet arcs of light shooting along its gleaming surface.

By his side the Archon took a flask from an inner pocket and sipped from it while they studied the towering bridge together.

'You Anwi think big,' Ash said after a time.

'Yes. It is our gift and our curse. We climb high and we fall far.'

'What is it, precisely?'

At last a look of surprise on the man's expression. 'A ladder, of sorts. Our way home, some day very soon.'

'Some day?'

The Archon noted Ash's tone of disbelief, and seemed more curious than amused by it.

'When it's completed. Right now it climbs nine-tenths of the way out of the atmosphere, yet we struggle to grow it any taller. The gravity well of this planet is an immense challenge to overcome. To grow it this far has taken us centuries of sustained effort.'

'But where will it lead you?'

'Back into the void, where we can build ships for the crossing. From there to our home of Sholos, the blue moon, where we will take back everything that we lost when we were cast out so cruelly.'

Was the man high on something? His pupils were certainly dilated, his eyes more glazed with every little pull of the flask that he took. He was drinking fermented Milk, Ash realized, catching a scent of it on the wind.

'There is a bridge like this one on the water moon of Sholos, which was used to banish our people to this planet millennia ago following the civil war, our punishment for siding with the ruling cartels and priesthood. It has been a long hard struggle to survive here ever since.'

With a scuff of his polished shoes the man turned his back on the bridge and gripped the platform's rail tightly, leaning back against the full stretch of his arms. His eyes ranged across the brilliant sky to the sister moons hanging there in the east, ghostly in the daylight, one white and one blue.

Hairs rose on the back of Ash's neck. In that moment he realized the Archon was sincere in all that he said, and that the Anwis' history was more than simple myth-making. He rocked on the balls of his feet, feeling as though his life's horizon had suddenly expanded beyond his reckoning. Ash thought of the lights on the moon he'd seen at night through a scope. People really lived up there, then. A whole living world hanging in the sky all this time.

'I understand you Anwi are not shy of exiling people yourselves,' Ash ventured, feeling a desire to know more.

'The Fallen Leaves, you mean?' The Archon tilted his head around to regard him with his intelligent gaze. He was rubbing

It was the one thing he had come here to achieve.

'Fine then. I will consider that much.'

Roughly the guards marched him towards the hatch. Before they [c]uld shove him down the steps, the Archon shouted back one last [ti]me.

'Tell me, assassin. I sense that you're dying, am I right?'

Ash stopped in his tracks. He looked up over his shoulder at the [fi]gure squinting down at him, taking another sip of Royal Milk.

'We all die. Even you, old man.'

'Don't count on it,' the Archon called back. 'I intend to live for[e]ver!'

his thumb and forefingers together absently, and the skin around them glimmered with bands of colour. 'Yes, regrettably we must exile our own from time to time. Mostly, though, it is for their own good.'

'You would say that.'

'Yet still it remains true. Even my own brother was cast out in such a way more than a century ago. And he went on to found the greatest empire on this planet.'

'You mean Nihilis?' Ash said in surprise. 'The first Patriarch was one of yours, an Anwi?'

But the Archon only twitched his lips and looked away, offering no more.

Even for the open mind of Ash it was almost too much to take in. At last he sensed the true age of this man, hearing it in the measured strokes of his words, which were almost glacial in their certainty, centuries of time borne behind them. Yet otherwise the Archon hid his years well, as though the near-immortality of the Elect was a preciously guarded gift, best hidden from sight.

Perhaps their influence upon the world was much the same.

Wind rippled their clothing and squeezed their eyes into squints. It was bitterly cold up here, though the Archon seemed oblivious to its touch. Ash had never stood this high before on anything made by his fellow humans. The limbs of the Sky Bridge alone made the sky-steeples of Q'os seem little more than toys in comparison. He leaned forward against the rail and looked around at the far horizon, wondering if it wasn't curved a little like the big round ball the world really was, then fixed his stare on the two moons again, his heart beating fast.

'My friend is no spy,' Ash said into the wind. 'You have sentenced an innocent man to death, a good and honourable man.'

'That may be. But my hands are tied. It is done. There is no changing it now.'

'He still breathes. You only have to give the command.'

The Archon peered at him closely. 'Your friend is anything but innocent, farlander. He is immune to truth drugs for one thing. And no matter how certain the Committee say they are, he's no Mannian agent either. Not if he's working with a Rōshun.'

'He has his secrets. That does not make him a spy. He was here in the city for a personal matter on my behalf. If anyone is responsible, he stands before you now.'

'Why *are* you here, farlander?'

'To fulfil a promise to a grieving mother. That is all.'

The Archon lowered his gaze and raised a finger to his pursed lips to stop himself from speaking. He turned his back to Ash, a powerful gesture in front of a Rōshun with motive enough to attack.

'How did you get here, I wonder?' he mused aloud. 'Your friend remains quiet on the subject. I doubt very much the Alhazii Guildsmen would have agreed to it. I should inform them to search every ship in the port.'

It was bait, though Ash went for it anyway. He grabbed the man's arm and yanked him around fiercely. Emotion blazed at last in those glazed eyes of his. Heat seemed to pulse in waves from his body.

Snapping the cuffs of his suit, the Archon spoke before Ash could. 'In these books I mentioned, this fluff about the exiled Rōshun, they forever claim that no one is safe from the reach of the Rōshun vendetta. I wonder though. Could you kill a Dreamer if you had to? Could you kill me, do you think, if it came to it?'

So it was a test he was after. A challenge for his powers.

'As easily as any other.'

The Archon's pupils were two vanishing points beneath his brows, drawing from deep within himself.

'How, may I ask?'

Ash said nothing, though he allowed a smile to spread across his lips. Just as the Archon opened his mouth to speak Ash slapped him hard and fast across the cheek, and in the same motion drove his pointed fingers at his larynx, stopping just short of the skin, just short of killing him. The Archon blinked in surprise.

'Timing,' Ash breathed.

'I could repair the damage quickly enough, you know.' His voice was strangled with self-restraint.

'Not if you were falling too,' said Ash, glancing to the rail at the Archon's back. His palm was tingling and the Archon's cheek was red with the print of it. The man's ears too had turned crimson.

'You go too far, child of Honshu.'

'Or not far enough.'

A sudden shout that was a roar. It hit Ash in the chest like the

kick of a mule and sent him tumbling backwards acro[...] form. His burnoose fluttered for a moment then lay sti[...] heaving chest.

Red pain flashing across his vision. Ash shook his head[...] then flipped to his feet with a practised ease.

Keep pushing.

'If you have any conscience at all, the fact that he is ar[...] man should mean something to you.'

'An appeal to my conscience. What an interesting choice[...]

'He is no spy,' Ash said, stopping just within reach of the[...] 'There is no need for this.'

'Really, farlander. You expect me to release your frienc[...] because it is the *right* thing to do? Is this truly what you came[...] ask of me?'

'Do it then for the sake of a Khosian mother grieving[...] lost son. A Khosian mother facing annihilation with the[...] her people, at the hands of a monster you released upon the[...]

'Enough of this,' snarled the man, and it was as though[...] had slipped from his face, all semblance of politeness fled.

Footsteps on the ladder now, guards climbing up to join t[...] though at some hidden sign. Without hurry they spread out[...] the platform to surround Ash, half a dozen of them with the[...] sticks crackling in their hands.

The Archon's thin lips stretched into a smile, and then[...] ished in a flash of white light. Ash blinked, thinking it was so[...] of trick. He glanced up to see the man perched on a high[...] above, looking down at him as though Ash was his prey w[...] guards did the dirty work of closing in.

So it had come to this already.

One of the guards stepped carefully behind Ash clutchi[...] of manacles, while the others held out their stunsticks read[...] him down. He offered no resistance, for his memories of g[...] by one of those things were fresh in his mind.

'Do one thing for me then!' Ash called out as he held[...] behind his back, allowing them to manacle his wrists.

'And what is that, farlander?'

'Stay the execution of my friend at least. Meer is mor[...] you alive than dead, I promise you.'

CHAPTER FORTY-NINE

Holding Fast

'Ash! So you're the reason they dragged another bunk into the cell.'

The hedgemonk Meer stood trembling in the centre of the cramped room with his reddened eyes staring out from swollen, battered features.

'They roughed you up, I see,' said Ash, turning the monk's face one way then the other, noting the cuts and bruised impressions.

Meer's eyes watered with emotion as he spoke. 'Some. When they found out they couldn't simply raid my mind. I'm fine though.'

Ash nodded. He had been interrogated too but only half-heartedly, as though they expected an old Rōshun to offer them nothing. They hadn't even bothered to get rough with him. Relaxing where he stood, he studied the small cell he had been roughly cast into: the surfaces of steel sheeting on its walls, the caged light embedded in the ceiling. A bright square of daylight shone from the rear wall; a deep-set window which he stepped up to smartly, finding thick glass held there behind a grille of steel.

Tentatively, Ash leaned forward and peered through the scratched glass and saw that they were in one of the legs of the Sky Bridge with the city arrayed far below.

He was tired now. And his head pains had finally returned for their daily hammering. An effect, it would seem, of being floored by the blast of the Archon's voice.

'How are you holding up?' he asked without turning from the scene outside.

'Oh, just fine,' quipped Meer. 'Save for the matter of an execution hanging over my head.'

No wonder he was so frayed at the edges, waiting here in solitary confinement to be killed. At least Ash could do something about that now to allay his fears.

'I shared some words with the Archon about that. I may have bought us some time, if nothing else.'

'Well, for all that and more I'm glad to see you, Ash. I can't tell you how good it is to see you. But I was hoping you would rescue me from this predicament, not join me in it.'

Slowly Ash turned with a finger held to his lips. The monk blinked. 'Eh?'

'We must be careful what we say here. You do not really believe they placed us in the same cell out of the kindness of their hearts?'

The monk's mouth formed a sudden O, and he looked to the walls and the ceiling with wide-eyed suspicion, tired and ragged in his filthy underclothes.

It had been hard on the man, but at least now he had hope.

'Hold fast,' Ash told him sternly. 'We are not finished yet.'

*

Down in Guallo Town, the longhunter was sitting there alone when Aléas clambered up the rigging of the *Falcon* on the side of the gently swaying loft. Cole sat in silence, nursing a bottle of potcheen, in the torrential tropical rain falling from the cloudy night sky, a rain which had been falling on and off for the last few days, announcing the beginning of the rainy season.

'Are you all right?' he asked the brooding longhunter, feeling somehow responsible for the man now that Ash and Meer were both gone. Carefully, Aléas stepped up onto the wooden platform that ran along the top of the silk loft, its surface wet and slippery.

Cole shifted where he sat in the gloom, and looked up at him with his scarred brows dripping above hooded eyes.

'Aye, lad,' he said with a slurred voice. 'Just thinking is all.'

'Something bothering you? You've been up here for hours, man.'

A sniff. A wipe of his nose.

'My family. Just thinking about my family.'

Aléas shook his eyes free of rain and felt the burnoose soaking through to his skin. Drops burst against the glass bottle as the longhunter raised it to his lips. The fellow was managing to sway drunkenly even though he was sitting down.

For weeks now he had seen this man wave away alcohol with a dark haunted look in his eyes whenever it was offered. Yet here he was, hammering the strongest of homebrew into his belly, so insensible that he didn't even know to come down out of the rain.

'Thought you didn't drink.'

'I don't,' grumbled Cole, hanging his bald head in the rain. He hadn't even bothered to wear his hat.

Aléas crouched down on one knee and wondered what he was going to do with the man. Since emerging from the Edge with the rest of the survivors, something had clearly changed in the longhunter. He had fallen prone to brooding silences, as though he had much to work through within himself; insular moods that seemed to only worsen with the prolonged spells of inactivity on board the *Falcon*. A man of action, used to keeping himself busy two steps ahead of his own reflection, now trapped on a ship with a crew of strangers all pretending to be Alhazii, facing inner demons stoked to life by his close shave in those tunnels of the kree.

'What is it you want anyway?'

A trembling hostility in his voice now. Aléas knew an angry drunk when he saw one. Maybe it was the reason he had been forswearing alcohol until now.

What to say though, without provoking him any further?

'Time to come down, don't you think?'

'So now you're my mother, is that it?'

'You said you'd help me when the rains came, and now they're here. I'll need that help any time now. Maybe it's best if you keep your head straight.'

A scrape of boots. The man staggering to his feet and swaying wildly. He faced Aléas crouched further along on the catwalk. 'I don't need lecturing from the likes of you, boy. A kushing Mannian pup barely plucked from the tits of your bitch mother.'

'You're drunk. You don't mean that.'

The longhunter staggered back a step merely to hold his ground.

'I said I'd help you and I will,' he grumbled, and swiped the empty bottle in his hand at the mountains over the town. 'What was Ash and Meer doing up there anyway? What's with all the secrecy, eh?'

'I told you already. He means to restore his dead apprentice.'

'What?'

'*He means to restore his dead apprentice.*'

'You're all moonbat crazy, you know that?'

'I won't argue with that.'

'So . . . you know this apprentice of his?'

'Yes. Nico was my friend.'

The longhunter tried to straighten.

'Nico?'

'That was his name. Nico Calvone.'

Cole took a few lurching steps towards him, his face screwed tight by rage. 'You think that's funny? You hear me kushing laughing, boy?'

'I don't follow.'

Aléas flinched as the man hurled the empty bottle at him, and watched it bounce off the catwalk instead even as Cole slipped and tumbled over the side after it, shocking to witness, even as he lunged and swept out a hand to grab the man but too late, too far away.

'Cole!'

Below him, the longhunter bellowed a curse in Khosian from where he dangled in the rigging of the loft. With a twist of fate his legs had snared within the ropes so that he hung over the long lethal fall to the ground.

'Be quiet, will you!' Aléas hissed down at him. 'We're supposed to be Alhazii here, you fool!'

'Blah-raddy-yah-yah-yah.'

Drunk beyond sense and reason, the young man thought to himself with a sorry shake of his head.

Thankfully the neighbouring ships of the skyport were dark tonight, though soldiers had been stationed not far from the *Falcon* in the shelter of a large tent, while others stood in the rain around the grounded vessel. They had been there ever since the searches had begun of the port following Ash's capture in the city. Only the medico Shin's quick work had held the searchers at bay for this long, after she had smeared the skins of the crew with a poultice to replicate the visible effects of Purple Fever, and then declared the ship under quarantine, no one to enter or leave. Fear of the fever had stopped the Alhazii from boarding the ship for inspection, but still they waited and watched with obvious suspicion from afar.

'Bastards! Bastards every one of you!'

For a moment only, Aléas was tempted to leave the longhunter hanging there for the rest of the night until he sobered up. But Cole was more likely to fall and break his neck than anything else, or else wake the whole skyport with his swearing, so instead Aléas scrambled down the netting where Cole was hanging and carried on to the deck, where he gathered rope and a few crewmen on watch to help bring the man down.

Aléas was soaked to the bone by the time they had the now unconscious man returned to his cabin, where Cole briefly awoke in his bunk and asked how he had gotten there and what was happening, all memory of what had transpired between them seemingly forgotten.

CHAPTER FIFTY

The Line Breaking

'Get a fire crew down to Lynch's position!' yelled a Khosian officer, standing in the middle of the street while another fireball hissed over their heads and exploded amongst the tents of the encampment. Soldiers scurried past him in every direction, frantic silhouettes backlit by the blazing inferno that was one of the forts down by the river.

Juno's Ferry was about to fall, Shard saw clearly enough, even as the party rode in from the Windrush sore and weary from their travels, hoping only to find shelter for the night. Indeed they could all see it, and they knew then that the Dreamer had been right in what she had seen in her visions back at the council: the Imperial Expeditionary Force attempting to break across the Chilos river.

Now, upon their return to Juno's Ferry, every shout from a soldier carried the high note of alarm through the smoking air, while the hospital tents were loud and overflowing with the bloody, shrieking forms of the wounded. From the back of her zel, Shard could hear the gunfire and clashes of battle down by the Chilos, where the Khosian defenders were fighting to hold the fortified bank against barges of imperial attackers. Cannon exchanged shells from dug-in positions and enemy ballista launched fiery missiles trailing arcs of smoke, which seemed to hang above the curve of slow red water – and the many bobbing bodies – before roaring downwards into the defenders.

More alarming than that though were the sounds of action to the south of the camp, between the river and the road that led to Bar-Khos. Explosions ranged along the line of earthworks there, and above them a pair of skyships were locked in a vicious dogfight, shedding parts of themselves with every strike of cannon fire.

The party pulled their mounts to a stop as they saw what lay to the south of them, shocked by the sight of what must be Imperials attacking the camp from this side of the Chilos.

'Looks like we're just in time,' growled the bodyguard Marsh from behind a scarf he had tied to his face against the smoke and fumes, his zel snorting and shaking its head beneath him. 'This place is about to fall.'

Captain Gamorre and the other surviving Volunteers stared at the scene with grim loathing. It was worse than any of them had been expecting.

'You think they're Romano's forces, or has the Expeditionary Force put aside its differences at last?' ventured the sergeant, musing aloud it seemed, for no one could know the answer.

She knew that Coya was stricken by what he saw, for his voice was thick when he spoke. 'With Contrarè aid we could be hitting their own flanks even now.'

A sigh escaped from the silent Dreamer's lips. All at once the cold air rushed in upon the group to chill them instantly in their cloaks, causing the zels to snort in complaint. Shard had dropped the cell of air around the party that had kept them warm during their long return.

'Can't you do something here, Shard?' Coya beseeched her.

For a long moment she appraised the encampment around her with her steady gaze. 'Maybe. If you give me some time to work with.'

'And risk getting trapped here?' Marsh snapped at the pair of them. 'Not bloody likely. If we want to make it back to Bar-Khos then we need to get out of here now.'

His words fell like rocks upon the weary rangers and the two medicos, none of whom had the same luxury of leaving. This was their base of operations after all.

'Well, better report in,' Sergeant Sansun announced, and he nodded to Coya before whirling his zel around.

'Sergeant!' Coya called after him, and then, more quietly, 'Captain. All of you.'

He had their attention.

'I can see our skyboat is no longer waiting for us in the field. It would appear I require an escort back to the city, if you'd be willing.'

The Volunteers exchanged surprised glances with each other.

'We'll still need to report in,' Captain Gamorre replied. 'Let them know that some of us made it back.'

'You will accompany us though, once you have?'

They all nodded their consent, save for Xeno, who already had his rifle unwrapped for action.

'Tell them I need you,' Coya said to the captain. 'Then meet me back here at the soonest.'

'Very well.'

She rode off at a canter with Sergeant Sansun following behind. 'And be quick about it!' Marsh shouted after the pair. 'We'll meet you out on the road!'

In their wake Shard watched them go, then craned her neck to stare back at the dark impression of the Windrush forest.

She thought of the man Sky In His Eyes just then. She pictured his startling gaze holding her own and wondered when they would meet again. But the concussions of the raging battle kept jolting through her. Distant screams assaulted her ears.

Shard turned to survey the fighting taking place around her.

'Probably too late to help much here anyway,' she murmured into the night.

Marsh shifted in his saddle.

'Probably.'

Neither had to say how glad they were, to be soon leaving this place behind.

CHAPTER FIFTY-ONE

Release

A bell was ringing from somewhere outside the prison cell, muffled by the heavy metal slab of the door which Meer had pressed his ear against moments before. The hedgemonk straightened and turned to his fellow captive with a shrug.

'Could be a bird attack on the city,' the monk suggested. 'We're certainly due for one now the rains have come.'

A grunt sounded from the old farlander slouched against the wall. Ash watched the monk return to a sitting position on the opposite bunk, where the younger man folded his legs together and settled his hands in his lap once more, his eyes lively with excitement. Together, their attention remained focused on the door and the alarm ringing on the other side of it, the only thing of interest to have happened in days.

*

'He should be fully grown by now, your boy,' ventured Meer, turning his mind to other things. 'I wonder if he will be himself again when he wakes?'

Ash nodded and tried to picture it in his mind, his apprentice alive again, right now at this very moment – but he could only summon up the memory of the strange spectralgraph Meer had sent him, that ghostly image of flesh and bones forming in a glass tank filled with Milk. It was all too unreal to properly grasp.

A strange sensation, nonetheless, to be this close to Nico yet unable to reach the boy, for his apprentice was in a different leg of the Sky Bridge, and Ash remained firmly imprisoned. Getting to him would be no easy matter.

But first he had to get Meer out of here, and before the hedgemonk's increasing need for conversation drove him crazy with distraction. With every passing day of confinement Meer was growing ever more chatty, unable to stop himself it seemed, despite Ash's lack of responses. Now that it was clear that neither of them were due to be executed, the man's tensions had gathered instead around the sheer soul-crushing banality of their confinement, and so talk had become a form of escape to him, a welcome release from circumstances beyond his control; much to Ash's ire, for he had never enjoyed idle chat, was frankly bored by it.

Meer was peering at him now in anticipation of a response. What to say, though, that hadn't been said already?

Instead Ash climbed onto his bunk to look out of the window, squinting through the rain-smeared glass at the twilight skies over the surrounding peaks.

At last the rainy season had arrived.

Between the grilles it was clear how thick the window pane was by the raindrops dribbling down the outside of the glass. Through the downpour he could see the leg of the Sky Bridge sloping down below him and the netting stretching away on either side of it into the haze, its skirts extending over the outer rim of the caldera. Beneath it the streets of the city looked empty, save for the odd smudge of motion that was a speeding groundcar.

A flash of violet light drew his eyes downwards, but he saw nothing except a lingering afterimage in his vision. Ash stared a while longer but did not see it again.

Come on. Where are you?

'Maybe we're only dreaming,' Meer said out of the blue. 'Maybe we're in something like the Black Dream, a fake construction, and they're only toying with us, hoping we'll confess our crimes.'

Over his shoulder, Ash cast him a doubtful look of concern.

Together they listened to the natural music of the rain, loud now that the alarm had finally stopped ringing. The rain was the only sound of the real world they had.

Ash thought he glimpsed movements in the grey skies between the peaks, something soaring out there in the obscurity of the rain. He leaned closer to the glass.

'We're never getting out of here, are we?' Meer suddenly blurted, and his tone was one of bitter regret, as though he was saddened by all the things he would never again experience, the places he would never travel to, the people he would never meet. 'They're going to keep us here until we wither away to husks.'

'Relax. They say you get used to imprisonment after the first few years.'

Meer managed a smile. Once more Ash settled his chin on the back of his hand and squinted out at the rain.

'You keep standing there at the window watching out for something, but you never tell me what!'

Ash blinked. Had he just seen something out there through the haze? Wings extended to catch the air?

Again he glimpsed a winged shape through the haze. His heart skipped a beat.

They're here!

Lightly he hopped from the bed and started to pull on his boots, humming something under his breath.

'What is it?' the monk demanded when Ash grabbed the headstand of his bed then dragged it across the floor towards the door, where he flipped it onto its side. 'What's going on?'

Without comment, Ash crouched down behind it for cover.

'Should I be doing that too?'

'I strongly advise it.'

Meer grabbed up his own boots and crouched down next to him for cover. A toothy grin split his face in two. Tears sparkled in his eyes. 'It's an escape, you bastard, isn't it? All this time you've been letting me wallow in my own misery and you've had this brewing all along!'

'I told you to hold fast,' Ash remarked, and lightly punched the monk's arm.

Suddenly the cell erupted in a clap of air and noise, and then a wind was blasting through the space, shocking in its coldness, whipping at their clothes and their heads and the fluttering lashes of their eyes. Together they peered curiously over the top of the bed, and saw the gaping hole where the window had once been and the figure dropping in on the end of a line, clad in a strangely bulky suit of brilliant yellow. Violet sparks flashed around his feet.

'Still think you are dreaming?' Ash asked the monk.

'I knew it!' Meer declared as Ash dragged him to his feet. 'I knew it!'

Amongst the flying rain the figure in yellow yanked down his hood. It was Aléas, and the young Rōshun apprentice raised an eyebrow at the sight of them standing there in a huddle, then smartly tossed a bundle of bright clothing on the floor before their feet.

'You fellows about ready to leave?'

*

The suits were bulky and stiff to move in, and with the wind and rain and downrush of hot air it was a desperate climb up the rope ladder to the craft hovering above.

Cole hauled them up the last few feet into the rear compartment of the flying machine, slapping each of their backs in turn. There they lay gasping and wiping their faces clear as the contraption tilted and turned away from the white leg of the Sky Bridge and the gaping hole of their cell. Through the open doorway behind Cole, the netting over the city flickered by, incredibly close.

'Keep your eyes open,' called the longhunter across to them, dressed in a shiny yellow suit like their own. His voice was shaky and dark rings underlined his bloodshot eyes, as though the man was badly hungover. 'We've got some big birds up here with us. And they don't look to be friendly.'

'They're harmless!' shouted a voice from the front. 'Nothing to worry about!'

With the compartment jostling this way and that, Ash made his way to the front, where the Anwi man Juke sat in one of the forward seats with his hands gripping the controls, grunting and cursing under his breath as he wrestled with the craft. Juke glanced over his shoulder and said, 'Just the man I was hoping to see.'

The nose of the craft was transparent, and through the smearing windscreen a far leg of the Sky Bridge was looming closer, shifting left and right in their view as Juke tried to keep them steady. Ash pulled at the tight neck of the suit stretched around his throat, and wondered if stealing the craft had been as easy as the Anwi man had claimed it would be.

'You sure you can fly this thing?'

'Of course I can fly it,' Juke called back over the noise of the thrusters, and Ash saw the sweat beading on his black skin. 'I was practising all night at home.'

'He means it,' Aléas muttered, standing next to Ash with a hand gripping the webbing over his head for balance. 'I sat and watched him.'

'Hey now, that was only a refresher. I've flown plenty. In the Dream I'm a damned good pilot.'

'The Dream?'

'The Black Dream,' explained Aléas. 'They can create dreams inside of it somehow. He's a good pilot in his dreams, is what he's telling you.'

'I'm coming back to the Free Ports with you by the way!' shouted Juke. 'Always wanted to see that big world yonder.'

'What about that woman of yours?' Ash asked him.

'Triqy? She barely tolerates me. Minus the great sex there isn't much left between us but air.'

'Here,' Aléas said. 'You'll need these.'

The young man passed him his sword, which Ash grasped eagerly, then a collection of smaller weapons from a canvas backpack, typical equipment of their trade. Ash fixed them onto the belt of the suit and into the deep pockets on its legs.

'You're going after your boy!' Meer shouted in delight. 'I knew it!'

'Better hold on to something,' Juke announced as the craft tilted sharply. Through the side doorway a limb of the Sky Bridge swung crazily into view. At once the nose of the craft tilted sharply upwards and Meer went tumbling while the rest of them clung to the straps on the roof. The tail lifted up and then the craft levelled off again, its great wings folding to cup the air.

'I think I see it,' Cole called out from the doorway, staring down at the slope of the leg. 'A maintenance gantry with an open door.'

Rain and wind smashed against his face as Ash leaned out to take his bearings. Below his feet the end of the rope ladder was swaying near the gantry that Cole had just indicated.

'Bring it closer,' Ash shouted, and he didn't wait for Juke to respond but climbed down onto the first of the rungs, pausing only to look up at Meer's startled expression.

'Make certain Juke keeps the craft here until our return, you hear me?'

'Of course! Good luck!'

With the sword over his back Ash scrambled down the swinging ladder with Aléas and Cole following after him, the city sprawling far below their dripping feet. He glanced down at it once then focused on the nearby gantry, made a grab for it but missed. The rain and the bulky suit were hardly helping matters.

'Keep it steady!'

*

In a shower of rain, all three staggered through the doorway and stood in a carpeted corridor inside the leg, panting and dripping water while they stared at the tall Anwi woman before them.

Triqy wore a sky-blue one-piece suit, and her blonde hair was tied back in a bun.

'Where's Meer, is he safe?' she asked them nervously.

'Don't worry,' answered Aléas. 'He's waiting on the Vulture.'

The Anwi woman's smile made her look much younger. 'Here, put this on,' she told Ash, and slipped another kidney-shaped farcry around his neck and tucked it in against his skin. 'You can talk with Juke with this. Quickly now. *Follow me.*'

Triqy led them down the corridor in their bright yellow suits, past a row of brightly lit windows which looked onto enclosed bays filled with foliage – spindly plants with their roots dangling in bubbling tanks of water – a few figures in white suits and hoods stepping amongst the humid air. The walls of the corridors here were convex and the same blue as her overalls, and her soft slippers padded across the floor with little rips. Their breaths were trails in the cold air.

Directly behind her, Ash suddenly stopped when she halted before a door next to a window in the wall. Through the glass he could see a chamber and the dim shapes of equipment illuminated by red light. Triqy checked left and right along the corridor then opened the sliding door with a slap to the wall. Warmer air wafted over them.

This was it then. The reason he had come all this way. The reason Kosh had given up his life in the Hush.

'He is ready?' came his whispered voice.

'Only just.'

The room was a long oblong chamber with pale red lights along the ceiling which brightened as they entered. Behind them the door slid closed with a hiss of air and Aléas and Cole stationed themselves on either side of it.

'Here,' said the Anwi woman and yanked a lever out from a wall hatch next to the door. 'Hold this down to keep it locked.'

Triqy moved deeper into the chamber and pulled something else from the wall: a steel slab with a body lying upon it rigged up to a series of tubes. Ripping sounds erupted as she worked over the prone form. Liquid dribbled onto the floor at her feet. Ash forced himself to take a step closer, and then another.

'Is that him?' hissed Aléas from the door.

'Yes!' replied a startled Ash in his native Honshu, and for all that the world turned beneath them he was rendered still.

CHAPTER FIFTY-TWO

Fear of Big Birds

It was the boy all right.

It was Nico, his apprentice, lying there as though dead within a tight transparent wrapping that reached up to his neck, his pale exposed face gleaming wetly. Ash could barely believe what he was seeing.

'*Nico,*' he breathed and cupped the boy's head in his palm, seeing the curls of his hair and the slightly upturned nose.

From the door, the longhunter Cole shifted around to stare. '*What did you say?*'

But Triqy was ripping more of the wrapping away, and she yanked a pair of paddles from the side of the slab trailing cords and placed them against Nico's bare chest. 'Stand back,' she declared, and the boy jerked and arched his back for a moment, then lay there suddenly breathing. Even as Ash watched he saw colour returning to his blood-less skin.

'His signs are good,' she said, producing something else from the side of the slab, trailing more cord. She clamped the device around the boy's forehead, talking rapidly as she did so: 'He's still a blank page, though. Normally we'd have a good working image stored on a heartstone to work with. Same things as your seals before you twin them. But since we don't have *that*, we'll have to do it the old-fashioned way.'

She snapped her fingers to gain Ash's attention. Placed something cool into his grasp.

It was Nico's hand.

'What do I do?'

'Call for him.'

'How?'

'In your mind. Call for him like his life depends on it.'

Nico!

'Think of a memory you both share. Relive it intensely.'

His mind went blank for a moment. But then he thought of autumnal leaves swirling around his ankles as he'd called out for the boy back in Q'os, waiting for his apprentice to return long after he knew that something had gone wrong.

No, you fool. Nico wasn't even there.

Flames rose up in his vision. A great pyre burning on the floor of an arena with his apprentice staked upon the top of it, struggling and crying out in pain. The last memory they had ever shared.

Nico!

A shadow crossed before his eyes, cast from the window of the room. An Anwi guard in a black uniform was peering through the glass at them all. A moment later, someone started thumping on the door.

'*Usht!*' cursed Triqy, and pulled a white breathing mask onto her face to cover it. 'Keep your hand on that handle whatever you do,' she told Aléas, for Cole had left him to it and was approaching the slab.

'It isn't working,' she announced with disgust, checking a glowing square of lights on the surface of the slab.

But Cole shoved her out of the way and looked down on the young man lying there breathing softly.

'*Nico?*' he croaked in amazement, and his scarred forehead wrinkled in a knot. It was as though Cole no longer heard the banging on the door. With all the time in the world the longhunter reached out to touch the boy, though he flinched back when their skins connected.

What's this? wondered Ash in confusion.

Before he could react, the longhunter was rounding on him with eyes wild with rage, grabbing at his suit to shake him roughly. 'What are you doing with my son, old man? *What's he doing here?*'

'Whatever you two are fighting about we haven't the time for it,' Aléas called out from the door. Blue sparks were flying through the metal and lighting the young Rōshun's grim features. The red lights of the room started to flash on and off above their heads.

'This is your apprentice?' raged Cole. 'All this time and you didn't tell me?'

Ash swept the man's clawed grip clear of him. 'You know this youth?'

'Know him? He's my son, you kushing fool! Nico Calvone! What's he doing here of all the damned places?'

His son?

In the midst of Ash's stupefied silence, Triqy held up a hand to placate them. 'You're his father?' she asked.

'Yes damn it!'

'Maybe you can help then. Here. You try.' And she thrust Nico's other hand into the longhunter's grasp. 'Call for him.'

'I don't understand.'

'You don't need to understand. Just call for him!'

Outside, a guard struck the window of the room with an axe. A starry crack appeared in the glass. The guard leaned back to swing again.

'Nico!'

'Do it with more meaning.'

'*Son!*'

'Again. But in your mind. Put all the meaning in the world into it.'

Ash glanced across to Aléas. A guard was shouting through the glass in muted silence, glaring and jabbing his finger at the apprentice. In reply Aléas pointed at the lever he was holding – *this? – this thing here?* – and dangled from it with a shake of his head.

Again Cole shouted in anger. 'Just tell me what's going on here!'

'I think it's working,' Triqy announced in a whisper. 'Yes, that's it,' she said to Ash and straightened over the slab. 'That's all we can do, for now anyway.'

'You found him?'

'He found us. What impression was left of him, anyway. We'll have to see how well it worked.' She wiped her forehead as she looked to Ash, who stared down at the young man with his mouth still gaping open.

'We really shouldn't be moving him in this condition.'

Ash blinked, and forced himself to the business at hand. 'No choice,' he told her. 'Cole, can you carry him?'

The longhunter stood dumbly looking down at Nico too.

'*Cole!*'

He started. Gathered up the boy in his arms, crushing him to his chest while glaring at Ash and the rest of them.

Now, to get out of there.

*

Dust roamed the gloomy maintenance passage behind the rear wall. Ash almost sneezed when he pulled his head back into the chamber and motioned Cole through the open panel.

'Go left and follow it round until you can find somewhere clear to come out,' Triqy instructed him, and then the longhunter vanished with Nico in his arms.

'Good luck,' she panted at Ash then stepped into the passage too, though she looked to the right.

'You aren't coming with us?'

'No, I have an alibi to get to. Tell Meer I'm sorry I didn't have a chance to say goodbye. Tell him . . .' she shook her head and motes of dust flew about it. 'Tell him it was good to see him again.'

'I will. Thank you, for everything.'

She nodded, then a moment later she was gone too.

'What about this damned door?' Aléas gasped, drawing Ash back to the door.

The guards were almost through the glass now, though he ignored them, and instead grasped the lever holding the door in place. 'Go. I'll catch up shortly.'

'I'm not going anywhere.'

'On three then, release together and run for the hole in the wall.'

'You must think me an idiot.'

'Aléas, it is no trick. On three and we both run for the wall. Now stop messing around.'

'Fine, fine.'

'One. Two. Three.'

They released the lever at the same instant and Ash pushed Aléas ahead of him towards the back wall. Almost at once the door slid open behind them.

Ash ducked behind one of the steel-sided trolleys occupying the room. Waited until Aléas was through the open wall panel then drew the sword on his back, feeling the heft of it in his grip.

A gunshot rang out, bouncing off the wall around the opening and forcing Aléas back inside. But the young Rōshun was armed too, and he fired back with his own pistol, toppling a guard entering the room before he swung out of sight to reload.

'Go now!' Ash shouted back at him, hearing the window crashing to the floor in pieces.

A pair of boots scrunched into the room, stepping across shattered glass towards his position.

Now.

With his naked blade Ash lunged up at the approaching guard, who was crouched down for cover, and speared him cleanly through the neck. Ducked down again just as another shot whipped past his head. The other guards opened up wildly and Aléas fired back again, but Ash could only huddle down as instruments and debris flew all around him and bullets spat through the metal of the trolley. He hunched lower and lower until he was sprawled on the floor, seeing the boots of more guards between sets of rubber wheels.

Shouts sounded from outside and the firing ended.

Silence fell amongst the gun smoke. Something dripped nearby. The red lights of the room still pulsed on and off. Ash checked to see if he was hit and felt a hole in the left sleeve of his suit, but no broken skin.

He hoped that Aléas had sense enough to stay back. Wondered how long Cole would need to make it back to the Vulture with Nico. Tentatively, he raised his head until he could peer through a ragged hole in the side of the trolley.

The fallen guard he had poked was gasping and clutching his bloody neck and trying to push himself back towards the broken window, where other guards had taken cover. One was trying to reach out to grab him. Beside them, a figure stepped through the open doorway wearing a fine black suit with tails.

The old Rōshun grinned.

*

'I did not think you were the kind to get your hands dirty,' he called out to the Archon.

Through the hole in the trolley he watched the thin man sniff something from a vial in his hand, then take a step further into the room.

'Consider it a compliment,' came the Archon's smooth reply. 'A professional courtesy, if you will.'

The Archon uttered a sound from his throat and swept his other hand through the air, causing one of the wheeled trolleys in his way to race to one side. He stepped into the space it had left, then swept his hand again and forced another trolley out of his way.

Getting up close and personal with this man was likely the worst tactic to follow here, Ash thought, running through the inventory in his head of the weapons Aléas had given him. He dug into one of the pockets on his leg for a throwing star he recalled placing there then rose to a crouch, just enough to throw it with a whip of his arm.

The disc spun at the Archon then veered past his head sharply.

'For all I know, you could be the last living Rōshun of your order. Your people could be moments away from extinction.'

His fine shoes crunched on the shattered glass. Ash gripped the hilt of his sword and readied himself to strike out, but suddenly the trolley before him swept to the side and he was hit in the chest by a force which threw him back skidding across the tiles.

Gasping on the floor, he called out weakly, 'Aléas?'

'The gun's jammed! It just jammed up on me!'

Gasping, rolling over, he snatched up his blade and gained his feet again, but another blow picked him up like a massive hand and swung him high into the wall by his legs.

Ash blacked out for an instant, and found himself on the floor bleeding from a head wound. He pushed himself through the familiar sickening grogginess of the knockout.

'Go!' he croaked to Aléas. 'Make sure the others wait for me. Tell them to give me a hundred counts.'

It was all he could think of to make the lad leave this scene, to save his young skin.

It was hard to breathe, hard to see straight. Like a pitfighter, Ash used the precious moments on the floor to regain his senses.

'I have to say,' declared the Archon, striding towards him where he lay on his back. Beneath the white streaks of his hair the Archon's temples were throbbing from his efforts. Sweat glistened on his face, cut trails down through his dark lips so that his chin was streaked black. 'I fear the fictions of the Rōshun may be as inflated as any other.'

At last Ash found it in a pocket – what he was groping for with his scrabbling free hand. Pain stabbed at his side as he staggered to his feet. For a moment Ash leaned on his sword as though it was a cane, observing the Archon with a calm and unforgiving outlook.

Make him bleed.

With a hiss Ash bounded forwards, swinging his blade up too fast to follow. Still it slid past the man's shoulder as though he knew it was coming.

The Archon swept his flat hand at Ash, and Ash ducked as a slice of air whipped across him.

Stinging pain across his left cheek. No way, it seemed, to get through with the sword. Nothing left for it then.

With all his strength Ash grasped the Archon in his embrace and felt the hoary force surging around the man's body and then his own, surging like muscles where Ash held him, surging as Ash fumbled to place something in his grasp, clamping the man's fingers around it.

Ash met the Archon's fervid gaze only briefly, and then he launched himself backwards over a trolley for cover.

He had just enough time to see the Archon glancing down at the live grenade in his hand, his expression curious and amused, before the thing exploded.

Smoke and shrapnel ripped through the air. Cries rose out and then the gunfire started again, shots whipping blindly through roiling smoke. When Ash glanced up, the Archon was standing there gaping in shock at a blackened stump where his lower arm had recently hung.

The rest of him seemed entirely unscathed.

Time to get out of there.

Ash's ears were ringing when he scrambled over the tiles and dived into the maintenance passage with the Archon's rage roaring after him.

'Rōshun!'

Like a gleeful rat, Ash scurried along the passage with the hood of his suit fluttering in the wind of the man's fury, letting the shine of his sword lead the way.

Nico, he's alive!

*

Ash, are you almost here?

It was Juke, his voice suddenly loud in Ash's head.

On my way.

We just took some incoming fire. We'll have to swing around and come back for you.

Understood.

Ash rounded a corner in the passage and spotted the light pouring from an open panel ahead. Behind him he could hear the footsteps of the guards pursuing him. He ran for the end of the passage, ducking his head out then back again as a bullet skipped off the floor before him.

Another quick fumble in his suit produced a smoke grenade. He pulled the fuse to let in the moist air then tossed it out into the corridor. Took a deep gulp of air then leapt out after it.

Blindly, Ash sprinted through the billows of black smoke until he could see again. Ahead lay the open maintenance door where the rain was coming through in gusts. He gripped the door frame and pulled himself through onto the maintenance gantry outside, looking about through the downpour.

No sign of Juke or the flying craft anywhere.

A guard rushed through the doorway and Ash kicked him back inside and threw the hatch shut, trying to find a locking mechanism without success. He leaned his back against it and looked down through the grilled floor of the gantry, taking in the vast sweep of netting stretched between the legs of the Sky Bridge and over the distant streets below. A winged shape sped towards the netting, and then with a violet flash it was falling, rolling and spinning down the flexing slope with sparks trailing in its wake. In the bursts of light Ash spotted other shapes soaring through the rain. Gunfire sounded from the Sky Bridge, heavy and rapid percussions which caused another winged shape to drop from the air.

They were the birds that came with the seasonal rains. The birds that Meer had first mentioned and Triqy had explained further, giant featherless carnivores that always returned to these mountains to prey on runs of fish and the yearlings of the wild goat population. Fairly harmless by the sound of them, rarely known to attack humans save for in a few instances of confusion, yet the Anwi apparently waged a defensive war against them every year, shooting the creatures on sight whenever they came too close to the city.

Accordingly, all winged craft should now be grounded while the city defences targeted the birds, including the security craft that would normally be shooting any escape attempts out of the sky. It was the perfect cover, the perfect time, in which to make their escape back down to Guallo Town, where the Alhazii too would be seeking shelter. Chaos was their best chance now, so long as they could avoid being shot at by the Sky Bridge itself.

The door bounced behind him and Ash pushed back harder, struggling to keep it closed. His boots slipped on the wet gantry. He glanced about for any sign of the returning craft.

Juke!

No response and the door was swinging outwards against him, pushed by several guards at least. Guards with guns and stunsticks no doubt. He had run out of options here. The only way remaining was down.

Perhaps it was a form of madness that allowed him to do these things in such moments as this, though to Ash it was a simple matter of faith, of taking whatever step needed taking next and hoping for the best. His eyes and nostrils flaring, Ash launched himself over the rail and toppled through the air.

He had time enough to straighten in his fall – and to glimpse the peaks made black by twilight – before the slope of netting was rushing up at him, and then he crashed into it, trying to loop an arm around a cable, but his weight bounced from the netting and he felt the wrench of his arm popping from its socket.

Violet sparks seemed to be bursting all about him.

He didn't bounce on his next landing, and with his good arm he clung on tight to the dripping wire and waited for the bobbing motion to settle. Rain and sparks blasted his eyes, though the yellow suit he was wearing seemed to be protecting him. Ash glanced between his feet perched on another thick bundle of wire, saw that he was about halfway down now, where the netting flared out like the skirts of a bell.

Juke, where are you, man!

Almost finished our circuit. We're heading back now. Where are you?

Hanging onto the netting. Look for the sparks!

A growing orb of light drew his gaze upwards and Ash narrowed his eyes, taking in the far gantry he had just plummeted from. A tiny figure stood up there washed in brilliance, with a lone arm held high.

Oh no.

What is it?

Ash gritted his teeth and stared back at the distant Archon with all his will.

Forget about me. Turn away.

Don't tempt me, old man.

Juke. Turn away!

Silence, while up there the figure was dropping his arm dramatically. At once a ripple appeared across the netting at the Archon's feet and pulsed downwards, narrowing as it picked up momentum.

Wildly, Ash started to scramble to the side as best he could with his one working arm, but the descending wave shifted across to follow him.

He would have sworn his defiance to the wind and rain just then had something not struck him hard on the back. It was the rope ladder, swinging away from him even as he spotted it.

Ash swept around and pressed his back to the netting. As the ladder swung back towards him he grasped for it and stuck a boot onto the lowest rung, then stepped out into the air, glancing up at the underside of the craft with its wing thrusters blasting him with hot air.

Juke! I told you to stay clear!

Even as he spoke the craft pitched to one side and slid away from the Sky Bridge with its twisting wings roaring hard. Ash hung with his limbs dangling into space, his head turned to the distant speck of light that was the Archon.

A screech of metal over his head, one of the thrusters exploding in the wing of the craft. Flames and debris trailed from the gaping hole. The craft tilted some more, picking up speed as its nose pointed towards the ground. Wind smeared Ash's face against his skull.

Ahead, below, all at once, the city was rushing up towards his feet.

It's all right, it's all right, I've got it! Juke yelled in his mind while the city swung at them with all its might.

CHAPTER FIFTY THREE

Reese

The road was empty in both directions for as far as Reese could see, an eerie sight for this early time of day when normally carts and riders would be making their way to the markets of Bar-Khos.

Reese stared again at the bruises hanging in the sky to the north-east, still unable to tell whether they were rain clouds or columns of smoke rising from a fire.

Sweating from her exertions, she pulled the handcart as fast as she could, cursing herself now for having left it so long, this flight to the city; cursing Los too for taking Happy, her single draught animal. Only rarely did she glance to the white-capped sea on her left contained within the Bay of Squalls, for time and again her attention was drawn towards the north, where the Mannians' slaver parties were said to be close.

Silence all about her, Reese noticed, save for the distant cries of gulls out in the bay and the rumbling of the handcart's wheels on the stones of the road.

The cart was laden high with everything she had been able to fit onto it from the cottage, even her oldest cat, Solberry, a plump ginger creature perched on the chest of clothing at the very top of the load, watching everything around them with half-blind eyes, too old to be left behind to fend for herself. Reese was making good progress considering the heavy load she was hauling, for the south-ern coastal road was a relatively smooth surface of flat stones bedded in gravel, and much of it was downhill. Overheating already, she left her blue cloak hanging open to sweep about her in the wind.

Panting, wiping her forehead dry, Reese followed the road down through a vale of swaying yellow grasses framed by white cliffs ahead and a gentle grassy slope to the north, the cart rattling and bouncing behind her along the stones, the ginger cat gripping on with her claws gamely.

She knew the vale to be a good spot for a rest on the long journey to and from the city. A peaceful place to enjoy a quick bite to eat while watching the waves crashing against the foot of the cliffs, listening to the sighs of the grasses in the wind. Not now though, with the smoke hanging there beyond the solitary tree on the crest of the northern slope. Reese felt only trepidation in this place now, and her eyes danced for a sight of what she did not wish to see most of all, signs of Mannians.

She stopped dead, blinking up at the solitary tree on the hill.

Something moved up there, parting from the tree so she could see it clearly now: a rider watching her.

The breath hitched in Reese's throat as more riders appeared over the crest, joining the first in a long line. Dark cloaks swirled in the offshore breeze. Steam rose from the snorts of their zels. They were armoured, their heads masked by helms that had slits for visors in a fashion not at all familiar to Khos.

'Oh no.'

They were coming, picking their way down the slope in a meandering column, long poles held upright in their grasps with nooses dangling from the end of them.

Reese looked about for somewhere to run, but there was nothing except the sea and the empty road. She'd freeze out there in the water, and she would never outrun them on the road.

She could only stare frozen on the spot as the lead rider spurred his zel into a canter, and then suddenly they were jingling towards her, spreading out in a line once again and bringing their poles down at the ready, the ground trembling just as she trembled.

She had left it too late. Much too late.

'Oh Sweet Mother, no!'

CHAPTER FIFTY-FOUR

Old Dogs

'Nico?'

The longhunter's voice croaked from all the shouting he had been doing, all the yelling in anger at the old farlander and the others since discovering his own son mixed up in their crazy scheming.

'Nico,' Cole tried again, from where he was perched next to the cot staring down at his son, but again there was no response, no indication even that the boy heard him.

Nico lay against the pillows with a heavy wool blanket pulled up to his chest, sipping from another mug of water, all he had been able to do since they had brought him here to the *Falcon*'s infirmary. The dark hair on his head was starting to curl once more as it dried. His wide blue eyes shone over the rim of the mug, observing them all without comprehension.

The boy had been dead, the old farlander had claimed, though Cole could hardly reckon it. Even Reese knew of the boy's passing, he had said. She must be tearing her hair out in grief, his wife who Nico reminded him so much of now, the boy of his memories grown into a young man and looking even more like his mother than before.

Whatever it was they had done to him back in the Isles, during that frantic procedure in which he had been revived, Cole was beginning to suspect that it hadn't truly worked.

Nico seemed barely there at all.

'I can't believe it's really him,' spoke the young man Aléas quietly from the doorway.

'Nor I,' replied Ash from the other side of the cot. The farlander sat with his arm cradled in a sling, black stitches running across a deep cut in his face. He looked tired but contented as he gazed at Nico lying there between them.

'Can you hear me?' tried Ash, as though he would have any better luck than Cole, but still those eyes stared and blinked above the mug, the boy sipping quietly, not answering.

'Give him time,' advised the medico Shin from her small desk, where she was writing something in a notebook. 'By the sounds of it he's been through a tremendous amount.'

Haven't we all.

A lantern over their heads was rattling lightly, and the soft roar of the thrusters filled the air like the rush of a nearby river as the ship sped across the sky. Hours had passed since the *Falcon* had taken off from the port of Guallo Town under cover of darkness and bird activity, lifting her nose to the sky while Alhazii soldiers ran at them firing their guns wildly but without effect.

It had been easy enough, the *Falcon*'s escape. Too easy in fact, and no one seemed in the mood for celebration just yet. Even now, hours clear of the Isles of Sky and heading north back to the known world, they seemed convinced that they were being pursued through the night by other skyships, and that messages were being sent ahead to cut them off.

But for now, in this moment at least, they appeared to be safe from harm. For now, Cole had time enough to take in a deep breath and fathom what all of this was supposed to mean.

'I don't understand,' he said aloud. 'How can something like this be down to coincidence?'

'The Way often leads to strange and useful congruences,' grumbled the farlander unhelpfully, and the old fellow even had the gall to shrug. 'These things happen.'

Clearly Ash had little interest in the how or why of it, content to sit by the boy's side watching the life shine from him.

'But of all the people you could have chosen to guide you into the Hush, you chose me.'

In the doorway, the Rōshun apprentice Aléas reached down to stroke the cat between the ears, lying there curled against the wall watching Nico with her curious eyes.

'Sometimes,' said the young man casually, 'it seems to me the Great Dream enjoys a good story, is all.'

'Well that explains it perfectly then, doesn't it?'

The cat looked to him then back again to Nico. She had seemed to recognize Nico when they had first brought him on board the ship, showing an interest in him as they laid him on the bed, though she had only known him briefly, back when Cole had brought her from the tunnels of the Shield on home leave, while he recovered from his wounds. For a month she had lived at the cottage with Nico and Reese and the family dog Boon, a month of peace and idle play in the sun where the tunnels faded to a faraway memory; before Cole had taken her away from it all by fleeing one night, deserting everyone that he knew for fear of what he had become.

Maybe the cat was recollecting that brief time again, some vague sense of it anyway, hoping to return to the peaceful farm even now.

Cole followed her stare back to the young man on the bed. Strange. The two childpox scars seemed to be gone from Nico's forehead. As though he was some kind of copy of himself, not the real thing at all.

Hairs rose on the backs of Cole's arms. For all the excitement of the others he felt unnerved by every aspect of this situation, like some kind of twisted joke was being played out at his expense.

He could still barely fathom any of it, least of all the thought of his son living as an apprenticing Rōshun, or so Ash would have him believe. What had Reese been thinking? Had she gone and lost her mind?

This is what happens when you run out and leave your family to fend for themselves in the midst of a war.

Cole pinched his brows into a scowl.

'He's coming with me when we return. Get used to the idea, both of you.'

Now the farlander pinched his brows.

'And where is it you propose to take him?'

'Back to his mother. Back to the family farm.'

'As I already intended to do. I will accompany you there.'

'Oh you will, will you?'

The two men stared at each other as though in challenge. Between them Nico lowered the mug from his mouth, but it was only so that he could look up at a scuff of boots in the doorway.

It was Captain Trench standing there in a rainslick and hat, looming over the shorter form of Aléas. The captain looked to Nico staring back at him, then nodded curtly to Ash.

'You made it then.'

'Of course,' replied Ash. 'Are we clear yet?'

'Aye. If you don't count the three skyships in pursuit.'

Heads turned in the direction of the captain.

'Can we stay ahead of them?'

'There's nothing in the sky we can't stay in front of. I'm more concerned with what might be waiting for us ahead. We need to talk.'

*

'You see them?'

Cole and Ash were both squinting through mounted eyeglasses on the quarterdeck of the ship, past her trailing Alhazii flag to the moonlit night sky behind them, where distant bulbous clouds sailed against the stars, and where three yellow lights glimmered faintly from the skyships in pursuit.

'Yes,' they both said at the same time as they straightened from the lenses, Cole pulling down his hat once more. Far beyond the trio of lights, right at the edge of visibility, stood the mountains running into the sea, topped by the faint glow of Mashuppa and its Sky Bridge.

'So,' said Ash wearily to the captain, 'what is there to discuss?'

'We're heading north for the Sea of Doubts. Crew decision. Faster than returning the way we came, even if we have to dodge a few Alhazii squadrons on the way.'

'And?'

'And a few of us can return even faster than that,' spoke Meer the monk through the darkness.

Meer stood with his back to the rail and his hands buried in the sleeves of his burnoose, his freshly shaven head gleaming in the moonlight. 'That craft Juke is flying alongside us,' he continued, and they all looked over the port rail to see the winged craft that Juke had stolen flying alongside the *Falcon*, a ghostly green light bleeding from its forward windows, a dim form sitting at the controls.

After almost crashing into the city, Juke had wrestled the controls long enough to bring them down from the peaks of Mashuppa to the skyport of Guallo Town, where they had settled right beside the *Falcon* before any of the Alhazii soldiers on guard could react. With the rest of them scrambling across to the skyship, Juke had lifted off again to patrol the air for hostile craft, and then had accompanied them during their escape, not wishing to give up the vessel now.

'The Vulture? What about it?'

'It carries six people in all. And Juke told me he brought along enough charge coils to make it all the way back to the Midèrēs. We'd be home in no time.'

It was the first time Cole had seen the farlander betray his surprise.

'Truly?'

'Yes!'

'It's the fastest way to get those charts back to the Free Ports,' added Trench. 'And if we risked our lives for anything, it was for those charts.'

Ash was nodding his agreement.

'When do we leave then?'

'Soon as we can pack.'

'*Charts?*' exclaimed Cole suddenly, and they all looked at him. 'I thought this was some noble mission to save my son?'

'You thought wrong then,' snapped Trench, turning back to the others. 'Get packed, and I'll tell the men to string across a line for you.'

'Wait! I'm getting damn well tired of being the last person to know anything on this ship. I've earned a right to know. Or have you forgotten I just helped break your sorry asses out of a prison cell back there?'

At last he had their full attention.

The monk stepped closer to his side and spoke softly, not wishing to be overheard by the crew. 'Full charts to the Isles of Sky and back. The greatest secret in the world, the location of the Isles, and now we have it.'

There was a sheen of fervour to the monk's expression as he spoke. An intensity to his words as though what he said meant saving the very world they were flying over.

'You mean to save the Free Ports with these charts?' Cole replied in surprise.

'We do. They offer us great leverage with the Alhazii Caliphate, in return for keeping the location to ourselves. Maybe, with their aid, we can even end this war once and for all.'

Cole favoured each of them with a quick glance, somewhat shocked to realize that perhaps they were not so crazy after all. Their plan sounded a plausible one. With the location of the Isles they might indeed buy a bargaining position for his people in the war. He glanced to the winged craft flying alongside the ship, and thought of returning home to Reese and his son and the rest of his family back in Khos, and helping to save them from the Empire's tightening grip, redeeming himself from his burden of guilt.

It was as though the pieces of his life fell into place at long last, every so-called coincidence leading him to a fate which had been there for him all along.

'Well,' chuffed Cole from beneath the tilt of his brim. 'What are we waiting for?'

CHAPTER FIFTY-FIVE

Final Flight

'Captain,' called Ash, meaning to say farewell to the man after all these years of acquaintance, of hiring the *Falcon* in his work as Rōshun, while the others hurried off to grab their packs.

But Trench had time only for the three lights in the sky trailing behind the ship, and the trim of the sculls and the direction of the wind and the dozen other details that were always on a skyman's mind when in the air. In his ringing voice he shouted down to the crewmen on the weatherdeck below, directing them to set up a line between the ship and the winged craft. The Anwi man Juke stood in the doorway of his stolen Vulture while the vessel somehow flew true and level by itself, grabbing the rope thrown across to him which he ran through a loop in the doorway before throwing the end back to the ship, so the crew could begin hauling a simple rope bridge between them.

'Trench,' Ash tried again, louder this time.

This time the captain swung his gaunt features towards him, his long oiled hair blowing in the breeze. Trench was barely thirty years of age yet the war had aged him prematurely. He had seen too much with those eyes.

'My thanks for getting us this far,' Ash replied, but the captain wasn't looking at him any more, was staring over Ash's shoulder at something in the sky.

A lookout shouted something from the loft above their heads. Something loud and panicky.

Suddenly Trench was bellowing to take cover even as a winged shape swooped out of the night sky and swept past the *Falcon* with its guns blazing, the sharp percussions pounding Ash's ears – another Anwi Vulture like the one Juke was flying.

Between himself and the captain a line of splintered wood erupted across the planking of the quarterdeck. Ash stayed on his feet while crewmen dived for cover, shifting his balance as the *Falcon*'s deck began to tilt. He glanced around to see old Stones the pilot still standing by the wheel and spinning it fast, turning the ship hard to starboard while the attacking Anwi craft banked around their prow. Its shots had chewed up the decking around his feet, taking out the speaking tube mounted next to the wheel, somehow missing him entirely.

Now a second Anwi craft was diving towards them with thrusters roaring, its guns spitting a curling trail of shots at the gas loft of the ship, where men scrambled across the rigging. Skymen fired rifles back at the attacking craft. Teams ran to the small hand cannons mounted on the prow and stern, loading them in haste.

Ash yanked the arm sling over his neck and cast it aside, ignoring the shooting pains from his shoulder. Trench had stationed himself near the wheel and the wrecked speaking tubes, still shouting at the top of his voice. The captain looked about as though for his second-in-command Dalas, but he spotted Ash instead and surged towards him purposefully, something of his old steel returned in those frantic moments of surprise.

'Get down to the tail!' he bellowed to Ash. 'Tell Nelson to give us all the black smoke that he can! Go. Go now!'

*

Down into the lower deck with his sword over his back and his boots clomping hard and fast, Ash staggered past the ship's hold, where crewmen were trying to calm a pair of zels that had broken loose from their pens, the animals' hooves flashing over their heads. With the ship suddenly diving he steadied himself against a door frame, feeling the clatter of the zels' hooves through the decking beneath his feet, and then the deeper shudder of the ship's cannon blasting from the starboard side.

He carried on into the chaos of the tail room, where men were coughing and yelling at each other through an acrid atmosphere of smoke that was slowly venting itself through ragged fresh holes in the hull. A group of crewmen were shouting down at a bleeding form lying beneath dials large enough to read from across the room, every needle pointed in the red. Other tailmen rolled casks to the great powder feeders on either side of the curving hull, where figures fed the external thruster tubes with their faces bound in leather breathing masks.

Nelson, the *Falcon*'s chief engineer, was bent over the port feeder like a loving father, listening to the inner workings of the tiq-encased mechanism with a long and narrow-stemmed listening horn; a lean and stiff-backed figure in dirty overalls with his patchy hair sweeping about in a draught from the holes in the hull.

'The captain wants all the black smoke you can give him,' Ash shouted into the man's ear, gripping the feeder casing to hold himself steady.

A tense nod from the sweating chief. A quick bark of orders.

'How is it up there? I can tell we're losing gas.'

Ash shook his head for lack of a ready answer.

Not good.

*

Past the mess room that had now become the gun room, the air thick here too with powder smoke, figures struggling through the haze to reload the cannons or to haul them back into their firing positions. The ship had levelled off again and Ash hurried past the scene, stealing a glance through an open port window. They were turning in a tight circle, creating a cloud of black smoke which poured from the rear thrusters. He spotted a starry sky and the sea glimmering far below; a shape glinting in the moonlight as it swept towards the ship, shots from the crew streaking into its path before the smoke engulfed it.

The din of gunfire was deafening as he stopped at the doorway of the infirmary and caught his breath. Nico was already gone from his cot though, and Shin was bent over a wounded man sprawled on her table, working to staunch a wound.

'I've got them!' shouted a voice and he saw Meer coming along the corridor from his cabin. The monk flapped a large leather tube in triumph. 'I've got the charts, thank Mercy.'

'Then get above with them, man.'

'I'll see you up there!'

With the *Falcon* pitching over again Ash clung to the door frame and felt an explosion shudder through her wooden bones. For a moment it seemed as though he couldn't move from there.

Get it together, he told himself sharply, but he couldn't help how he felt just then. It had just struck him that he was deserting Shin and the rest of the crew to their fate, and the knowledge was a deepening pit in his stomach.

Skymen shouldered past him with another wounded companion, laying the man down unconscious on a cot. Shin told her assistant to take over and moved across to inspect the newcomer. A quick check of his eyes, a moment to feel for his pulse. She shook his head. Told them the man was dead.

He was about to call out when he realized what he would have to say to her, that he was leaving the ship, and in the midst of the action.

Ash turned and strode away quickly. He had made four strides along the corridor before the ship's nose lurched downwards, sprawling him to the floor. A bucket went clattering past his head. People shrieked throughout the ship. Ash rolled across to the side of the passage with butterflies fluttering in his belly.

The ship was falling.

On all fours he scrambled back to the doorway of the infirmary while the *Falcon* dropped from the sky. He clung to the bottom of the door frame while he looked inside for Shin, seeing figures writhing about on the floor. He spotted Shin lying motionless near the table, her head bent at an impossible angle, her eyes glazed and lifeless.

There was nothing he could do here for any of them. It was like the revolution all over again, that feeling of dread as you left behind your companions under fire.

His face locked in a grimace, Ash struggled down the slope of the passage towards the steps leading up. In the gun room beyond, the men were yelling in fright and gripping onto whatever they could. Their cries followed him as he crawled up the steps and through the hatchway.

Up on the weatherdeck it was much the same, crewmen sprawling on the deck and shouting through the wind. The timbers of the ship were trembling now against his touch. Hanging there from the hatchway, Ash's heart almost stopped when he saw the front portion of the ship's loft gone entirely, and the *Falcon*'s nose rushing towards the gleaming silver of the sea. Torn silk flapped back along the surviving loft behind. He spotted flashes of flames back there in their smoky wake, the ends of the tattered silk burning.

Not quite free fall then, for all that it felt that way. Falling like a leaf rather than a stone, thanks to the remaining loft.

His head jerked around until he saw Juke still flying alongside the diving ship, and once more his heart skipped in his chest. A simple rope bridge had been strung across from the deck of the *Falcon*, though the end of it had broken away so that figures clung on to the bridge dangling from the open doorway of the craft.

Ash gritted his teeth and forced himself to move. He made it stumbling to the port rail and gripped it hard, from where he saw Aléas reaching out from the doorway of the winged craft with the cat crying out next to him, trying to haul Nico up from the hanging rope bridge. Below Nico swung Cole, and at the very bottom of the bridge dangled Meer, the monk flailing his legs wildly.

Suddenly the craft swung upwards out of sight, taking them all with it.

Ash gasped, blinking his eyes clear of sweat. *They're fine, they're going to make it*, he told his thundering heart.

Somehow it felt better this way. To go down with the rest of the crew while the others made it to safety. Spreading his legs wide for balance, Ash leaned out to look back along the hull of the ship. The tail room was partly gone now and debris tumbled out from it. Even as he looked a man toppled out head over feet and plummeted through the darkness.

Ash tore his gaze away and looked ahead. Despite the damage, the smaller forward thrusters were still burning on full and pushing them faster into their dive. They were falling in an arc.

'Full lift on the fore-sculls!' screamed Trench up there on the quarterdeck at old Stones the pilot – the grit of them both, trying to wrestle some kind of control even now. '*Get her nose up!*'

Past Ash's position, Berl the ship's boy was trying to climb back up the sloping deck with his face set in a determined grimace, using his crutch for purchase. Another skyman staggered towards Ash groping for the rail. It was one of the Caffey brothers who had come with them into the Edge, the man wide-eyed with panic.

Over the man's shoulder, a scull tore free from the other side of the ship and whipped away into the night. The *Falcon* dipped over violently, bucking the skyman right into Ash so that they both crashed against the rail, then spilled right over it.

Weightlessness. His burnoose fluttering around him as the old Rōshun snatched the cargo netting hanging from the side, yanking himself to a stop. From his good arm he hung there alone with his feet dangling in the air, like his plight on the Sky Bridge all over again. The Caffey brother was gone.

Without warning the *Falcon* started to roll upright again and his body pressed against the hull, allowing Ash to get his other arm hooked through the netting – the screams of the crew and the shouted commands of Trench still filling the dying ship with purpose.

When the *Falcon* carried on rolling over to starboard, Ash placed the soles of his boots squarely against the side and stood up and outwards, squinting ahead along the sleek curve of the hull to see the nearing sea below them, feeling the mighty heft of the ship roll against his feet.

There were worse ways to go, he knew. At least it would be quick.

Ash glanced down past his feet and saw Juke's craft flying just beneath him, wings flaring as it dropped at the same speed as the *Falcon*. The Anwi man's face stared up at him through the forward windscreen.

Juke waved for him to hop on board, as though it was as easy as that.

Maybe it was.

The old Rōshun dropped and landed on the metal wing of the craft with a jolt. His boots slipped from under him and his feet went out over the forward edge of the wing, dragging the rest of him behind them, hands clutching for a purchase that wasn't there. Ash toppled off the wing, snatching out for whatever he could. He glimpsed Aléas's fierce expression in the doorway before he tumbled and hit the trailing rope bridge legs first, snaring himself upside down with a wrench of his back.

Pain blinded him for an instant, almost drove him into unconsciousness.

'Ash!'

Meer's gleaming face beamed up from the end of the rope bridge, his feet trailing free. Ash dangled just above him.

He shook his head, the blood rushing to it now, the burnoose flowing all around him. His left leg seemed to be tangled in the ropes, and he felt someone press against it, Cole maybe.

Beside them, the *Falcon* creaked and groaned in her burning descent.

'I can't hold on,' yelled the monk below, his hands gripping a single loop of rung.

'Climb up!' Ash called down to him.

Something flapped in the wind between them. It was the leather tube containing the charts – Meer was holding it out to him. 'Sweet Mercy, will you take the charts, man!'

With a deep exhalation Ash stretched out his body and arm and snatched the heavy tube from the air. A tricky business, though he managed to stuff it safely into his belt, and then he stretched out once more to reach for the monk. 'I have them. Grab my hand!'

But Meer could only hang there gripping the loop of thin rope with his fingertips, the last of his strength seemingly spent on passing up the tube.

He tossed his head back so he could look up at Ash.

'No regrets!' yelled the hedgemonk in triumph, and then his fingertips slipped from the rope and Meer was falling through the dark void of the night towards the sea, his robes billowing up around his tumbling body.

Ash held a hand extended after him and watched his companion disappear from sight.

'Ash!'

He swept the burnoose clear of his head and looked up at the voice calling from above. Now Cole was shouting down at him. He didn't catch the longhunter's words, but he saw Aléas in the doorway struggling to pull up Nico. The boy was clearly still weak.

An awful crackle sounded out from the *Falcon*. It was the surviving loft of the ship exploding into silk tatters. The ship dropped away from them, falling faster now so that clouds of smoke tumbled up around him.

Choking, near blinded from the smoke, Ash heard another shout above him. He looked up past his own legs to glimpse Nico falling towards him as his tunic slipped from Cole's grasp.

Ash caught Nico's arm on the way past so that the young man

hung below him where Meer had so recently been. He gripped Nico like a vice. Beyond the young man's kicking feet, through tears and brief breaks in the smoke, he spotted a startling white splash interrupting the dullness of the sea where the *Falcon* crashed through its surface.

Smoke engulfed them momentarily. In his grasp, Nico struggled like a bitter prize.

'Boy!' Ash yelled down with all his might.

At last the smoke cleared as the winged craft tilted away. Nico was still hanging there, blinking up at him in startled fright.

'What?'

CHAPTER FIFTY-SIX

Damnations

General Mokabi was up at that late hour, as always after the brief time of the little sleep, that first slumber of the night from which people often rose for a short spell to relieve their bladders or read by candlelight, to contemplate the day behind or the day still ahead, to snack or have sex or a quiet conversation with a loved one, before lying down again for the long sleep.

With so much to be done tomorrow, overseeing another day of assaults against the walls, Mokabi had opted to have his hair and beard trimmed tonight in his personal salon while he caught up with the Dreamer's progress, a man who seldom seemed to sleep at all.

'More time?' he asked incredulously of the cloaked man standing by the window of the room, his back turned arrogantly towards him. 'How much longer do you need?'

'A few days, at most,' replied Seech without looking at him.

'You said that last week, and the week before,' Mokabi growled with a slap of his chair, and the barber behind him straightened with his scissors, waiting for him to remain still.

'Yes,' admitted the Dreamer. 'I did.'

'Don't play games with me, Seech! I'm just about reaching the end of my patience with you, are you comprehending that yet?'

The Dreamer turned sideways, framed by the night's darkness outside. He looked at him distastefully down his long nose. 'Listen, you idiot,' he retorted like the sting of a slap, and Mokabi gasped at the insolence of the man, gripping the arms of his chair to still his trembling hands. 'You're asking me to shake loose a wall that's over a hundred feet in height. Such techniques take time to perfect, techniques which I have now achieved to my satisfaction. What remains is the performance itself. Perhaps, if you try hard enough, you might just sense an inkling of the reserves this task will demand from me. I will need a few days to prepare myself adequately, that is all.'

I should have him killed in his sleep. Those quarters he's staying in – I should have them blown to smithereens. Let us see how well he is protected against that.

'This has something to do with that Dreamer of theirs, hasn't it?' General Mokabi retaliated, and when he caught the sidelong glance from Seech he knew that he was right. Anger shook through his words. 'You're waiting until she returns to the city, so you can show off to her with your latest trick!'

'I've told you my reasons. I care not one whit whether you believe me or not.'

Mokabi breathed deeply, red rage nearly firing him from the chair at the Dreamer's throat. It was all he could do to hold himself where he sat. The impudence of the man, stalling like this for his own personal reasons, now of all times with Sparus and Romano finally pushing hard across the Chilos. Here at the Shield, Mokabi had a hundred thousand men hanging back from the daily action, ready for a major surge against the walls. His suicide ships were ready. All they waited for now was the Dreamer himself, holding up the entire assault.

Never in his entire life had he met such an infuriating individual. *Easy, old boy. You still need him.*

General Mokabi, ex-Archgeneral of Mann, bunched his jaw muscles together hard enough that his teeth hurt. 'The Lord Protector,' he rasped. 'Tell me that Creed remains clear of the picture, at least?'

'Of course. My leech continues to suck him dry. He remains infirm and confined to his chambers.'

That was something, anyway. But keeping the Lord Protector out of the picture was about all the Dreamer had been good for so far. It seemed little enough for the fortune he was paying the man.

It was bright in the small salon with the lanterns hanging from the ceiling. Bright enough to see his own reflection in the window glass that Seech stood beside. Mokabi's eyes stared back at himself with a dark intensity. Even with regular infusions of Milk, he saw how he was turning to fat around the neck and jowls.

He breathed until his throat had relaxed again, so that he could speak with some dignity, allowing the snips of his barber's scissors to lull him down from his fury.

In the warm and luxurious setting of the salon it was hard to believe they were within his mammoth warwagon, which was acting as both his command post and personal quarters during the campaign, outfitted with all the rooms of a small fort. Mokabi had ordered it hauled by the giant shaggy-haired mammoots to the northern reaches of Camp Liberty, where he could observe the Shield from a safe distance. At nights, he fell asleep to the soft percussions of the guns.

'Perhaps, then, there is something else you can help me with,' he said with his composure restored.

'Yes?'

'It appears the Khosians are constructing something behind Singer's Wall. Digging up large amounts of earth for some reason. So far, we've been unable to find out why. Perhaps, with your link to Creed, you could find something in his head which would explain what they are doing there?'

'It's not impossible,' mused Seech. 'But I would advise against it. If I go sniffing around Creed now it might give away my leech.'

'*Damn it, man!* Can't you do a single thing for me? What am I paying you a king's ransom for if you can't even fetch me some simple intelligence?'

A man of surprises, always, the Dreamer sighed with resignation and nodded curtly. 'Anything else?'

'Yes,' Mokabi barked. 'If that wall doesn't come down during the surge, you can say goodbye to the rest of your payment. In fact, if you fail me, you should leave as quickly as you can while you still can. You understand?'

'Threats, Mokabi?' retorted the man with a dry chuckle. 'Are you so desperate now you would threaten a Dreamer?'

'Get out. Get out of my sight and do not return until you are ready.'

'As you wish.'

In his cloak of ribbons he strode from the room, leaving the doors wide open behind him, letting the warm air flood out into the corridor beyond. A masked Acolyte leaned in and closed it quietly.

Next to the door, his personal bodyguard Nil offered a single shrug: *what can you do?*

*

Nil seemed alert tonight, as though the bodyguard could sense something out there on the wind, assassins coming for the general through the darkness perhaps. More paranoia, he hoped, though Nil had every right to be suspicious, given that Mokabi's top officers were still being killed one by one during the late nights, cut through by blade or crossbow bolt. It seemed the Khosians had assassins every bit as skilled as the Empire's Diplomats.

Snip, snip from his barber, who was humming to himself now, lost in his simple work.

Ah, to be this slave for a day, thought Mokabi wistfully. *Free of responsibilities, nothing worth losing but your own life. No reputation, no great wealth, to place on the line like this.*

It must be starting to get to him, he realized grimly, if he was longing for the simple contentments of a slave. Mokabi had almost forgotten what the pressures of absolute command were like. Colossal in magnitude. Like standing on a mountaintop yet with everything inverted, so that the mountain was also on top of you, the loneliest of all the peaks in the world. For who could he share it with? Who would not consider the voicing of his burdens as a weakness, as a possible chink in his glamour?

There was a constant tension in his stomach now that never left him – a nugget of dread that was there when he first awoke and still was there when he lay down to sleep.

Mokabi unclenched his fists in his lap and tried to soothe himself by staring through the window, the glass panes reflecting the light of the room's lanterns so that it appeared darker outside than it really was. Fires were shimmered amongst the distant ramparts of the Shield after another day of attacks.

His grand plan for the final conquest of Khos, his great chance at redeeming his name as the greatest Archgeneral of all, and once more he was running out of time.

It was the height of irony, considering that Kharnost's Wall had fallen as quickly as he had anticipated it would. But of course it had fallen. It had barely been standing by the time he had arrived here with his forces, worn down by more than two years of attacks by the Imperial Fourth Army. Against that fractured bulwark, Mokabi had successfully thrown the largest assault ever seen in this world, and even that had been but a portion of the resources available to him here, this vast horde he had assembled on the narrow strip of the Lansway around Camp Liberty.

To think of the expense of it so far was to momentarily rob him of breath. His vast fortune would be blown on this enterprise, all the wealth of the southern continent, as much as could be rifled into the coffers of the Archgeneral who had conquered it, gone in the storming of this one damned city, this gateway to the Free Ports.

A single wall taken and three remaining in his way, when ten years ago six had stood at the Shield. With newly built walls the Khosian defenders had dragged out the siege indefinitely, falling back to them when the originals had been taken one by one. Now, with the fall of the ragged battlements of Kharnost, the new front line in the war had become Singer's Wall, where the defenders had once more dug in their heels, stubbornly refusing to give further ground despite the overwhelming numbers thrown against them.

The daily casualties were as staggering as the costs in gold. Never had he read such casualty reports before. His own forces were taking the vast brunt of the losses in both men and skyships, in those daily slaughters that were their frontal assaults on the Shield. But the vastly outnumbered defenders were feeling the hurt too, and even with Bar-Khos filled to the brim by reinforcements from the rest of the Free Ports, they were dipping deep into their reserves. The majority of the Khosian forces were now committed to holding Singer's Wall.

Cannon fire flashed amongst the distant ruins of the walls, ruins that were the remains of walls taken by Mokabi himself during the early years of the siege, victories which had meant little while the remaining battlements still held the Empire at bay.

It was a bind that was fast approaching once more. The Khosians refused to be broken, and now Sparus and Romano had united the Expeditionary Force again in the north and were moving across the Chilos, soon to turn south for Bar-Khos. Sparus, the Little Eagle, the very man who had replaced him as Archgeneral after his earlier failure to take the city.

Mokabi couldn't bear it, the thought of being beaten to his victory at the very last moment. He would rather take his own life than live with such shame.

I stalled too long in Sheaf. I shouldn't have held back so many reserves from the assaults. I should have thrown caution to the wind and hit them with every-thing right from the beginning.

But that was hindsight, a nearly useless vantage for his present situation. Besides, Mokabi hadn't become the Empire's most famous Archgeneral by being reckless. No, he had risen to that exalted position by the relentless, grinding inevitability of his conquests.

It was only now, with his window of opportunity diminishing, that he prepared for one grand throw of the dice heavily loaded in his favour.

If he could take Singer's Wall decisively, causing as many enemy casualties as possible in a single fateful stroke, he could well defeat the remaining walls in a matter of days. Which was precisely what Mokabi intended, just as soon as the Dreamer finally declared himself ready to shake the wall: an unstoppable all-out surge against the Shield with everything that he had to seize the city for himself.

CHAPTER FIFTY-SEVEN

Vigil

With a start the Dreamer Shard awakened in a cold sweat, the beads cooling upon the surface of her glimmersuit. She grunted in pain as she sat up in her cot and tried to recall where she was.

Of course. They were travelling by road back to Bar-Khos after finding their skud gone from Juno's Ferry. She recalled that they had stopped for the night in a lonely wayhouse by the roadside, halfway to the city.

In the darkness of her tiny room she gritted her teeth and clamped an arm around her abdomen. The cramps were so bad now that fear washed through her for a moment, for there was no doubting the savagery of these pains. She had been vomiting blood on and off for a day now. In a mirror in her room, her eyes had looked yellow and bloodshot. The worm was slowly killing her. Soon she would have to think about getting it out of her body.

Not long now, she told herself for reassurance. *We're nearly back in the city.*

All she needed to do was return quickly enough to confront Seech while her focus remained acute, finish him with powers she knew were approaching their apogee thanks to the sensee bark she'd been given by the strange, blue-eyed Longalla man at the council, and then she could be rid of it. If only she could hold on until then.

Shard thought about getting up and fixing herself something for the pains. But then she realized that her glimmersuit was tingling across her skin, pulsing to a particular rhythm.

One of her vigils was trying to alert her to something.

As easily as she commanded her muscles, Shard called up a column of glyphs in her vision, each pulsing in and out of existence.

Quickly she scanned through them until she saw what she was looking for.

Ah!

After all this time of doubting, one of the vigils she had lain
around General Creed had finally been tripped.

In excited haste Shard cast the blanket from her naked body and
swung her legs to the ground, warmed by the second skin that was
her glimmersuit. In her mind she selected the glyph that was pulsing
faster than the rest of them and closed her eyes, slipping free of her
body and its discomforts.

She found herself floating in the darkened bed chamber of General Creed.

Easy now.

There – a shell of light dancing in the blackness over the sleeping
form of the Lord Protector. A disembodied intruder, betraying himself without knowing it in a gentle halo of light, his aura unique to
him alone, unmistakable.

Tabor Seech.

Back in the waking world, the scarring of her face itched from the
immediacy of the man.

Carefully Shard whispered her tree of offensive glyphs into
creation around the left edge of her vision, and then her defensive
ones too along the opposite side, running through her head the
order in which she would use them. They were symbols she had
crafted herself, customized and refined like the glyphs she used
within the Black Dream. With practised grace she swept them into
different strings, preparing the order of her attack. Willed to life a
pair of her fiercest barbed snares and filled them with burgeoning
early life, making sure they were primed and ready to go.

Let's have a peek at what he's doing first.

Carefully she edged closer, as fully cloaked as she could maintain,
close enough to see the glyphs that Seech was spinning out before
him. The man had his own unique symbolisms too, impossible for
her to read. But she could tell he was trying to crack into the Lord
Protector's sleeping mind.

She itched to launch everything she had at him, but something
held her back. On a hunch, Shard raised the focus on her scanning
glyph. Traced the faint web of energy sparking out from the light

that was Seech, connecting with his glyphs and then wrapping around Creed himself. She increased the focus a little more, spotted a lone ghost glyph fixed to the body of Creed.

A leech, hooked up to the Khosian general!

Suddenly Seech's spark danced upwards and swept around in a circle until he was close above her.

Shard? Is that you?

It was that damned sixth sense again, that connection between the two of them.

Do it now!

Shard launched her snares right at the dazzle of light, but it was too late.

A whisper of energy washed across her like ripples in water, and then Seech was gone.

She hung back, scanning around her, her suite of remaining glyphs throbbing like her fast-beating heart.

Next time, she promised fiercely.

CHAPTER FIFTY-EIGHT

Landing with a Crash

Rain spattered against the windows of the Vulture, though it was only the dark clouds they were flying through now, threaded with irregular streaks of lightning.

The flashes of light illuminated the faces of Aléas and Nico sitting on the other side of a folding table, both strapped into their seats and dozing lightly, heads rocking from side to side with every lurch of the winged craft. Up front in the green glow of the instruments, Cole sat listening to the Anwi man's quiet chatter as they rode through the storm.

Absently, Ash stroked the cat sitting by his feet, and stared down once more at the charts spread out before him on the trembling table. Meer must have drawn them up with help from the ship's navigator, Olson, for they were precise in their graphical descriptions, dissected with lines of latitude and longitude, marked with scales of distance in laqs. Each unrolled sheet described a certain region they had passed through, leading to the final one, the most important one, a complete chart ranging from the Midèrēs all the way to the equator and the Isles of Sky.

Ash kept seeing flashes in his mind as he stared at the white spaces of parchment. Images of the *Falcon* crashing into the sea. The white froth spilling away from it in every direction. The remains of the skyship slowly sinking into the water.

Hard to equate these paper charts with the lives of all who had been lost.

If there had been survivors amongst the crew, they were on their own now. Ash and the others had been chased away by the pair of Anwi attack craft, fleeing north in their own Vulture until Juke had managed to lose them. Stunned silence had been their companion for the rest of the flight.

North-west they had sped with the thrusters blasting and the wings vibrating through the air, plotting a course which they hoped was aimed directly at the Free Ports, Juke occasionally changing the charge coils when needed. Over clouds and highlands they had flown, and then the great range of the Aradèrēs itself, a crossing made easy this time by the great height at which they flew. Somewhere not far from Lucksore they had entered southern Pathia at last, with Juke nursing the craft now at minimum speed, trying to save what power was left in the last few cells.

Ash gazed down at the charts blindly. He blinked for focus, and tried to imagine the importance of these parchments to the people of the Free Ports, the leverage it would offer them in their dealings with the Caliphate, even with the Empire of Mann; if the walls of Bar-Khos were still standing.

He glanced across to Nico, dozing away in all his ignorance. What was Ash bringing his apprentice back to, besides war and a grieving mother?

A face flashed in his mind: Meer falling away from him into the night. The horror of it bore down on Ash.

The cat was purring at his feet.

'Thank you,' said a quiet voice.

It was Nico, watching him from half-closed eyes.

'What for?'

The boy blinked with those big eyes of his, so much like Ash remembered. A shiver ran up his spine; sitting here talking to a ghost.

'For not letting me go.'

Something in the way he said it made Ash wonder if he meant more than hanging on to him on the dangling rope bridge. But then the boy closed his eyes fully, and there and then seemed to drift into sleep again, exhausted and still weak.

*

'What's happening?' Cole hollered.

Ash opened his eyes to find the craft diving sickeningly towards a canopy of forest and the others gripping their seats with their wide stares fixed ahead, looking past Juke at the controls.

'Port thruster,' grunted the Anwi man from the cockpit, one hand wrestling the control stick and the other flicking switches over his head. 'It just died on us. Hold on!'

The forest was rushing fast towards them, but at the last moment the craft's nose swung up so that they crashed belly-first through the canopy – bare tree limbs clattering past the windows – then dropped to the ground, hitting it with a shock that threw Ash forwards in his seat, the straps biting into his flesh as water swept over the front canopy.

At last they came to a rocking stop. Juke was flicking switches as fast as he could, shutting everything down.

In moments they were sitting in silence save for the dying whines of the craft.

'That's it,' said Juke thickly. 'End of the ride.'

*

'Where are we?' Aléas asked with the rain drumming against the metal hull over their heads, and Nico glanced through the windows as though wondering the same thing. It was getting cold in the cabin of the craft, their breaths rendered visible in the air.

'Near Sheaf, I think,' rumbled the longhunter, peering outside at the tall reeds surrounding them, for they seemed to have come down in some sort of forested marsh. 'I recognized the harbours of the city on the way down on the coast of the Sargassi. We must be in the marshlands to the south of it.'

'Northern Pathia,' scowled Aléas. 'We almost made it back to Khos!'

'So what now?' Juke asked, turning from the cockpit to look at Ash standing there peering out – as though Ash had all the answers in the world.

He shrugged, tightening his lips.

'I guess we walk.'

A curse from the longhunter uttered beneath his breath. 'We just walk to the Lansway and knock on the Shield to be let into the city?'

Ash sat down heavily, needing to lighten his burdens. He reached for the leather tube containing the charts and gripped it hard in his hands, aware of Nico watching him and his father from his seat on the opposite side of the cabin, the boy's hands kneading themselves on his lap.

Give him time, Ash decided. Let him settle into himself.

'Tell me if I'm wrong,' said Juke from the front. 'But they have farcrys in the Free Ports, do they not?'

'What of it?'

Juke raised a kidney-shaped device that dangled around his neck, and grinned.

'Then maybe we can use this one to contact someone, and arrange for help?'

*

Far, far to the north of their position, beyond the bridge of land known as the Lansway connecting Pathia with the Free Port of Bar-Khos, Shard the Dreamer sat with closed eyes communing silently within the Black Dream, seemingly oblivious to the freezing wind blasting her in the face.

Around the Dreamer, the rest of the party sat waiting upon their zels in two groupings: the surviving rangers and medicos, and Coya and Marsh. All of them huddled in their cloaks and watched the hundreds of men and women training in the fading light of day, squads of Specials running and shooting on the windswept plain before the northern city wall of Bar-Khos.

Coya gritted his teeth against the chill gusts and looked on without expression. He had been told the winds of the plain here were a constant presence during winter, pouring down from the far Reach where the lands and mountains were frozen hard now by snow, gathering speed across the open land around Bar-Khos to scour flesh with their bitter cold, making a misery of everything.

No wonder they had built the northern wall of the city so high all those centuries ago.

Before Coya, shots and gun smoke quickly sheared away to nothing, though he could tell that the Specials were only firing blanks out there on the open ground. It had been their gunfire which had first drawn his interest in his typical nosey fashion, as the party rode along the road towards the gates of the city, nearing their journey's end – a quick look, he had told them, drawing grumbles from the cold and weary riders who wished only to see a roof over their heads before the setting of the sun.

Now, however, the rangers showed some interest in what they were witnessing, enough at least to quell their impatience. Partly screened from the city and road by the broad depression they worked within, the hundreds of Specials were clearly practising for a raid on Camp Liberty, the Mannian siege town to the south of the Shield. For it was all there before them – the layout of the northern side of Camp Liberty, staked out using sticks and lengths of bright string, through which hundreds of figures moved quickly in the fading light of day and hundreds more fired blanks or blunted arrows from an array of defensive positions, their shouts carrying in the breeze.

Intrigued, and unaware of any planned attack on the Mannian camp, Coya spotted a group of black-robed Rōshun sprinting on their own mission through the stakes and string, their curt calls sounding like birds on the hunt.

He sat up straighter in his saddle, or at least as straight as he could.

Baracha was there, the big tattooed Alhazii looming over everyone around him. And the others too who had accompanied him here in his skud.

If this was a planned raid on Camp Liberty, then the Rōshun must be using it as cover for their own purposes. He looked closer. Sure enough, the Rōshun practised just beyond the staked layout of Camp Liberty, working through a separate floor plan strung out across the short grass of the field; a small and self-contained area, a single building with different floors laid out side by side.

Mokabi, Coya thought in a flash. *They're going after Mokabi at last.*

Such had been their intention all along, just as soon as they found a way of getting to the Mannian general. Until then they had planned on targeting his top personnel and learning the lay of the land. Maybe a full-blown raid on the camp had been their idea then, the very opportunity they had been waiting for to strike the head from the snake.

The sight of the familiar figures made Coya want to ride over and greet the men, but they were in the midst of their operation, and he had more pressing matters at hand.

'Well?' Coya asked quietly, for he saw that the Dreamer had opened her eyes at long last, returned to the waking world.

'The Khosians are right,' she offered in reply. 'It's the expedition all right, speaking through a man named Juke. He claims to be with Ash and a few others. He says they have the charts you wanted.'

'*They have them?*' Coya gripped the pommel of his saddle and swayed in his own sudden excitement, his ailments at once forgotten. 'Then we must do all we can to get them here. Where is Ash now?'

'Just south of Sheaf. On foot, apparently. They ask if we can send a skud or a boat to pick them up.'

'Sounds good. Let us do that then.'

'We can't. The Khosians say Mokabi has sealed the Pathian peninsula tight since his arrival. No way to slip a ship through, sky or water.'

'So what do we suggest to them?'

'I was hoping you could tell me.'

Coya ruminated where he sat in his saddle. He should be dead by all reckoning, for the bolt was still firmly lodged in his bandaged skull. Yet so far he had suffered only headaches and some minor memory losses, while his sense of taste seemed to have gone awry, everything tasting of garlic, even the hazii cake he munched away on for relief. Otherwise he was fine, in that he was still alive. He might even get to see his wife again, if he did not drop dead first from a sudden jolt to his head.

It was a miracle, whatever Shard had done for him, as slight as she claimed her touch to have been at the time. Coya had seen men robbed of vision, language, all recollection of who they were, from much less serious injuries than his own.

Shots rang out from a group of Greyjackets stationed in the replica camp, sending puffs of white smoke into the air, the figures crouched down on one knee and reloading after every shot they fired, taking it as seriously as they could. Through the scene walked a few sergeants of the Specials with hands behind their backs, shouting through scarves at people, telling them if they were dead or not.

The battle was impressive to watch for all that it was only an exercise. Though it was still nothing compared to the scene at the city's northern wall, which stretched from east to west across the plain. In the weak afternoon sunlight, thousands of people laboured across a great slope of earth they were building against the wall, citizens by the dress of them, frantically erecting a defence against the imperial guns that would be heading here just as soon as the Expeditionary Force completed their capture of Juno's Ferry, which by the accounts of couriers on the road was now surrounded and barely holding on.

Even as they laboured, Coya could hear the rumble of cannon from the Shield to the south, low vibrations that matched the grumbling wheels of the wagons on the road behind him, bearing wounded fighters evacuated from Juno's Ferry before it had been cut off.

If only he had those charts to play with, to wave in the face of the Alhazii and demand of them aid in this war.

'But they're so damned close!' Coya exclaimed in frustration. 'There must be some way we can bring them home.'

'This raid,' said Marsh, and his bodyguard nodded to the figures running through the gun smoke. 'Find out when it's due to happen. Find out how the Specials intend to make it back through the Shield.'

'Of course,' said Coya, seeing it now too. 'If they can make it to Camp Liberty in time, they can return with the Specials under cover of the raid.'

Shard closed her eyes again in her silent communication.

Moments passed in silence, in which Captain Gamorre nudged her zel towards Coya. The other rangers watched her in glum impatience. 'Well, we got you here safely.'

'Yes, you did.'

'We'd like to head into the city, if that's all right with you. We still need to report in and sort out a billet for the night.'

'Of course,' said Coya distractedly. 'And thank you again, Captain. Thank you all. We could not have done it without you.'

She nodded, then whirled her zel around and led the others off across the field through drifting tatters of smoke, the rest of them offering their farewells. Sergeant Sansun raised a hand. Young Xeno waved a salute in the manner of the imperial military. The medico Kris nodded.

'Stay safe,' he heard the girl Curl say to the Dreamer, and then she too wheeled away.

Across the plain a gust of wind howled fiercely, making the world seem larger than before.

Good fortunes, he thought after the line of departing riders.

Shard stirred in her saddle and inhaled the cold wind. 'They're raiding Camp Liberty in two nights' time, if the weather stays dry.'

'That's a lot of ground to cover in two days,' observed Marsh. 'From Sheaf to the Lansway. Will the Khosians push back the raid I wonder?'

'I already asked. They say they can't risk waiting any longer. They suspect Mokabi is preparing to launch a major offensive against the Shield any time now.'

'Then tell them,' Coya urged with his voice raised. 'Tell Ash they must find a way to get to the Lansway in time. Tell him to hurry!'

CHAPTER FIFTY-NINE

The Pathian Arrow

In the darkness of the night a cone of light swept around the low bank of earth and raced towards him, trailing ribbons of smoke and a sequence of lesser lights framed by windows. The longhunter Cole stood watching with narrowing eyes, one boot propped on a felled tree that lay across the iron tracks, one hand perched on the barrel of his rifle, smoke rising from a burning roll-up hanging from his lips.

'Hurry up, you fool, it's coming!' came the voice of Aléas from the nearest trees.

The longhunter's wide-brimmed hat tilted as he scanned the trees bordering the track, where he glimpsed the young Rōshun hurrying deeper into cover.

Closer the light came, spearing along the track and narrowing his eyes even further. Cole stood his ground, caught in a sudden mood of daring as he watched the smoke trailing from thrusters on either side of the approaching rail liner, felt the vibrations rising up from the stony ground and into his boots. Moments before the beam struck him, he tossed his roll-up to the ground and hitched up his rifle. Casually stepped aside into the gloom beneath the trees and followed after Aléas, hearing the rail liner's thrusters cutting out and brakes screeching in their place. Lights flickered through the trees from the passing windows, faces staring out from the comfort of their carriages.

The rail liner was a recent innovation by the Empire of Mann, a form of fast transportation that was being unrolled across the far northern continent by competing cartels and now in Pathia too, where a track connected the capital city of Bairat with Sheaf, and which was being extended northwards onto the Khosian Lansway. Still unfinished, it should take them close enough to Camp Liberty to complete the rest of their journey by road in the day they had remaining, if only they could avoid unwanted attention until then.

Not an easy task in this land suffering under Mannian occupation.

In the gloom a pair of eyes swung to watch him approaching. It was Nico, crouched down next to Ash and Juke. The cat sat at his side.

His son had barely spoken to him since they had left the Isles, seemed to hardly even know who or where he was. It stung Cole's heart, such indifference from his only child, no matter that the lad hardly seemed himself yet.

Without acknowledging him, Nico stared out at the strange contraption arrayed along the track, its carriages jostling together one after the other as they came to a stop.

Voices shouted as men jumped down from the forward draught carriage to inspect the fallen tree in their way. Silently watching, Cole and the others waited until the sounds of chopping axes rose into the night air, and chatter came from passengers climbing down from the carriages to stretch their legs or relieve themselves in the bushes.

'Now,' announced Ash, and they stepped out from the tree line and made their way towards the last carriage on the rail. A group of Mannian priests stood clustered in their robes of white further along the liner. Soldiers passed the time with remarks and leers towards a pair of women.

'Quickly now,' Ash urged, and they climbed steps into the heat and light of the carriage and sat down at the back in empty seats. Cole whistled softly and the cat scurried down under the seat, her nails clattering against the wooden floor.

Soon enough, the passengers were stepping back on board and returning to their seats as a horn wailed outside, stamping their feet and blowing into their hands for warmth. The thrusters roared and fired brightly, and then the rail liner was in motion again with a sudden lurch.

No one paid them any heed. Outside, the world accelerated ever faster until they were shooting through the night like an arrow, heading towards the far Lansway in the north.

CHAPTER SIXTY

Siege Town

The lights of Camp Liberty smouldered beneath the late-night stars, its jagged skyline sprawling across the Lansway surrounded by earthworks and endless encampments of tents, with the sea washing gently ashore on either side. None of them had ever seen such numbers of tents before, choking the breadth of the isthmus on either side of the road for laqs on end, before spreading around the camp itself.

Mokabi's army, a quarter million mercenaries strong. Drawn here from every corner of the Midèrēs and beyond, their flags and pennants flapping in the intermittent sea breeze.

Weary and footsore, Ash and the others scouted the western perimeter of the armed camp, listening to the percussions of explosions and cannon fire from the besieged Shield to the north of them: a dark form spanning the width of the isthmus, lit by flashes and fires. Beyond it lay the city, blocked by sight. More glitters lit up the sky above it. Fires reflected from the bellies of passing clouds. It seemed a sky raid was hitting the besieged city.

'Bar-Khos,' Nico exclaimed at the sight of it, and both Ash and Cole looked at him in surprise.

The young man blinked quickly, glancing around at his companions in darkness softened by the lights of the camp. The fire was back in his eyes again, and Ash's pulse quickened at the sight of it.

In his mind he saw teeth flashing in triumph; a hand holding out a dripping pelloma egg above a dark pool.

Your turn.

'We're going home?' asked Nico.

'Aye, son,' his father told him. 'That's where we're headed.'

With Ash leading the way they crept past dug-outs protecting the camp's western flank, where sentries played dice near the heat of braziers and paid little heed to their duties, hardly expecting an attack. Ash settled down occasionally on one knee, sniffing the air and watching for a while without moving, before setting off again at a crouch, seeking a safe way into the town.

'Where did you think we were going?' he heard Aléas asking of his apprentice behind.

'Don't know. I hardly knew where we were until a moment ago.'

'You even know who *I* am?'

'Should I?'

'Well that's great, after everything I've—'

'Relax. I know who you are, Aléas.'

'*Sshh!*' Ash hissed from up front, spotting an opening in the defences at last.

Stealthily, they approached an area of pens holding hundreds of zels, and with care made their way through the crowds of snickering creatures without causing a panic. On the other side they were startled by the sight of a patrolling sentry, but Ash knocked him out from behind then beckoned the others to follow. Together, they slipped into the town without raising an alarm, the sun just beginning to rise over the eastern sea.

*

The streets of Camp Liberty were quiet at this early hour, though they began to grow busier as the sun rose weakly. In some places the night's festivities seemed to be still ongoing; music and chatter drifted from the many brothels and tavernas along the streets, while drunken soldiers and mercenaries sprawled in the dirt roads or wove their way blindly back to their billets.

No one paid the party any attention as they made their way to the north end of the town. Nearing the northern perimeter of buildings they stopped and looked about, rubbing their hands for warmth in the freezing air.

'What now?' Aléas asked in a cloud of his own breath.

'They told us to wait here until nightfall for the raid,' Ash told him, staring towards the walls of the Shield wreathed in smoke. 'So we wait.'

'Well we can't just lurk around the streets all day. We'll freeze to death, for one thing.'

The Anwi man Juke was suffering worst of all, arms stuffed into his armpits and teeth chattering. He looked to a nearby taverna and gestured towards it. 'Don't know about anyone else,' he said, 'but I could do with a hot drink.'

The taverna was called the Beggar King according to the sign over its door. Inside the warm interior, soldiers played games of Rash or slumped drunkenly in their seats, though a few heads turned as they entered before looking away again in disinterest. Around the upper storey ran a balcony with more tables and chairs, and the party made their way up the steps, letting the cat choose an empty table for them by curling up beneath it.

They ordered hot drinks to warm their bones, cautiously eyeing the other customers around the room. From where they sat a window of glass overlooked the distant fighting on the Shield. Ash could see the walls clearly now in the daylight, ranks of fallen ruins stretching across the breadth of the Lansway, swarming with a mass of figures beyond counting, and past the ruins the foremost surviving wall, a cliff of black stone faced by a rampart of earth, hazy in the white smoke of cannon fire.

Juke rose and stood next to the window to gaze at the sight of the Shield, his expression tinged with what appeared to be disappointment.

'They sound a lot bigger in the stories,' he grumbled to no one in particular, to the world perhaps.

They seemed smaller than Ash had remembered them too, though they had been soaring cliffs when first he had witnessed them, and from a distance similar to this one.

A throat cleared. Nico staring at him.

'What happened to me?' he asked Ash, and Aléas turned his head to regard the young man who was his friend, and to listen to the reply. Cole seemed to be holding his breath.

'You have no memory of it?'

'Only parts,' replied Nico, then stared down into his mug of chee. 'Q'os. I remember the imperial capital, and being captured by the Mannians.' A shudder ran through the young man's thin frame. In the glow of weak daylight he held up the fingers of his hand as though to study them for injury. 'And the arena. They brought me to the arena to fight. After that . . .' Nico shook his head.

Best if he remembered none of it, Ash considered with feeling. Who would wish to recall such a thing, tied to a stake and burned alive for the benefit of thousands of spectators?

He reached over and gripped the boy's bony shoulder hard. 'Let me tell you of it another time. If you still wish me to.'

Nico nodded. He looked to his father's scarred features and a frown crept onto his own. 'We'd given you up for dead,' he remarked flatly.

'No, still working on that.'

Something unspoken passed between their stares.

'It broke her, you know. You shouldn't have left us like that, even after what you did. You should have stayed and made it right.'

'I know, son. I know.'

*

By late afternoon the taverna had filled with soldiers and mercenaries eager to drink away the siege and the winter cold. Showing his usual initiative, Cole purchased a deck of cards from the bar, and while he and the others played casual hands of Rash amongst the scattered remains of the food they had ordered, pretending to ignore the many fighting men and women around them, Ash was content to sit relaxed in the warmth of his companions' presence, knowing that hiding out in plain sight was their best option for now until the raid commenced some time in the night.

Slouched in his chair, Ash listened to the easy banter passing between Nico and Aléas now, reminding him of a time not so long ago, when they had travelled together on vendetta to imperial Q'os with Baracha growling constantly at the two young men's exuberance, the pair like old friends already.

Even now it was hard to grasp that Nico was really alive and breathing again. Such a physical shock to the system, each time Ash turned and caught an unexpected glimpse of his apprentice, a dead person sitting there in the flesh; as though his death had been a dream or imagining and nothing more. Every instance of this seemed to cause a split-second revaluation of his memories, resulting in Ash blinking startled from flashbacks of a fiery pyre, seeing his apprentice burning to death upon it.

So much life in the boy's eyes now, so much animation. It seemed that in almost reaching home he had remembered himself again. What was he thinking right now? What did he make of these strange events he had awakened into? To see him playing cards it was easy to imagine that he was taking it all in his youthful stride. But whenever Nico glanced his way, Ash could glimpse the conflicts quietly surging within the young man.

Yet he lived, and that was the important thing after all. Nico would be fine, given time. Ash was as certain of it as he was of the sun rising on the morrow.

We did it, Kosh, he thought with a silent pat of his own hand beneath the table. *We brought him back from the dark.*

Ash might have been content just then had so many losses not lain on the path behind him, and if the boy's presence had not stirred his usual melancholy for the past – for watching Nico smile at Aléas's humour was like watching the son he hadn't seen in thirty-something years, springing back to life sharper than any memory, sharp as life.

Ash turned away to look out of the steamy window. The short winter's day had almost passed by then, and the foremost wall was dull in the deepening twilight. He thought of Nico's mother Reese, her surprise and joy as he returned with her living breathing son by his side, fully restored.

His heart was warmed by the thought of such a reunion, even if the walls of the Shield and several hundred thousand armed men presently stood in its way.

*

'It's a little late to be drinking, don't you think? The surge is set for tonight.'

'Never too late. Now get it down you.'

'If we start now I'll be blind drunk by the time we muster.'

'That's the idea, laddie. When you're charging those walls you'll be glad you're blinded out of your senses, believe me – you'll be shitting your trousers and you won't even know it.'

Ash stirred where he had been quietly dozing in his chair, ears pricking to the conversation from the table behind him. A mirror was set into the far wall, and through it he could see a pair of merce-naries dressed in leathers, one bald and one blond, knocking back stiff drinks at their small table.

'You think this surge will work then?'

'Certainly. Even if it takes fifty thousand corpses to do it. Trick is not to be one of them.'

'I hear those Khosians are stubborn bastards.'

'They fight hard, I'll give them that. I didn't sleep for a week after my last assault.'

'I don't want to be doing this, Cheeros.'

'No, few men do.'

'I don't even want to be here.'

'Who would?'

'Yesterday, when I was passing an infirmary with Hermet, I saw a pile of arms as tall as my waist, just lying there in the mud. Arms! Left arms and right arms all bloody and tangled together, just heaped in a pile.'

'Calm down, will you? Losing an arm's nothing. Just pray you don't lose your legs or your balls.'

Ash smiled grimly, reminded of the dark humour of his rebel companions during the days of revolution. Horrors softened by words.

'I thought the damned siege would be over by now. Thought I'd arrive here just in time to take part in the sack.'

'Aye. Didn't we all, laddie.'

Movement in the mirror caught Ash's eye. He watched as a hooded man climbed the steps into sight, his shadowed gaze scan-ning around the upper balcony, looking at each face in turn. Behind him, more hooded men were stepping up into view.

Beneath the table, Ash nudged Aléas with his boot.

Trouble? motioned the young man with a subtle gesture in Rōshun sign.

Maybe, Ash responded with a tilt of his head, and drew the leather tube of charts slowly out of sight, squeezed it through his loose belt, straightened where he sat.

The fellow swept his hood back as he approached, displaying the pallid features of a northerner, while beneath the table Ash gently lay his sword across his lap.

He stopped and clasped his hands behind his back in a deception of openness, and looked to each of them in turn.

'I take it you are mercenaries, here to enlist then?'

The cat growled from where she lay curled on the floor. Warily Ash nodded, and hoped the others had sense enough to act their parts, for he had already noted the shortsword hanging from the fellow's belt and the bulge of a pistol, not to mention the repeating crossbows in the hands of a few of his companions.

Regulators, Ash thought in alarm. Mannian secret police.

He felt the leather tube pressing hard against his ribs, and it struck him just then the enormity of what was inside it.

All of this time focused on Nico, and here he was in possession of something that could either save the Free Ports or doom them. If the charts were to fall now into the Empire's hands it would be disastrous for Nico's people. The Alhazii Caliphate would turn against them for threatening their monopoly with the Isles of Sky, while the Empire would find a way to use the charts for its own advances.

It could change the world, this stiff tube of leather stuffed with parchments.

'Mind telling me where you've been billeted?' asked the Regulator, hands still behind his back. His companions were spreading out along the balcony, observing the other patrons with suspicion.

'What's it to you?' Cole snapped, throwing down his hand of cards.

'Maybe nothing. Or maybe you're the reason I've been tramping through the cold streets all afternoon. Tell me. You didn't happen to rap a sentry over the skull last night, did you?'

'Who are you?' demanded Cole.

'Camp security. Now answer me. Where are you billeted?'

The longhunter barely hesitated. 'Haven't gotten around to it yet.'

'Nonsense. They wouldn't have allowed you into the camp without assigning you billets for the night.'

The talk had ceased from the tables around them.

No. We're too close now for this to happen.

Ash tried to think of the right thing to tell the man, but he was distracted by the cat growling even louder now from the floor. Nico stared down at the table with his shoulders hunched while Aléas casually sat back with a hand beneath his cloak.

Juke watched it all with the fascination of a tourist.

Their silence stretched on, every passing second adding another measure to their guilt.

They had been found out, and all knew it.

There was no warning, just the act itself – Ash lunging up with the edge of the table in his grasp to overturn it with a crash. His blade swept free over his companions' startled reactions.

'Run!' he shouted. 'Get out of here!'

And then he vaulted over the table, bounding in amongst the Regulators like it was sport.

A pistol pointed at his face and he swept his blade up and knocked it flying. Another man fired his crossbow just as Ash ducked beneath it and impaled his side. He swept around and the rest of them hopped backwards, stunned by his ferocity, tripping over tables and chairs suddenly cleared by the scattering patrons.

Bedlam behind Ash too; all around him, in fact. Soldiers shouting and joining in the fight. Cole swiping at a pair of fellows with his longrifle. Aléas swinging his shortsword. Juke throttling a fellow from behind. Nico throwing a steel mug at someone and then a chair.

'Get out!' Ash shouted again, but to little effect.

He glimpsed another pistol rising in someone's hand, saw that it was aimed right at Nico's back. Ash hurled his sword into the man's chest then surged after it, even as the Regulator fell backwards with his pistol flaring.

A slap struck the farlander's side, harder than he thought for it bowled him over onto the floor. Winded and gasping, Ash lifted his chin from the planking to see the boots scuffling around him as though it was all a grotesque dance.

He gripped his side with shaking hands and felt the hot wet flow dribbling between his fingers, where the bullet had grazed his ribcage.

I'm shot!

Six feet away Juke was down too, though he was still heaving beneath a mound of soldiers. Above him, Cole's arms were pinned while the cat snarled and bit at his captors. Only Aléas and Nico were still standing, the pair pressed back to back, his apprentice wielding a chair against the flash of swords, his face grimly desperate.

It was horror that gripped Ash right then. They were going to capture the boy just like back in Q'os. Nico would fall into Mannian hands and the nightmare would become real all over again.

Nausea washed through him like a fever. He reached for his sword, instinctively knowing where it lay. Grasped it up and swept it at two Regulators bending towards him with blades, forcing them back. With an effort he staggered to his feet, barely feeling any pain in his side at all, just a dull throb of presence.

Too many of them, he saw in a single glance of appraisal. Most of the balcony's occupants had risen up to fight.

Save the boy later.

Save the charts now.

He glanced to the nearest point of escape, a glass window, and saw three soldiers standing in his path to it, all three catching his eye as they drew their weapons.

With a lurch Ash kicked the nearest fellow in the groin then snatched up the pistol flying from his grip. He stepped to the side as he aimed the gun at the man's head, lining up his two companions behind him, then fired a shot that went straight through all three heads before crashing through the pane of the window.

Even with the glass shattered, Ash was hopping over the trio of dead bodies like useful stepping stones, using the last to spring through the window.

Ash toppled outside, tumbling once before he landed on his back on a sloped side-roof amongst the crash of broken shards.

He slid with the pieces of glass down the tiled slope of the roof, shooting off the edge as he grabbed for the rain gutter and hung there dangling for a moment as he checked below him, before he dropped down into an empty back yard.

Faces at the broken window above. Shouts of anger cast down at him.

Ash hated himself just then, but still he gripped his sword and the wound in his side and staggered off into the twilight, deserting the boy to his fate once again.

CHAPTER SIXTY-ONE

Fighting Spirit

Shard and Coya walked through corridors blackened and still reeking with smoke damage from last night's sky raid, no doubt why the many windows of the Ministry of War were propped open a little, so that the halls were chill and they walked through their own spurts of eager breaths.

Their boots rapping on the smooth marble of the floors, together they marched for the private chambers of the Lord Protector Creed as fast as Coya could manage, which was to say in a stiff amble.

Shard pretended not to mind, but really her body hummed with impatience.

They had just come from the dusky streets below, where the dead were passing in carts led by shaven-headed monks ringing bells in sonorous percussions, and waving burning incense to mask the stench. Nearest to the Shield, a thin pall of smoke had blanketed the southern quarters of the city, diffusing the fading daylight so that the living stood like murky spirits lining the streets. They watched the corpses go by in the backs of the wagons, casualties from the walls wrapped in cloaks, blankets or nothing at all, jostling and bouncing as the wheels clattered over the cobbles, crudely animated in ways that could never be mistaken for life.

The people had been hit hard by last night's sky raids in those southern quarters closest to the Lansway. Marsh had stared darkly in the worst-hit districts, where figures still stumbled around in shock, filthy faces made clean where tears had cut their stripes. Terror had clearly fallen from the sky. Rows of buildings still smouldered where stooped figures clawed through the smoking ruins, searching for survivors or simply what was left of them.

On one corner, Coya had stopped abruptly with a tut and a pull of his face. He was looking across the street at a man holding a woman, both of them visibly distraught and with something clutched tightly in her arms. A young child. The mother was soothing the still form and sobbing and shaking like the man who held her. Two small bare legs poked out from their embrace. Burned flesh dangled from them like socks of skin.

Shard had looked away quickly.

Onwards they had continued, eager to reach the Mount of Truth and General Creed. But even in their haste the news had caught up with them, panicked citizens and street-criers shouting it aloud: Juno's Ferry had fallen. Even now, elements of the Imperial Expeditionary Force were pushing south towards the city.

Bar-Khos would soon be surrounded on all sides.

*

General Creed sat where he always sat these days, on his wheeled chair on the balcony of the Ministry of War overlooking the Lansway, pale and slumped in the twilight. Alone.

There had been a lull in the fighting on the Shield today, though the pounding of cannon fire continued unabated, smoke and fire rising up from the defences where the specks of men hunkered down along the battlements of the walls. Creed watched with darting eyes.

'Coya,' he breathed with the scent of wine on his breath. 'Come to see the show, then?'

'Show?'

'Mokabi marshals his forces for a major offensive. We expect an attack tonight.'

'We just heard the news about Juno's Ferry. Why haven't the Al-Khos forces to the north launched an offensive in support of them?'

'Because Al-Khos is commanded by mutinous Michinè fools who think they know better. Believe me, there will be a reckoning when I am back on my feet again.'

'Good. But by then the Expeditionary Force will be ensconced outside the northern walls.'

Creed's expression stiffened. The Lord Protector of all of Khos, helpless while the city was slowly surrounded.

'Tell me, then,' he said quietly, and glanced up at Shard at last, catching her eye, 'of your jaunt in the forest.'

Coya bristled and shot her a dark look.

'Best if we speak on that later. For now we have something more pressing at hand. Shard, if you please.'

In her cloak and black leathers, Shard squatted down next to the wheeled chair and lay a hand on the back of Creed's. The general's eyes widened in surprise.

'It's all right, Marsalas. She's here to help you.'

'Miracles, is it?' said the general into her face. 'It's a miracle you've brought me, then?'

She called up her tree of profiling glyphs and called one to life. Carefully, she scanned around the body of Creed and the pulsing aura of his presence, simmering like the banked coals of a fire. She sought out the hidden glyph which Seech had left there, the leech that was sucking Creed of his spirit.

Despite its layers of protection, it was an easy thing to remove now that she was this close to its victim, touching him in fact.

'You have a leech fixed to you,' she told the general quietly, the tip of her tongue poking from the corner of her mouth. 'There. It's gone.'

She released her touch and stood back from the chair, studying Creed closely.

'Explain yourselves!' demanded the man with sudden colour in his cheeks.

'The change is fast,' Coya remarked, clearly impressed. 'You see how the glaze in his eyes is fading already?'

'Yes, it happens quickly.'

Creed growled.

'One moment, man,' Coya admonished him, then opened a vial of rush oil from his pocket and tilted the end over his forefinger. Restraining a smile, he bent down and smeared the liquid over the general's lips as though the man were a child.

Creed slapped the hand away and struggled unsteadily out of the chair to glare at them with his nostrils flaring. He opened his mouth to shout his anger then looked down at himself, swaying there unsupported.

'What did you do?' he asked her.

'You had a leech fixed to you by Tabor Seech. It was draining away your life.'

In his long nightrobe Creed straightened with surprise. Stiff muscles carried him across the small space of the balcony before he swept around to face their stares.

It was Creed the fighter, the general, the hard-headed bastard that Coya had always described to her with so much admiration, standing there before them now.

'I thought I was cursed. Truly. I hadn't known you people could do such things.'

'I hardly know what we can do yet either. But you're safe now. I've placed protections around you to keep away anything like this in the future. A few traps too that will burn a mind if they try to break them.'

He grunted, arching his back so that his bones crackled loudly. '*Ahhh.*'

'You should take it easy for a while,' suggested Coya. 'Allow your body to recover.'

But the Lord Protector dropped his arms and flashed that wolfish grin he was so famous for.

'Gollanse!' he shouted with a voice of steel through the open doorway to his chambers. 'Have my armour brought to me, at once, you hear?'

'Your armour?' came a creaking voice a few moments later.

'Yes, old man. Do it quickly now. And make ready to send a message through our farcry.'

Creed's old attendant poked his greyed head through the doorway and saw him standing there swaying. He cast a quick, fearful look at the Dreamer before vanishing back inside.

'Give me that,' said Creed and snatched the rush oil from Coya's hand to apply some more.

In the gathering gloom, the Lord Protector of Khos observed the range of his battered city and then the walls of the Shield, where the bombardments were raining down in the fall of twilight, and then beyond that scene to the far smudge of light that was Camp Liberty.

Mokabi, said the spite in his eyes.

CHAPTER SIXTY-TWO

The Raid on Camp Liberty

'Sir, message received. The Dreamer confirms that he's ready. We may begin the night assault at once.'

'Very well,' snapped General Mokabi from where he stood on the upper deck of his warwagon, his clammy hands resting on the wooden crenellations.

Squeezed into the muscular form of his decorative white armour, Mokabi stared ahead at the distant, foremost embankment of the Shield that was Singer's Wall, and watched the lights of explosions along its dark slope still at play, his hands clenching and unclenching.

He needed that damned wall to fall tonight. He needed his surge to wash over the battlements like an unstoppable tide, sweeping away the defenders with it, so that he could finish off the remaining two walls with haste. What he needed was an outright massacre.

Behind him to the south, the small squadron of powder ships – or suicide ships, as the squadron itself was calling them – was preparing to launch. They had successfully refined their technique over the previous few weeks, though it remained a hit or miss tactic in the extreme. Either the ships would end up being as vital to Mokabi's plan as anything else tonight, or they would betray themselves as little more than the world's most expensive fireworks.

No, they had to work. They had to punch holes right through that wall, and quickly enough that his forces could surge through and surround its defenders. Otherwise the success of the attack would likely hang on Tabor Seech, the very last person Mokabi wished to rely upon – fixated as he was on some personal feud with the enemy Dreamer. For Seech had claimed he could shake a portion of the wall loose. He had sworn to bring a portion of it down.

Mokabi frowned, thinking of what lay ahead.

A surprise night attack, throwing everything he had at the Shield under cover of darkness, supported by siege towers, mammoots, sky-ships, flying mines and a Dreamer shaking the very walls. It should be unstoppable.

Yet it was a risk, committing everything to a single offensive. As remote as the chances were for disaster, Mokabi had never been the coolest of gamblers, not when everything lay on the line. The general's palms were sweating. His guts churned loudly enough to be heard by his attendants.

It shamed him enough that he spoke aloud, addressing his old officer Fenetti by his side.

'So it all comes down to this, eh, Fenetti?'

'Aye, my lord,' the man replied without commitment.

Mokabi bristled, feeling the isolation of command like never before.

*

Deep beneath the Shield, hundreds of stooped figures shuffled through the tunnel while the dull thud of explosions shook the ground above their heads and rattled the string of lanterns hanging from the beams, filling the tight passage with their acrid smoke. Ash-blackened faces glanced up nervously. Men muttered to those before them to hurry up, to keep the pace going.

For many of the Specials, it seemed as though they had been moving along this tunnel for an endless time, their slow progress marked by the occasional whitewashed number on a beam that told them the distance they had made so far. An eternity ago they had passed beneath Singer's Wall. Now they were beneath the enemy's foremost positions, passing below the feet of imperial forces hunkered down in the ruins of the fallen walls while Khosian guns pounded their positions. Onwards still the head of the line pushed, heading deeper behind enemy lines. In the smoky air between their pinched, ash-smeared faces their mood was a palpable one. They were on their own now, with no one to rely upon but themselves.

The hundreds of Specials wore enemy uniforms weighed down with webbings and belts of weaponry. Many carried heavy packs of powder mines on their backs, which they would use to blow up the arsenals of Camp Liberty during their raid.

Amongst the airless press of them, a group of Rōshun splashed through the half foot of water that filled the tunnel, nine figures dressed in black and lightly armed in comparison.

'Who did they think they were making this tunnel for,' complained one of the Rōshun, the biggest one. 'Women and children?'

The figure was Baracha, stooped low at the front of the small group, his scalp scraping against another roof beam, his shoulders brushing along the bare earthen walls.

'I doubt they had a seven-foot Alhazii in mind,' said young Bones with the crazy blue eyes.

Another explosion overhead caused the beams to creak loudly and loose earth to trickle down on their heads. Baracha glanced back without expression to take in the line behind. He showed no fear, as usual, only that vague annoyance his expression always seemed to carry whether there was reason for it or not. The Alhazii brushed the back of his sleeve across his sweating forehead, careful of the punch-spike he had fixed to the arm where the hand was missing.

In a long steaming line they passed the last of the lanterns strung along the ceiling and entered a stretch of pitch blackness.

'We're close,' someone hissed after a few moments. 'I can feel the air on my face.'

Baracha was seeing spots from the last lantern he had just passed, though gradually he discerned a dull light coming from above. It was the glow of the two moons.

A pair of legs were climbing out of sight above him. A Special, lugging a scoped longrifle up a vertical tunnel on a high wobbling ladder, scattering a fleck of mud from her boot. He wiped it off irritably.

When it was his turn, he found that the rungs of the ladder were wet and grimy with mud and his boots wanted to slip clear of them. Baracha gritted his teeth and followed the Special upwards.

At last, a breath of icy air on his face and the night sky partly masked by clouds.

On the surface once again, the Rōshun hunkered down together to take their bearings amongst the hundreds of Specials. Cannon rumbled from the distant Shield, imperial artillery embedded between the ruins of the fallen walls blasting thunder and lightning into the night sky. Behind the ruins, the dark shapes of siege towers pulled by mammoots rose above an army filling the entire breadth of the Lansway, all of them moving slowly forwards. A surprise night attack, though the Khosians were waiting for it.

To the south, the bright lights of Camp Liberty shone beneath a night sky thinly populated with moonstruck clouds. On a wide road riders sped back and forth between the forward positions and the sprawling town, which was not as far from the tunnel mouth as he had been expecting, and was occupied to the east and west by endless tents and the sparkles of fires.

Already the large raiding force of Specials was sweeping silently towards the town with their equipment jingling, many of them wearing Owls.

The Rōshun fixed their own goggles to their eyes, looking to the north where they knew Mokabi's warwagon to be sitting behind his massed forces. Baracha flashed a signal with his hand and then they were speeding off into the darkness, the Rōshun jogging in a ragged V-shape, wild geese in the night.

*

A roar rose up from the high battlements of Singer's Wall at the sight of General Creed stepping up onto the parapet, his personal bodyguards forming a powerful wedge around him.

The defenders pumped their fists in the air, acknowledging the Lord Protector as he towered there above the raised shields of his men, with his long black hair shearing sideways in the gusts, his eyes filled with the spurts of dirt and blossoms of fire rising up over the crenellations behind which the defenders had been huddling.

Creed was panting in his heavy armour after their short ride to the front line and the steep climb of steps to the very top of the wall. Too long spent in his chair and bed while his muscled condition wasted away. The soldiers' shouts revived him though, lifted the general's chin from the thick collar of his bearskin coat, tightened his throat with sudden emotions as the word of his arrival passed along the battlements like fire in the wind, until it seemed the whole laqwide span of the wall was resounding with the roar of throats and banging of shields, and a few yipping hunting horns in celebration.

'Good to see you, General,' a Red Guard shouted from where he stood amongst a group of reserves around a burning brazier. Creed nodded to the man and flashed his teeth to the others. 'Damned cold up here!' he called out as though it was his first time on the Shield on a winter's night. 'I'd almost forgotten!'

Beyond the brazier's glowing coals he saw a line of sharpshooters positioned at the forward crenellations, men of the famed Grey-jackets, comprised of refugees from lands already fallen. Their attentions were returning to the scopes of their longrifles pointed down at the Lansway, where the isthmus flashed beneath a night sky feathered with clouds.

'Where's Halahan lurking?' he called to the foreign fighters at the crenellations, asking for their commander, and a sergeant signalled along the wall to the nearest turret.

'Darl,' Creed said to his fastest, smallest bodyguard. 'Find Hala-han for me. And get a hold of General Tanserine too. Quickly now.'

To the rest of his guards, wanting rid of their protective press around him: 'Go and warm yourselves, lads, I know where you are if I need you.' They feigned their reluctance, but the night was a bit-terly cold one and the braziers had been banked high.

'*I thought you'd given up on us,*' shouted Halahan himself in his tight-fitting jacket of grey, stepping out from the arched doorway of the turret. Soldiers parted before him as he limped towards Creed, grinning lopsidedly.

The two men embraced as brothers, slapping backs and shaking each other with the boyish grins of friendship. Soldiers watched them from the circles of light around the fires.

'You picked a good night to join us,' the old Nathalese veteran said at last.

Creed released him and they grew sombre.

'They're still massing, then?'

'Reckon as soon as this barrage stops, they'll be upon us.'

Together they stepped to the crenellations, where Greyjackets made room for them, and Creed and Halahan looked out upon the Lansway with the whips of the wind narrowing their eyes, the stone of Singer's Wall shuddering beneath their feet from every nearby explosion. The isthmus was a black road before running out before them across the pale sea, filled as far as they could see with a rash of torchlights which culminated with the distant shine of Camp Liberty.

Mokabi was out there somewhere, Creed knew, perhaps watching this wall even now.

'You ever hear of what Mokabi did to Hano, the Nathalese queen?' asked Halahan over the din of falling mortar rounds, sharing something of the same thought. 'After Nathal fell to the Empire, he had her impaled on a hundred-foot spike along with as many others as would fit onto it. Then he left them there to die.'

It was the first time in years Creed had heard his friend speaking of his past, this man who had once been a Nathalese preacher before joining the fighting in defence of his homeland; who had cast his religious convictions into the gutter after the ruin and enslavement of his people. But then it was that kind of night, for Creed could feel it himself; a night for reckonings.

'I'm told the raid on the camp was your idea,' Creed said.

'No, I only pushed for it. Though if they manage to hit the powder stores I'll claim it was all mine.'

'Let's hope the Rōshun can get close enough to slice his throat.'

Teeth shone in the moonlight.

'Listen,' said Creed suddenly, looking out over the killing ground beyond the wall. The enemy barrage had stopped. Long moments had passed without any incoming fire. Already, the Khosian guns along the parapet were falling silent in response.

An eerie hush fell across the darkness of the killing ground. Creed's armour creaked as he leaned closer.

All was blackness out there save for the lingering flashes of fire in his vision. By his side Halahan snuggled the butt of a longrifle against his shoulder and peered out through the scope with a pair of Owls.

'Anything?'

Halahan grunted, quickly swinging the rifle left and right across the width of the isthmus.

'Someone send up a flare!' hollered Creed, though other voices were already calling for them too.

Within moments five green flares were arching out over the killing ground, spreading like fingers across the isthmus, hissing and dripping as they rose. In the distance stood the black jagged ruins of

Kharnost's Wall, foremost line of the Mannians' position. To either side of the field the smaller coastal walls flickered in the ghostly light.

Creed settled his chin on a crenellation, and waited.

As the sputtering flares descended, their circles of light spread across the cratered killing ground, growing brighter.

'There!' someone shouted as a sudden mass of running men crossed into the emerald cones of light, with ever more coming behind them in waves.

A roar rose from the enemy throats as the lights of the flares gave them away. The very air shook with the volume of their voices.

'Gods, will you look at that,' Halahan exclaimed, squinting though the scope eagerly. 'A hundred thousand at least. Acolytes and heavy infantry at the front. They're sending in their finest first.'

A change in tactic then. Mokabi had been playing it cautious and smart up until now, as was his way, nursing his reserves while he used his weakest fighters to grind down the defenders, getting rid of the chaff on both sides. Now he had ditched that entirely, in a change of pace that was uncharacteristic of the old Mannian general. He was sending in his hardest steel first with everything else behind them. All or nothing.

Creed's chest tightened within his armour.

'He's going for the knockout,' growled his voice. 'He wants it all tonight, never mind the cost.'

One hundred thousand attackers with the same again in reserves, versus sixteen thousand defending the wall, and another eight thousand more defenders on the next wall behind them, the fall-back position in the event of a calamity.

'Some siege towers coming in,' Halahan observed. 'Lots of ladders and shields too.'

But Creed was paying more attention to their own situation now. He looked down from the great height of Singer's Wall to the slope of earth fronting much of it, then surveyed its breadth across the Lansway, its parapet thronged with defenders firing and shooting down from their positions.

Cannon opened up along the top of the wall, sending grapeshot down into the enemy ranks, cutting through their numbers in bloody swathes. Defenders pulled on hand ballistas to toss bundles of grenades into the enemy midst, while larger catapults rained down showers of jagged rocks. It was murderous ground to be crossing. The ragged front of the enemy wave faltered, thinning out as men fell all across the isthmus. But those behind quickly filled their places, screaming their war cries to blast the crippling fear from their hearts – for it was a soldier's worst nightmare this, even drunk and drugged as many of them would be, ordered to storm a heavily defended position at any cost.

Not that Creed felt pity for a single one of them.

We can hold, the Lord Protector told himself fiercely. *These walls have never fallen without first being breached.*

Calmer than he had any right to be, General Creed dabbed some rush oil onto his lips from the vial he'd taken from Coya, and felt its quick release of energy surging through him. Just as coolly, Halahan squeezed off a shot then broke open the rifle to reload it.

In ragged waves the enemy reached the earthen slope facing Singer's Wall and started scrambling up it, many with shields over their heads for protection, heavy infantry and white-clad Acolytes just as Halahan had said. The defenders rained down rocks and arrows and bolts and shots and flaming casks of oil, felling them in droves, thinning their ranks enough that all along the line they once more faltered, broke, started taking cover where they could.

On the flat ground before the slope imperial missile troops took up positions behind wicker screens they swiftly erected, returning fire and offering what cover they could to the assault.

More waves rolled in, whittled down by missile fire, joining those hunkering down in cover to fill out their numbers, prompting renewed charges up the slope. Onwards they came like an unstoppable tide.

Around Creed and Halahan, his bodyguards bunched tighter in protection. The Nathalese Greyjacket blasted away as fast as he could shoot and reload.

'Time for a few words, General?' shouted a voice nearby.

Creed spotted the familiar face of Koolas darting around the circle of his guards, the plump war chattēro who had accompanied them to the battle of Chey-Wes, and had since made a legend of Creed from his published accounts of the action. He was holding a battered helm firmly on his sweating head.

'Get out of here, you bloody fool! Can't you see we're busy, man?'

With a crack of wood the top of a ladder slapped against the stonework before them, then began to shudder as men clambered up from below. Still the ladder shook as Halahan shot down at them.

Creed's sword came out with a breath of steel; Sharric steel, finest in the world, forged in the heart of Khos itself. He planted himself squarely before the ladder. Swung his blade down at the white-masked head of an Acolyte, cleaving it in two as easily as a melon. With Koolas as his witness, the Lord Protector yanked the blade free and leapt up onto the battlement, steadying himself with a slick palm.

'Make them pay!' he yelled at his men around him, and his boot lashed out and kicked the next masked Acolyte climbing into view, toppling him from the ladder. Something shot through the sleeve of his bearskin coat. He barely noticed. It felt good to be on his feet again, good to be in the heart of the action with his men once more.

Exultant, Creed spread his legs wide and gripped the sword with both hands, then whipped it down again cleanly through another skull.

'*Make them pay!*'

CHAPTER SIXTY-THREE

Reckonings

Dearest Ennio.

My thanks for your heartfelt concerns over my poor health. I am much restored now, you will be gladdened to hear. By the way, I am told your Dreamer's work was of the highest order.

Ennio Mokabi. When we snap your neck here at Bar-Khos, which shall be soon, I will not claim the credit for it. It will be the people of Khos and the Free Ports who do the felling. They, and some friends of ours.

I expect you will meet them soon enough.

Try to greet your end with honour. Know, at least, that the evil you unleashed here upon Bar-Khos will be long remembered.

Marsalas Creed

General Mokabi set down the letter that had been delivered to him only moments earlier, and looked up from the fortified deck of his warwagon at the fighting raging on the Shield, wondering if his rival Creed was watching it too.

So Bearcoat had read his earlier missive after all. Yet his response was hardly the dejected tone Mokabi had been expecting from a man supposedly leeched of his spirit. Indeed, he sounded quite the opposite. He sounded as though he had somehow freed himself from the Dreamer's influence.

In a burst of annoyance, Mokabi crumpled the letter in his hand and cast it over the side, then regretted it instantly. He called to one of his men to go down and fetch it from the ground, feeling strangely troubled by what he had just read and wanting to read it again.

"'I expect you will meet them soon enough.'"

Mokabi glanced about the deck as though looking for assassins, but saw only the familiar faces of his field officers, and his personal bodyguard Nil standing close by with his scratch-gloves sheathed, and the detachment of white-armoured Acolytes posted around the deck's crenellations.

Is he trying to spook me?

'Any reply, sir?'

'What?'

The young aide was still waiting by his side. Next to the steps, the Acolyte courier who had delivered the letter stood wearily in his hooded white armour. The courier had arrived on a steaming zel fresh from the camp, where Creed's communication had been sent to an imperial farcry.

'No. That is all.'

He was about to turn away when he noticed something next to the courier's boot – a small black pool spreading onto the decking.

'You're bleeding there,' he called across to the man. 'Are you wounded?'

But before the courier could answer, an explosion lit up the night sky over his shoulder to the south, right above the skyline of Camp Liberty, followed by a brilliant flash of light so dazzling that it cast livid shadows from the hand Mokabi threw up before his eyes.

Squinting through his fingers, the general watched as a massive mushroom cloud rose high over the town.

He gasped as the rumble of it swept through him, feeling it shudder through the wood of the warwagon. He saw debris flying hundreds of feet into the air.

They've hit a powder store! he thought in alarm, and at last a cold worm of doubt entered into the equations of his mind. Was it a raid? Had they found a way to get behind his lines?

Moments later a second explosion lit up the skyline of the camp, another arsenal going up in a blossoming pillar of flame and smoke. Someone shouted out a curse.

The general slapped his palm against the parapet and gritted his teeth in silent fury. All of that black powder, one of the most expensive substances in all the world, going up in great clouds of smoke.

In a rage he turned to bellow a command just as something dropped around his neck, tightening with a cinch. Mokabi froze, aware of the cold press of a gun barrel against the side of his throat.

His eye flickered to the side. He saw that the bleeding courier had somehow managed to position himself by his side, and that the pistol was tied to a loop of cord fitting snug around the general's neck.

'Easy there,' came the courier's muffled voice through the holes in his white mask to Nil, the bodyguard. 'One press of this trigger and *pfff*, no more.'

Nil paused in mid-step, flexing the small poisoned blades of his scratch-gloves keenly, his shaven head reflecting the distant flames from Camp Liberty. No one else had even noticed yet, too busy taking in the flames rising from the camp.

'Are you mad?' Mokabi rasped. 'You'll never get away with it, man.'

Gripped by shock and the tightening cord, Mokabi watched the courier tear the mask from his face to reveal the black-skinned face of an old farlander, and a pair of dark eyes promising his death.

No, not now, not like this!

Mokabi steeled himself as the farlander leaned closer to speak softly into his ear. 'Your people are holding some friends of mine back in the camp. I need them released and delivered here now.'

'What? I don't know what you're talking about.'

'Four people, captured in Camp Liberty by your Regulators earlier today. Have them brought here now!'

Sudden action around them now, his officers noticing his plight at last, the slow-witted fools, calling out to the Acolytes around the perimeter. Mokabi held up a hand to stay them. There wasn't a chance that any could dispatch this assassin without his finger pulling the trigger in the process.

Still, he wasn't dead yet. For an assassin the old farlander seemed more concerned about the fate of his friends. Mokabi could use that to buy himself time.

'Do it, pass out the order!' snapped the farlander.

Mokabi tried to take a deep breath, then spoke out with the firmest steel that he could muster, passing on the instructions to his nearest aide.

'Do as he says. Bring the prisoners here, and try nothing in the meantime!'

Quickly the aide hurried below decks.

'Good,' panted the farlander by his side, swaying as though he might collapse at any moment, the blood continuing to pool around his boot.

*

The night burst alive with fountains of fire jetting high into the sky. Even in the midst of the fighting on the wall, eyes turned to the startling sight of them, where they rose above the distant glimmers of Camp Liberty, heart of the enemy. A moment later their concussions shook the wall and the bones in their bodies; *crump, crump, crump*.

Few knew that the Specials were raiding the imperial camp, but it was a victory for the Khosians anyway, and cheers and shouts of triumph sounded from the battlements of Singer's Wall as the defenders hurled themselves at the enemy with restored vivacity.

'*They've bloody done it!*' Halahan exclaimed to Creed as he cracked an Acolyte's head with the butt of his rifle. 'They've hit the bloody arsenals!'

Eyes reflecting the distant fireballs, General Creed gritted his teeth in a primal grin.

*

How much time had passed he could not say precisely – standing there rooted to the spot while he held his finger to the trigger, his other hand clutching the bandaged wound in his side. Time enough for Ash to mull over his situation, at least, and to wonder how much longer he could remain on his feet without fainting from loss of blood.

After his flight from the taverna, Ash had eventually lost his pursuers by hiding out in a crowded stable of zels. In the moonlight pouring from the doorway, perched trembling on a water trough next to his sword, the old farlander had washed out the wound in his side so he could have a better look at it, long inured to the pain of such injuries. It seemed he had been lucky, for the bullet had grazed off a rib, gouging out a bloody furrow of flesh along his side. Gamely he'd swept the blood from it with his hand, seeing the whiteness of his rib bone shining through for a moment.

He had needed stitches, or the kiss of a red-hot poker to seal the flesh. Lacking either, the farlander had torn up his undershirt to use as a pressure bandage, and had fixed it in place with its twisted sleeves wrapped around his torso, tying them as tightly as he could. And then he'd wondered how he was going to save Nico and the others.

Hours later, with two Mannian Acolytes left dead in the settlement of Camp Liberty behind him – one of them missing his white cloak and armour – Ash had followed their directions to the warwagon of Mokabi, and from there he had watched it from afar until spotting the hooded courier riding towards it along the paved road from the camp.

With no time for anything else he'd simply acted on the spur of the moment, propelled by the simplicity of his sudden, audacious plan.

And somehow he had made it work.

'These friends of yours must mean a great deal to you,' came the voice of Mokabi, breaking the long silence between them. The Mannian general sounded calm, almost disdainful, as though it was nothing to have the end of a loaded gun tied to his neck with a grizzled farlander holding the trigger.

'A great deal more than your life, certainly.'

'Come now. We both know you need me alive here.'

'Do not mistake what I need with what I am willing to do.'

'You're bleeding out, old fellow. I doubt you'll be in a position to threaten me for much longer.'

'Better hope my companions arrive soon then. If I drop first, I take you with me.'

Bursts of light in the night. Skyships fighting up there in the sky above the Shield. Mokabi watched them with narrowed eyes, though Ash returned his gaze to the Mannians on the deck around him, the bodyguard hovering nearby with his deadly claws, refusing to retreat any further, the others waiting for a chance to jump him, a few edging closer whenever they thought he wasn't looking.

Steady, Ash told himself as he swayed on his feet, applying more pressure to the bandage under his clothing. His legs felt weak. His arm was growing tired simply holding the pistol in the same position for so long. It helped that the end of it was tied to the loop of cord around Mokabi's neck. Give it long enough, and Ash would be hanging from it for support.

'Know this,' he growled at the figures around him loudly. 'The next man who moves will be the reason I put a bullet through your general's throat.'

'Stay back!' Mokabi spat at them, and they obeyed.

Ash's nostrils flared, scenting something new in the air. Over the side of the wagon a white mist seemed to be rising. A cry rang out.

Along the western crenellations an Acolyte suddenly toppled backwards to the decking, something black sticking out of his eye.

Two more Acolytes fell back from the edge before anyone could react. Shouts were rising from below now, from Mokabi's cavalry detachment stationed on the ground around the wagon, from where sudden clouds of white smoke were rising to obscure everything.

Suspecting some kind of rescue attempt by the Imperials, Ash gripped Mokabi and pressed the gun harder into his neck. But then he saw that three, four Acolytes had fallen now, along with the pair of drivers too, and he knew that this was something else entirely. Grim-faced, the huge bodyguard Nil took up position over the fallen drivers, his back turned as though Mokabi was no hostage at all. Beyond the bodyguard's armoured shoulder, Ash glimpsed hooded figures bounding over the backs of the massive mammoots, the foremost of them leaping for the cupola that was now clear.

Ash barely believed what he saw next. It was Bones, the young Rōshun who had once been an apprentice of Kosh, his crazy eyes flashing.

The bodyguard Nil snapped into a fighting stance and swayed aside from a slash of the young Rōshun's blade, then thrust out with both scratch-gloves. Twisting desperately, Bones lost his footing and pitched over the side, but his place was instantly filled by another leaping figure, and this time Ash knew how it would turn out – for it was Wild, one of their deadliest, coming in through the rising smoke like a thrown spear. Nil lashed out but Wild spun past him like a dancer to pierce his back, then ducked beneath a reply of steel, twisting the blade that was still deep in the bodyguard's body.

Boots clattered on the decking as more robed figures leapt in around the falling bodyguard to attack the other defenders, Wild amongst them. Smoke blew thickly across the scene. Through the clouds Ash saw a massive form stepping over the fallen bodyguard, a large axe in his grasp. It strode towards Mokabi, lifting his axe to strike.

'Not yet!' Ash shouted to the robed form and held up his hand. 'I need him alive!'

And in that moment he saw the tattooed face of the big man before him, saw that it was Baracha himself.

The big Alhazii lowered his axe and leaned closer for a better look. '*Ash?*'

CHAPTER SIXTY-FOUR

Tremors

Shard stepped onto the parapet as the fighting raged along the battlements, at once shocked and awed by the desperate battle before her, all of it taking place against the backdrop of giant plumes of fire and smoke hanging over the distant Camp Liberty.

So this was war at the front then, what it was like for the defenders of the Shield; what it had been like for ten long years.

In the bloody dazzle of it all Shard hesitated, as any sane person would have just then. She'd been drawn here with Tabor Seech in mind, sensing her ex-lover at work tonight on the Lansway, seeking him out for their reckoning; but now it was the battle which filled her senses to overloading, sweeping her up in them.

Lit by torches and braziers, groups of defenders were clashing hand to hand with figures struggling up between the crenellations. Even as soldiers heaved and cast the ladders sideways from the parapet, grappling hooks sailed up and over trailing knotted chains, accompanied by grenades and firebombs blossoming wherever they landed. Some distance away, out there in the killing ground, a siege tower was burning brightly like a torch, its huge form dwarfed by the even greater bulk of Singer's Wall. Other wheeled towers continued closer in jerks and lurches, pulled along by lines of armoured mammoots. Flashes could be seen at the tops of them, the enemy shooting up at the parapet of the wall with rifles.

Further along the thronged run of the wall stood General Creed, surrounded by his bodyguards, unmistakable with his bearskin coat and naked head, his sheer black hair flying as he swung his sword at a white-cloaked Acolyte scrambling over the wall.

Dark smoke rolled over her head. She couldn't seem to move for a moment, frozen there in the midst of the action. With explosions rippling along the wall, Shard fired more of her will into her hastily improvised body shield, an invisible barrier encasing her body, hungrily seeking further protection from its presence, awfully aware that it would stop only small masses, nothing larger.

Still, it was something. The Dreamer straightened in her cloak and took a few purposeful steps in General Creed's direction, but then she stopped, feeling the stones beneath her feet begin to tremble. She swayed for balance, seeing everyone else sway too, the whole wall seeming to shudder and shake beneath them so that men were staggering now, falling even, from the shifting force of it.

An earthquake, here of all places.

'*Seech,*' she hissed aloud.

*

Speckled in other men's blood and panting fiercely, General Creed backed away from the crenellations and shook his blade dry, seeing whole gutters of the stuff flowing blackly down the flagging and over the rear edge of the wall. He swayed unsteadily on his feet.

Catch your breath, man, before you drop.

The space he left was quickly occupied by Red Guards taking their turn at the front. The enemy had largely been beaten back along this section of the wall, though they rallied below at the base of the slope in preparation of another charge. Elsewhere, Mokabi's forces clashed in whatever toeholds they had gained on the parapet, fighting for time and space so that more of their companions could join them from below, the waves of enemy fighters still surging up the slope and the upper face of the wall. Defenders were surrounding them, though, in overwhelming numbers.

His own hands shaking, Creed took out the vial of rush oil and sipped a mouthful, letting it burn his gums for a few moments before squirting the foul stuff out again onto the flagging. Strength shot through his weary muscles.

Where was General Tanserine? It seemed like ages since he'd sent out a runner for the man.

Glimmers over the eastern coastal wall, high above the Bay of Squalls, where the thin clouds were afire with the blasts of skyships circling and fighting like dogs over a prey that was the two moons.

Along with the initial assault had come the first wave of Mannian birds-of-war, sweeping in at the wall from across the bay where Mercian squadrons had jumped them swiftly. The sky battle had grown larger and more intense as ever more squadrons joined in from both sides, until it was clear the Mannians had launched everything they had in one big pulse across the bay. There was no telling who was winning and losing up there.

Creed stared along the length of the parapet, taking in the measure of their position. Explosions bloomed along the line. He could hear shouting from the defenders in the distance, shouts which seemed to be passing along the wall and sweeping his way.

'What is it?' asked Halahan, turning to look.

Suddenly, all around them, men began to stagger as though they were drunk. Creed blinked in surprise, feeling the growing tremor of the wall shaking through his boots.

He caught Halahan before the man lost his footing. Others were gripping onto whatever they could. It was an earthquake, no mistaking it now. Shouts of panic filled the air as Creed made his way to the back of the parapet and leant out far between the smaller crenellations. From there he glanced along the rear face of the wall, seeing the torches and braziers along a single portion suddenly vanishing in a cloud of dust and a rumble of collapsing masonry, men disappearing down into it.

Part of the wall was collapsing, spilling backwards as it fell.

They've breached us!

His hands gripped the edges of the shuddering stonework to keep him upright. The shaking was growing even more extreme now, as though the quake was moving closer to his position. In that moment he spotted the Dreamer Shard not that far away in her feathered coat.

'Dreamer!' he shouted across to her. 'Can't you do something?'

But she already was. Her hands were rising into the air with her head thrust backwards, skin glowing where it was visible. A gust of wind swept out from her along the battlements, driving before it a hiss of dust and grit until it veered out over the crenellations and the killing ground beyond, picking up the ends of the soldiers' hair and cloaks so that everything seemed pointed at the enemy.

*

Shard was feeling strong tonight, focused like a lens. So much so that when she shed her body and launched herself into the night, she felt a wind of dust following after her disembodied form.

Like a bird seeking prey she flew up over the battlements and the men fighting desperately along them. She raced out over the killing ground and the masses of enemy forces running across it, drawn towards the echo that had returned from her glyph searching out for Tabor Seech.

With the help of the sensee bark in her veins, her mind was clear enough tonight to master the potent juices of the worm. Confidence lent her speed. Racing onwards, Shard called up the three trees of glyphs she had been preparing for their confrontation. The glyph she wanted most of all was shaped like a shower of falling stones. It took all the will she could muster to ignite it, draining her of strength as it sprang into life. And then it was as though a great hand was raking up the stones and pebbles on the ground that she passed over, pulling them up into her wake – a trailing cloud of debris, clattering like a stony beach dragged through the air in a vast net.

There! Standing alone on the open top of a turret amongst the ruins of what remained of Kharnost's Wall, the one most recently fallen – the tiny form of Tabor Seech in his swirling dark cloak.

Shard sensed the colossal effort he was expending on shaking the opposite wall with his will, and even then, she saw, he was targeting only a small section of it at a time. An impressive feat, regardless, and part of Shard wanted to know how he was doing it even as she dived downwards, intent on stopping him.

At the last moment Seech's eyes snapped open, finally noticing the swirling cloud rushing towards him. Seech threw up a body shield just as her storm of stony hail fell upon him, slashing out of the night sky.

Tabor Seech reeled backwards with his face bloody, throwing up his arms to protect himself and strengthening his shield to ward them off. A flash of light pulsed off him, almost blinding her despite her protections; Seech seeking her out even in the heat of saving himself.

Shard launched everything she could at him.

CHAPTER SIXTY-FIVE

No Regrets

'They're here,' said Ash, pressing forward for a better look.

Shod hooves clattered on the road behind as riders emerged out of the night. They slowed, milling around the rear of the warwagon while riders dismounted.

'Can you see Aléas?' Baracha asked by his side.

Even now, Ash kept the pistol pressed against Mokabi, and stood with him at the edge in clear view of all, the general gagged and his hands bound for good measure.

'Yes. And the others.'

A soldier was yanking Nico from the saddle. Another pair shoved Cole against his protests.

In moments a call sounded from below, telling them that the prisoners were coming up.

Boots clamped on the steps, and the old farlander straightened when he saw Aléas staggering up into view, and then Nico, Cole, Juke – all of them, still alive and breathing. He grinned at their dazed expressions blinking across the decking, stunned by the sight of him standing there with a pistol jabbing into Mokabi's neck.

'You are well, all of you?'

'Chirpy,' Aléas answered, his own two eyes blackened. 'Baracha!' he exclaimed, taking in the big fellow at last and the rest of the Rōshun arrayed around the edges. 'What are all of you doing here?'

'Saving your skins, by the looks of it.'

All at once they crowded across the deck to surround Ash and Baracha, stepping over the dead Acolytes sprawled between them.

'Don't suppose you've seen the cat about?' the longhunter enquired, taking in their delicate situation here with concern.

'No. But if she is free I am glad of it.'

Bruised and battered, Nico was clearly shaken by his recent captivity, but his large eyes shone with a defiant spirit.

'I'm losing count,' said the young man. 'Does this make us even?'

'Almost. Just as soon as you are home.'

They clasped hands, and then Nico embraced him awkwardly while his father watched on, something unreadable in the man's gaze.

Strange to feel Nico in the flesh like that. Too real almost, too much for his senses to take in; like the ragged bleeding wound in his side that only throbbed dully now.

'So this business of getting out of here,' Cole reminded him tersely. 'Your hostage there. We walk out with him?'

General Mokabi bristled, chomping at his gag to be released.

'Not a chance,' answered Baracha. 'We do that and we lead them straight back to the escape tunnel they're using for the raid. A lot of Specials are still going to be needing it.'

Heads turned to Ash.

'So what do we do?'

'What we always do,' he told them. 'We make a way out.'

*

'Safe passage!' Ash hollered down to the imperial forces below them. 'Safe passage for my people, and I will not shoot your general.'

'Do as he says,' called Mokabi, buying himself time. 'Let them through, and no tricks!'

And under his breath he added, '*You will pay for this, all of you!*'

Stuffing the gag back into the general's mouth, Ash spotted Baracha staring at him without expression. It was the look he always bore whenever competition arose between the two of them. Whenever he believed Ash to be trying to outdo him.

'I have a better idea,' rumbled the Alhazii. 'We get this wagon going. Break out with it.'

But Ash shook his head. 'Safer my way. Now go. All of you. When you make it back to the tunnel safely, send up two flares to let me know. Then I will make my escape.'

Grumbles from the Rōshun, who made no effort to move.

'Go!' Baracha shouted at them suddenly, surprising Ash as much as the others. 'I'll stay here too, make sure he makes it out of this. Wait for us as long as you can at the tunnel.'

The Alhazii's words sounded false to Ash's ears. They were enough though to get the Rōshun moving towards the stairs.

Yet still Nico and Aléas stood there unmoving. It took Cole to forcefully push the pair towards the stairs.

'We're coming down,' shouted one of the Rōshun as they descended the steps with their weapons at the ready, and each one glanced back before disappearing from sight.

'See you soon?' ventured Aléas, looking between Ash and Baracha.

'Aye, lad,' replied the Alhazii.

'Soon,' said Ash.

No shouts or gunfire from below yet. It seemed the Mannians might let them pass after all.

'The charts!' Cole shouted back in a panic. 'Where are they?'

Sweet Mercy, Ash had almost forgotten about them, too busy again thinking of his apprentice.

'I buried them,' he told the longhunter. 'Head along the road that runs west from here to the coast. There is an old stone marker not far along it. The charts are buried under some rocks.'

'Good luck to you, farlander.'

Ash nodded, feeling faint now, almost spent.

'Nico,' he called out, taking a step forwards, and the young man stopped at the head of the steps, resisting the shove of his father.

Nico cast him a smile.

'No regrets!' his apprentice shouted back, just as they'd heard Meer shout as he'd fallen.

Ash lifted a hand in farewell, his blood surging, his own mouth stretching tight. It was hardly how he had imagined their final parting, but it would do. The boy was alive and soon to be home again; one single broken shard of the world restored to its rightful place.

'I would have been honoured to call you my son,' he called out to the young man, and realized how much it was true. There was so much to impart just then. So much he had learned in this life over sixty years and more – the whole map of his soul. 'Follow your heart, Nico,' he shouted across to him. 'Do it all for the passion!'

Even as Nico was pushed downwards by his father, he called out to Ash.

'Make sure you follow after us when you can!'
Nico shot him a final fateful glance.
And then he was gone.

CHAPTER SIXTY-SIX

A Fighting Retreat

When the earth tremors finally stopped, abruptly, beneath their feet, Creed surged to the front of the parapet to find the enemy gathering for another charge, and saw how a single breach had dissected Singer's Wall in the middle of its span, where dust still settled over thousands of toppled stone blocks. He hurried to the rear of the walkway to see the same thing. Down there on the ground behind the wall, some of their reserves of Khosian chartassa, heavy phalanxes, were moving in to stand before the hole and its ramp of rubble, the foremost ranks levelling their great spears in anticipation of the enemy now pouring through.

At least the damned wall had stopped shaking.

Creed wiped a hand across his brow and glanced with gratitude towards the Dreamer. But the woman remained locked in her own ongoing battle. Moments earlier, she had flung herself aside just as a block of masonry had hurtled from the sky, scattering men in all directions as it bounced clean off the walkway.

Now, with a sweep of her hand, the Dreamer flung her own block of stone in a high arc above the killing ground, up there where skyships were circling fiercely, aiming the block at someone on the far ruin of Kharnost's Wall. Soldiers watched her with open mouths.

'She must be going for the enemy Dreamer,' Creed said in wonder. Halahan was turning to look when a blast of heat and light struck them from the side, and every man on the wall turned to see a section of the battlements going up in a fountain of fire and debris.

Holy kush, that's big!

'Have they mined us?' Halahan called over the noise of it.

'No!' Creed shouted back, leaning out over the side, his gaze filled with the brightness of the flames. 'The base of the wall's still standing.'

'Well something just took a big chunk out of the wall. Looks like it hit the rear of it.'

They both looked to the sky, back in the direction of the city. A crackle of fire lit up the clouds and then a chorus of others followed it like a display of fireworks, the sky defences further back on the Shield firing at something up there.

Creed furrowed his brows and spotted a ship dropping towards their position, a fast skud with its thruster tubes blazing on full, its empty silk loft rippling behind it. The diving ship drew some rounds from the ground and the next wall behind them, green tracers streaking through the night and zipping over or under or into it.

'Suicide ships,' cursed Halahan with snarl. 'We used them back in Nathal against the Fourth Army.'

Creed was speechless, caught up entirely in the moment.

The small ship was tilting as it fell, spilling debris from its deck. He swore he glimpsed a man floating down on what looked to be a parachute, drifting out towards the sea. As the skud fell closer he saw that it was going to strike a section of the wall not far to the east.

Again the wall shook beneath their feet.

This time the explosion was so close it made them shield their faces with their arms.

Already, where the first skyship had struck, Mannians were rushing through the sudden gap in the wall under cover of dust and smoke. From the Khosian side a horn sounded out, urgently calling for reinforcements. More rang from the Mannians' side, triumphant and piercing.

'To arms!' a sergeant was shouting over and over, shoving the men around them from their shock. The Mannians were renewing their assault on the battlements with all their fury.

Ashen-faced, General Creed looked about for one of his signallers.

'Tumus!' Creed called with a wave of his arm to the young woman huddled down with her horn and flags. 'Send out the call,' he bellowed through his cupped hands. 'Full counter-attack now, damn it! Full counter-attack now!'

The woman had to wet her lips first before she could get a sound from the horn, and then she blew a long single note with her cheeks bulging, and waved a flag striped yellow and black at their rear positions. Distant horns called out in reply from their deepest reserves. Another mass of infantry chartassa rose up from the foot of the next wall behind them, began marching across the field towards the phalanxes already there.

Just pray they're not too late, Creed thought to himself grimly, watching the enemy fighters pouring through the breaches like a flood.

*

Shard was struggling to breathe now.

The Dreamer had snapped back into her body just as Seech had hurled the first block of stone at her, the man retaliating with a fury that had momentarily knocked her off stride. He had missed, though only just, with a stone that might have crashed right through her personal shield had it taken her by surprise.

Now she could hardly breathe because Seech was sucking the air out of the space immediately around her body like a great squeezing fist, and it was all she could do to maintain an open funnel that drew in enough air for her lungs, a long and winding vortex revealed by the drifting smoke of the battlements.

But Seech was fast, as fast as she was even now on the worm juice. He was attacking her vortex of air as she fought to keep it open, their conflict made visible by the smoke compressing and stretching at the mouth of the spout.

With a gasp of effort, Shard mentally picked up another lump of masonry and tossed it high over the parapet at where she knew him to be. She was aware that she did not have the strength left to throw many more of them; wondered even if such brute tactics were worth their expenditure. But it had become a kind of challenge between the two Dreamers, flinging rocks back and forth like this. A game of dare and distraction while they tried to snare each other with cleverer, more subtle tricks of the mind.

Right now, gasping for air as though Seech was physically gripping her throat, part of Shard's mind was watching her ex-lover through the eyes of a circling pica bird that was vaguely consenting to her prompting, using it as a forward scout. Through its lensed sight she watched Tabor jumping aside from the boulder she had just cast at him, and this time he didn't allow it to crash off his body shield as before, but instead danced out of the way amongst the debris she had already thrown at him. His shield was finally weakening like her own, more and more of his effort going into his grip on her.

Almost casually the man launched a block in reply. She hopped to one side, trailing her winding pipe of air with her. Saw Seech's stone crash against the flagging.

No sense assuming he wasn't watching her closely too in some way. Shard waited until she was engulfed in a passing cloud of smoke then sent a boulder out hard and fast towards her opponent. A second stone, much larger, she heaved up with a heft of her mind, and with her remaining strength fired it in a steep arc upwards into the sky until she lost sight of it.

Heat roared against her face. A fireburst, one of Seech's old favourites. Not a problem with her body shield still active, or so she thought, until she realized that Seech was maintaining its existence in the air, so that the flames were wrapping her entirely, and even feeding down into her tube of air.

Fear of agonizing death flooded Shard with her reserves of strength, her second wind. She forced the flames back from the tube so that she could breathe again, the air scorching her lungs nonetheless. Drenched in sweat, she pushed against Seech's will, forcing him to focus his own ever more on their struggle. With what fraction of concentration she had left over, Shard used her bird's eye view to watch Tabor on the far tower, skipping aside from her missile.

Through the bird's sight, Shard judged the path of the heavy block still up there, tumbling now on the apex of its arc. She nudged it a little to correct for Seech's change in position.

Seech! she shouted in her mind in the fiery heart of the inferno.

Shard! he shouted back.

I just gave our child a name, she told him.

What? What child?

She choked down her bitter retort, galled by his ignorance.

Tippetay. It's what I named him. A Contrarè name.

He would hate that. Seech had always held a low opinion of all things Contrarè. What was he pondering, in the silence now hanging between them?

Shard. It didn't have to end that way you know. We could have left the oasis together, all of us.

As murderers. As thieves in the night.

As a family.

Stunning, the things he could say to her even now. Playing with her mind, she knew, just as she was playing with his. As they had been speaking, Shard had pumped her lungs full of hot air before holding her breath. Now, she allowed the flames to creep into the vortex once again, feigning a weakening of her power. Sensing it, spurred on by hope, Seech put every last effort into finishing her.

He was so focused right then that he failed to notice the block suddenly dropping straight down on top of his head, at least not until the last moment, glancing upwards, and then it crashed onto him and he was lost beneath it, gone from the bird's line of sight.

Shard! came the faint echo of his voice, and then the flames instantly vanished around her. Fresh air flooded back into her lungs.

Shard sagged to the ground with a growl.

*

'We've lost the wall,' General Tanserine was shouting at him, having come to him at last. 'Marsalas! We must sound the retreat!'

But Creed shoved the old veteran of the Shield out of his face, then pushed his way clear of his circle of guards to take in the breadth of the action, oblivious to the defenders beside him fighting tooth and claw to hold the battlements.

There were breaches on both sides of their immediate position now. Dark earth and rubble half-choked each one, but their tongues fell out onto the open ground before and behind the wall, so that they formed ramps for the enemy to rush across them in their roaring thousands, tiny figures struggling over the debris with Mannian flags streaming behind them. Warheads glittered in the darkness down there where they ran head on into the squares of chartassa.

Occasionally the pinprick figure of a man would fall where Creed was looking, yet his eyes roamed onwards to the rampart that was their fall-back position, Xeno's Wall – where the second line of defenders stood watching on helplessly.

'Marsalas!'

The Lord Protector tottered on the edge of the parapet with his balance shifting around him, his body still weak for all he was demanding of it. He leaned against the hard stone for support, the wall holding him up on his feet. If only he could return the favour.

Shouts of alarm on the nearest steps; Acolytes trying to fight their way up to the top.

'Marsalas, they've enveloped us!'

In brooding silence Creed appraised their sudden, drastic change of situation, shedding any illusions of hope for cold reality instead. He stood in an eye of a storm in the huddle of men surrounding him, letting it all sink down into his stomach, where his best judgements were always made at times like these.

To lose another wall, so quickly after the last one.

'Marsalas, we must do it now!' General Tanserine shouted again. 'We need time if we are to open the flood defences.'

Creed could smell the reek of the men's fear in the frigid air, floating off them in waves of vapour. His bodyguards shifted uneasily. General Tanserine looked old for all his thirty-two years.

'He's right,' snapped Halahan, and his hard stare forced Creed to listen. 'If we pull back now in good order, we can save most of these men.'

The leader of the Greyjackets knew all to well what it was like when a wall fell suddenly. They all knew.

The rout, the mad desperate scramble of it, the unfolding massacre. Wounded men left where they had fallen. Their screams as the Mannians made sport of them sounding long into the night.

But Creed was thinking of what Tanserine had said. The flood defences behind the wall. They would never have a better chance of taking out so many of the enemy, not in one fell swoop.

Once more he looked to his signaller standing there waiting with her flags and horns. 'Sound the retreat,' he said even as the words tried to strangle him to silence.

'General?' she asked him, not certain if she had heard him correctly.

'Sound the bloody retreat, and quickly now!'

CHAPTER SIXTY-SEVEN

Run to Ground

Two flares rose up into the night sky burning green and bright, not far to the south-west of their position on the warwagon.

It was a signal from the Rōshun, telling him they had safely reached the tunnel with the others, the tunnel which would bring them back beneath the Shield.

'They made it,' said Ash with relief, crouched down next to General Mokabi, who sat on the floor with his hands behind his back, eyes glaring above his gag.

Baracha stood at the top of the steps where he had thrown the hatch across before bolting it shut, the chops of an axe sounding through its wood now. 'I think they plan to storm us. Any thoughts on how we get out of this?'

Nothing had come to Ash yet. They were surrounded up here on the high deck of the wheeled fort. A skyship circled far above, maintaining its distance for now. Light cavalry roamed on the ground where snipers were hunkered down in cover. The warwagon was trapped from behind by barricades sealing the ruins of an old fallen wall. Ahead, more ruins led to the Khosian defences, swarming with tens of thousands of the enemy.

'I think we should get this thing rolling,' the big man suggested again, and Ash suspected it was only because he liked the sheer scale involved in the idea, this huge wagon rolling through the enemy ranks. Though now that he thought it over, so did Ash.

'Head deeper into the ruins of the Shield, you mean?'

'Why not? Can't be any worse than here.'

Blind optimism was hardly Baracha's style. Ash suspected it was only for his own benefit, and he realized then how poorly he must appear to Baracha, an old bloodied farlander crouched there breathing raggedly.

'Either way, time to finish him,' the Alhazii declared as he looked to Mokabi, and drew a wicked blade from his belt. 'Before we lose the chance to.'

Mokabi had been still ever since hearing they were Rōshun, consigning what time he had left to containing his fears. Now, though, he struggled at the sight of the man approaching with the knife. He shouted through his gag and speared Ash with panicked eyes, breathing so fast through his nostrils that snot flew from them and his face turned red, the man choking.

Ash tugged down the gag then slapped the general hard across the face, stunning him to silence.

'You have something to say to us?'

'We had a deal!'

'Aye, that I would not shoot you.'

Mokabi glanced up wide-eyed at Baracha's blade.

'I can make you both rich,' the man panted, his beard glistening with perspiration. 'You don't have to do this.'

Baracha towered over him, death from above. 'No one asked you to come here and wage war on these people,' snarled the Alhazii. 'You reap what you sow.'

'Wait!'

'What is it?' snapped Ash.

'It isn't meant to end like this,' Mokabi exclaimed with a passion. 'Not now!'

Ash snorted. Baracha rolled his eyes. The hubris of the conqueror.

'Make it quick,' Ash said as he stood, holding Mokabi's glistening stare. But his companion was looking off to the north just then, his attention caught by something else entirely.

Horns were blaring from the distant rampart under attack, which Ash could just see over the low rubble of a previously fallen wall; high wails of alarm calling through the din of the battle.

'They're falling back from Singer's Wall,' realized Ash. 'Those are horns of retreat.'

'So?'

'If the Khosians are falling back there must be a breach in the defences. A place for us to get through.'

'Ah!'

Quickly Baracha strode to the front of the deck and climbed up onto the driver's cupola, partly covered by a weather canopy. As he gathered the heavy reins in his single hand he shouted down to the enemy forces surrounding them below.

'Any of you sons of bitches take a shot at me, your beloved general is dead, you hear?'

In the ensuing silence the Alhazii flicked the barbed reins across the backs of the first pair of harnessed mammoots. There were six of them in all, chewing on great mounds of shorn grass while they waited. 'Yah!' he shouted, and one of the shaggy-haired creatures flicked its tail, but neither moved.

'Ash. Throw me a pistol there.'

He spotted one lying next to a slain Mannian officer. Checked that it was loaded and tossed it across to his companion. Baracha turned back with it pointed in his hand, aimed along the barrel then fired it squarely into the rump of one of the lead mammoots.

At once the creature reared up with a trumpeting roar from its trunk and pulled against the harness, prompting the others to do the same until the wagon was slowly creaking forwards on its man-sized wheels. The whole thing started to shudder.

A shot sped in from the darkness, tearing a hole through the canopy by Baracha's head.

What did I say, you son of a bitch? What did I tell you?

Another shot whipped past him, and then gunfire was erupting all around them, dissecting the air above the deck and forcing Baracha to duck low in his seat. 'Go!' Ash shouted from behind a crenellation. 'Go!'

'Yah!' Baracha yelled again with another heave of the barbed reins across their backs, and this time the animals responded by picking up speed, the warwagon rocking now from side to side along a paved road which it filled entirely, scattering men out of its way as it headed for the ruins of the Shield.

*

Ash swayed unsteadily as he made his way towards the driver's seat. An axehead was splintering through the hatchway covering the steps, and he paused to haul a table onto it, and then as an afterthought some heavy corpses too. The deck was rolling crazily now. He glanced up over the side, saw that the mammoots had built up enough momentum to enter into a run, pulling the wagon along the road at a terrific clip, the huge rolling fort creaking and rattling as though it was about to shake apart. Voices rose up through the decking loud and frantic, people jostled about down there. Glass crashed to pieces.

'Anyone following?' Baracha asked with a grin when Ash dropped into the bouncing seat next to him.

'A skyship. Some cavalry.'

Soldiers on the road ahead were scattering out of their way. The ruins of a wall were rushing towards them, the road leading through it via a levelled gap. The wheels bounced going over and then they were through and into the old killing field beyond, filled with tents and great crowds of soldiers. He spotted the breached remains of another wall far ahead, and then he was gripping his seat as the wagon veered off the road out onto the frozen ground, Baracha manoeuvring around a line of smaller wagons with hard tugs of the reins.

Startled faces flashed below them in the night. Screams as the team of mammoots charged through tents and camp fires like a sudden hurricane, trampling anyone caught in their way. A sound rose to Ash's ears, a low rumble of snaps and cracks; rocks exploding into dust beneath their iron-clad wheels.

They were through the next line of ruins in a flash of passing masonry. General Mokabi was on his feet back there, leaning against the rear crenellations and shouting out to their pursuers. Ash rose and staggered across the deck to him with his naked sword in his grip. Somehow Mokabi sensed his approach and spun around, hands still bound behind his back.

'Come to finish me?' the general shouted, spitting white froth from his lips, incensed by this mistreatment. 'We had a deal! You swore on it!'

'Jump,' Ash commanded, pointing the tip of the blade at Mokabi's throat, and Mokabi faltered back a step, pressing against the wooden crenellations. Ash stepped forwards to push the steel against the man's skin, pricking it, and Mokabi leaned back even further, out over the rear of the wagon.

His eyes flashed down at the road in panic, a good thirty feet below them.

'Jump and take your chances,' Ash said again. 'Or I kill you myself.'

There was hatred in Mokabi's eyes now. They were so intent upon each other that neither noticed the wagon bouncing through a gap in a ruined wall.

'You think this will change anything?' spat the general into his face. 'You think it will stop the Empire from taking the Free Ports? You fool. You bloody fools all of you. The creed of Mann will still—'

'*Jump!*' Ash commanded with all the projected will his voice could muster, and Mokabi flinched back just as the wagon jolted violently, tipping him over the edge.

He screamed, his body vanishing over the side and his legs following, and Ash looked down to see the general crashing to the ground head first, where he lay there unmoving in a heap.

'Is it done?' Baracha wanted to know when Ash returned to the driving seat.

'Aye.'

Ash's heart pounded within his ribs. His gaze was struck by the great rampart they were bouncing towards, Singer's Wall, foremost surviving wall in the Shield – though by the looks of things no longer.

Several breaches stood along the cliff of stone like the gaps of missing teeth, where Mannian forces were surging through like a rising tide. Between there and the wagon, tens of thousands of fighters swarmed across the vast killing ground, parting before the roaring team of mammoots.

They passed a siege tower burning there on the field, men jumping from its heights; a pair of panicking war mammoots thrashing about with their curved tusks. Corpses lay scattered across the ground, crunching beneath the wheels like the many rocks, and growing in numbers as they neared the wall. Ash finally spotted the breach that Baracha was heading for. In a flash of an explosion he saw the ramp of rubble that led up to it, jagged and uneven.

'This wagon will never make it over that breach,' he offered.

'Oh, you heathens of little faith,' replied Baracha, and with a thrash of the reins drove the team towards it, towards the tongue of earth covered in swarms of charging men, many of them looking back now at the approaching thunder of the warwagon.

Barely slowing, the six mammoots charged onto the gentle slope of earth pulling the mighty wagon behind them. Its deck pitched upwards, pressing Ash and Baracha back against the seat, the Alhazii whipping hard with his reins, the wheels jolting over the loose earth and rocks. Upwards they climbed through a breach filled with thousands of running figures – startled faces in the moonlight – cutting a path through them like the bow wave of a ship, while the wall's great height rose raggedly on either side like a canyon.

He was holding on for dear life as they made it to the top of the ramp where it levelled off, the wound in his side spilling freely again.

'Never make it, you say!' Baracha shouted wildly, even as the wagon pitched from side to side right on the very limits of toppling over.

But Ash was already thinking ahead, trying to squint at the killing ground beyond lit brightly by falling flares. He could make out masses of the city's defenders rushing back to the safety of the next wall, pursued by an ocean of baying enemy forces. It was a rout.

Faster, Baracha whipped the trumpeting mammoots onwards with the wagon rumbling down the other side of the breach, both of them gripping the sides of their seats with their boots braced against the footrest. On the uneven slope the wagon lurched sharply to one side and Ash and Baracha exchanged panicked grins. The wagon pitched further, its great mass tilting onto its side, until Ash felt a lurch in his stomach as it toppled over.

He was flung clear from the seat with his arms and legs wheeling through the air. Tucked himself into a ball just as he crashed amongst a cluster of men and bowled through them, hitting the slope of earth and rocks before rolling down it in a cloud of choking dust.

Bruised and winded, he lay there for a moment regaining his senses, surprised that no bones were broken.

Get up. Get up, you old fool!

Ash gasped for air and ignored the flares of pain as he staggered up onto one knee. Men were running past without paying him any notice, keen to join in the pursuit of the fleeing defenders. He tried calling out to Baracha, but he had no breath to lend to his voice.

He rose to his feet and staggered towards a still form lying on the ground not far from him. Found that it was indeed Baracha, lying there dazed and with blood smearing his face and head.

'Can you move?'

Baracha blinked up at the night sky.

'I think so.'

'Come on, then,' Ash gasped, and draped an arm over his shoulder and helped the Alhazii to his feet. Baracha hissed, hopping on one foot, the other leg dangling broken.

'Busted some ribs too, I think,' growled the man, clutching his side. Blood was trickling from the corner of his mouth. Ash hid his concern.

Together they shambled down the rest of the ramp and out across the open field, Baracha hopping as best he could with Ash's support, two figures in a sea of thousands. Baracha was even heavier than he looked.

'We almost made it,' the Alhazii gasped.

'You did not have to stay with me.'

'What, and let you steal all the glory?'

'Save your breath. We can still do this.'

But just then Ash glanced up over his shoulder and saw the skyship still following overhead. A beam of pale light shone from the lens of a mirrored search lantern, pointing down at where they stumbled.

It was like the Isles of Sky all over again, pursued by a flying craft with stabbing lights betraying his location.

He felt the shudder of hoof-beats behind before he heard them. Looked back to see two Acolyte riders coming in at them with their swords drawn.

Yes. We almost made it.

'Do what you can,' he said to Baracha, and released the big Alhazii so he could draw his sword from the sheath on his back.

Ash ducked a swinging blade then sliced through one of their sides as the fellow flashed past him. He turned for the other rider, just in time to see Baracha still somehow on his feet and punching the zel hard across the head, knocking it out cold so that its rider toppled to the earth with a crash. Baracha fell on the sprawling man and broke his neck with a vicious twist.

A fast wind whipped past Ash. More riders coming in to surround them, armed with small bows. On the ground, Baracha swore in defiance.

'Come on then, you bastards!' the big man roared, and then the Alhazii's tattooed face flinched in surprise and his spine arched suddenly, two arrows sprouting from his back.

Ash ran for him as Baracha lurched up onto his knees. Another arrow streaked into his chest and he fell sideways against the zel he had just knocked unconscious. Blood was spilling from his lips as Ash reached him.

'Baracha!' he whispered fiercely, clutching him with claws, but the man only rolled his eyes and gasped for air, too busy dying.

Szhip! An arrow shot into Baracha's throat. He sagged in Ash's grip, lay still across the belly of the zel.

A roar gathered then in the old farlander's throat, and it propelled him over the fallen zel towards the nearest rider, the naked steel of his sword flashing. The rider fell, and then something hit Ash hard in the back, and he twisted around to see the feathers of an arrow sprouting from his body. Another blow struck his back. Another arrow sticking out of him.

He staggered round, his throat uttering a guttural growl.

Foot soldiers were gathering around them now, drawn to the sight of an old farlander surrounded by Acolyte horse archers. Someone was shouting over their heads to stop, one of the masked riders, he thought, telling everyone within earshot that the farlander had murdered General Mokabi, and that he was to be taken alive.

Too spent to run, too spent even to stand any longer, Ash sagged against the flank of the quivering zel on the other side from Baracha, bloody sword in hand.

*

The great horns were blaring out too now from the city's Stadium of Arms, declaring to the whole of Bar-Khos that a wall was falling and that every fighter was needed on the Shield.

Across the ground behind Singer's Wall, the rout of defenders withdrew to their fall-back position on Xeno's Wall, from where the pursuing enemy forces were driven back with heavy barrages of missiles.

The forward lines of the Mannians hunkered down and returned fire, buoyed by the knowledge that behind their backs came tens of thousands more through the breaches to join them, and that Singer's Wall was now theirs.

Across the open ground, yells and whistles of triumph shot back and forth between the two walls.

When the trap was fully loaded, the Lord Protector himself raised his hand from the parapet of Xeno and gave the order smartly.

Nothing happened for a moment, and then from the lesser seawalls on either side came a ripple of explosions that caused the air to shudder in succession, ringing out across the vast swarming army of men. It was the sound of the freshly installed floodgates along their dug-out foundations blowing open one by one.

Even as the echoes faded away, they were replaced by a rising, thundering roar of sea water suddenly flooding into the open ground.

*

The old farlander gritted his teeth and struggled to push himself to his feet, but his boot slipped in the dirt and he sagged back against the zel with a wince of pain, gripping the bleeding wound in his side, the pair of arrows sticking from his back like quills.

Around his feet lay five dead Acolytes. About him in a great circle, a thousand eager faces stared with fascination in the light of a falling flare, pressing closer with the trepidation of hunters closing on a wounded tiger. Beyond them, hundreds more shouted and jostled closer for a better look at this enemy they had been told lay within their midst, though even in such numbers they were merely a knot of interest in a great sea of the enemy still rushing towards Xeno's Wall.

'Hold your fire, I say!' an Acolyte officer on a zel was shouting at a few fellows flexing their bows. The rider pointed his mount towards Ash and shook his sword at him. 'Let's see how you like the fire, old farlander. Let's see how well you hold up when we roast you slowly, over the coals.'

'Come and get me then!' Ash spat back, and the effort of it caused his head to swim sickeningly.

The arrows in his back were not deep. He could hardly feel them in fact. It was the wound in his side that was flaring with pain now, and spilling the life-blood out of him.

He tried to breathe stillness into himself, seeking the calm centre of everything. Awkwardly, he twisted his head around until he could see the still form of Baracha sprawled across the zel, the Alhazii's glazed eyes reflecting the light of the moons.

So this was how it was going to end then, just as Ash had always expected it would. Death by the sword, alone without friends or family to witness his passing, to soothe the passage from this world to whatever came after, if anything at all.

It was not so bad a fate after all, he realized now, facing it at last. What regrets he still carried seemed old and stale, belonging to a different person.

He gazed out at the sea of faces surrounding him, nursing what time was left to him.

Out there amongst the surrounding crowd a young mercenary was weeping quietly from shock, from the terror of the bloody assault he had been taking part in, from all that he had so far witnessed. Another fellow quenched his thirst from a bulging skin of red wine as the liquid spilled down his chin like a painted moustache, gasping as though breathing it in.

'Water,' Ash croaked aloud, his tongue dry and limp in his mouth.

'Give him nothing,' retorted the mounted officer. 'Now get in there someone and take him!'

The more eager souls braved another step closer, nervously eyeing the blade in his grasp, the bodies of the slain Acolytes at his feet, felled when they had gotten too close.

Ash's head lolled back. He was panting lightly like a dog.

Far above him, the arch of the Great Wheel soared across the starry firmament. Ninshi's Hood blazed up there amongst the other constellations, named after the goddess who favoured the dispossessed. Fervently, he sought out the ruby star that was Ninshi's Eye, the star that sometimes blinked to absolve the wrongdoings of whoever witnessed it.

Perhaps there was a meteor shower tonight, for another streaked across the night sky leaving a trail of smoke in its wake. It vanished over the horizon even as the press of the men closed ever tighter around him.

Ash blinked the sweat from his eyes, saw how the shooting star's trail of smoke lay directly across the Eye of Ninshi. For a moment the star was entirely obscured by it, and then the trail began to slowly fade, so that Ash saw the speck of light trembling there, appearing and vanishing again.

He coughed, his throat raging with thirst.

For the love of mercy, will someone give me some water.

What was that in the distance, like the sudden shudders of rolling thunder?

Loud explosions boomed across the space between the walls. All heads turned to seek them out.

The ground was trembling beneath him. More riders approaching perhaps, a great number of them. With a jerk Ash sat upright, coming back to the situation at hand. The armed men closest to him had stopped to look back in puzzlement. A distant roar filled his ears.

Over the din he heard the shouts of panic rising in the distance, spreading throughout the enemy forces arrayed across the killing ground.

A sudden cool breeze played across his face. Stirred all the loose cloaks around him. Closer came the cries of alarm until the men around him were shouting too. He blinked, marvelling at what he saw. A wall of white water was tumbling towards them a good twenty feet tall, brighter than anything else in sight, picking up specks of debris that were men and zels and wagons alike.

Ash snorted his disbelief. Once more he jerked around towards Baracha. Saw another flood surge roaring towards them from the other side of the Lansway.

'Hah!'

So the stubborn Khosians weren't so beaten after all.

A flood, sweeping inwards from the two opposing sea-walls to meet in the middle. Somehow, the Lansway here must be lower than the level of the sea. It seemed the Khosians had laid a trap the size of no other.

In a single instant the mass of fighters around him broke apart in disarray, men stampeding against each other to run for their lives.

The old farlander laughed aloud and dropped the sword from his grasp, too heavy to hold now anyway. He lay back against the flank of the zel still laughing up at the sky, laughing from right down in his clamping belly.

As the ground shook beneath him and his ears pounded with the nearing thunder of the white water, his laughter turned to a roar of defiance, so that Ash was howling with eyes wide open as the flood rushed in to take him, sweeping his body up in its maddening chaos, carrying the old man tumbling away with everything else in its path until there was nothing left but crashing, foaming waves.

CHAPTER SIXTY-EIGHT

Hereafter

High above the Shield, a trio of thunderhawks were at play in the night sky. They had eaten their fill from the grisly scene on the Lansway below, picking the choices parts of the corpses clean, gorging themselves on the bounty of eyes and tongues. Now their spirits soared as their bodies soared, rejoicing in their temporary freedom from hunger.

Far below their dives and circles, the flooded killing ground between the walls lay as a lake of scummy black water covered in floating debris and bodies, their numbers too thick to count, like jams of logwood from one side of the Lansway to the other. A feast for all the birds of the city, and they flocked above it now, crying out in the moonlight in their excitement.

North the three thunderhawks flew, sisters all of them, chasing each other as they veered off towards the city's coastline, headed for the cliffs overlooking the shanty-town that was the Shoals – where a prickly old thorn-apple tree stood perched on the very edge, holding their permanent nest and food store in its crown.

In the waning darkness before dawn the birds spotted flames on a lawn of one of the many mansions built back from the cliff's edge. They circled in interest, calling out to each other. Watched the flames burn in a great cross.

A shape emerged from the sky above them, dropping fast towards the fire. A small skyboat, its thrusters burning softly. Gracefully it circled the lawn too before dropping down next to the burning cross, settling onto the grass without a sound.

The thunderhawks called out once more before tilting away for their nest and their day's refuge, a lone moon shining low over the western sea.

*

The light was brightening as the crew of the skud tied down the vessel, preparing for Kira's stay in Bar-Khos. The spymaster Alarum had chosen well when he had selected their hideout in the city. The area of mansions belonged to Michinè and independent merchants alike, a place where private skuds were often seen on their grounds. Flanked on one side by a cliff and surrounded on all others by a high barbed wall, their own rented mansion was the perfect place from which to stage their operations without notice.

'Kira,' said a voice across the lawn, addressing the old woman stepping down from the landed skud.

'My dear Alarum,' she replied in her husky, croaky voice, and the woman's pale eyes darted to the figures hurrying across the grass towards the fires, watching them coolly as they cast buckets of sand over the burning oil of the cross. Against the mansion's white pillars, the reflections of flames began to die down. A figure approached her, plump Alarum the spymaster, only just arrived here himself in the previous day. 'Report,' she snapped at the man.

Not caring to hide his annoyance, Alarum frowned and said, 'Come, let's get you inside first and out of sight.'

Kira, mother of the deceased Matriarch Sasheen, bristled visibly before him. 'Mokabi's surge,' she declared, noticing that the guns on the distant Shield were silent. 'Has he taken the wall yet?'

Alarum, spymaster and envoy, rubbed the hair on his scalp and looked away, plainly embarrassed.

'He failed to take the wall?' she asked, incredulous.

'Oh, he took the wall all right. And then his forces walked straight into a trap.' Alarum had been up all night, she could see. His eyes were red-rimmed, his jaws set to the clenching of a perpetual yawn. 'Looks like the Khosians dug out the ground of the Lansway between the walls so all of it was below sea level. And then they rigged flood-gates in the sea-walls. Blasted them open when Mokabi's surge took Singer and poured in with all their numbers. There's a seawater lake there by all accounts now, stretching between the walls and with no way across it. Effectively the Khosians have cut the Lansway in two, making Khos a true island. The whole southern campaign is stalled in its tracks.'

The old woman hissed through clenched teeth.

'How many did he lose?'

A shrug in the darkness. 'Hard to know right now. I just received a Khosian report suggesting a hundred thousand men or more. An exaggeration, I hope. There's word too that Mokabi might be dead.'

'He took his own life?'

That vain old bastard had better have taken his own life, after such a calamity as this one. Mokabi was finished after tonight. Alive or dead his reputation lay in tatters, an embarrassment to the Empire.

Silently she cursed the general and all his easy promises to take the city. Her last hopes of stopping Romano from taking Bar-Khos and becoming Holy Patriarch were gone now, gone with the hope of Mokabi achieving the same feat first.

In that practised way of hers Kira calculated the adjustments to her own position, and decided there was nothing else for it. They still had a city to take here. Anything could happen to the young pretender before then, especially if Kira had her way.

'Tell me some good news,' she said. 'Have the Khosian traitors reported in yet for their briefings?'

She referred to the Khosian prisoners that had been captured after the battle of Chey-Wes, their minds warped by drugs and suggestions until the order had feigned their escape.

'Some. Others remain missing. Indeed, we have a visitor right now.' And the spymaster looked towards the mansion, where a figure was leaning against a wall with an outstretched arm.

The fellow was shivering, whoever he was. Kira watched him slowly wipe his mouth with the back of a hand, as though he had just vomited.

'He turned up at the drop point tonight. Claims to have been laid up suffering dysentery for all this time. I've given him a trigger phrase and confirmed that we captured him at Chey-Wes. He's one of ours.'

The order had grown skilled over the years in conditioning the minds of others. Those Khosians they had captured after Chey-Wes had been primed to report to their new Mannian handlers once they had escaped and returned to the city of Bar-Khos.

Yet the procedure still remained something of a hit or miss affair. There was no telling how a person would react when those dormant suggestions were first activated.

'He appears to be taking it hard,' she noted. 'How long before his conditioning fully asserts itself, do you think?'

'Only time can tell.'

'Yet time is what we are lacking, spymaster. The Little Eagle and Romano push south down the Chilos even as we speak. We must ensure the traitors are ready to let them into the city once they arrive.'

'We have others who are ready for that task. This one is special, though.'

'Special?'

Alarum called over to the slouching figure.

'Step forwards, soldier of Khos!'

Across the lawn and into the light the figure approached them cautiously. He did indeed look like a man who had been suffering dysentery, his appearance gaunt in the extreme.

'Introduce yourself, soldier,' commanded Alarum.

'What?'

'Your name, man!'

The Khosian peered with confusion in his raw eyes.

'Bahn. Bahn Calvone.'

When Alarum looked to Kira his own gaze was shining excitedly.

'The fellow is a lieutenant in the Red Guards. An aide to General Creed himself.'

'Really?' she said, and Kira leaned closer with sudden, acute interest, lifting a bony hand to his shoulder.

'Then you may be of great use to us indeed,' she told the shivering man in her grip. '*Hm?*'

The Khosian lowered his head and sniffed loudly, then offered a reluctant nod.

CHAPTER SIXTY-NINE

Once Were Brothers

Cole was thinking of the cat as he approached the house behind the others, for he had lost her during their capture back in the imperial camp, and hadn't seen her again.

She's fine, he told himself now for the tenth time. *She knows how to look after herself.*

Neither was he the only one to be worried over a lost companion. Aléas and his son both remained wrapped in their thoughts since the failure of Ash and the Alhazii man Baracha to return through the tunnel before its collapse – a tunnel which Cole had been glad to get clear from himself. Safe in the city at last, they had refused to leave the tunnel exit until Cole had pulled them clear.

Now he breathed in the early-morning air of the city and looked at the house they were walking up to, seeing movement in one of its upper windows.

His stomach churned.

So strange to be back in Bar-Khos where the war rumbled on even more fiercely than before, everything the same and yet different. There were too many desperate people in the streets now, too few faces that he recognized. A mood of perpetual threat hung above it all.

Cole felt the familiar tensions rising in him again, wanting to be gone from here.

Ahead he heard the door open and a woman's voice shout out in surprise as she laid eyes on Nico, a young man believed to be dead. It was Marlee, his brother's wife.

Cole had never heard her so excitable before.

They disappeared indoors, and Cole sighed and stilled his racing heart as he stepped up to the house, knowing that his wife Reese might be inside even now.

*

Inside the front hallway, Cole was sniffing at the fragrant incense that Marlee liked to burn just as the woman herself appeared before him, still dressed in her nightgown and shawl.

Marlee froze, and her widened eyes narrowed into a frown.

'I thought Nico was joking.'

Cole stepped forwards and saw her tense as though in loathing of him. 'Reese. Is she here?'

'Reese? No. She's still out at the cottage.'

'What, even now? I thought imperial forces were to the north of the city?'

'They are. I've tried and I've tried but she refuses to come in. She's in love with that farm of yours, Cole.'

Inwardly he swore with a passion. It was just like Reese to dig in like that in her stubbornness. He'd always been endeared to that quality in her character, yet now it caused a heavy dread to settle upon him.

Just then Nico's face appeared in a doorway, one cheek filled with a bite from the round of bread and jam he held in his hand. He leaned against the varnished door frame with a worried frown that said he had already heard this news, and was still coming to terms with it.

'Aunt Marlee,' he said. 'Any chance you can put two heads up until we return with my mother? Aléas and Juke need a place to stay.'

'Of course. Your friends are welcome.' A brief glance at Cole. 'You all are.'

Cole didn't have the patience for this. Reese was supposed to be here. They had a reunion to work through, tears and accusations and all.

'Why hasn't that brother of mine gone out to fetch her yet?' Cole wanted to know.

Marlee glanced to the stairs behind her. Lowered her voice to a hush. 'Bahn went missing, Cole. Until yesterday we thought we had lost him.'

'Is he here?' he demanded, stepping around her. 'Bahn!' he shouted up at the stairs.

'Please, the children are sleeping.'

'Bahn, where are you, man!'

A soft press upon the front of his tunic. He looked down to see Marlee's hand pressed firmly against his chest, trying to calm him.

'Your brother came back to us yesterday with the last of the wounded from the Chilos. He's been ill with dysentery, lying in an infirmary cot in Juno's Ferry all this time. Please, go easy on him. I don't think he's himself yet.'

'What do you mean?'

'The Mannians held him captive for a while. I think they did something to him before he escaped.'

Torture, thought Cole with a shiver of emotions.

He needed to see Bahn. Needed to see that his younger brother was alive and well.

The stairs creaked, and then a pair of legs appeared followed by a stick-thin figure wrapped in a blanket. Cole looked up to see a face sunken into itself, the eye sockets a pair of deep hollows, the skin sallow, darkly shadowed.

'Bahn?'

'Brother,' said the man in a hollow voice, stepping down carefully to meet him in his bare feet.

They both stopped a few feet apart, as though some barrier existed between them. There was a shadow in his brother's shifting gaze. Emotions so consuming he bore them only by holding onto something else even stronger; hatred perhaps, or bitterness; something black.

Without a doubt the war had changed him. Cole hated to think of what he had been through as a captive of the Mannians.

He and Bahn had been inseparable during their youth, getting into constant trouble while their eldest brother Teech had busied himself with becoming a man. But then wives and children had come along, and the war, and they had grown apart during the long course of the siege, each man falling further and further into himself under the growing pressures.

'I can hardly believe it's you,' Cole said with a tremor of a smile.

For a few moments Bahn seemed his old self again, embarrassed and looking down at his toes.

Cole grabbed hold of him and embraced the man tightly. 'Good to see you, Bahn. Good to see you.'

But in his arms he felt only the stiffness of his brother's posture, the resistance of his body against his own.

A chill ran up Cole's spine, as though he embraced a stranger.

They parted, not looking at each other.

'Hey,' said Cole, and he tugged the leather tube of charts from his belt. He had found it right where Ash said he would, under a pile of rocks by a road marker, the charts to the Isles of Sky still safe within it. But he hadn't wanted to simply pass them on to the first officer he came to, not when they were of such importance. 'Can I trust you with something, maybe see that it gets to the Ministry of War? I need to go chasing after my wife.'

'What is it, something important?'

Cole handed him the charts with his eyes dancing.

'You'll see.'

CHAPTER SEVENTY

Homewards

Two cloaked riders cantered along the road leading along the coastline, heads turned to the north where ribbons of smoke were slanting across the morning sky.

'*They're close*,' a passing Khosian outrider had told them at a crossroads on their way towards the Chilos. '*They're coming down the Chilos on rafts!*' And he had pointed northwards, over a road choked with the wagons of refugees and soldiers falling back in ragged columns, where the Imperial Expeditionary Force was marshalling against the city.

Eastwards, crossing the Chilos at last where the steaming waters ran into the sea, and warned at the fort there of slaver parties roaming beyond the river, the two riders had ventured onwards into a land that seemed deserted now, the windswept road ahead empty of life.

Now they cantered along with the shod hooves of their borrowed zels clopping against the rocky road and their rising fears tightening the screws on their silence. Finally one of them could take no more of it, and spoke out aloud.

'What's wrong with you, boy?' asked the taller rider, Cole.

'What do you mean?' his son Nico snapped back at him.

'I mean, why do you look like you've seen a ghost?'

Nico was quiet for a long moment, chewing on the long stalk of grass between his teeth. 'He's dead, I think.'

'The old man?'

'Yes. I think I can hear his crazy laughter in the wind.'

Cole studied his son, painfully aware of how little he knew him any more.

'You need sleep. We both do.'

We need to find your mother.

The day was dull beneath the clouds sweeping in from the bay. It was a good day for passing showers and watching the tracks of rain approaching from across the white-capped sea, clouds channelled between the snowy mountains along the coast and the far southern continent. Features that he loved about this part of Khos; the drama of its big skies and the constantly changing weather that you could watch sweeping past your position; the drama of the mountains running down into the wild sea.

On a ridge to the north he saw a small herd of untamed zels against the skyline, pulling lazily on the grasses. Cole bent in his saddle, ran his fingers through a stand of swaying lemon grass still wet with dew. He straightened while his son slyly watched him, and lifted the bright scent to his nostrils, letting it spark memories within him.

'I think I dreamt of you, you know,' came his son's voice from behind. 'One time when I was with Ash in the mountains of Cheem. We took something strong and I saw you in a vision. At least I think it was you.'

'And what was I doing?'

'Sleeping beneath a tree. Something big was running in at you, a whole gang of them, and I yelled to wake you but nothing happened. And then the last seed on the tree fell loose and landed on your face, and you awoke.'

Cole stopped his zel to look back at his grown son.

The longhunter said nothing, but a rash of goosebumps had risen across his flesh as though someone had walked over his grave.

Spooked, he spurred his zel onwards.

Together they rode up the rise of the road and over the crest, squinting down at the small vale below. In the middle of the road sat an empty handcart, its load scattered all around it. They picked up speed, trotting down to it.

'Father,' came Nico's voice.

The boy was staring up into the bare branches of the tree, from where an old ginger cat looked down at him.

'That's Solberry, mother's old cat.'

With sinking dread, Cole stared down at the luggage spilled across the road. The longhunter spotted a chest with clothes strewn out from its open lid, recognizing its carvings instantly.

He tried to speak, and found that he was shaking.

'Look,' he said. 'That's her clothes chest there. Her mother gave her that before she died.'

There were tracks all over the ground, Cole saw now. Zel prints, leading off north across the vale towards a solitary tree on a hill. Multiple riders weighed down with weapons and armour.

'You think the Mannians have her?' Nico asked.

Cole shot him a dark look from beneath his brows. 'You think they don't?'

His son was chewing on the stalk in his mouth, cheeks rosy with growing anger, his hooded eyes staring off towards the north where smoke was still rising.

The enemy, coming ever closer.

'We have to go after her,' Nico said with sudden conviction, and in that moment he was no longer a boy in Cole's eyes.

'Aye, son. We do.'

Thirst

Something of hope shone from that early morning sunlight filtering into the sky to the east, yet it was a deception, Ash knew, or at the very least a promise broken even as it was being made.

Naked and gasping like a beached fish, the old farlander lay across two corpses bobbing just beneath the scummy waters, his clothes gone in the forces of the flood, his head turned to the side with bloodshot eyes staring through a collapsed portion of sea-wall to clouds approaching across the bay, dragging dark curtains of rain.

Hurry up, then, Ash told the clouds in his near-delirium. *Before I die of this damned thirst.*

As he bobbed in the freezing sea water he saw warships out there in the Lesser Bay of Squalls, turning their sails now from the incoming weather. His eyelashes fluttered in the sudden breeze pushed ahead of the rain, though he barely felt its cool touch across his skin. Some time in the previous hours of daylight, his teeth had stopped chattering along with the trembles of his body. His breaths came now in irregular sips and sighs.

Ash knew that he was nearing his death.

Still, bad as things were, at least the rain was falling at long last; a fine drizzle at first, then plump drops crashing all around him. The old Rōshun was able to open his mouth wide and drink it down a trickle at a time, wondrously cool, reviving him a little. The rain thinned the caked blood from his face and naked body, washed the cuts and scratches on his skin. Ash sighed with relief, nothing more to be asked for now.

All was as it should be.

His head lolled to the side, letting him watch the blood from his wounds trailing away in the minor currents of the water. He followed the trail as it curled towards the nearest logjam of bodies, where it merged with a larger cloud of blood darkening the water all around them. It was the same wherever he had been able to glance so far. Bodies *everywhere*.

It was as well there were few man-eating sharks in this region of the world, though around him a feeding frenzy was taking place anyway, for the city's thousands of birds perched on the floating dead, pecking eagerly at their soft tissues, with hundreds more wheeling and squabbling overhead.

Two mighty walls of the Shield stood at equal distance to the left and to the right of him, one held by the Khosian defenders and the other having fallen to the Mannians during the night. From both opposing parapets, thousands of grimy faces stared down at the flooded space between the walls, rendered mute by their mutual shock.

Only occasionally would someone on a wall point a hand and holler down to the crews in the row boats working through the scene for survivors, calling out to them of some sign of movement. The Khosian and imperial crews passed each other without challenge, even without banter. A truce held between both sides, it seemed, at least so long as it took to recover their comrades.

The boy Nico had made it home safely. He felt it in the fibre of his being; life where once there had been death.

And even though his son Lin remained there in that inner place of loss, the pain of it seemed more muted now, less jagged; as though in making up for one tragedy he had redeemed himself – irrationally, in some small measure – in relation to the other.

He had done all that he could for the young man and his mother. More than had ever been expected of him.

Tiny waves lapped against the farlander's neck, growing into the bow wave of a nearing boat. Ash heard the chatter of Khosian voices drifting closer. He had no strength left in him, none at all to raise a hand and signal help.

Instead he closed his stinging eyes, fearing nothing, hovering on the very brink of the world.

He had travelled the surface of the planet in his years. He had seen it in all its glory and its madness.

Clear as day, Ash watched his old comrade and mentor Oshō leading the charge across the Sea of Wind and Grasses, the dust rising in a plume as thousands of Shining Way followed him into the maws of the enemy ranks and the bitter climax to the revolution.

Lightning flashed. A storm was raging at sea. He saw young Baso lashed to the mast of a ship, shouting his challenges to the gale and the heaving waves.

A sweep of sunshine, dazzling, through the gauzy air. Now he was watching his old friend Kosh as he sat in peace sketching the Rōshun monastery of Sato on a sunny day, becoming looser, better, the more that he worked through the warming skin of wine by his feet.

Aurora, flaming in passion across the night sky.

Ash recalled nights when the winds came as storm and vied to have his tent away with them, shoving him as he held down canvas with tired muscles and idiot grins.

He remembered sharing his thoughts with his son on a wintry night on the outside porch, while the frost had crept towards their feet.

A funeral march in Perfume City where he'd watched the people's grief from behind.

A robin sheltering under a thorn bush in the forest, watching him getting drenched in the rain.

No one there but the trunks swaying in the deep woods.

His wife. Ash thought of his sweet, kind wife. He thought of their first bed, much too small for them, and how they had made do; her pitched stare as they made love. Soft mornings in the glade where she had scattered the crows from her stride, a pretty woman he loved even now.

'You took your time,' said a voice of milk and honey.

Ash blinked his eyes open, crusty with blood. Took in the sight of his young wife standing before him, standing there in the green dress she had worn at their joining as husband and wife.

Her dark hair stirred in a breath of wind. Startled, he saw that his own hair hung across his shoulders, long and fine as all northern highlanders of Honshu. Ash was young again. He had his hair again!

'*Butai*,' he breathed in surprise.

'All that time,' said his wife brightly, radiant in the sunshine, 'and you never took another, never started a new family. What a waste! What a foolish waste of a life!'

'I still lived it,' he croaked back at her. And for all his longing for the remembered past, Ash recalled why he had always been so restless in his early life, why in the deep calculation of things he had found his rightful place as Rōshun. His great desire to see the world. To live with new horizons daily.

'Yet here you are,' she said. 'Home again.'

'Yes!'

A breeze rustled through the long summer grasses, drawing his gaze to their simple cottage perched on a mound of ground before the stony face of the hill. Butai was walking towards it now, glancing over one delicate shoulder.

A roar filled his ears.

'Your eyes,' Ash called after her. 'They're as beautiful as I always remembered them to be.'

In reply his young wife trailed her open hand.

'Are you coming or going, my love?'

Her love inflamed his own. A boyish smile twitched his lips.

Ash inhaled the sweet winds of the mountains as they flowed through the grasses, through his hair, marvelling that he was home.

extracts reading groups

competitions books new events

discounts extracts extracts reading groups

competitions extracts discounts

books new events

events reading groups

new books extracts reading groups

interviews events extracts books

events

discounts

new books events interviews new books extracts

discounts extracts discounts

www.panmacmillan.com

extracts events reading groups

competitions books extracts new books